# A TASTE OF POISON

TESSONJA ODETTE

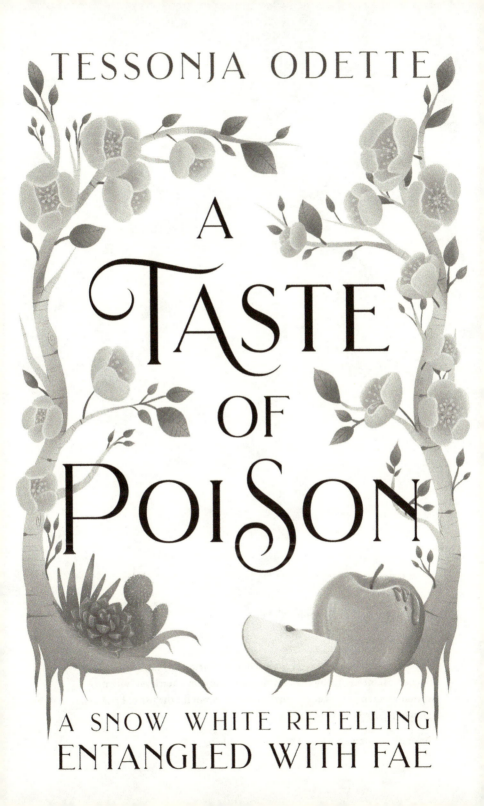

TESSONJA ODETTE

# A Taste of Poison

A SNOW WHITE RETELLING
ENTANGLED WITH FAE

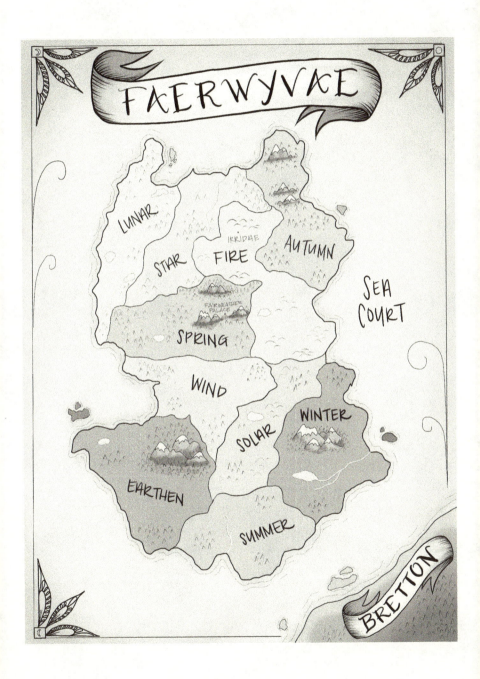

# PROLOGUE

*ASTRID*

The woods outside Fairweather Palace have never looked so sinister as they do now. The dark closes in around me the deeper into the forest I go, a sliver of moonlight my only guide. Branches reach out like clawed hands, scraping my cheeks, snagging loose tendrils of my hair. I ignore them, fixing all my attention on my next step. My breathing grows labored as I pump my legs faster. I lift the hem of my skirt and petticoats to avoid them snagging on the underbrush. Beneath the tattered shreds of my silk stockings, my legs burn with fatigue, my muscles begging me to stop.

But I can't stop. Not yet. Not until I'm far enough away from the palace.

*You have to run, Astrid. It's your only option.*

Marybeth's words echo through my mind, urging my feet to move faster. Faster. No matter how badly my heart yearns to return and see my father properly buried, my lady's maid was right. She knows what I am. Knows my magic will never cast me in a favorable light. Not where murder is involved.

*The queen won't give you a trial. She'll kill you herself. You have to run.*

Marybeth spoke only the truth.

With almost three years of hate and envy standing between me and my stepmother—the Seelie Queen of the Spring Court —I know she'd never believe me innocent. I'm lucky she didn't kill me the moment she discovered me next to Father's dead body.

A body that is now growing colder by the minute.

A body I'll never get a chance to say goodbye to.

The thought almost crumbles my resolve, but I remind myself of the fae queen's terrifying fury, how her lips had curled into a snarl before she said, "You did this."

As if I was the one who killed her husband. *My* father. *My* favorite person in the whole world.

After that, she had her guards haul me away from Father's corpse and into my bedroom, but it might as well have been the dungeon for the threat the gesture posed. I knew then that it wouldn't matter whether I'm innocent or not, only that Queen Tris blames me. She was biding her time by locking me in my room. Putting on the act of being a just ruler, waiting to gather evidence before condemning me for the crime she was already convinced I'm guilty of. If my lady's maid hadn't snuck into my room through the servant's passage and spirited me away, I might be dead already.

Like Father is now...

I swallow down a sob building in the back of my throat. It sears my lungs like flames. I can't cry. Not a single tear. I can hardly see as it is.

Blinking furiously to clear my eyes, I lift my skirts higher, sprint faster.

Father's face fills my mind. The smile that stretched over his lips for all of a second before he staggered away from the dinner table, clutching his throat.

A cry escapes my lips. I shake my head, but the vision is replaced with the sight of him stiff on the floor. Veins of black trailing over his skin from his lips to his ears and down to his neck—

A heavy feeling tugs on my heart, which in turn frees the sob from my throat. My knees buckle, and I almost collapse in place. Grasping the nearest tree to steady myself, I gather in a lungful of air to counteract the violent weight of my sobs. I keep my eyes pressed tight, but my father's face remains. My chest heaves with a whimper, and I pry my eyelids open.

The first thing I see is a tall slender shape leering before me. I nearly jump out of my skin, my mind reeling with the fear that Queen Tris has found me. I see her lithe form, her brown bark-like skin patterned with beautiful whorls, her head crowned in brambles and pink cherry blossoms in place of hair.

I blink a few times, and my vision turns sharper, clearer. It is not Tris who stands before me but a cherry tree like every other in the Spring Court, its bark and blossom-covered boughs cast beneath the pale light of the moon.

I gasp with relief, my sobs having fled during my momentary panic. In its place, logic forms. I have no time for grief. I'll never make it far from the palace with such sorrow dragging me down.

With another heavy breath, I reach into the pocket of my wool coat and extract a vial. My hands shake as I turn the cap and remove the dropper from the ruby liquid. Tipping my head back, I lift my tongue. One drop. Two.

No sooner than I secure the cap do my nerves begin to settle. Calm spreads from my chest to my head, then down to my toes. My mind spins with a slight euphoria, but I know it will pass. It always does.

"Poison." The voice comes from my left, ethereal yet chilling.

The vial nearly falls from my fingertips, but I close my hand tight around it, shoving it into my pocket as I whirl toward the speaker.

An enormous male equine creature steps from the shadows between the trees. His black mane ripples as if on a wind I don't feel. I avoid meeting his eyes, but their red hue glows brightly enough for me to see their shade nonetheless. The size of his massive hooves sends a shudder down my spine.

"Kelpie," I say under my breath as I take a step back. The tincture warming my blood and calming my nerves is all that keeps my fear from taking over. It's bad enough that I already get an irrational sense of panic when I'm around horses of the regular sort. Kelpies, on the other hand, are meant to be feared by all. They may have somewhat recovered from their once-deadly reputation in recent years, but that doesn't mean this one is harmless. Even though Faerwyvae is an island where humans and fae live in unity, there are still just as many vile creatures as there are bad people. The laws enacted by the fae royals forbidding trickery by magic and malice can only go so far.

"Crimson Malus," the kelpie says. "I smell it." The voice comes not from his lips but somewhere inside of him. Some fae creatures are like that—able to communicate without shaping words with their vocal cords or mouths. He steps closer again, making me take two steps back, my heart lurching at the nearness of those too-large hooves. "If you can stomach such a poison without dying, then you must not be human."

He's right. I'm only half human, but I don't say so.

"You must be lost," he says, voice laced with false pity. "Come, I will take you where you need to go."

That phrase is enough to tell me this kelpie is not the benevolent sort. "I know what you would do to me," I say, trying to keep my voice level. "You'd take me on your back, wrap your mane around my hands, and drown me in the nearest source of water. Am I wrong?"

The kelpie rumbles with something like a chuckle.

There's only one thing left to do.

With a deep breath, I force away the terror churning my stomach and turn myself over to the effects of my tincture, letting it soften the edges of my fear. I summon whatever pleasant thoughts I can muster. Soft textiles. Baby animals. The sparkle of morning dew on bright green grass. As soon as my emotions lift, I lock my eyes with his. The low hum of my ever-present magic surges outward, wrapping me in an invisible shroud. My magic is normally the bane of my existence, but right now it's my only weapon.

The kelpie stiffens.

It's my turn to take a step closer. "How do you know I wouldn't do the same to you? How do you know I am not a kelpie too? Dragging me into a lake just might be exactly what I want you to do, for perhaps then I can do to you what you were just imagining doing to me."

The creature assesses me for a silent moment. When he speaks, his tone takes on a curious quality. "Yes, we are similar, aren't we? You are fearless. Dangerous."

"I am." A bold-faced lie. But it doesn't matter. People only see themselves when they look at me through the lens of my magic. He won't see my trembling legs or my quavering shoulders. He will only see his own qualities reflected back.

I don't wait for him to say another word. Pinning him with a glare, I say, "Don't follow me."

Then I run.

I run until I can't breathe.

Until I can't feel.

Until my father's lifeless, poison-laced face slips to the back of my consciousness.

# 1

**TWO MONTHS LATER**

*ASTRID*

Thousands of people have seen my face and yet no one knows what I look like. People see me, but they don't really *see* me. That's the nature of being a mirror. People may notice things about me, may see what I'm doing, how I'm sitting, where I'm standing, but once I leave another's proximity, I'll remain faceless. Featureless. Forgettable. A frame without a painting. It isn't until one meets my eyes that a true impression begins to form. What passes in that instant of eye contact is so strong, it shapes how one sees me thereafter.

And it all depends on my blooming mood.

A twinge of pain flutters in my heart. The first sign that my emotions are slipping. That the calm buoyancy I feel now will soon descend into neutrality. Then apathy. After that, I'll be left with...I don't even want to think of it.

I scan the cafe, finding no one looking my way. Not that it would matter much. Even if I were caught doing something unseemly, I can change that impression with a meeting of the eyes. Angling my body toward the back wall behind my corner table, I extract my vial from my skirt pocket. With a flick of my wrist, I bring the dropper under my tongue. One drop. Two.

I sigh as I swivel back to face the rest of the dining area and pocket my tincture. The twinge of pain leaves my chest, replaced with a warm melty feeling. Of spring afternoons and the brightest shades of watercolor spreading over paper textured like clouds.

My lips curl into a placid smile as I scan the room. Breakfast was served an hour ago, but there are still several patrons lounging at their tables, sipping tea from porcelain cups, gossiping with their companions, or partaking in breakfast pastries. The windows at the far end of the cafe blaze with the bright morning sun. Thankfully, the cafe is cooled by iced fans that are powered by electricity that runs through the magic-infused ley lines that traverse the isle of Faerwyvae. Otherwise, the persistent daytime heat of the Fire Court would already be smothering the room, even this early in the morning.

Nearly every building at the Seven Sins Hotel is adequately cooled, something that makes the resort so popular in the city of Irridae. As a hub for trade between three of the northeast courts of Faerwyvae—Fire Court, Star Court, and Autumn Court—the city hosts a constant bustle of residents, tourists, and merchants; human and fae alike. The premier establishment to cater to these guests' every need is the Seven Sins Hotel. The resort is like a small city in and of itself, with seven departments each catering to a different vice. The cafe I'm sitting in now is situated on the second floor of Department Gluttony. The first floor is reserved for the butcher, grocer, and other daily food stalls, while the higher floors host finer dining. All the way up on the highly restricted eighth floor, those who are granted access can find delicacies that are of a more illicit or taboo nature. Not that I've ever been there. I mostly frequent either the market or cafe.

I sip the final dregs of my tea—cooled, thankfully—and settle my attention on the table I've been watching for the better part of an hour. A gentleman in a fine gray suit and silk cravat sits alone, oblivious to how I watch him over the rim of my teacup. He's human. Middle-aged. A well-groomed mustache hides his curt upper lip while his receding hairline reveals a severe forehead. Yet his sharp jaw and sparkling blue eyes are proof of why he's constantly referred to as handsome by many marriage-minded women of Irridae. However, I'm certain it isn't his looks that prompt women to speak so favorably of him, but the fact that he owns one of the fastest trade ships in northern Faerwyvae and possesses a covetable fortune.

With his breakfast long since finished, the man peruses the broadsheets, pausing only to sip his tea or check his brass pocket watch now and again. Based on what I've witnessed during my prior days' spying at this same hour and at this same cafe, he'll soon depart for his first business meeting of the day.

Which means it's time to do what I do best.

Leaving my table and my empty teacup, I smooth down my blue satin skirt—more out of habit than necessity—and straighten the rolled-up sleeves of my white blouse. Then I stroll to the man's table and stand before it. Without looking up from his paper, he says, "I don't need anything else."

I'm not at all surprised that he assumes I'm waitstaff. It's understandable considering I'm merely a hazy shape to him at the moment. Were he to glance away from his paper, he might notice a thing or two more. A feminine form perhaps. My posture. My white lace gloves. Still, it's worth noting that he assumes anyone approaching him without invitation is in a position to serve him. I reach for the chair across from him and pull it away from the table before sliding into it. That catches his attention.

Slowly, he lowers his paper and frowns at me.

Our eyes lock.

A spike of panic squeezes my chest, something that isn't uncommon when I make eye contact with someone, especially a stranger. Whether it's due to my magic or some automatic reaction of my own, I know not. I let the uplifting effects of my tincture carry the momentary discomfort away and shift my attention to how my magic feels. It surges from its constant low hum to a roar. As it blankets me in its smothering embrace, his expression shifts. Annoyance turns to curiosity as his impression of me forms. Were I in a sour mood, he'd see his worst qualities reflected back at him. But since the Crimson Malus tincture has me as content as a bunny in a meadow, he'll see what he considers his best assets.

I keep my lips curled in a neutral smile as I study him. He too changes before me. Or—more accurately—everything about him becomes more telling. The set of his shoulders radiates arrogance, the tilt of his chin screams superiority, and the cut of his jacket is edged with pride in his wealth. He relishes his own confidence. He considers his domineering nature a great virtue.

As he straightens in his seat, I know this is what he sees in me now too. Instead of my secondhand skirt and blouse, he'll get the impression I'm wearing something custom-tailored and new. Instead of the bobbed cut of my blue-black hair, he'll perceive perhaps an immaculate updo, not a strand out of place. He'll interpret every one of my features and characteristics as qualities he likes best in himself. Nothing of my true face will show through.

Now that his impression has formed, it's time to see how he responds to it.

He stares at me a few beats longer, cheeks blushing pink.

Finally, his eyes turn hard. "You are too bold, Miss. We are unacquainted. You should not sit with me so brazenly."

"Then let us be acquainted, for I'd much like to meet you," I say, even though I already know exactly who he is. Lies roll off my tongue with ease. That's the benefit of the human blood I inherited from my father. Unlike full-blooded fae, I can lie. "My name is Miss Mallory Mansfield. And you are?"

A tic forms at the corner of his jaw. "Onto your scheme," he says, rising to his feet. "I'll not fall for it. You can try to swindle another man's fortune. Good day, Miss Mansfield." He takes his paper and leaves.

I purse my lips to suppress a chuckle as I return to my table. The man must value his own cunning for money to have reacted to me in such a way. Despite our meeting being far briefer than I expected it to be, it tells me everything I need to know.

"Orson Carver likes submissive women," I say to the human female sitting at the table across from me. The room is warmer than the cafe was, with only a small iced fan to cool the heat streaming through the shuttered windows. The space is modest in size and lit only by the muted sunlight, the walls papered in crimson damask that casts everything in a pink glow. Yet it does nothing to mask the red burning in Miss Hampstead's cheeks. Even more telling is how her face falls.

I'm not the least bit surprised by her disappointment. I knew from my first meeting with Miss Hampstead that she was a bold woman, much like the version of myself Mr. Carver saw an hour ago. The fact that he reacted so adversely to me tells me exactly why Miss Hampstead has never been able to catch his favor.

"Submissive women," she repeats.

I nod. "And he has no patience if he thinks a woman is after his money. He seeks a wife who is quiet and demure and will allow him to take the lead. He does not care for an attractive mate, only an obedient one." These observations were some of the first I made over the last few days I've spent spying on him. It was easy to catch the changes in his composure when he'd interact with different people. I can't fathom how Miss Hampstead didn't see it herself. Then again, I've grown adept at noting such subtle shifts in other people. Being all but invisible myself, I've had many opportunities to practice the art of studying other people's reactions.

Miss Hampstead lifts her chin. "I don't know how you can call yourself a matchmaker, Miss Lottie Lovecraft, if that's all you can do for me."

I shrug. With the Crimson Malus still warming my blood, her irritation has no effect on my mood. "I described my services to you in full detail during our first consultation. You knew the information I brought back would tell you precisely how to best earn Mr. Carver's favor. The rest is up to you."

"You are blunt in your honesty, I'll give you that."

I don't bother with a response. So many times I've heard the phrase *you are* followed by everything I'm not.

*You are kind.*

*You are cruel.*

*You are beautiful.*

*You are the most hideous girl I've ever met.*

There was only one person who was ever immune to my magic. One person who saw the real me.

And that person is dead.

"Very well," she says and hands over a small velvet pouch.

I peek inside and find six spheres of glittering opal—the currency of the Fire Court. "We agreed on ten opal rounds, Miss Hampstead," I say flatly. I anticipated her attempt to underpay me as much as I expected her disappointment in my report on Mr. Carver. She may be ridiculously wealthy, but I knew she valued being a miser from the first time I met her eyes.

With an exasperated sigh, she opens her small, beaded purse, takes out four more opal rounds, and places them on the table. "Good day, Miss Lovecraft." In much the same manner as Mr. Carver departed my company an hour ago, Miss Hampstead leaves the room, not bothering to close the door behind her.

I rise from the table and tidy the little room in her wake, arranging the red silk pillows against the walls in neat, comfy-looking piles. Not that they're anything more than props to help set a mood appropriate for a brothel. In the adjoining rooms, the pillows and furniture are used for all manners of romantic transactions—ones I'd rather not ponder too long. Ever since I set up shop at Madame Desire's Pleasure House, the only thing that ever gets used in this room is the table, and that's only for the sake of consultations with my clients. Still, I keep the pillows. I like the way they look. They're cute and they make me feel warm and cozy.

A figure darkens my doorway, and I find Madame Desire leaning against the doorframe. She wears a red, skintight, spider silk dress that covers nearly every inch of skin while somehow leaving very little to the imagination. The skin she does show is pale pink, standing in contrast to her crimson hair that flows around her in rippling, weightless curls. One side of her perfect tresses is pinned up with a heart-shaped comb, revealing a pointed ear—a sign that she's full fae. My ears, on the other hand, are round like a human's.

Madame Desire's voice comes out soft and sultry as she bats dark pink lashes at me. "Remind me why I allow you to work for me when half your clientele leaves in a huff."

With a grin, I approach her with an outstretched hand. She opens her palm, and I drop five of the opal rounds into it.

Whatever I make, Madame Desire gets half—unlike her courtesans, who she pays handsomely and treats like queens. That
isn't to say she treats me badly, only that I haven't been here
long enough to prove I'm worthy of a raise just yet. "Because I
still get paid, which means so do you."

She drops four of the rounds down the front of her dress
but keeps one in her palm. She runs her thumb over the
smooth surface of the opal. "I suppose our arrangement is
adequate, *Miss Lovecraft.*" She says the name with a note of
taunting. Even though she knows it isn't my real name—in fact,
everyone goes by a pseudonym at Madame Desire's brothel—
she's never inquired about my true identity. She has no clue I'm
Astrid Snow, fugitive princess. Nor does she seem even
remotely curious. I appreciate that about Madame Desire and
the Seven Sins Hotel. The Seven Sins is a place of escape. Of
pleasure, vice, and fantasy. Not truth. Which is why it's the
perfect place for me to hide.

"Although," she says, tapping a fuchsia fingernail to her
chin, "I can't imagine why you wouldn't rather work for me like
my courtesans do. With a lovely face like that, you'd make us far
more than a dozen opal rounds a week."

I nearly scoff at that. A dozen opal rounds is hardly what I'd
consider measly. Opal rounds are the highest form of currency
in the Fire Court, with opal chips being the lowest. Besides, she
hasn't the slightest clue that her brothel's patrons wouldn't see
me the same way she does. She perceives me as beautiful.
Desirable. A being of supreme sensuality. Instead, I'm a half-
human fugitive wanted by the Queen of Spring for murder. I'm
nothing like the sultry, seductive nymphs and succubi the
brothel is renowned for. They are what make Madame Desire's
Pleasure House different from any other brothel in Faerwyvae.
It's the only one that legally utilizes fae courtesans. All other
fae brothels were outlawed decades ago. Furthermore, I have

no desire to work in the sex trade. "I prefer my line of employment, Madame Desire."

She studies me, eyes narrowing as if noticing something she hadn't before. My pulse quickens, half with panic, half with hope. Even though no one but my father has ever seen through my magic, I can't help but humor the possibility that it could happen again. Sometimes I'd give anything to be truly *seen*. To hear someone say those dreaded words *you are* followed by something true for once. I wonder if I'd even recognize the truth if I heard it. I've spent so much of my whole life being told what I am, described as nothing more than another's reflection, that I'm not even sure there's a real me to be seen.

Madame Desire stiffens, a slight curl to her upper lip. Disappointment and relief flood me at once. I recognize that look. I've seen it more times than I can count. Her momentary scrutiny wasn't due to her seeing through my magic but discovering something new in her reflection. Or, more accurately, something familiar, beloved, cherished. Something she loves about herself...but not in others.

She tilts her head to the side. "I do wonder when you might just use this *line of employment* to steal one of our client's objects of affection for yourself and leave me with a sobbing girl and a lawsuit on my hands." She says it with a smile, her tone light with jest, but I know her concern is real.

"Love isn't in the cards for me, Madame Desire. I prefer to serve others." It's only half true. Less that I prefer to serve others, and more that I know finding love for myself is folly. I've already learned what it means to be courted by a person who's only in love with themselves.

Her grin widens as she pushes off the doorframe. "If you say so, Miss Lovecraft."

As she leaves, I wonder how long it will take before she turns on me. They always do. It's the downside to being a mirror.

Once I make an impression on a person, I'm stuck with it. Every time I meet that person's eyes, the same impression snaps into place. I can't turn my magic off. I can't reverse it. The best thing I can do is manage my mood and try to make only positive impressions. But even that comes with risks. Not all people enjoy seeing their most cherished attributes in another person. And when they do, there often comes a time when the dynamic shifts. Admiration turns to envy. Respect turns to disdain. Especially when one's best qualities are deeply entwined with their worst. I only hope Madame Desire's benevolence outlasts my most recent employer's, because I'm not ready to leave. I've only been at the Seven Sins Hotel for a month, and I like it here. I like the music, the lights, the vibrancy. I even like the darker aspects, like the fighting pit in Department Wrath. Most of all, I like using my magic in a way that feels useful.

It reminds me of how things were when Father was alive. Back when I would use my power to aid his work as a portraitist. I would sit in on his sessions, tap into my magic to see what his clients valued most about themselves, and relay my findings to him. It was our secret, and what he claimed was his key to success, allowing him to paint hidden qualities into every portrait and satisfy even his most demanding patrons.

That was before he painted Queen Tris. Before he won her heart three years ago with his breathtaking talents. Before he died and left me at the mercy of his vindictive widow, a woman who would sooner sever my head from my shoulders than consider me innocent of the crime she blames me for.

I shudder as her final words echo through my mind.

*You did this.*

At least I have one consolation. My nemesis has no idea what I look like. Only she could ever recognize me by the impression we first formed three years ago, when I sat in on Father's session with her, whispering my findings and watching as he brought her best qualities to life in vibrant shades of brown and pink. She can send all the bounty hunters and assassins she wants. None of them will find the girl she describes.

Unless the Spring Queen comes for me herself, no one will ever find me.

# 2

*THE HUNTSMAN*

She's here. I know it as soon as I crest the dune and catch my first sight of the sunstone arch that marks the entrance to the city of Irridae. And thank the blooming hell my target is close, for the sooner I get this done, the sooner I can get out of this infernal heat. The Fire Court is no place for a bear. At least not one used to the cooler climate of Spring.

Warm air ruffles my fur as a train rushes by on the tracks to my right. I inhale, catching aromas of coal, steel, and an assortment of cargo. At the very back of the train is a passenger car. The faint whiff of skin, hair, and sweat tells me it carries mostly humans, although I catch scents that are undoubtedly fae too; something woodsy from an earth fae, the salty tang of a sea fae. A pinch of envy strikes me as I imagine the cooled interior of the train car. I'd have taken the train too had I not been so determined to follow my target's scent trail on foot. Had her scent diverged between stops, I wanted to know about it with enough advance warning to change course with it. Something that wouldn't be so easy to do while blazing across the desert at a breakneck pace. Though, in the end, it seems the runaway princess rode the train with no deviation, straight from Lumenas to Irridae.

As the train pulls into the city, it takes the temporary breeze with it, leaving me panting in its wake, my tongue lolling from my muzzle. I claw at the ground beneath my paws, seeking cooler sand beneath the sunbaked top layers, and watch the entrance to the city for a few moments longer. With a deep inhale, I home in on the singular scent I've been following for two weeks. It's the strongest it's ever been.

Which means she *must* be here.

Anticipation buzzes through me as I transfer my weight to my hind legs, then lift off my front paws until I'm standing upright. With a shudder that ripples from my ears to my claws, my body begins to contract, my brown fur shrinking into my pores, replaced with smooth flesh. Claws become fingernails while paws shrink into hands. Soon my unseelie bear form gives way to my seelie form. The ability to shift between the two forms is common amongst faekind. Our unseelie form is our natural manifestation, while our seelie form is modeled after a human likeness. Not all seelie bodies mimic humankind so convincingly, though. Many retain animalistic features—ears, tails, antlers—or other inhuman characteristics. My seelie form, however, is as inconspicuous as they come. Save for my pointed ears and towering height, I could pass for the average human male.

My loss of fur brings some relief from overheating, but I'm still dressed in the last thing I wore in seelie form—full evening attire. It was an outfit appropriate for hunting my target in the theatrical city of Lumenas, but not at all suited for this new climate. I frown down at the sand slowly swallowing my polished shoes and shrug off my frock coat. With it slung over my shoulder, I roll up my sleeves, remove my cravat, and unbutton my waistcoat. Then I proceed toward the city.

Once I reach the sunstone arch, I cross under it and step onto the sidewalk. Phaetons and other open-air carriages pass down Nieman Avenue—the main thoroughfare that spans the length of the city—while the sidewalk crowds with pedestrians stopping at storefronts and market stalls.

I brush past them and continue down Nieman Avenue, following the scent trail that is undeniably Astrid Snow. It's an aroma I've grown keenly attuned to, reminiscent of morning dew, apple blossoms, and lemon. A personal scent like all beings have, one derived from a medley of body, mind, and soul to create a perfume unique to the individual. Were she but a stranger in a crowd, I'd give her fragrance no more than a cursory sniff. But since Miss Snow is my target, her scent stands out amongst the sweat, sand, and bodies like a golden thread in an otherwise plain tapestry.

I try not to think about what I'll have to do once I locate the runaway princess, only *why* I must do it. There's no way out of it now. I made the bargain.

*Find Astrid Snow and bring me her heart.*

As personal bounty hunter to the fae royals, conscripted into service as punishment for the mountain of debt I've collected, I don't get to say no to jobs ordered by the kings and queens of Faerwyvae. It's work I must do until I've served the term of my sentence, so I do it, no questions asked. But I could have said no to the last part. I could have agreed to do only what I'm known for. Find the fugitive. Bring her back alive for trial.

*Bring me her heart and I'll erase your debts and consider your sentence fulfilled.*

Freedom. That's what drives me now. What drove me to say yes two weeks ago when the Spring Queen asked me to commit a vile act well beyond what is required of me. All I have to do is take one life, then my hundred-year sentence of servitude will be over, completed in just five years. Only then can I start earning money of my own. Only then will I have the chance to buy back the inheritance I so recklessly gambled away. I may have an immortal life span, but every minute I bear the weight of my shame is the purest agony. If I have to kill one murderous girl to reclaim what my father left me, I'll do it.

It isn't anything less than she deserves, considering the crime she committed, the unforgivable method she utilized to kill Edmund Snow. Her own father. I may bear the guilt of gambling away my deceased father's fortune, but at least I know what I did was wrong. At least I now do whatever I can to honor his memory. Unlike Miss Snow, a girl whose guilt I confirmed within moments of finding her scent, a fragrance that told secrets I'm sure she thought no one would ever uncover. Besides, what I must do to her will be a mercy compared to whatever punishment her stepmother would design for her.

Sweat beads my brow as I cross Darton Street to the north end of the city. There I catch my first glimpse of the enormous structure perched at the far end of Nieman Avenue. The Seven Sins Hotel. It spans nearly the full length of the city behind a tall sandstone wall lined with palm trees. Rumor has it a portion of the hotel was once the palace of a fae queen before she had a new residence built following the war that united the humans and fae. Seeing the hotel for the first time now, I believe those rumors are likely true. Everything about the Seven Sins is palatial, from its construction of sandstone and white marble to the elegant towers glittering with sunlight.

The streets and sidewalks grow more crowded the closer I get to the hotel, the establishments far finer to compete with the high-priced vices that the Seven Sins offers. Here, pedestrians wear their finest daytime attire complete with straw hats or parasols to defend against the relentless heat. I feel somewhat out of place with my dressed-down evening wear, but no one pays me much heed.

I reach the wall outside the hotel and cross under yet another sunstone arch. Here it's even busier with patrons coming and going or lounging by the palm-shaded pools flanking the red tile walkway that splits an enormous courtyard in two. The walkway leads to the main entrance—Department Pride. Adjoining Pride is Department Sloth, where all the suites are located. If the rumors are true, these two departments comprise what was once the original palace, while the remaining five buildings stand separate, divided by small alleyways. My fingers flinch as my gaze locks onto one particular building to the right, a marble behemoth of twelve floors topped with a gold-plated pyramid. Although I've never laid eyes on the building before now, Department Greed is well renowned as the largest, most extensive gambling house in all of Faerwyvae.

Shame mingles with a sharp yearning for quick wins, easy money, and the spike of euphoria that comes with both. Being so close to card tables, roulette wheels, and betting machines is all it takes to set my teeth on edge. It was bad enough having to follow the runaway princess' scent through Lumenas, a city with its fair share of vice. But this...this is worse. Everything inside me begs to enter that building, to try my luck at dice before unleashing my true talents at the Poker and Doubt tables. Where one's lies are whispered to me on the winds of scent fluctuations, where I can't possibly lose—

*No.*

I stop myself midstep, realizing I'd already begun heading for Department Greed.

Even after everything I've lost, after everything I've done, the dark allure is still so strong. I should know better. And I do. I also know that Greed is unlike any other gambling hall. There are very few limits to what one can wager. Not only money but limbs, teeth, lives. So long as it is one's own property, it can be placed on the table. The danger of such a gamble should turn my stomach. Instead, I can only think of the rewards I could receive if I bet everything left to my name—which is only my flesh, life, and blood—and won.

I clench my teeth so hard, pain pulses in my jaw.

I wonder if Queen Tris had any inkling as to where my mission would lead me. She knows why I lost Davenport Estate. She knows I gambled everything my father had left me in a bet that was supposed to be a sure win. If she *did* know I'd be forced to confront such temptations on my mission, then she's a crueler woman than I thought. Then again, perhaps that's why she offered me such a favorable bargain.

With a deep inhale, I reconnect to my target's scent trail, the whiff of apple blossoms and dew stronger now, saturating this very walking path, circling around every building. I tear myself away from the lure of Department Greed and follow the faintest scents first, acquainting myself with the areas Miss Snow first frequented upon arriving at the hotel. I don't enter any of the buildings yet. Instead, I put my hands in my pockets and stroll at a leisurely pace like the other visitors and guests, skirting around the enormous structure of the combined Pride and Sloth, then Gluttony. I weave around Department Envy with its four stories boasting the latest fashions and finest wares in every window. Then I pass the single story that is Department Wrath, rumored to host an underground fighting pit. Finally, I reach Department Lust. Here Miss Snow's scent is condensed, trailing all the way back to the first time she arrived, with the freshest still hanging in the air from no less than an hour ago. I stop outside the main entrance and stare up at the six stories, each lined with crimson shutters.

So she's a courtesan now.

Excitement bubbles in my chest. For one glorious moment, it feels too easy. I picture myself entering the building, requesting a night with Miss Snow, and completing my mission in the privacy of a pillowed room, where any shouts of alarm can be muffled by the sounds of pleasure emanating from behind adjoining walls.

It would be over so quickly. Quick enough that I won't have time to lament. To dread. To hate myself for the gruesome act I must commit.

Logic invades my mind, sending my hope fleeing as I realize it won't be as simple as I imagined. The girl won't be going by her true name here. And if I don't have her name, I can't request her at all, for I have no physical description of her to give.

It didn't take long for me to understand why no one was able to find Astrid Snow before Queen Tris called on my services. The princess' scent was faint by the time I arrived at Fairweather Palace to investigate, but thank the All of All it hadn't disappeared completely. Had I simply followed the queen's description of her runaway stepdaughter, I never would have found her.

*Skin like the eldest of trees. Hair like the first pink blossom of spring. Lips like the reddest poppy.*

I was confused over why the queen would describe her stepdaughter's appearance so much like her own when Miss Snow is only a princess through marriage, not blood. Even stranger was the fact that the princess was the daughter of a renowned painter-turned-king yet had never had her likeness captured in portrait. The princess' maid, a human girl named Marybeth, was the only person who offered anything helpful at all. I'd requested interviews with the palace staff who'd been closest to the princess, and none had given me anything useful. Not until I spoke to Marybeth.

"You will not know her by sight," the human girl said during our private interview. The way she kept her voice to a whisper, eyes darting wildly about as she spoke, told me such intel was known by few. Perhaps not even by the queen. "She will look different to you than she does to the queen, or anyone else for that matter."

Based on that, I've determined Miss Snow must be a glamourist. And if she has any wits at all, she'll most certainly be using a new glamour by now. Just like she did in Lumenas. While there, I followed her scent to a matchmaker's office, where a fae female claimed to have employed a young woman for two weeks. All she remembered of my target's appearance was the striking purple of her irises—the same shade as her own. Everything else she said revolved around what a swindling thief the girl was, which was why she dismissed her from her employ with a threat to turn her over to the city patrol officers as well. I find it rather odd that the woman only remembered one physical feature about Miss Snow—the feature the woman herself possessed— while everything else she described were personality traits. Perhaps the fugitive knows how to weave a forgettable glamour.

Regardless, I'll need to catch a glimpse of the princess' newest disguise if I am to request her company.

Keeping my attention fixed firmly on my target's scent, I round the building, leaving the main walkway to pass through the alley between Lust and Wrath. It lets out to an expansive garden brimming with fragrant roses, lilies, trailing jasmine, and other plants not often seen in the desert. The floral aroma is so heady that it overpowers Miss Snow's scent—and sends a throbbing to my skull in the process. I exhale, releasing my hold on the scent trail as I hurry past the noxious garden and enter the alley on the opposite side of the building between Lust and the towering perimeter wall. Breathing in again, I pick up the scent, surprised to find it startlingly potent.

I know she's there, even before I see her.

My heart thuds heavily in my chest as one of the alleyway doors opens to reveal a petite figure. I freeze as she steps into the alley and kneels beside a waste bin. She's facing away from me, so I can't make out her features, nor can I see what she's doing. My fingers flinch at my sides, my pulse hammering as I consider that *this* might be the time to act. *This* might be my best chance to fulfill the bargain I made. But no matter how many times I've reasoned that it must be done, it's one thing to commit to it and another to actually do it, especially when faced with my target for the first time. She's so much smaller than I expected her to be. And her scent...it's...changed. Or perhaps it's only grown more complex now that we're so close. There's something sweeter in the bouquet. Something softer.

I shake the notion from my mind and remind myself why I'm here.

*Bring me her heart and you'll be free.*

I curl my fingers into fists and start down the alley, my steps even. Casual. Silent. She keeps her back to me as she sets something on the ground. I take another step closer. Another. My next step brings us only a sparse few feet away. Just then, she rises to her feet and turns halfway around. Now I can glimpse her profile, but all my eyes seem to register is her posture. Her shoulders are relaxed, her arms cradled around a white bundle of fluff. It takes me a moment to realize it's a kitten. There are three more mewling around her ankles, plus a too-thin mother cat eating from a bowl Miss Snow must have placed on the ground. I try to study my target's face, but all I can make out is the curve of her jaw, the ghost of a smile on her lips as she brings the kitten to her cheek and nuzzles it.

I halt again, noting another strange shift in her fragrance. No, not a shift. A...scent memory. A familiarity. I shake my head. Of course her scent is familiar. I've been following it for two damn weeks. And yet, there's something different about it. Something I can't quite—

Astrid Snow whirls fully toward me with a startle. Only now do I realize I'd taken a step closer, and this one wasn't so silent. Our eyes lock, and my mind empties of all reason. I don't recall why I was momentarily confused. All I know is that my heart feels as if it's been torn in two, for no other reason but the agonizing urge to *protect*. But protect what? The kitten in the murderer's arms?

No.

My breath catches as the impossible answer crawls to the forefront of my mind.

The urge is to protect *her*. The girl I've been sent to kill.

I clench my jaw to fight the overwhelming instinct, one that has no place invading my good sense. Whatever magic she has, it's messing with my mind. My emotions. And it still has me in its grip. For a split second, I feel as if I'm a cub again, small and helpless in a rapidly changing world, where the safety of my forest home is replaced with iron traps and blood—

"Can I help you, sir?" Astrid Snow's voice cuts through my stupor. It isn't a gentle sound. It's a harsh tone laced with suspicion, at odds with the sweet aroma I breathed in a moment before.

It's enough to clear my mind and remind me who this girl really is.

A murderer. My target. My ticket to freedom.

With a deep breath, I stand tall and tear my gaze from her. My eyes land on a couple strolling up the path along the wall toward the mouth of the alley. The man looks our way and tips his straw hat before meandering on.

Damn. It's too busy to act now. Too bright.

The realization is almost a relief.

"No, Miss," I say, doing my best to keep my voice steady. "I am only cutting through." Since I'm full fae, I can't lie, which means I must follow through on my statement. I keep my distance as I pass swiftly by. Still, the smell of apple blossoms nearly robs me of my wits all over again, even with the waste bins so nearby. Every step I place between us sends my muscles uncoiling and provides a respite from the strange hold her magic had on me. I wasn't prepared for that.

But I will be next time.

And there *will* be a next time. I know where she works. I'll find out where she sleeps. I'm already getting an idea of which buildings in the hotel she most commonly frequents. All I need is the cover of darkness and a moment to get her alone.

As I stalk away from Department Lust, I realize that even though I saw her face—or whatever glamoured countenance she conjured—I still have no idea what Astrid Snow looks like.

# 3

## ASTRID

I've seen plenty of handsome faces in my day—something that comes easily when I can stare without being noticed —and the man marching away from Department Lust is no exception. However, there's something dark in his handsomeness, in the sharp edges of his jaw nearly hidden behind his overgrown beard, in the cruel curve of his full lips, in the angry shade of copper tinting his slightly mussed hair, in his broad, towering build.

His presence was startling when I first found him leering behind me in the alleyway, but I was more put off by his curled fists, his tense shoulders, the way he stared at me as if he'd expected to find me there. It's a rare thing for me to be noticed as anything other than a vague figure, especially before I've made eye contact. Perhaps the kitten had been what first caught his eye and not me. But what kind of lunatic sees a kitten and does anything but melt into a puddle of absolute bliss? I'd been too startled by his presence to get a clear read on the impression I made on him, but he seemed to be wound tighter than a clock.

"Maybe he's allergic," I whisper to the cuddly ball of fluff wriggling in my arms before casting a final glance at the man's retreating form. His hands uncurl finger by finger before he shakes them out at his sides. My lips quirk into a half grin. "Or maybe he just needs a tumble with one of Madame Desire's courtesans."

The kitten makes no reply, of course, for she's just a regular kitten, not a fae creature. It isn't always easy to tell the difference between the average animal and a fae in their unseelie form, but I've learned the hard way that fae are far less amenable to being petted by random strangers. Kittens, on the other hand, accept pets just fine. Not only that, but they don't seem the least bit affected by my magic. As far as I can tell, they don't see me as a mirror like humans and fae do. Which is why —in my esteemed opinion—animals are better than people.

Forgetting the handsome stranger, I crouch beside the waste bin and set down Madeline, the white kitten. Mama Cat looks up from her plate of salmon I got from the butcher at Gluttony this morning, giving me a grateful meow before returning to her meal. The other three kittens, whom I've named Abernathy, Natalie, and Grigg, scramble up my skirts for their turns to be petted. My smile widens as a hum of euphoria ripples in my chest. The way I feel around animals is better than even the temporary high I get from my Crimson Malus tincture. I've always felt this way. Animals—and the feel of fur and soft textures in general—have a way of calming me like nothing else. It's probably because my earliest memory is of the fur pelt my father wrapped me in when he first held me. What preceded that is far less pleasant, but thankfully I don't remember it. All I know is my water sprite mother gave birth to me, tolerated me for less than a year, and then left me on the bank of her lake for my father to find.

The thought has my emotions slipping toward anger, so I lift up Grigg, an orange tabby who looks just like Mama Cat. I bring him to my cheek and nuzzle his soft fur while Madeline climbs up my back and onto my shoulder to nibble the ends of my hair. Mama Cat must be doing her duties to keep them groomed, for they all seem rather clean and well-kept for a family of strays. Still, I wish I could do more for them. "I could probably sneak you into Department Sloth," I say to Grigg, but even if I were to take the family of cats into my tiny room at the hotel, I know they don't belong indoors without better accommodations.

My lady's maid, Marybeth, was always reminding me of this fact whenever I thought about sneaking a pet into the palace. Queen Tris would never allow it, of course, but that didn't stop me from plotting. Always the voice of reason, Marybeth made sure my plots remained in the realm of fantasy. She'd remind me how much trouble I'd be in should Tris ever catch me bringing animals into her palace. When that didn't work, she'd bring up the childhood stories I'd told her...and their disastrous consequences.

I can't count the times I snuck furry creatures into the house when I was younger, hoping I could keep them without Father noticing. Even when I did manage to hide them from his knowledge for a day or two, the evidence would eventually show up. Particularly the messes. Animal waste and nibbled bedsheets were only the half of it. The worst was when an injured squirrel—who clearly didn't need my care as much as I'd thought—found her way into Father's studio and nibbled two sketchbooks, four tubes of paint, and the corner of his current portrait commission. When Father found the critter invading his most sacred workspace, he laughed. Actually laughed. He delivered his scolding with a smile that crinkled the corners of his eyes. It made me feel guiltier than if he'd yelled.

Grief plummets my stomach, opening a chasm so vast that not even the four kittens climbing all over me can lift my spirits. I run my hands over my silk skirt, focusing on the smooth texture to distract myself from the oncoming wave of sorrow, but that doesn't work either. Even as I try to force thoughts of Father's loss from my mind, my previous musings about Marybeth remain, reminding me of how much I miss her.

She was more than just my lady's maid. She was my friend. The only true friend I've ever had. As a human girl, she related to that side of me. Since I'd come from living amongst a primarily human society only to be thrust into life in a palace teeming with fae, she was a comfort to me. She had a way about her that encouraged me to open up, always asking gentle questions and listening to my answers with quiet curiosity. When I finally took the risk and told her about my magic— something I'd sworn off doing after such actions wreaked havoc on my life in the past—she accepted me. No suspicion. No sudden awkwardness. I hate that I had to leave her behind, but we both knew she couldn't run away with me. We'd have drawn more suspicion as a runaway pair. Not to mention the fact that Marybeth can be recognized by physical appearance. Unlike me.

Instead, I'm alone.

Alone.

Closing my eyes against the well of tears that have sprung there, I reach into my skirt pocket and pull out my vial.

One drop under the tongue. Two.

Soon I'm back to content. Numb. Perfectly fine.

THREE DAYS LATER, I'M IN MY BEDROOM AT DEPARTMENT SLOTH, preparing for my night's work. I've secured two new jobs since finishing up with Miss Hampstead. My first new client is a fawn who works in the hat department at Envy. She's desperate to learn what it would take to win the heart of the well-dressed merchant she fancies. My second is Mrs. Haywood, a concerned mother of the fae aristocracy. Her youngest daughter is set on marrying a wealthy human who recently began courting her since arriving in Irridae. Mrs. Haywood, however, would rather her daughter wait until she's officially presented at the next social season, in hopes of snagging an even better match.

Tonight, I'll be investigating the latter case. I don't always work at night, but the intel Mrs. Haywood gave me is too good to pass up. Turns out the suitor in question, Mr. Donnelly, attends nearly every fighting match at Department Wrath. Who could blame him? I too find myself seated around the fighting pit several nights a week.

I glance at the clock perched on the nightstand beside my narrow bed—the only furnishings in my tiny room aside from the low chest I keep my clothing in. The clock reads eight forty-five. Fifteen minutes from when tonight's fight begins and my spying on my target ensues. I change out of my clothing in favor of a clean linen skirt and blouse that hasn't already suffered from the sweltering heat of the day and the unavoidable sweat that comes with it. Not that my new ensemble won't soon be exposed to much of the same once I enter the fighting pit. With my fondness for soft textiles comes a preference for clean ones too. They always feel nicer against my skin. More calming when I run my hands over the fabric. Not nearly as calming as fur, of course, but enough to have my clothing chest over-flowing with an abundance of simple comforts bought at Department Envy.

I only shop on the lower levels, where secondhand clothes and basic attire can be found. There's always something there that suits my needs—skirts in soft cotton, lightweight linen blouses, smooth satin. I have no need for the designer dresses with fancy trimmings found on the upper levels. Not when no one sees what I wear anyway. That and I'd rather not spend money on frivolous things. This is why I live on the bottom floor of Department Sloth, in a cramped unit with a single window and no iced fan to cool the room. I've saved a decent amount from matchmaking and could likely afford a room on the second or third floor, but I don't want to risk being destitute should I be forced on the run again.

At five minutes to nine, I leave my lodgings and head for Department Wrath. A breeze settles over my skin, the air cooled in the sun's absence. It dances up my neck, rustling my short tresses. I reach Department Wrath, a circular single-story building of brown sandstone topped with decorative crenelations. Instead of heading for the ticket booth at the front door where a long line of patrons file in, I skirt down the alley between Wrath and Lust, then around the back. I breathe deeply as I pass the fragrant garden, which is one of my favorite places on the hotel's property. Once I reach the rear of the building, I enter the back door to a dark hallway. Norace, the centaur working security, half rises before he recognizes me. What he recognizes is his own honesty, strength, and sense of justice. The only true thing he knows about me is that I'm an investigator of sorts working for Madame Desire. It's a true kind of lie that gets me free entrance to watch the fights. At least tonight I really am here on business.

Norace shifts on his hooves to allow me to pass. "Who are you spying on tonight, Miss Lovecraft?"

I wink at him. "You know I'll never tell."

He gives an appreciative grunt. "Client confidentiality. I respect that."

I follow the length of the dark hall until it opens to the brightly lit main building. It's comprised of a circular walkway with an obsidian marble floor edged in a black rail. The center of the room is hollow, ending at the fighting pit four floors down. The walls are papered with red and gold brocade while warm light glows from bright lamps encased with black metalwork, casting sinister shadows on the gilded frames lining the walls. Each frame bears a different painted portrait of the most renowned fighters who have graced the arena in years past.

The walkway is crowded with excited guests—men and women, human and fae—funneling in from the main entrance. I exit the hall to join the flow of foot traffic. The air fills with chatter as we circle the perimeter of the room, then descend the spiral staircase that continues down to the cylindrical underground portion of the building. The lighting grows dimmer the farther we go, the walls darker, the mood more excited. Finally, the staircase lets out to a walkway that surrounds the circular tiered seating. In the very center of the stadium is the sandy floor of the fighting pit. I continue around the stadium until I reach the aisle my client indicated at our meeting.

According to Mrs. Haywood, Mr. Donnelly owns one of the private boxes at the very front of the arena. The most dangerous—and most coveted—seats in the pit. His is just left of center, so I only leave the walkway once I've located the box I think is his. Instead of heading for the front, I slide onto a bench at the far back. This might be one of the least ideal seats in the house, but it means I won't be bothered much. No one would dare ask me to trade seats so their companion might sit next to them, nor will anyone notice a nondescript girl staring at the front box too long.

The arena fills up quickly, and I'm nearly bouncing in my seat with anticipation. I'm so excited that I almost miss the arrival of Mr. Donnelly. He claims his seat in the box with three other male companions, each with a drink in hand. That's another benefit to owning a box. Those patrons get meal and drink service while the rest of us must visit the concessions at the far end of the arena. Aromas of foods from said concessions waft into the air, filling my nose with the zesty tang of fruity ices, the mellow earthiness of chilled teas, and the heady sweet-ness of Agave Ignitus wine—Fire Court's signature spirit.

Any minute now, every aroma will be drowned out by the scents of blood, sweat, and maybe even magic. It's a morbid thought, yet it excites me nonetheless. I clamp my hands together at my chest, Mr. Donnelly forgotten, and lean forward with bated breath. I've been looking forward to tonight's fight for a week. An ogre will be fighting a griffin. Not just any griffin, but the famous Helody, who decapitated the last person she fought against with a single swipe of her claws. Helody doesn't appear in the pit often, as she isn't a career fighter. However, griffins are known to have no tolerance for bad manners. If someone so much as insults a single hair on one of her chil-dren's heads, she'll challenge the perpetrator to a duel. And this is the only establishment on the isle of Faerwyvae where such duels can legally take place.

That's what makes the pit in Department Wrath different from other fighting arenas. Where most sports were brought to Faerwyvae by humans, organized by careful rules and regula-tions, and host primarily human athletes, Wrath features fae fighters who don't often come from professional fighting back-grounds. These duels are personal in nature, granted only to those who can prove to Madame Fury—the head of Depart-ment Wrath—that their grievance is just. Unless you're an established fighter, petitioning her costs almost a hundred opal rounds. But it's a price many are willing to pay to claim vengeance at their own hands. To see justice served where Faerwyvae's legal system fails—or to die trying. There are very few rules aside from sound-minded consent to fight and a restriction from harming anyone but one's opponent during the duel. The fighters can battle to the death or until the other yields. They can fight with magic or they can use strength alone.

My favorite fights are the ones that utilize wits over all else. One of the first I witnessed was like that. A tiny fire sprite challenged a dragon over the murder of her soot sprite lover. Everyone knew the dragon would win. Even with both combatants being fire fae, the dragon had the advantage of size. And yet, the sprite was fearless, constantly baiting him to chase after her, tossing insult after insult. In the end, she tricked the dragon into confessing his crime. The sprite immediately yielded, losing the duel. But she won the war. After such a public confession, the authorities were able to act and arrest the dragon.

That's the kind of fight that makes me so determined to stay at the Seven Sins Hotel, fanning the flames of a hidden hope I hardly dare to acknowledge. A hope that, perhaps one day, I'll save enough opal rounds to buy a meeting with Madame Fury and earn my own shot at vengeance. A hope that, if I watch enough fights, sooner or later someone will set a precedent, and I'll learn how a powerless half-human girl can defeat a queen.

It's a childish hope, merely a fledgling fantasy that I know I'll never see materialized, but I cling to it nonetheless.

Hopes and frail fantasies aside, this fight will surely be one of brawn over brains, and I can't wait for it to start. As soon as I heard Helody was returning to the pit, I knew I had to be here. Based on how crowded the arena is now, I'm not the only one. Even the back bench I'm seated on has become packed. I've already been shuffled from one side to the other several times as excited spectators flank me until hardly an inch separates me from my bench mates. I glance down one end of the bench, finding it mostly occupied by young men dressed down to their shirtsleeves, probably laborers from the warehouse district. No one pays me the slightest heed, which suits me well enough. But when I glance down the opposite end of the bench, my heart nearly leaps out of my chest.

A pair of honey-colored irises stare back at me beneath two auburn brows. The man quickly looks away before we can properly lock eyes, but I can't do the same. For seated next to me, so close that the hem of my skirt brushes his pants, is the stranger from the alley. His appearance has somewhat changed since our encounter a few days ago. Hair no longer in disarray, his copper tresses are neatly styled in a light wave. His beard is trimmed close to his chiseled jaw. His outfit has changed too. Instead of evening wear, he's dressed in linen pants, a light-weight waistcoat, and a cotton shirt unbuttoned to the middle of his chest. The fact that each article of clothing is black makes him stand out against the lighter hues most people favor in the heat of the Fire Court. His pointed ears tell me he's fae while the set of his shoulders reveals the same tenseness he held in the alley.

Slowly, I drag my eyes away from him, but I can't help the uneasy feeling that settles in my gut. Is it only a coincidence that the same man from earlier is sitting next to me now?

The lights suddenly dim, sending a spike of alarm through me, but it's quickly washed away as three spotlights illuminate the sandy pit. My concern over the stranger trickles away as two gates on opposite sides of the pit creak open, splitting at the center to unveil two dark archways. Silence fills the arena, and I find myself scooting to the edge of my seat. Finally, after an unbearable wait, a taloned foot emerges from the shadows of the first archway, followed by an enormous birdlike head. Next, Helody reveals her lionlike midsection and hind paws. She snaps her beaked mouth and struts to the center of the arena, gold wings splayed wide while her slim tail whips side to side, painting her aggression in quick strokes. The audience erupts in a cheer, then begins to hum with an equal number of boos as her opponent marches out of his gate.

I read up on the match days ago, so I know the ogre is named Murtis. He's making his debut in the ring after he tried to eat Helody's youngest daughter. He must have been difficult to persuade to come here, considering the massive sum that will be awarded to tonight's champion. Each fight's prize is calculated based on the fame of the fighters and the cost of getting both parties to agree to fight. Since Helody's previous fights awarded no more than five thousand opal rounds compared to tonight's ten thousand, I suspect the latter factor had the strongest influence.

I honestly wouldn't blame Murtis for being hesitant to fight Helody, what with her fearsome reputation. He looks like he'll pose an adequate challenge for the griffin regardless. He's a head taller than her and twice as wide, dressed in only a loin-cloth. His skin is thick, green, and roped with scars. As he circles the arena, he gnashes his pointed teeth in an attempt to intimidate the griffin. She merely stands with her feathered head held high, patiently awaiting the Master of Ceremonies' announcement that they may begin.

Silence falls again as a fae in humanoid seelie form strolls to the center of the pit, dressed in a purple top hat and frock coat. His bellowing voice introduces the two fighters and recites the pit's few rules. Once the Master of Ceremonies concludes his announcements, he leaps into the air. A pair of violet wings sprout from his back and take him a dozen feet above the sandy pit. "Begin!"

Both the stranger next to me and Mr. Donnelly are entirely forgotten as the two fighters charge toward each other. I bite back a squeal and nibble my lower lip as Helody slices a wide gash across the ogre's chest. Murtis leaps back, his wounds closing up and leaving only three slashes of blood behind. Since fae are essentially immortal, they are very hard to injure, much less kill. Most fae—especially the pureblood kind—heal quickly from superficial wounds. The only way to reliably end another fae's life is to sever their head from their body. Other methods include trapping another fae in a bargain. If they fail to fulfill it, they die. The final method is to wound them using iron, but the metal is illegal in Faerwyvae. The last time it was seen on the isle was during a bloody rebellion several years back.

With a roar, Murtis charges and sends a fist straight for Helody's face. She weaves to dodge it and lands another swipe across his torso. I cheer with the rest of the crowd, sitting so far at the edge of my seat, I wouldn't be surprised if I toppled off. I grip the bench's ledge for good measure. Helody claws the ogre again, then lunges her beak toward his hand. She comes away, sending a spray of blood where she bit off a finger. A startled laugh bursts from my lips. Fae may be able to heal from almost any wound, but lost appendages don't tend to grow back.

The fact that Helody hasn't simply beheaded her opponent shows just how furious she is. She intends to make him suffer. As grim and unladylike as it might be, I can't help but enjoy every minute of it—

Something cold touches my wrist, followed by a snap. I glance down at my right hand, finding a brass band encircling it. It's curved on one end with a flat bar on the other. A chain leads from the flat side to another cuff. An open cuff held by my mysterious bench mate. I lift my eyes to his, but my gaze falls to his widening mouth as his canines slowly stretch into sharp tips.

I try to flinch back but the man on the other side elbows me in the shoulder, forcing me to surge up against the man with the cuffs. Before I can react, the mysterious stranger leans in and brings his lips to my ear. His voice comes out a low, deadly rumble. "Come quietly or I'll tear out your throat with my teeth."

# 4

*ASTRID*

The man waits for me to nod. I know better than to scream. Know better than to cause a scene. It wouldn't matter if I called for help now. Even with my last dose of Crimson Malus still warming my blood, I'm too shocked. Too frightened to feel anything but terror. Which means anyone who met me for the first time now would only see their worst qualities reflected back at them. I've lived with my cursed magic long enough to know that people may have a love-hate relationship with their best qualities, but their worst? They have a hate-hate relationship with those. No one would defend me now. My only hope is that maybe we'll come across Norace, the security centaur. Surely he'd stand up for me, with his admiration for justice.

For now, all I can do is follow my captor as he tugs me off the bench by my cuffed hand. "Struggle and I'll cuff the other one," he says as he drags me away from the arena, away from the seats, and up the walkway that leads toward the spiral staircase. With the hall lights dimmed, the stairs are dark, the only light coming from the arena behind us and a pale hint of light from the very top floor above. No one else is around. No patrons, no security officers, no waitstaff. As we begin to climb, he glances at me time and again, his sharp teeth glinting even in the dark. I don't doubt he'll make good on his threat. Handsome man or no, there's something supremely deadly about him. I still haven't made eye contact long enough to get a read on his qualities, but his actions tell me enough. He's working for my stepmother. I just know it. How he found me, though, is beyond me.

And if he brings me back to her...

Panic surges through me. Despite his threat, I know I can't succumb to whatever fate awaits me. At least now I have the cover of semi-darkness. We climb a few more steps, and I wait until he glances at me one more time. As soon as he turns away, satisfied that I'm still compliant, I tug my cuffed hand with all my might. The still-open cuff slips from his grasp and I quickly dart back down the stairs. While there's no exit outside on the bottom level, I can at least hope to hide somewhere and sneak back upstairs with the rest of the crowd after the fight.

I make it no more than two steps before I trip in my anxious haste. Muscled arms encircle my waist and drag me upright. I swing my arm, knocking the loose cuff into the side of his head. He bats it away before it can make contact, then tries to snatch it back. Before he can grab the cuff, I swipe my nails toward his cheek with my free hand. What I wouldn't give to have claws like Helody right now. Or any useful unseelie form. Unlike most fae—even those with only some fae blood—I don't shift between two forms. Instead, my seelie form is *me* while my unseelie form is the reflected version others see. Blooming useless, in all honesty.

But that doesn't mean I won't try to fight.

My blunted, futile, too-human fingertips are less than an inch away from his face before he grabs my wrist in one large hand, angles my back against the wall, and pins me there, wrist over my head. His other hand secures my shoulder against the wall. I swing my remaining weapon—the loose cuff—at his arm. Instead of striking his forearm or slicing a gash in his flesh, the curved end hooks around his wrist. His eyes widen as he stares down at the cuff. The flat end still hangs loose, open. He freezes, eyes darting from me to the cuff. As his gaze returns to mine, he speaks in a low growl. "Don't you dare."

That's all it takes for me to reach the rest of the way with my cuffed hand and slam the flat portion shut. With a click, it locks in place.

A cold terror shudders through me as I realize what a horrible mistake I just made.

His eyes snap to mine with a furious glare. "Why did you do that?"

I stare at the hand now connected to mine by a brass band and less than a foot of chain.

When I don't answer, he repeats the question, louder this time. "Why the *blooming fuck* did you do that?"

"Because you didn't want me to," I say in a rush. "I thought...I thought..." I don't know what I thought, for I couldn't have made a worse choice. Because now I'm firmly attached to a man who threatened to tear out my throat.

He mutters a curse under his breath and glances down the staircase, then up it. "Very well," he says through his teeth and takes another step closer. Even with one of his feet on the stair below mine, he still towers over me.

"What are you going to do to me?" I ask, my voice a trembling whisper.

"What you deserve." He purses his lips into a tight line and releases my uncuffed left hand. I'm only given a millisecond of hope before his fingertips come to my chest. My pulse thrums as he splays his hand just above my breast. Images of the worst sort run through my mind.

Then I realize something about his touch.

It isn't hard. Isn't groping, roving, or squeezing. Only the pads of his fingertips make contact with my blouse, and it isn't my mound of flesh he's after.

It's my rapidly beating heart.

The images in my mind take a far more gruesome turn, and I know then that he is going to kill me. He's going to rip my heart from my chest. Even with fae blood swimming in my veins, I can't heal as fast as full fae can. In fact, I've learned the hard way that I heal nearly as slowly as a human. Even if I did heal quickly, there is one way to kill a fae that I hadn't considered. Remove one's heart and it won't grow back. It's just as final as a beheading.

I bite back a cry and wait for claws. Surely if he can summon sharp canines in his seelie form, he can summon claws too. I haven't a clue what his unseelie form is, but many fae can partially shift between their two physical manifestations or summon only fragments of their other forms.

My heart slams against his fingertips, my chest heaving with sharp breaths. Breaths that will be my last.

My only consolation is the hope of an afterlife. Then I can be with my father—

With a growl, the man pushes away from me, tearing his hand from my chest. His breaths come out in ragged gasps, pointed teeth receding into his gums until they look square and flat. Ordinary. "What magic are you using on me?"

I meet his eyes, every inch of my body trembling, and try to see what he must see in me. No matter how long I stare, I can't make out the qualities that are normally so easy for me to decipher. For a second, I think I glimpse something—weakness, vulnerability—but it's gone as fast as it came. As I study him again, I see neither of those qualities written in his features. This giant of a man is anything but weak.

And yet...he didn't kill me.

A cheer roars from the arena below, making me nearly jump from my skin. From the pitch and volume of the celebratory noise, the fight must have concluded. I feel a mild pinch of disappointment over not having witnessed it, but my current situation is far more pressing.

"Come," the man grunts. This time, I don't even consider trying to fight him. It's more fruitless than ever now, with my hand chained to his. But if I can find where he keeps the key before he kills me...

"Aren't you going to unlock your cuff?"

"No," he says, and the bitter edge laced into that single word makes me wonder if he perhaps doesn't have the key at all.

My legs feel heavy by the time we reach the top floor of Department Wrath. A spark of hope surges in my chest as he guides me along the walkway and down the hall that leads to the back door. There I find Norace sitting where he always is. But as we draw near, my captor offers the centaur a nod, and Norace...nods back. He doesn't so much as look at me.

"He knows I work for the Alpha Council," my captor explains once the back door slams behind us.

I'm too stunned to say anything to that. I'd already grasped that he'd come for me at the command of Queen Tris, but the Alpha Council is the highest form of government, consisting of all the kings and queens of Faerwyvae. Since there are eleven courts on the isle, with each court being ruled by both a seelie and unseelie monarch, then he serves all twenty-two of them. No wonder Norace didn't question his authority.

Does that mean Tris has convinced the entire Alpha Council of my guilt? The council is supposed to stand for fair trials, not covert abductions and assassination attempts. My eyes unfocus as he leads me down the alleyway between Department Wrath and Lust.

"Is it a glamour?" he says, tone sharp.

I frown up at him. "What?"

"The magic that makes it impossible for me to hurt you. Is it a glamour?"

I blink a few times. "My magic doesn't work like that."

He releases a grumbling sigh. "Fine. I'll take you to her like this. When I bargained to bring her your heart, I didn't specify you wouldn't be attached to it. Although, I'm certain she'll be displeased—"

"No!" I dig my heels in and yank on my cuffed arm. While it sends a spike of pain through my wrist, it doesn't even make him budge. He yanks back and forces me to walk again, but after a few steps, I dig in once more. This time, I ball my fists and try to look as intimidating as possible. As ridiculous a notion as it is, there's a chance it could work. I still don't know what qualities he sees in me, but if he's planning on taking me back to my stepmother, I have to try anything. "You can't bring me back to her."

He halts and whirls to face me. As his eyes land on my balled fists and my half-crouched stance, he lets out a dark chuckle. "You're going back to your stepmother, and there's nothing you can do about it. Especially since you've so conveniently attached yourself to me. I didn't like the idea at first, but honestly," he lifts his cuffed hand, "this works. Now you couldn't get away if you tried."

I stand taller and lock my eyes with his. Once again, I get no clear read on him. What impression did I form? And why is it so unclear? "How do you know I'm not like you?" I say, attempting the same trick I used on the kelpie after I escaped Fairweather Palace.

"Oh, so you're a bounty hunter, then?" he says with clear disbelief.

"Whatever you think you can do to me, I can do to..."

My words dissolve as he steps closer, fully facing me. He looks more relaxed than ever, as if his attempt to kill me was all he needed to shed the tension I'd previously seen. He keeps one hand casually in his pants pocket while he wears the locked cuff like it's a fashionable accessory. He narrows his eyes at me. "Do you not deserve to die after what you did?"

"I didn't kill my father, I promise you."

"You're half human," he says with a derisive snort. "Your promise means nothing when you can lie."

"I'll make a binding vow. I'll do whatever it takes to prove I didn't do it."

His expression remains firm, revealing not an ounce of faith in my words. "Then why did you run?"

My answer comes easily. "Because I knew Queen Tris would blame me either way. She hates me."

He studies me for a few more moments, then leans close. I try to stagger back but he only pulls my cuff, forcing me to nearly collide with his chest. He places his free hand gently behind my back and brings his cheek next to mine. We're so close, I feel the slightest brush of his bearded jaw graze my cheek. I seize up, poised to defend myself against any attack when I hear him take a slow, deep inhale. Then he steps away and looks down at me with a smug grin. "Whatever magic you're using to cloak your lies, it isn't enough to cover the smell of Crimson Malus on you."

I swallow hard, my eyes going wide.

"There's the aroma of guilt I was waiting for," he says, his grin stretching. His elongated canines may have receded, but their absence does little to soften the threat of his very presence. "Now tell me, Miss Snow, if you didn't kill your father, then why the blooming hell do you carry the scent of the same poison that ended his life?"

## 5

## ASTRID

The blood drains from my face, taking all the strength from my knees with it. I stagger back, my free hand reaching blindly behind me for anything that could steady me. Finally, my fingertips brush the wall of Department Wrath. My captor steps forward. At first, I think he might attack again, but I realize he's only standing closer to give slack to the chain that connects our wrists. Only then do I allow myself to lean against the wall. It's all I can do not to collapse to the alley floor entirely.

My throat is so dry I have to swallow several times before I manage to find my voice. "Father...my father was killed by Crimson Malus?"

A furrow forms between the man's brows as he stares down at me. Then he steels his expression and grunts a gruff answer. "Yes."

"How do you know?"

"I'm a bounty hunter. It's my job to know as much about my case as I can."

I try to make sense of what he's saying, but the sudden wave of grief that has me in its grips is clouding my mind. My fingers itch to reach for my vial, to numb this awful emotion, but now would be the worst possible time to prove my possession of the drug. "I knew my father was poisoned," I say, voice small despite my efforts to keep it level. "So that part doesn't surprise me. But how are you so sure it was Crimson Malus?"

His jaw shifts side to side. At first, it seems he won't answer. Then he releases a heavy breath. "I have an impressive sense of smell."

"And you...smelled the poison? How? Where?"

"Two weeks ago, Queen Tris called me in to find you. She'd left the dining room in the same state it had been the night of the murder, cast under an enchantment to suspend decomposition."

My eyes go wide. "Even my father's body?"

"No, he had already been buried by then. But I'd seen the sketches taken by investigators."

I close my eyes against memories of Father's face, of the black veins bulging against his pale skin, running from his mouth to his neck. With a shudder, I force my eyelids open again. "So you investigated the crime scene by...smell. You smelled Crimson Malus. Where did you smell it?"

"I think you know that answer."

I do, but I want to hear him say it. "Tell me. Please."

"I smelled the poison in the pie he took a bite from before he died. The very pie *you* made for him."

Pain sears my heart, bringing tears to my eyes. I already knew it was the pie. Knew it as soon as he began to choke, as soon as I saw those black veins rise to the surface of his skin. Father had taken just one bite before he began to grasp at his throat, clawing the sides of his neck, his lips.

And there was nothing I could do.

Nothing but watch. Shout. Cry for help. Help that wouldn't come until it was too late.

A sudden wave of sound comes from nearby—the patrons from the fight emerging from the front door of Wrath. I almost forgot hearing the cheers that marked the duel's recent end, right before the bounty hunter dragged me up the stairs and into this alley. Now that the fight is over, the guests will spill out onto the walking paths and find vices at the other departments to enjoy.

My captor tugs my cuff, pulling me from the wall. "Walk. And don't cause a scene. My earlier threat remains."

I wonder if he's bluffing. He's already had several chances to tear out both my throat and my heart, and so far he has done neither. I still don't know what he meant when he asked me how my magic made it impossible for him to hurt me. It must have to do with whatever he sees reflected back at him. With my mood so low, my earlier dilemma remains. If I call for help from someone I'm not already acquainted with, they will find only their worst qualities in me now. And even if I were to find someone I know...

I remember how Norace—someone usually so friendly to me—let my captor drag me by like I was no one. All because of who the bounty hunter works for.

There's little else to do but to follow. For now. I've glimpsed...*something* in him a time or two. The way his brow furrowed a few moments ago when he looked at me. The way he tore his hand away from my heart instead of ripping it out. Perhaps there's a chance I can convince him of my innocence.

He leads me to the mouth of the alley where we are quickly swallowed by the crowd spilling out of Wrath. Several patrons stream straight into Department Lust while others head for Greed or Gluttony. The only building that sees less activity at night is Envy, for most guests prefer to do their shopping during daylight hours.

We bypass Lust and follow a slightly less busy path toward the back of the largest building—Sloth. Even with Pride comprising the front of the building, with its enormous lobby, ballrooms, and parlors, Sloth takes up the most real estate.

As we proceed down the path, I keep my eyes averted from those we pass by. I'm determined not to make any new impressions until I've steadied my mood with another dose of Crimson Malus. Still, I have to at least return the polite nods directed at us. I'm not used to such attention when I'm alone. Does everyone get noticed this much, or is it only my captor's towering height and confident bearing that has so many people tipping their hats and nodding? Is this what it's like to be...normal?

"Fine evening," one man says, stopping entirely. He frowns down at our hands, and I feel a flutter of hope in my chest. If he sees our cuffs, perhaps—

A warm, heavy palm presses against mine, claiming my hand in his. My heart lurches at the sudden touch, the feel of a man holding my hand. It's considered far more proper for a couple to stroll with a lady's hand at her companion's elbow. Some circles of society—especially the human upper class—find hand holding to be vulgar.

Heat rises to the other man's cheeks as he lifts his eyes from our joined palms.

"Evening," my captor grunts back. He doesn't release my hand as we brush by the man and continue our journey.

"Where are we going?" I ask, part out of necessity, part to distract myself from the heat of his hand.

"To my suite at Sloth."

Alarm surges through me. "Why?"

"Because there's something there that I need. Something that will allow us to travel quickly back to Spring."

"Please don't take me back," I say, pulling on his hand to no avail. I keep my voice low to avoid being heard by passersby.

And to keep on this side of *not causing a scene*. "Just hear me out. I didn't poison my father."

"Then tell me why you—a princess with a kitchen full of seasoned staff at her disposal—would make a pie with her own hands?"

"It was a gift. A peace offering."

He glances over at me, a knowing look in his eyes. "Because the two of you fought, correct?"

I purse my lips. Is there anything he *doesn't* know?

"If you want your chance to convince me you aren't guilty, then take it now," he says, although his tone suggests he highly doubts I'll succeed. "You have until we arrive at my suite. Answer every question."

"And you'll let me go?"

He says nothing, only quickens our pace. It makes Sloth loom even closer, faster. I understand his silent message. *Time is running out. It's now or never.*

The truth bursts from my lips. "We argued."

"Over what?"

"His wife," I say through my teeth.

"Elaborate."

I bite my lip, my craving for my tincture growing stronger with every step, with every dip my emotions take. I run my free hand over my skirt, trying to focus on the soft texture, but it does little to soothe my nerves or take the edge off my craving. "Queen Tris threatened to kick me out of the palace after I... rejected her nephew's marriage proposal."

He glances over at me. "Why did you reject it?"

I lift my chin, trying not to think about Albert or the irritation that comes with the memory. For one small moment in time, I thought I'd found someone to love. Someone who'd love me in return. But I was, predictably, wrong.

*What color are my eyes, Albert?*

*Your eyes? They...they're beautiful. Green. Just like mine. It's what I love most about looking at you. I can get lost in eyes like those.*

My eyes are not green. They are gray. The very thing he liked most about me was a lie.

"I rejected him because he did not love me."

"That's not what your stepmother said. She claims you broke his heart."

I burn him with a glare. "My stepmother doesn't know the first thing about me."

He assesses me from head to toe before averting his gaze. "How did your father feel about his wife wanting you out of the palace?"

My stomach sinks. I remember the argument that sprang between us after he told me he agreed with my stepmother. That he thought it would be good for me to get out of the palace and go my own way for a while. I recall the deep sense of betrayal I felt when he admitted he'd already enrolled me at university, and I would leave by the end of the week. I railed against his suggestion, but he insisted I should make something of myself. Do something *for* myself.

*You don't understand*, I said to him. *I don't exist outside of your eyes. There is no me out there.*

*It's time you let someone other than me see you.*

It was that last part that sent me into a rage. The way he suggested my unfortunate magic was somehow *my* fault. He knew better than anyone that my magic was beyond my control. He'd seen the consequences. To hear him suggest I'd somehow brought it all upon myself—

A fresh wave of anger surges through me until I remind myself...

Remind myself...

That there's no one left to be angry with.

Because he's dead.

I nearly sag against my captor, but his firm grip on my

cuffed hand manages to steady me. "He was going to send me away," I explain, voice quavering. "I confess I did not react with dignity. I said horrible things to him."

"Like what?" There's no judgment in his voice. Not even curiosity. His tone is so even, so dry and neutral, that it somehow soothes my mood. Slightly.

"I...I accused him of changing since marrying Queen Tris. I said he didn't defend me anymore. Didn't protect me. I stormed away from him, but I immediately regretted everything I said. That's why I made the pie."

Tears well in my eyes as I recall my hideous, horrendous, handmade pie. I thought the palace baker would sever my head when I insisted I be allowed to make it myself.

"Why, though, did you make it? What's the reason behind the reason?"

If I didn't hate my captor, I'd be impressed. He asks questions the same way I watch my targets when I'm matchmaking. Seeking beneath the surface. "I made it because I thought it would remind him of how things were before Tris came into our lives. Before they married three years earlier, I was the only cook in our home. Father was too busy to cook, always working odd hours. He'd have worked straight through every meal if it hadn't been for my awful cooking. My father was a painter, you see."

The nameless bounty hunter nods. "Yes, that is how he gained Queen Tris' favor. He painted her portrait."

"He did," I say, not mentioning that I had a hand in that very portrait. It was one of the last times Father and I worked as a team. Thanks to my magic, he was able to highlight the three things Tris liked most about her appearance—her hair, her skin, and her lips—as well as working in the other qualities she favored. Beauty, charm, and lovability. Queen Tris was so enamored with the end product that she made him one of her prized artisans and gave us rooms at the palace. Not long after, she and Father fell in love. She made him her husband, then her king—a true honor, considering royal titles are not automatically given to the husbands and wives of the isle's ruling monarchs. Tris loved Father so much, she wasn't willing to let him remain merely her consort. However, he wouldn't accept the honor unless I was named princess as well. Tris grudgingly complied.

We approach the rear entrance to Department Sloth, and two doormen open the set of double doors. They don't bother looking our way, not even at our still-clasped hands as we step over the threshold. Panic climbs into my throat as he guides us down a plush, purple-carpeted hall, silver sconces glowing with orbs of light illuminating our way. Depending on where his suite is located, we could be mere seconds away from the end of our journey. The end of how long he promised to listen to me.

We bypass the corridor that leads to my tiny room and proceed to a silver gate. Next to it stands a muscular fae. His legs end in wide hooves, and his head sprouts curved horns. The sight of large hooves always makes me anxious, eliciting almost the same level of panic I get around horses, but what stands beside the fae is nearly as dreadful. The elevator. I've only ridden in it once, but that was enough for me. "Can't we take the stairs?" I whisper.

"Not to the top floor."

I blink at him in surprise. The top floor hosts the finest rooms. I'm given only a moment to gawk before the horned fae opens the gate and nods at my captor, who in turn leads me into the narrow boxlike alcove. The muscular fae closes the gate as we turn to face it, then steps out of view. I hear him turn the crank just as the floor begins to lift. Against my will, I cling to the bounty hunter. He, on the other hand, leans against the back wall as if riding in a moving box is the most normal thing in the world.

Urgency thrums through me, reminding me my time is

running out. If I'm going to convince him not to take me back to Spring, I need to do it now. I must get him to trust me.

"What's your name?" I ask, my voice unsteady as my stomach lurches with every inch the lift climbs.

"You don't need to know my name."

"But I want to." I try to add something sweet in my tone, but I think it comes off more frightened.

I glance up at him in time to see his jaw shift side to side. He refuses to meet my eyes but manages to give me an answer. "The Huntsman."

"Your name is Huntsman?"

"That's what you can call me."

"All right, Huntsman. I implore you to believe me. I didn't kill my father. I would never do such a thing. I loved him more than anyone in this whole world and love him still with every beat of my heart."

He turns his gaze to mine, expression full of surprise. The single light in the lift illuminates the honey tones of his eyes, the fiery copper in his hair.

My breath catches in my throat. Only now do I realize how close we're standing. Despite our lack of audience, our palms remain clasped. My free hand, having reached for him when the lift began to move, is still clenched around his arm. I stare down at my hand, painfully aware of the hard muscle beneath my palm. He might not be as muscular as the elevator operator, but the firm bicep under my hand...

With a lurch, I pull my hand off his arm and step as far from the Huntsman as my bonds will let me go. Our palms are no longer clasped, but my skin tingles in the absence of his heat. We ride the rest of the way up in silence while I try to come up with something that will make him see that I'm innocent.

When the lift comes to a stop, the silver gate opens to a dimly lit hall with white marble walls lined with elegant paint-ings and gold sconces. The floors are fiery pink and orange sunstone. I've never been to the top floor of Sloth, but it certainly puts the first level wing I live on to shame.

The Huntsman leads us down a quiet corridor, his steps too quick for my liking. I have to rush to keep up with him lest I be dragged by my cuff. Clearly, he's eager to get to his suite. What did he say about it? That there's something there that will allow us to get to Spring quickly? I try my appeal one last time. "Please don't take me back to her. She'll kill me."

"I know," he says, tone dark. "I was sent to do that very thing. I made a binding bargain to bring her your heart."

"But I didn't—"

He stops and rounds on me, fury in his eyes. "There's still the most damning evidence of all. Your blood smells of the same poison you killed your father with. Additionally, I can smell that you carry a vial of it now. Why do you take it? To build a tolerance?"

I blink at him a few times. "I don't need a tolerance. I'm half fae. It can't kill me." I swallow down what I've left unspoken. That it's only deadly to humans. Like my father.

"Then why do you take it?"

The truth settles like an iron weight in my heart. It isn't something I like to remember, much less talk about. I give him the simplest answer. "I was injured a few years back. Trampled by a horse. I nearly died from my wounds, even with my fae heritage. The healer used a tincture of Crimson Malus to speed up my recovery. I...I would have died without it." I shudder at the thought. Crimson Malus might be deadly to humans, but when used on fae, it speeds their healing tenfold. It is rarely used in such a way since fae can normally heal well enough on their own. But for someone with only some fae blood— someone who won't die from its poisonous effects but won't heal quickly enough on their own—it's lifesaving.

He looks me over. "You're healed now. Why do you still take it?"

I nibble my lip before answering. "I use it to manage lingering pain."

His lips turn up at the corners, quirking into a cruel smile. "That last part was a lie, wasn't it?"

The blood leaves my face. He starts to turn away when I blurt out my confession. "I use it to manage my mood."

"Why?"

"Because my mood influences my magic, all right?"

"Tell me about your magic."

I clamp my lips tight, the prospect of telling him the truth almost too painful to bear. My magic has gotten me into some unfortunate situations, but so has confessing my strange abilities. It's brought me enemies in the past, just like my sour mood has. The only people who have ever accepted me after knowing about my magic are my father and Marybeth.

As much as I'd rather not tell the Huntsman any of this, I doubt he'll take silence as an answer. "I'm a mirror," I say, my voice almost a whisper. "All you see right now is a reflection of yourself. If I'm in a pleasant mood when I meet someone, they'll see their best qualities reflected back. But if I form a first impression when my mood is low, their worst qualities are all they'll ever see. Sometimes these qualities have to do with physical appearance. Other times they're emotional or more of a personality trait. Either way, the impression is permanent. I can't turn my magic off or change how someone perceives me. It's...it's dangerous for me. That's why I take the tincture. It keeps me safe. At least safer than I'd be without it." I close my eyes on the memories that flood my mind, of horse hooves crushing my ribs, a pair of sinister eyes, and a vicious trill of feminine laughter echoing in my ears—

"Your injuries weren't an accident, were they?" The Huntsman's low, rumbling voice has my lashes fluttering open. I see that same furrow between his brow that I glimpsed earlier.

I shake my head.

He assesses me for a few silent moments, then gently tugs my cuff. When we start walking again, our pace is slower, a somber quality to the air between us.

We reach a door at the end of the hall.

The Huntsman stops before it, fingers frozen on the handle, his posture suddenly rigid.

I look from him to the door and back again. "What is it?"

His expression darkens. "Someone has been in my room."

## 6

## THE HUNTSMAN

The aromas of roses and jasmine are so overpowering, I don't know how I didn't smell it before. No, I know exactly how. Before now, I've been too focused on the girl at my side. On her unsettling nearness, the feel of her small hand in mine when we rode the lift, on every shift in her fragrance that marks a change in her emotional state. I've been so wrapped up in trying to get a read on her that I failed to note the floral trail that led straight to my door.

But I notice it now. It drips from the door handle, threads itself through the rug outside my door. Based on the dual flow of the scent trail, whoever has entered my suite has already left and went back the way they came. I'm torn, eager to follow the trail now before its source gets too far, but there's a cold dread sinking my stomach, one that has my fingers digging my room key out of my pocket and unlocking the door at once.

Astrid Snow's voice cuts through the roar of urgency burning my veins. "It was probably just the cleaning staff, wasn't it? No need to get worked up."

"Staff is forbidden from entering my suite. I left express instructions with the front desk at Department Pride."

"Perhaps your note got lost," she says as I push open the door.

I stride inside, bringing the handcuffed girl with me.

Her steps falter, and I hear a gasp escape her lips. "Your suite is enormous."

"Didn't you live in a palace?" I bite back, my patience wearing thin. Or thinner, I should say. It's been fraying to threadbare scraps ever since she fought my attempts to complete what should have been an easy mission. I'd be impressed by her if I wasn't so on edge. I reach the other side of the room, my eyes fixed on the center window on the opposite wall. It remains open the way I left it, and the flower box affixed to the outer sill reveals the tops of succulents. I reach inside the flower box—only to have my dread darken to a gaping hollow.

I slam my hand on the sill. "Blooming hell, it's gone."

"What's gone?" Astrid's voice comes out with a note of hope, reflected in the subtle brightening of her scent. She must be able to tell that my plans have been thwarted.

And thwarted they are indeed, for in that flower box I left one of the most important items I've ever had—a Chariot. It's a rare device invented long ago with Star Court technology that allows instantaneous travel. There are restrictions, of course, like the need to clearly visualize one's destination, meaning one can only travel to places they have been before. Even so, the technology is considered so dangerous that only a limited number have ever been made, and most—if not all—are possessed by a select few fae royals.

How I came by my Chariot was pure luck. When I arrived in the city of Lumenas to seek out Miss Snow, I received a correspondence from King Ronan of the Sea Court. He requested a favor from me, asking that I relay a message to his daughter— yet another runaway princess, a selkie who'd been hiding out on land for over a year. I found her with ease, delivered my missive, and received a message in return for me to pass on to her father. But that wasn't all she gave me. She handed me a Chariot as well, one she was determined to see turned over to the Alpha Council. Which I was planning to do, of course. Eventually. Maybe.

For now, I thought I'd keep it to make my job easier. That's why I brought my captive here, so I could leave with her at once. That, and get the key to the handcuffs I so stupidly forgot in my room. I had it all planned out. I was supposed to stroll into my suite, grab the key from my jacket, retrieve the device, and use it to transport us back to Fairweather Palace.

But now...

Now the most important part of the plan is missing.

I run a hand over my face and stare at the flower box. My eyes dart all around it, seeking any sign of the silver, hexagonal compact. I left it tucked underneath the largest succulent, hidden from unwitting eyes but still able to absorb starlight—a necessary component that allows it to harness the energy required to operate it. Now I wish I never parted with it. And yet, I had little choice. A Chariot can only be used twice before requiring starlight, which means each time I've used it to make a report to Queen Tris—traveling to Fairweather Palace and back again—it's drained of power. My most recent round-trip use was this morning. That's why I left it under the stars tonight.

While I could have kept my possession of the device a secret in the first place and sent my status reports by letter, flaunting the Chariot was a calculated move. When I made my first in-person report upon arriving in Irridae, demonstrating just how I was able to make it there so swiftly, the queen was impressed. Envious. Willing to sweeten our bargain.

*Turn the Chariot over to me when you've finished your mission, and I'll see that you are compensated. Not only will your debts be paid and your service as Huntsman complete, but I will return Davenport Estate to your name.*

I agreed to that bargain without falter, entering a secondary bargain that will result in my death if I fail to fulfill it. And if I've lost the damn thing...

"Fuck!" The word comes out like a roar.

If Astrid is offended by my use of profanity, she doesn't show it. "Tell me what's going on, Huntsman."

"You are in no position to make demands of me," I say as I dart for the black coat I left strewn across my bed. I find the key to the handcuffs and slide it into my trouser pocket, making no move to unlock my cuff first. When the princess first locked me in the spare cuff, I'd been furious, especially as realization dawned and I recalled the last place I'd tucked the key. But after coming to terms with my inability to take her heart like I'd planned, I'm now aware of the benefits that come from being handcuffed to the girl. Trapped to my wrist, she isn't going anywhere. I'll haul her before her stepmother exactly as she is now and be done with this whole mess. First, I need to find my damn blooming Chariot.

I race for the door, and she jogs to keep up with my pace. "Have you changed your mind? Are you not going to take me back to Spring?" Her tone brightens. "Please say you have. I will be so grateful—"

"I haven't changed my mind." I slam my suite door behind us, not bothering to lock it this time. The only valuable thing in that room has been taken. And I'm going to get it back.

"Where are we going? Is it the key to the cuffs you've lost?"

"No."

"What did you take out of your jacket and put in your pocket when we were in the room? Was *that* the key?"

When I say nothing, her emotions brighten like the freshest slice of lemon. If she thinks she's being subtle, she's not. I can almost smell her schemes to steal the key from me, can almost feel her calculating gaze burning into my pocket.

When I lift my eyes to hers, Astrid's expression falls behind a milky haze. No matter how hard I try, I cannot see her face clearly. I can look. I can *know* what her features are doing—whether she's smiling, frowning, or glowering—and interpret her expression, but I can't process anything beyond that. Not the color of her eyes or the shape of her lips. My mind goes half empty when our eyes meet, providing a simple perception of her and nothing else. All I'm able to see clearly is her body, her gestures, her posture. I can see her clothing too, although there's a similar haze about it, as if at any moment her attire could shift.

*I'm a mirror*, she said. *All you see right now is a reflection of yourself.*

I was wrong about her being a glamourist, and I suppose it also explains why some accounts of her appearance have included no physical attributes at all. If one only sees their best or worst qualities reflected back when they look at her, then they may not notice any of her features unless they love or hate their own. Like her former employer who claimed Astrid had violet eyes. Or Queen Tris who mentioned her pink hair and brown skin.

When I look at her, though, I see nothing distinct. Nothing that makes sense.

I expected her magic to explain why I found it impossible to do my duty. Why I couldn't tear out her heart, even when my mind was screaming to do it, even when I told my fingers to extend into claws, to just finish this task and beg the All of All for forgiveness later. But this feeling I get around her, this awareness of how small and vulnerable she is, this inconvenient need to do whatever it takes to protect her...it doesn't align with how her magic supposedly works. *Small* and *vulner-*

*able* aren't qualities I possess, nor do I value or condemn such attributes.

Perhaps I hated being small and weak once before, but that was long ago...

I shake the thoughts from my mind and continue down the hall, bypassing the elevator and taking a corridor to the left. Breathing in deep, I bite back a gag as the floral aroma intensifies. Strong floral scents are my demise. Aside from the subtle fragrance of fruit blossoms found in my home court of Spring, flowers are repugnant to me. They're cloying, invasive. In too large a quantity, they can overpower my ability to smell anything else, like what happened when I passed the garden behind Lust the other day. Thankfully, this floral trail belongs to a single person and not an entire garden. Although, I get the sense that this aroma isn't a true scent trail, but an artificial fragrance masking its bearer.

My dread deepens.

If the person who stole my Chariot wore a floral aroma on purpose, then that means the device's theft was no accident. It isn't a matter of cleaning staff unwittingly entering my room, seeing a priceless item, and stealing it out of a naive intention to pawn it for a few opal rounds. Whoever took it knew my weakness. Knew I had the Chariot to begin with.

"Huntsman, what is going on?" Astrid asks, a note of hysteria in her voice. "Why are we racing through the halls?"

"Quiet," I bark as I push open the door at the end of the corridor. It opens to a dark, narrow hall that looks like something used only for hotel staff, dimly lit by the occasional wall lamp. The floral scent veers off to the right and down a flight of stairs.

I descend the first step, but Astrid yanks hard on her cuff, her other hand wrapping around the top of the rail. "Don't you dare just tell me to be quiet."

I charge back up the step and round on her. "We don't have time for—"

My words snag on the back of my throat as I feel something move against my thigh. Eyes wide, I glance down and find her hand in my trouser pocket. I know she's only reaching for my key, yet her bold touch stuns me nonetheless. So much so that by the time I gather my wits and try to knock her hand away, she already has the key in her fingers. With a triumphant grin, she brings the key to her cuff and slams it into the lock—

Her colorless, shapeless eyes go wide, and she tries the key again.

A dark laugh rumbles in my chest as I watch her futile efforts a few seconds longer. "That's my room key," I say as I reach into my pocket—the same one her hand was so brazenly buried in—and pull out a much smaller key. "*This* is the key to these cuffs."

She reaches for it, but I pull it far out of reach. With a growl, she edges closer until her body is pressed against mine. She all but climbs up my chest in her attempts to reach the key. With a quick swipe of my leg beneath hers, she loses her footing. I wrap both my arms around her before she can fall on her ass, but I don't let her up all the way. Instead, I keep her in an angled dip so that she can't gain purchase with her feet. My face hovers mere inches from hers. The smell of lemons turns bitter, almost strong enough to bury the floral trail I'm still desperate to follow.

I meet her eyes and feel something tighten in my chest. It's that urge again, that need to protect her. My next word comes out far softer than I intend. "Enough."

She pushes her free hand, still clamped around my room key, against my chest.

But I don't budge. "Enough," I say again.

"No! I won't stop fighting you. Not if you're so set on taking me to my death."

Another squeeze to my heart. "There's something I need to retrieve right now. If I don't do it soon...just...I already told you I'd rip out your throat if you don't come quietly."

Slowly, she lifts her chin, then angles her head to the side, exposing the length of her neck to me. It would be seductive if not for our violent topic of conversation. The scent of bitter lemons darkens with a heavy wave of fear. "Do it then."

I stare down at the delicate flesh she's exposed—flesh I can clearly see. Her pulse leaps at the base of the column of her neck. My heart slams against my ribs in echo.

Something stirs inside me, something warm and unwelcome. It takes its place next to that damn instinct of mine to protect her. Mingling with it. Taunting me.

"Blooming hell," I curse as I pull her upright and step as far away from her as our chained hands will allow. "Every moment we linger here is another moment the thief can get away. I need to get what they stole."

She tries to cross her arms but gives up when she realizes her cuffed hand won't allow such a gesture without forcing her closer to me. Instead, she plants her free hand on her hip. "Why should I care?"

Annoyance burns in my chest, chasing away the other less convenient emotions. I need to get her to comply. Fast. "Look," I say through my teeth, "come with me calmly right now and I will...I'll allow you a full hour to tell your side of the story."

She blinks at me a few times. "You will?"

"Yes."

"Promise me," she says, stepping forward. "Promise you will give me a full hour to tell my side. Promise me that you will listen with your undivided attention and actually *try* to decipher whether I could be innocent."

My mind blares a warning that fae promises are nearly as binding as bargains. But this is a promise I can keep. Even if I vow to give her a chance to prove her innocence, it doesn't mean I won't still take her to Queen Tris. "I promise," I rush to say before she can add any stipulations. "Now, let's—"

She lunges forward, swiping her fingers at my hand. Once again, I lift the key to the cuffs out of reach. I pin her with a glare. "That isn't what I call coming calmly."

She shrugs and glares right back. "I was very calm about it." Her tone tells me that she'll likely try again.

Which gives me an idea.

Holding her gaze, my lips curl into a devious grin. With my cuffed hand, I tug on the waistband of my trousers. My other hand drops the key straight into my underbritches. "Try and get it now."

She gasps, the apple blossoms in her scent profile growing almost as strong as the bitter lemon. It's a dynamic I haven't witnessed in her before. "You're disgusting," she says, averting her gaze from my crotch. If I could see her face better, I'm willing to bet I'd find her blushing.

It gives me no small amount of smug satisfaction.

I gently tug her cuff, and she starts walking without any further retort. Meanwhile, I force away memories of Astrid's hand in my pocket and return my attention to the thief's trail.

## 7

*ASTRID*

Why do his pants have to be so damn tight? That's all I can think as we make our way down the narrow staircase through Department Sloth. When I reached into his pocket to grab the key, I was immediately alarmed by how little room there was between his firm thigh and the linen my hand was plunging into. I blame his unnecessarily slim trousers for my inability to grab the right key. Not that I had much hope of getting away even if I had found the right one. It was worth a shot. At least now I have his binding promise to hear me out, for there's no way I'll get a chance to retrieve that key where he hid it now.

I blush at the memory of where my eyes locked when he slipped the small piece of brass behind his waistband. Even though I didn't glimpse what hides within his underbritches, the form-fitting linen was more than enough to offer a...preview.

Damn those tight pants. Surely they make them large

enough to fit a bear of a man like him. Why couldn't he have chosen something more sensible?

The Huntsman quickens his pace as we reach the bottom floor. He's been hellbent on following the trail of the supposed thief. A thief who took some important thing that he won't tell me about. All I can do is follow.

He leads us out an unmarked door, and warm air greets us on the other side. I glance around, finding us behind Department Sloth near the walkway we traversed not long ago. Instead of going back the way we came, however, the Huntsman leads us down a smaller path, one flanked with shrubs and beds of cacti. Hardly a soul lingers around, as most patrons have found their vices for the rest of the night. Strains of music pour out of Lust, Greed, and Gluttony—three separate tunes that somehow manage to encapsulate the sins behind their doors—while Wrath and Envy are silent and will be for the rest of the evening. The music grows louder as we reach the end of the path. The trail lets out onto the main walkway, and the Huntsman takes a sharp left.

"We're close," he mutters under his breath as he guides us down the alley between Lust and Wrath.

"Close to what?" The dark alley paired with the sultry beats pounding from behind every window in Lust sends a wary chill through me. It suddenly seems foolhardy to be chained to a man preparing to confront a thief. "Shouldn't you separate us before you go about your...unsavory business?"

He scoffs. "Not a chance."

I try another angle as we round the back of Lust toward the garden. "What if...what if I'm injured? What if I'm killed? I take it you care a lot about fulfilling your mission, and you can't cut out my heart if someone else gets to it first."

That gets his attention. He pulls up short and frowns at me, mouth open as if on the verge of speaking. Then he purses his lips and tugs me forward without another word. He takes only a few steps more before he stops again, turning this way and that. "Fucking flowers," he mutters, pinching the bridge of his nose. Then, with a frustrated growl, he heads straight for the garden.

The entrance is a sunstone trellis draped with climbing jasmine. It opens to an array of dirt walking paths lined with opal stepping stones. Aromas of lilacs and roses fill my senses, which manages to calm my nerves—a welcome thing, considering I still haven't managed to sneak another dose of Crimson Malus. My mood will matter greatly should we come upon the thief. I might even get them on my side if I can mirror back a positive first impression.

I breathe in deeply, allowing the lovely scents to soothe me further. "I love flowers," I say, my whispered words carried on a sigh.

"Of course you do." He says it like it's a bad thing. I glance over at him. He's grown tenser since we entered the garden and no longer seems to be following a straight path like he had inside Sloth. Instead, he takes us through turn after turn down the maze of walking paths only to change direction time and again. I also catch him covering his nose or pinching its bridge now and then, as if he can't handle the delectably sweet aromas that surround us.

Then it occurs to me. If the Huntsman has such a keen sense of smell, then something like a garden might be a bit overpowering to him.

"Blooming hell," he says through his teeth as he pulls up short and runs a hand over his face. "I can't stand this place."

Seeing him so undone makes me realize *this* would be the perfect time and place to try and escape him. I bite my lip, cursing myself for my foolish attempt at stealing the key earlier. If only I'd waited until now—

Something thuds nearby, so heavy it makes the opal stepping stone shudder beneath my feet. We whirl toward the sound but see only shrubs and trees silhouetted in the darkness.

Another thud. This time one of the trees moves.

Or...perhaps it isn't a tree at all.

The silhouette shifts, sending the stepping stone rumbling once again. Then the shadow angles to the side.

Toward us.

The Huntsman takes a step back, pulling me with him. Just then, the towering shape emerges from the trees and steps onto the path.

My breath catches as the moon illuminates green skin, enormous meaty hands, and a mouth full of sharp pointed teeth.

An ogre.

Not just any ogre, either.

This has to be Murtis, the ogre who fought Helody in the pit. He wears the same loincloth, has the same fierce expression. If that wasn't evidence enough, I catch sight of a missing finger on his right hand—the finger Helody bit off. I can't fathom how he survived the duel. The griffin is known for her swift beheadings. Which means either she lost, or the ogre yielded.

Neither scenario is comforting.

Not when the vicious fae stands before us, saliva dripping from his maw, hunger burning in his yellow eyes.

Murtis glances from me to the Huntsman, as if debating which of us to devour first. Attacks like this are highly illegal, whether on humans or fae. It's a fact that comforted me when I first went on the run, living alone for the first time in my life. But now...

Now such laws and prohibitions don't seem to matter one bit. Who cares about the protection of the law when I'm about to be eaten by an ogre?

The ogre's lips curl into a wicked smile, revealing even more of his razor-sharp teeth. He staggers his legs, sending the ground thudding yet again.

"Get back," the Huntsman barks, and it takes me a moment to realize the order was for me. He throws his arm out in front of me, but with his hand cuffed to mine, it only makes me hit myself in the stomach with my own arm.

I grunt, and he tosses me a wide-eyed look, gaze moving from my face to my cuff. "Sorry," he mutters, then ushers me behind him, angling his arm to allow me to be fully hidden behind his broad back. "I'm going to have to ask you to retrieve that key now."

A spike of alarm rushes through me. "What?"

"Reach around the front of me and get the key."

"Get it yourself!"

"I have to fight him! Do you want to be attached to me when he attacks?"

I glance around the Huntsman's torso just in time to see Murtis bend into a crouch, readying himself to charge us. "Get the key. Now."

That's all I hear before the ogre races forward.

The Huntsman retreats, forcing me to lurch back in turn, but we only make it three steps before Murtis' enormous hand closes in on the Huntsman's head. Even with his missing finger, the ogre's grip seems impossibly strong. Time almost stands still as I watch with horror, bile rising in my throat as Murtis wraps his fist around the Huntsman's neck. A small part of me wonders if I should let it happen, let the ogre kill my captor. But that sentiment is quickly burned away by shame. Guilt. Disgust.

I may not like the Huntsman or appreciate his attempt on my life, but I'm not a killer, despite what he thinks. And if I let him die...

My eyes widen as Murtis squeezes harder. There's something large and furry working to pry the ogre's hand from around the Huntsman's face. Enormous claws sprout from the brown mass. Is it...an arm?

"The key," the Huntsman says through gasping breaths, his voice strangled, muffled behind the ogre's palm.

Without a second thought, I swallow my panicked squeal and press myself against the Huntsman's back. With my free hand, I reach around to the front of his britches...and then plunge my hand beneath his waistband. This may not be the time for modesty, but my cheeks heat nonetheless as my palm slides down the warm front of him, discovering yet more proof of what I glimpsed from the other side of his linen trousers. I angle myself closer to his ribs to get a better reach, grasping certain *things* I really ought not to grasp. He doesn't seem the least bit perturbed, for he has far more pressing matters to attend to than being unceremoniously groped by his captive. Still, my work is made all the more difficult by how he shifts and lurches in his attempts to fight off the ogre.

I hazard a glance up and see the furry brown mass inside Murtis' fist has grown. In fact, that's all I *can* see. The Huntsman's head is now fully obscured.

His voice reaches me all the same. "The key, damn it!"

"I'm trying," I bite back, renewing my efforts.

"I can't fully shift with these cuffs connecting us."

"I said I'm trying." I reach farther, deeper. Finally, the feel of metal reaches my fingertips. With the key grasped between my fingers, I pull my hand free. I take a step back, the key trembling in my grip. I'm not sure who to unlock first—myself or him. If I free myself, I can run, get far away before the Huntsman can even think to find me again. Now that I know floral aromas bother him, I might have an advantage.

But can he shift with the cuff still around his wrist? I know fae can shift between their seelie and unseelie forms in full clothing, causing no harm to their ensemble even if they sprout wings or claws through them. But do metal cuffs count?

"I better not regret this," I mutter as I shove the key into his lock first. My heart slams against my ribs as the sounds of struggle increase. Finally, the flat end of the cuffs comes open. With a tug, I unhook the curved side from around his wrist.

The Huntsman swings his newly freed fist into the ogre's belly. I slowly back up a few steps, eager not to attract Murtis' attention—

Too late.

The ogre's yellow eyes snap to mine. With a growl, he releases the Huntsman's neck. All I catch is a blur of brown fur, linen, and skin before Murtis rakes sharp green claws over the front of the Huntsman's torso. A spray of blood strikes the ogre, and the creature tosses the bounty hunter aside like he weighs nothing more than a rag doll.

Then Murtis lunges for me.

# 8

ASTRID

All I can do is run. I don't have time to free myself from my cuff. Instead, I let the loose end dangle from my wrist and pour all my attention into getting away from the charging ogre. I don't dare look back, not even as the sound of shuddering bushes and crushed flower beds gains on me. Finally, I make it to the sunstone arch and dart through it, my sights set on the alley between Lust and the hotel's perimeter wall. Panic crawls up my throat, setting my pulse pounding, prying tears from the corners of my eyes. If I can get to Lust, I can call for help. So long as I can find someone I already know—someone like Madame Desire—I don't have to worry about making a poor impression in my perilous emotional state.

I reach the mouth of the alley just as I hear a loud thud behind me. Only then do I hazard a glance over my shoulder. Murtis is half a dozen feet away, and the sunstone arch lies in ruins in his wake. I pump my legs faster and sprint down the alley. Despite my cries for help, my every word is swallowed by the sultry music still emanating from behind Lust's closed shutters.

If I can get to the front door...

If I can only get inside...

I'm almost to the other end of the alley, mere feet from the safety of the front end of the building, when an enormous hand closes around my middle. My breath heaves from my lungs, my stomach lurching as the ogre drags me from freedom and tosses me back the way I came. I land on my side near one of the waste bins. A surge of pain ripples up my hip, my elbow. But I have no time to dwell on it, for the ogre is already gaining on me yet again. He's moving slowly, however, as if he doesn't see me yet. His eyes dart from one side of the alley to the other. Either the shadows cast by Department Lust have compromised his vision, or he hadn't expected to throw me so far.

Inch by inch, I lift myself halfway off the ground and crawl closer to the wall.

Maybe he won't see me.

All my hopes plummet as his eyes lock on me. Quickening his pace, he closes the distance between us. Despite the pain in my hip, I force myself to my feet. If I have any hope of getting away, I need to use his size against him. He may be strong and heavy, but he's a lumbering sort of giant. If I wait until the moment he tries to grab me again, I can evade his clutches and run for Lust's front door before he even turns around.

My breaths come out in rapid bursts as fear twists my guts. I watch his enormous form close in on me, watch his fist come open, reaching for my middle—

Murtis lurches to the side as a mass of brown fur collides with his shoulder.

A bear.

I can't tear my eyes away as the ogre goes down with a rumbling thud, the bear on top of him. A green fist collides with the bear's side, then its head, but the bear doesn't balk. Its lips are pulled back in a snarl, revealing a mouth full of vicious teeth.

I realize what this bear is. *Who* this bear is.

It's the Huntsman.

Whatever injury the ogre inflicted when he clawed the bounty hunter must not have been too grave. With the Huntsman's pure fae blood, he would have healed quickly. But now more blood sprays from the bear's hide as the ogre digs his claws into the Huntsman, pounds his fist into the bear's face. This time, the Huntsman isn't the only one bleeding. He gnashes his teeth, rakes claws over the ogre's arms and face.

I'm torn between seeing how the battle ends and getting to safety. I choose the latter. With trembling steps, I edge around to the other side of the waste bin and begin to creep down the opposite end of the alley from where the fight is. It will take me to the back side of Lust instead of the front. Unlike Wrath, Lust doesn't have a rear entrance to sneak into. But as long as the two fae males are locked in combat, I'll have a chance to slip away. I glance at the fighters one more time.

Then I run.

A bellowing roar shatters the air around me, piercing my ears and setting them ringing in its wake. My heart plummets as the sound of pounding footsteps surges behind me. With my feet still flying, I glance over my shoulder, hoping beyond hope it isn't Murtis but the Huntsman.

No such luck.

The ogre jogs after me, face twisted in fury. Jagged gashes crisscross his face, but it doesn't slow him down. Too soon he'll be upon me—

The bear slams into the ogre's back, sending the creature sprawling forward. I nearly trip in my haste to evade being crushed by him. At the last moment, I whirl to the side toward the building just as the ogre falls. The Huntsman digs his claws into Murtis' shoulders, pinning him down. Then, in a flash, the bear sinks his teeth into the back of the creature's neck. Once. Twice.

The ogre twitches, but the bear's third bite has his body going still. For that's the bite that severs Murtis' head from his body.

I stare at the gruesome sight for several moments, watching as blood soaks the alley floor like a macabre pond—black beneath the dark night sky. I can't blink. Can't look away. Nor can I stop myself from shaking.

The ogre is dead.

There's no coming back from a beheading.

Movement catches my eyes, and I lift my gaze from the dead creature to the bear slowly edging off his victim's back. Blood drips from the Huntsman's muzzle, mirroring his gore-drenched claws.

Then my attention slides to his rounded ears, his brown flank.

The bear takes a hesitant step toward me. Then another.

My legs are too weak to move.

I swallow hard, my throat as dry as sand. "You're... you're..."

"Frightening?" His low voice emanates from deep inside his bear form. Like the kelpie I once met, his lips don't move when he speaks.

My eyes return to those round ears. "You're so..."

Another step closer. "Terrifying?"

Something melts inside me, a calm breaking through the dark storm of my emotions. "Fluffy."

He halts. "What?"

I take a step closer, ignoring the pools of blood all around us. "Can I please touch your fur?" Even as the words leave my mouth, I know they're ridiculous. But my mind isn't in the best state. I'm teetering on the edge of hysteria, balanced between safety and the dangerous chasm of grief that lies gaping beneath me. I need comfort right now. Either that or my tincture.

He pads a few more steps closer, his tone taking on a tenuous quality. "I suppose."

That's all the permission I need before I reach out and bury my hands in his soft hide. A hum of bliss rolls through me as I stroke my hands over his silky fur. My rational mind tries to remind me that he's likely coated in blood, but all I care about now is soothing my emotions, numbing my panic, my sorrow, my agony. "You are so soft," I say, only half aware that I'm speaking. "It's taking all my restraint not to squeeze you hard and bury my face in your neck right now."

His thick, warm hide ripples beneath my hands. Then the bear is gone.

I blink at my hands, finding them no longer buried in brown fur but...pressed against the Huntsman's chest. "What is wrong with you?" he asks.

I frown up at him, finding narrowed eyes beneath a quirked brow looking back at me.

It cuts through my momentary haze of comfort and reminds me where I am. What just happened. Whose chest I'm touching.

My cheeks turn warm. "I like the feeling of fur, all right?" I take a step back and snatch my hand away. Just then, I hear a click.

The Huntsman's lips twist into a sideways grin. He lifts his hand to show that he's locked himself back in the cuff—the cuff that had still been dangling open from my wrist.

My eyes go wide. "Why would you do that?"

"It's a convenient solution to prevent your escape."

I try to cross my arms, but it's no use with our cuffs connecting us yet again. "I liked you better as a bear."

"And I don't like you much at all. Give me the key."

I curl my fingers into fists, but that brings a startling realization.

I'm no longer holding the key. I shrink down as I say, "I don't have it."

"What?"

"Did you expect me to keep hold of it while I was being attacked by an ogre?"

His expression softens before he brings his hand to his face and pinches the bridge of his nose. "Where do you think you lost it?"

I'm about to say it could be anywhere, but my gaze lands on the ground near the waste bins where the ogre first tossed me. The Huntsman follows my line of sight. Before I can say a word, he drags me there. It takes all my willpower not to glance at the hulking dead body as we skirt around it.

"Look for the key," he demands.

I obey, for finding the key serves me just as much as him. And if I can get to it first...

Moonlight glints off something peeking out from the nearest waste bin. I bend down, wincing at the pain that surges through my hip. Elation floods me as I snatch up the key.

The Huntsman pulls me to my feet before I get the chance to pocket it. He holds out a hand. "Give it to me," he says through clenched teeth.

I stare back at him with defiance. Remembering how he'd hid the key in the absolute last place he thought I'd try to retrieve it, an idea sparks in my mind.

His tone darkens with warning. "Give it to me or I'll take it through force."

My hand slowly moves toward my chest...

"Don't you dare," he hisses.

I bring the key closer, preparing to drop it down the front of my shirt and bury it in my corset.

He huffs a laugh. "Do you think I won't retrieve it?"

That gives me pause. "It wouldn't be very gentlemanly of you."

"Nor was it very ladylike for you to grope my nethers the way you did." A suggestive lilt plays in his tone.

I burn him with a scowl. "You made me do that."

His crooked grin grows devious. "Is that why you want to put the key down your shirt? Because you like the thought of where it's been? Does it give you pleasure to think of my big, hard...*key*...pressed between your breasts?"

I don't think such fire has ever filled my cheeks before now. I can only hope he doesn't see it, that his impression of me is strong enough to hide everything about my true face.

Based on the smug confidence in his eyes, I'm starting to fear he *can* see my blush.

"You do know that thing is probably covered in ogre blood. Do you want that touching your—"

With a frustrated growl, I thrust out my hand toward him. He doesn't hesitate to take the key from me. I note that instead of slipping it into his underbritches, he slides it into his pocket. Probably doesn't want ogre blood touching his private bits either.

He gives my cuff a gentle tug and we take a step toward the front end of the building. The Huntsman stiffens and pulls up short. It takes me a moment to realize what startled him. My mind goes to the worst possible scenario—that the ogre managed to survive the bear's deadly blow and is preparing to attack again.

Then I see the silhouettes crowding the mouth of the alley.

It appears we have an audience.

## 9

## THE HUNTSMAN

Men and women spill into the alley, halting when they glimpse the scene before them. Based on the half-dressed state of our spectators, they must be patrons from Lust. Despite the music coming from the brothel, I suppose the ogre's final, rumbling fall was loud enough to catch someone's attention from inside. Still, I curse myself for not having sensed their presence before we were spotted. The aromas of ogre blood mingling with the floral fragrances from the garden behind the building are too strong, clouding my sense of smell.

Damn. It seems we won't be able to flee the gory scene without notice like I'd hoped.

I take a steadying breath, wincing against the cloying, searing odors that flood my nostrils. Then, with my cuffed hand, I take Astrid's palm in mine, once again masking our bindings beneath the guise of overly familiar touch.

I lead us toward the group of people. As we reach them, a tall, slender figure parts the crowd to confront us. She's a fae female with pink skin and ruby-red hair. A sprite, perhaps, in seelie form. Her eyes land on Astrid, then widen.

"Miss Lovecraft!" the fae woman says with a gasp. Her gaze slides to the body behind us, and she launches a step back. Her lips curl into a sneer. "Is that...blood?"

Astrid's scent flares with panic. "Madame Desire—"

"What have you done to attract such...such," she points down the alley at the silhouette of the dead ogre, "such a repulsive spectacle to my establishment? Do not tell me this is the result of your...line of work."

Astrid opens her mouth, but I speak first, choosing my words carefully to ensure they are true. "I rescued this woman from an ogre attack. Had I not acted, there's a chance he could have targeted your brothel next." The last part rings with a hint of untruth, but my use of the word *chance* allows me to utter such a statement. There's always a chance anything can happen.

Madame Desire's irritation softens the slightest bit, especially as she looks me up and down. "How lucky Miss Lovecraft was to be protected by such a handsome savior." Her eyes briefly land on our clasped hands, sparking something like envy in her eyes.

To ensure further cooperation, I reach into the pocket of my torn waistcoat and extract a large gold coin stamped with an intricate sigil bearing the letters *AC*.

I hand it to Madame Desire. She examines it for only a moment before her eyes fly back to mine. "You serve the Alpha Council." Her statement elicits awed looks and a flurry of whispers from the crowd behind her.

My skin crawls to have this information so freely shared before spectators. I work best when I can keep a low profile. And yet, sharing my identity so publicly might be our only way to avoid further complications. Killing a fellow fae, even in self-defense, normally comes with a hefty dose of legal proceedings.

But not for the Alpha Council's appointed Huntsman when he's on duty. "Yes, and I am on private business here at the hotel."

She hands the coin back to me, and her expression turns sickly sweet. "You must be a very important man. Please take my gratitude for protecting my humble establishment from such vile characters as that...monster." Her expression flashes with disgust as her gaze darts back to the dead ogre. She lowers her voice. "I will speak with Madame Honor and have this matter taken care of discreetly."

Madame Honor must be the head of Department Pride. It makes sense Pride would encompass such aspects as cleanliness. And the disposal of dead bodies. "I accept your gratitude and your cooperation, but I will ask for one more thing."

"Anything." Madame Desire flutters her lashes and bats a flirty hand toward me, as if she intends to brush her fingertips over my chest. Astrid's palm goes rigid in mine, and I feel a sudden tenseness radiate up her arm. Madame Desire's fingers stop inches away from my torso just as her gaze locks on the bloody gashes in my clothing. She snatches her hand back and places it on her amply curving hip instead.

"I request a room for the night. Any room you have available will suit, but I ask that I be granted permission to stay overnight. You may charge any expense to the Alpha Council."

She lifts her chin. "I can give you a room. The best room, and more. I'll send my prettiest girls to you as well. Three of them."

"I'd like to request—" I'm about to say *Miss Snow* when I recall Madame Desire referring to her as *Miss Lovecraft*. "I request a night with Miss Lovecraft, if you will. *Only* Miss Lovecraft."

Her expression shifts to one of surprise. "Miss Lovecraft?"

Astrid gives my hand a squeeze. From the way her nails dig into my palm, I think it's meant to be a silent threat. I can feel her gaze burning into the side of my face, but she doesn't argue.

"Yes," I say, and Madame Desire continues to blink at me in a perplexed manner. Did I perhaps come to an inaccurate conclusion regarding Astrid's profession? "She does work for you, does she not?" I ask.

Astrid opens her mouth but only manages to utter a sound before her voice is drowned out by Madame Desire's fervent tone. "Yes, she does! She very much does." Her gaze slides to Astrid's, and there's a clear warning brimming in her eyes. "She *will* spend the night with you. Because she works for *me,* and she doesn't dare forget that."

Astrid's hand turns rigid in my palm yet again, but all she says is, "Of course, Madame Desire."

A FEW MINUTES LATER, ASTRID AND I STAND ALONE IN A bedroom on the top floor of Department Lust. The room is spacious with floors of fiery opal, pink papered walls, and plush rugs woven from ruby wool. The lamps give off a rosy glow, casting the brightest light upon the bed. The latter is the only piece of furniture in the room, aside from two narrow nightstands.

It sends a clear message that this room was designed for one thing and one thing only.

Astrid seems equally aware as her gaze wanders every-where *but* the bed. She steps as far away from me as our linked cuffs will allow. "I take it you'll claim the floor."

I huff a dark laugh and guide her to one side of the bed. "Sit."

She glances from me to the bed. A note of panic rises in her scent profile. "Why?"

I tilt my head toward the ewer of warm water left on the nightstand. It was the final request I made from Madame Desire. "You're wounded. You need to clean up."

She looks pointedly at my chest with those unsettling eyes of hers. Eyes I still cannot see. Eyes I can only comprehend. "You're wounded too. Why don't *you* clean up?"

"I will after. Besides, I'm full fae. My wounds have already healed."

"How do you know mine haven't also? I'm not fully human, you know."

I shift my jaw back and forth. Must she argue with everything I say? "I know your wounds haven't healed because your elbow is dripping blood."

She glances down at her free arm where a scrape runs from her wrist to her upper arm. The most severe part of the wound is at her elbow. It gapes open, dripping rivulets of crimson. I can only imagine how much worse it must have been when she first sustained the injury, before her innate healing kicked it. Or has it not begun healing at all? Regardless, it shouldn't be this bad for someone of fae heritage.

She lurches forward as if suppressing a gag and brings a hand to her lips. "Oh no. It's bleeding."

"I said as much." I lift a brow. "Are you sensitive to the sight of blood?"

She nods and plunges a shaking hand into her skirt pocket, swaying a little as she extracts a small vial. I narrow my eyes while she turns the lid and draws out a glass dropper. My blood goes cold at the aroma of Crimson Malus filling the air.

Poison.

The very same that killed her father.

"Don't judge me," she says, voice strained. With shaking hands, she tilts her head back and places two drops under her tongue. Then she seems to think better of it and drops a third.

My shoulders tense, my muscles rippling with rage. Crimson Malus is a vile drug, one that harms more than just humans. It can hurt fae too. Destroy lives. Families. And here she is, brazenly swallowing it down like it's some prized nectar.

How could she be so reckless as to take that drug in front of me, knowing what I know?

She returns the vial to her pocket and releases a slow breath. Her eyes flutter closed. "I really needed that."

Her scent grows dimmer, mellower, the lemon, apple, and morning dew components of her aromatic profile blending into a harmonious concoction.

I stand stiffly beside the bed, unsure how to react. Unsure how to swallow down the anger twisting my heart...and the memories it forces to the surface.

*A soft, mellow voice, devoid of all feeling.*

*A placid, vacant expression.*

*Cold, limp hands...*

Astrid lets out a dreamy sigh, rousing me from my thoughts. Her voice takes on an airy quality. "I feel so much better now."

"You're high on poison," I say with a glare. I'm vaguely aware of a soft smile playing over her lips, although her mouth remains just behind the haze forever marring her face.

She meets my eyes. "I told you. I take the tincture to manage my mood."

"I thought you did it to control what impression you make when meeting new people."

"I do," she says, a note of haughty indignation in her voice. Then her scent flares with guilt. "But I use it for me too."

"Why?"

She shifts from foot to foot. "My emotions haven't been as... as tolerable since Father died. I don't like how I feel when the Crimson Malus wears off."

"That's probably more due to withdrawal from the drug than anything else."

"No," she says in a rush. "It's...it's...you wouldn't understand. You think I'm guilty, so you can't comprehend the grief I feel." Her voice begins to quaver at the end.

That's all it takes to shatter some of my composure, cutting through the anger I felt a moment ago. The truth is, I know the grief she feels. Just like I know that she truly feels it. A dark note lingers just beneath her scent profile, where the aroma of dew dips into the fragrance of a stormy sea.

It's sorrow. I'm too keenly familiar with that emotion not to recognize it, no matter how one's personal scent profile expresses it.

"Sit down already," I say as I retrieve the cloth from the ewer and dip it into the warm water.

This time, she obeys. Perhaps I should be grateful for the mellowing effect the poison has on her. I bend down on one knee and bring the cloth to her arm. She snatches the limb back before I can make contact with her wound. "What are you doing?"

I cut her an irritated look. With her sitting and me kneeling, we're nearly eye to eye. "What does it look like?"

"Don't touch it. It's going to hurt." She glances at her elbow and quickly averts her gaze. Her voice rises nearly an octave. "It's still bleeding."

I encircle her wrist with my cuffed hand so she won't pull away this time, and bring the cloth to her arm. Softly, I dab at the dried blood, starting at her wrist. She closes her lips on a whine, her eyelids pressed tight, head angled as far from me as it can go. I roll my eyes. "What is with you and blood?"

"I don't like it."

"You didn't seem too shaken when you watched me bite off an ogre's head. Nor did you cower when you saw me covered in blood. And you seemed fully captivated during the fight at Department Wrath. Were you not aware the duel might end in bloodshed?"

Finally, she opens her eyes to glare at me. "I don't like seeing *my own* blood."

"Well, that must be inconvenient," I say with a smirk. "Do you not have monthly courses?"

"That's different." Her scent profile flares with embarrassment. "You shouldn't even mention such a thing. Have you any idea how private a lady's courses are?"

I shake my head. "You really are half human, aren't you?"

With a huff, she angles her head away again.

I continue to clean her wound, slowly working up her arm. Quiet falls between us, punctuated by the occasional hiss of pain. Finally, I reach her elbow, which I know will hurt. Even though I'd prefer to work in silence, I figure it might be best to distract her. "You work for Madame Desire."

"Yes." The word dissolves into a wince.

"But not like the other girls do."

"No," she bites out. "I'm a matchmaker."

So I was wrong about her after all. "Why didn't you beg your employer to save you from me when she found us in the alley? Not that I'm complaining."

"I promised to come quietly in exchange for a chance to prove my innocence, didn't I? Besides, as soon as you flashed that coin, I knew she was lost to me."

I dip the cloth back in the ewer and wring out rust-colored water. When I bring it back to her elbow, I ask, "What do you mean she was lost to you?"

She releases a sigh. "It's because of my magic."

I consider what she could mean by that. Based on what she's told me about how her magic works, I can imagine one explanation. "Did you form a poor first impression when you first met her? Because of...your mood?"

"Well, no, but even if I do form a positive impression, there often comes a time when someone's best mirrored qualities evoke negative feelings from the other person. It doesn't always happen, but where envy is involved, things can go badly. Madame Desire has always been good to me, but I can tell her opinion of me is starting to change. She suspects me of possessing the worst aspects of her best qualities."

I ponder that for a moment. Astrid's magic is strange indeed, a kind I haven't encountered before. I still can't fathom why I see her the way I do. Why I so badly want to protect this aggravating stranger.

"Why did you bring us here, anyway?" she asks.

"I needed a place for us to stay." I almost leave it at that, but there's a truth I can't help but confess. "The ogre attack was no accident. Someone lured me into that garden. Someone broke into my room and stole my Chariot."

She looks over at me with a furrowed brow. "What's a Chariot?"

"A device that allows for instantaneous travel. Whoever stole it knew I had it. How else could the thief have found it? It isn't some mammoth contraption. It's small. Unimportant to the common onlooker. Anyone who didn't know exactly what to look for would think it a cosmetics compact or a snuff box. The thief had to have known I possessed it and understood how it worked in order to guess where I'd left it."

"That's the object you were so determined to get back after we left your room?"

"Yes, and I wasn't willing to take us back to my suite tonight. The fact that the ogre went after you as well told me we might not be safe in your room either."

"Does that mean you think some other person was working with the ogre?"

I nod. "Murtis couldn't have gotten to my room so soon after the fight at Wrath. To the garden, yes, but nowhere else. Based on the scent trail the thief left behind, they'd been inside my room during the duel and left just before it ended. They purposefully cloaked their scent in a floral aroma and led me to the garden where my senses would be too overwhelmed to smell the ogre."

Astrid shifts anxiously on the bed, and it isn't from me

cleaning her wound this time. "If the thief is still out there, what makes you think we're any safer here?"

I finish cleaning her elbow and run the cloth over the rest of her arm. The gash seems to have stopped bleeding now, so I gently rotate her wrist in search of other injuries. "I can't be certain. The fact that the attack was set up at night, long after the hotel's patrons ceased to linger outdoors, suggests our hidden assailant wanted everything taken care of covertly. This room at least offers some semblance of protection. I assume Madame Desire doesn't let just anyone into her brothel."

"No. Certainly not this late. I'm assuming the only reason she allowed you to purchase an overnight visit was because you gave her permission to charge the Alpha Council. Overnight stays are very expensive."

I grunt a response and finish examining her arm. When I'm certain the limb has been properly tended to, I wring out the cloth again. Rising to my feet, I hand her the rag. She meets my eyes with a questioning look before taking it. "I...I can't see if there are wounds on your face, so you should clean them yourself."

She snatches the cloth from me. "I could have done all of that myself, thank you very much."

I scoff. "I didn't see you doing a very good job while you were whimpering at the sight of blood."

She has no argument for that and reluctantly brings the cloth to her cheek. I find myself staring, wishing I could make out more than just a hazy impression of her face. Even as I watch her scrub furiously at her skin, my eyes refuse to take in anything tangible. I know she's frowning, but her lips are devoid of color. I know she's scowling but her eyes have no distinct shape. Her hair is just a dark blur. Does everyone see her this way? Am I only perplexed by what I see because I know to look? I suppose any unsuspecting spectator would simply lose interest in such a hazy perception and move on.

Astrid finishes cleaning her face and brings the cloth to her other arm. "So..." She draws the word out slowly. "Someone lured you from your room into the garden where we were attacked by an ogre. That same someone knew where to find you, understood your weaknesses, and stole a strange device that I'm guessing very few people know you have."

"Yes, and I'm going to find out who it was."

She finishes cleaning her arm and returns the cloth to the ewer. Her shoulders sink, and her scent profile takes a dive, clouded with something like grief. "I already know who it was. It's the same person who *really* killed my father."

I'm torn between shock, curiosity, and suspicion that she could be baiting me. My first two instincts overpower the third. "Who?"

She meets my eyes. "Queen Tris."

## 10

*ASTRID*

The Huntsman blinks back at me for several moments, expression blank. After a while, his stony mask slowly begins to crack. First with a narrowing of his eyes. Then a stretch of his lips. Finally, he throws back his head...and laughs.

"It's not funny, Huntsman. I'm being serious."

It takes him several moments to even remotely sober from his amusement. All the while, my cheeks grow redder. I'm not sure whether I'm more embarrassed or angry. When he does manage to stop laughing, he's left with a smile that crinkles the corners of his eyes. The sight of it does something strange to my belly.

"You could have come up with a thousand other possibilities to explain your innocence," he says, "but Queen Tris murdering Edmund Snow, her beloved husband? Nice try."

"You're laughing over my father's death, Huntsman."

That wipes the smile off his face.

"I meant what I said. Queen Tris is the real killer."

His brow furrows as he studies my face. Or what he can see of it. I stare right back, seeking my reflection in his eyes. I've only managed to glimpse it a time or two, but it always shows me the same thing as before—something small, weak, and vulnerable. Qualities that don't seem to exist in my captor at all, neither as positive attributes nor negative ones. The impression itself feels threadbare, fraying at the edges. I've never had this happen before.

He lets out a grumbling sigh. "Fine. I'll humor you. Why are you so convinced the queen killed your father? What motive could she possibly have had?"

I nibble my bottom lip, preparing my words. This is my chance. Stating the truth won't be enough. Whatever I say must be convincing. Logical. "Queen Tris never meant to murder my father. She was trying to poison me."

"Why would she use a poison that is weak against someone with fae blood?"

That's a question I've had ever since the Huntsman told me Crimson Malus had been involved. Before he told me that, I'd already deduced that poison had killed my father. I'd also guessed the pie had been the vehicle that delivered said poison. The type of poison used, however, throws a hitch in my theory. "I...I don't know. Maybe she didn't realize it wouldn't work on me. I wouldn't be surprised if she never bothered to learn of my fae heritage. Honestly, I doubt she'd have let me into the palace, much less married my father, if she knew what sort of creature my mother was."

"What sort of creature was she?"

I bristle, annoyed at myself for even bringing my mother up. She's the last person I want to talk about. "A water sprite. An unsavory unseelie type. You know, the kind Queen Tris finds far beneath her. She abandoned me when I was a baby. So, on second thought, perhaps they'd have been kindred spirits."

The Huntsman's eyelids narrow to slits. "I sense much disdain for the queen."

My eyes fly to his. "Of course I have disdain for her."

"Because she tried to make you leave the palace?"

"Because she *killed my father*."

He folds his arms over his chest, a move that drags my cuff with such force, it pulls me to my feet. I nearly collide with him, but he braces my shoulders with his hands. I'm so caught off guard my breath hitches. His hands are warm and strong on my shoulders, and when I tilt my head back, I meet his eyes. Their honeyed hue glitters in the lamplight. Warmth rushes through my chest and spreads outward. A buzzing heat sizzles every inch of my skin his palms touch, even through my shirt—

In an abrupt move, he releases my shoulders and takes a full step back.

I blink at the space between us as my mind clears a little. Only then do I realize I'd been trapped in a moment of euphoria...over my captor. Damn that tincture! I shift to the side and run a hand through the ends of my hair to distract myself from my embarrassment, but my moves feel slow. Heavy. Perhaps taking three drops was a little too much this time.

"Blooming hell, you really are high. I should not be entertaining murder theories from you right now. You aren't in your right mind."

I scoff. "My mind is just fine. My tincture only affects my mood. And...and maybe my body a little."

He shakes his head. "You should get some sleep."

"No," I say, fully facing him again. "I'm not done talking about this. You promised you'd hear me out. That you'd give me a full hour."

"I never said when I'd give that hour, nor did I say it would be one consecutive hour."

"Please," I say, infusing my voice with desperation. "I need you to listen to me."

He moves his arms as if to try and cross them again but seems to think better of it last minute. Instead, he tucks his free hand in his pocket and slouches slightly to one side. On anyone else, such a stance would look casual. But on him, it looks as intimidating as ever. "Is this truly the hour you wish to waste?"

"Yes, this is the hour I wish to *use*."

"Fine," he bites out. "Go ahead. Tell me how your step-mother murdered her beloved husband using *your* pie and the poison *you* carry at all times."

A flutter of satisfaction ripples through me, made all the more enjoyable by my tincture's influence. "First of all," I say, sifting through everything I want to say, "Let us speak about *my* motive. I had no reason to kill my father."

"Aside from the fact that he agreed with his wife about sending you away from Fairweather Palace, and that you had a very heated argument over that."

I clench my teeth. "That's hardly worth killing someone over. Children argue with their parents. It isn't a revolutionary concept."

"Very well," he says. "Explain the use of poison then. Even if I were to accept that you held no ill will for your father, could you have accidentally poisoned the pie while taking your tincture?"

"No," I say, tone firm. "I'm careful with it. I never take it around someone else's food or drink, nor could I have accidentally used actual Crimson Malus fruit. Had it been an apple pie, I might understand the possibility of such a grave mistake, but the pie I made was strawberry. *Only* strawberry."

He lifts his chin, his countenance taking on a smug quality. Or smugger, I should say. The Huntsman is already smugness incarnate. "What would you say if I told you the poison wasn't inside the filling but coated onto the pie crust?"

My mind goes blank at that. "That's where the poison was placed?"

He nods. "It was laced into the butter that greased the pie tin."

I place my hand on my chin and begin to pace, only to remember I can't get very far in these cuffs. "That proves it," I say, half to myself, half to him. "The pie tin is the only component that was out of my hands for any amount of time."

The Huntsman takes a sudden step forward until only a foot of space stands between us. He lowers his head, and I pull back, but he doesn't come closer. Only...breathes in.

"What are you doing?" I ask.

He breathes in deeply again, then steps back to where he was. "Smelling for lies."

I cut him a glare. "Then sniff away, bear man. I'm telling the truth." When he says nothing more, I continue. "Queen Tris was alone with the pie tin. She came to speak with me when I first entered the kitchen to start the pie. She sent everyone out of the kitchen, the cooks, the servers, even my lady's maid."

"What did she come to speak with you about?"

My fingers curl into fists. "To remind me how serious she was about seeing me gone."

"All because you rejected her nephew's marriage proposal?"

I shake my head. "That was only the most recent fault she found in me. Her animosity for me had reached a boiling point long before then."

"Why?"

I lift one arm in a half shrug. "Why do you think? Because of my magic. Because—like Madame Desire—she was envious of the reflected qualities she saw in me. More condemning is the fact that she had the opportunity to poison the pie. When she asked me what I was doing in the kitchen and sent everyone away, I told her I was making a pie but never said who I was making it for. While we spoke, I began to gather my supplies—pie tin, measuring cups, butter. By the end of our conversation, I was so upset, I stormed out of the kitchen in a huff. I didn't bother to see when she left."

"So you think Queen Tris poisoned the pie tin—or the butter—after you left the kitchen." His tone suggests he's still only humoring me, but at least he's listening.

"Yes."

"Was anyone in the kitchen when you returned?"

I suppress a groan, knowing my answer will give more space for doubt. "Yes," I begrudgingly admit. "When I returned to the kitchen, the staff had already returned too. But none of them did it. It *had* to be Tris. She did it before she let the staff back in the room."

A few quiet moments pass between us before the Huntsman poses his next question. "How would the queen have come by the same poison you use to manage your mood? We've already determined the poison had been laced into the butter and did not come from the fruit itself. Which means it had to have been delivered in liquid form." His eyes narrow yet again. "Like a tincture."

"I understand your conclusion, but regardless of what form the poison was delivered in, it was not placed there by my hand."

"Tell me this, Miss Snow. Where do you source your tincture?"

My stomach sinks. Not with guilt but with the knowledge that my answer will cast me in a suspicious light. But if my captor can smell lies, I have no choice but to answer honestly. "I make it myself."

He gives no indication whether he's surprised by that. "Where do you brew it? The same kitchen you made the pie in?"

"Of course not! That would be highly irresponsible." I take a deep breath before I explain. "I brew it in my room. I learned how to make it from the fae who healed me. When I was recovering, I asked a few questions. I hadn't had any intention of making it then, but I was so curious about the poison that I wanted to understand more. I asked how to identify the variety from regular apples."

"And how does one distinguish Crimson Malus from a non-poisonous apple?"

I assume he's testing me. With how thoroughly he seems to have studied this case, he probably knows the answer already. "Crimson Malus drips dark red nectar when it's ripe, and the grass and soil beneath the tree will be the richest shades of green and brown."

"All right. So, how do you explain how Queen Tris got hold of your tincture? Does she know about your reliance on the drug? How many others know?"

"Only Father and Marybeth," I say. "But that doesn't mean Tris couldn't have found out. It's possible that she discovered my vials in my room. I...I didn't think to count if any were missing. I only briefly checked my stash when I grabbed an extra vial right before I fled the palace. That's the only one I have left." I don't mention that once my current vial is gone, I'll need to make more of the tincture. Which will be difficult, considering Crimson Malus only grows in the Spring Court and sale of the fruit itself or any products made with it is illegal. I suppose I could buy access to the restricted top floor of Department Gluttony. That's the only place I can imagine finding it around here.

The Huntsman rubs his bearded jaw. "While I can see how you *might* be innocent, your case against Queen Tris is weak, if not downright ridiculous. It makes very little sense why she would use a poison against you—an ineffective one, I might add—that she found in your possession. You also suggested she was behind the ogre attack and the theft of my Chariot. What you failed to reason is that she hired me to find you. She wouldn't try to kill me or send an ogre to do what she already sent me to do. Why would she intervene when all she wants is you dead? She's a queen. She has better things to do than go through all the trouble of hunting down her stepdaughter. If she lets me do what she asked me to, she gets the same result for a fraction of the effort."

I hate that he's right about that. Even though I know my stepmother is guilty, I can't imagine her traipsing around the Seven Sins Hotel, getting her hands dirty, meeting with ogres in dark alcoves. But still…I'm not ready to let this go. "What about the floral aroma? You've obviously met my stepmother. Her hair is made of cherry blossoms. It doesn't get more floral than that."

He shakes his head. "Fruit blossoms are one of the few floral fragrances I can tolerate. More importantly, I know Queen Tris' scent profile. The trail we followed earlier did not belong to her. That was a false fragrance. An unnatural perfume."

"Couldn't she have used a perfume to cover her innate scent? I take it she knows of your weakness to floral aromas?"

The tightening of his jaw tells me I'm onto something. "She might have inferred as much when I demanded all floral arrangements and bouquets, unless directly related to the case, be removed from the palace before my arrival. It helps assure my senses are clear. It's the same demand I make every time I'm called to a location to pick up a scent trail."

"I'm assuming she knows where you are now? Where you're staying?"

His throat bobs. "Yes."

"Is that not all the proof you need? How else do you explain that someone knew exactly where to find you? The way the ogre tossed you aside when I freed myself from the cuffs makes me think he was really after me all along. And not to kill me but to capture me. To bring me straight to Tris so she can do the killing. Don't you see that she could have been using you to get to me? She needed *your* sense of smell to find me."

He furrows his brow as if he's truly giving my question serious thought. "I suppose the last part could be true, but it still doesn't make sense that Tris would be behind it. Why offer me a bargain if she was only going to follow me and kill you herself? As Huntsman, I'm supposed to find fugitives for the fae royals, no questions asked. If she only wanted my sense of smell to find you, she could have left it at that. She offered me a bargain to bring her your heart knowing I had no obligation to say yes."

I shudder at the thought of what he agreed to do for her. She must have kept the terms rather vague, though, considering what he said last night. *When I bargained to bring her your heart, I didn't specify you wouldn't be attached to it.*

I rub my free arm over the other to ward away my sudden chill. "What did she offer you in return for your bargain?"

His eyes go distant before he answers. "Freedom."

"What do you mean?"

"I only serve the Alpha Council as their bounty hunter because it is my punishment. I'm on year five of a hundred-year sentence. This is not the life I chose to have, only what I deserve for my own reckless actions."

I take a hesitant step back, one that has him assessing me with a frown. Forcing myself not to cower, I ask, "What was your crime?"

He releases a slow, grumbling sigh. "Gambling."

I pull my head back. "Is gambling a crime?"

"It is when you wager more than you have and wind up in a mountain of debt you can't pay back."

His answer sets my nerves at ease. Even though I know the Huntsman is hardly an innocent or kindly soul, I would have felt far more wary had I learned his crimes were of a more sinister nature. "So Queen Tris offered to release you from your service to the Alpha Council if you found me and brought back my heart. Does she even have the ability to release you? Are you not bound to the council as a whole?"

"My debts were accumulated in the Spring Court. Since my crimes were a matter of finance, it was up to Spring's seelie ruler to dole out my punishment. Tris sentenced me to my term as Huntsman, which means she has the right to end that sentence."

I suppose that makes sense. Each court in Faerwyvae is ruled by two fae rulers—a seelie monarch and an unseelie monarch—who live in separate palaces and reign in different ways. The seelie monarch, like Queen Tris, oversees matters of day-to-day life and finance, while the unseelie ruler oversees nature and advocates for the unseelie fae. Since the Huntsman's crime involved gambling debts, it would have fallen under Tris' jurisdiction. "How much time did she give you to fulfill your bargain?"

He hesitates before answering. "I have until the seventeenth of this month."

My throat goes dry. "That's less than two weeks away!"

"I'm aware."

"And you'll die if you fail to fulfill it?"

"Yes. That's how bargains work."

I'm surprised at how my heart clenches at the thought of him dying. Why should I care? My eyes go unfocused as I try to fit this whole bargain business into my theory. If I'm right and my stepmother only needed the Huntsman's sense of smell so she could follow him and kill me before he got to me, why would she offer him a bargain at all?

Realization begins to dawn. "Huntsman, what if...what if Tris never wanted you to succeed at fulfilling your bargain? What if she never intended to set you free?"

"What would be her motive?"

"Well..." I draw out the word slowly as facts and figures lock into place. "You seem to have become valuable to the Alpha Council. With your sense of smell, you must be able to find fugitives no one else can."

He waves a flippant hand. "That's exactly why I was appointed to this role as my punishment."

"I imagine letting you go would be quite a blow to the council. Especially when they are expecting ninety-five more years of service from you."

He releases a slow breath that has his wide chest deflating. "I see the point you're getting at, but it still doesn't explain the bargain. If I fail, I'll die. If I'm so valuable—" His words cut off as if he has reached the same conclusion I have.

"The bargain was only meant to motivate you to find me quickly," I say. "What she really wants is to kill me herself. Once she does that, you will be forced to fail your end of the bargain. However, she won't let you die. She'll revoke your bargain at the last moment and, in turn, keep you in service to the Alpha Council."

A hollow look crosses his face. He rubs his jaw again, eyes distant, searching. "I'm still not convinced it was Tris. Not everything about your theory lines up. Besides, she can't lie, and I would have smelled any fluctuations in her scent profile had she tried to deceive me."

I take a step closer to him. "Then you at least believe I could be innocent."

He gives me a pointed look. "Heavy emphasis on the *could*. But I won't know anything for certain until I find the thief who stole my Chariot. I will not return to Tris without it."

My chest buzzes with excited warmth, and only half of that is due to my tincture. The other half is from hope—the most he's given me yet. It's the same spark I've felt every time I've fantasized about facing Tris in the fighting pit. Of outwitting her, tricking her into confessing her crimes, or finding some other way to defeat her and see my father's death avenged. No matter how much money I've saved, no matter how many times I've analyzed the duels, I've never fully believed I had a chance to see my impossible fantasies fulfilled. But now...now I have a chance to do more than petition Madame Fury. More than gamble on a duel I might not win.

With the Huntsman's help, I can uncover solid proof.

See justice served.

Claim vengeance.

"Then let's put all our efforts into finding the thief," I say.

"*Our* efforts?"

I lift my chained wrist and quirk a brow. "Your refusal to let me out of your sight paired with your statement that you will not return to the queen until you've found the Chariot tell me I'll be trailing along whether I like it or not. And I want to come along. If finding the thief means proving my innocence, not to mention the guilt of the real killer, then I want to help. I know I *can* help. You might find clues that only mean something to me. Furthermore, because of your bargain, both of our lives are on the line. It makes sense that we'd work together."

"You do realize that working together won't stop me from hauling you back to your stepmother, don't you? If we find evidence that Tris killed your father, I can petition the other royals on the Alpha Council to intervene. But if we don't, or if it was someone else, I'm still bound to fulfill my bargain with her."

That turns my stomach. But on the off chance Tris wasn't the one who poisoned the pie, then finding the culprit could still save my life. Tris will have no choice but to spare me if we prove I'm innocent, and she'll certainly revoke the Huntsman's bargain.

But if it *was* her, we'll need damning evidence. Evidence he might never find on his own. Not with his strong bias to believe her. Not when it would be so much easier to just bring me to her and let her kill me.

Damn it all. I need him more than he needs me. Which means I need to sweeten the deal.

"If you agree to let me work with you as an equal and not as a captive," I say, "I promise not to run away anymore. I promise not to fight you. And...and I'll come willingly back to my step-mother when the time comes, regardless of whether we've found the true killer." That last part is a gamble. If we don't prove my innocence by then, it will mean my death.

He reaches into his waistcoat pocket and extracts a brass pocket watch. He returns it with a frustrated groan. "I'm not agreeing to anything tonight. I need to get some sleep if I'm to utilize my senses at their sharpest."

I narrow my eyes. So, he needs adequate sleep to function at his best? I file that intel away in case I need it in the future. "You'll consider my proposition though?"

"I'll consider it tomorrow. Now, we sleep." He angles his chin at the bed.

I lift my cuff. "We can't very well sleep soundly while chained together. Not if I'm on the bed and you're on the floor." I give a halfhearted chuckle, but it quickly dissolves as the Huntsman does nothing but stare blankly back at me. "You're sleeping on the floor, right?"

His lips twist into the slightest hint of a grin that somehow manages to brim with all the smugness in the world. "No. The bed is big enough for two."

The blood leaves my face as I lift my cuffed wrist higher. "You're unlocking these, though, right?"

A snort of laughter. "Not on your life."

# 11

*ASTRID*

This is by far the most uncomfortable night of my life. I don't know how late it is, but it must not be terribly so, for the brothel is still very much active, as evidenced by the grunts and moans humming through the walls. Apparently, the Huntsman isn't the only one wealthy enough to afford an overnight stay.

Since I only use my rented room during the day when Department Lust sees far less activity, I've never had to witness such...acoustics. Let me just say the sounds are far from soothing. Instead, they have my every muscle coiling tight while a strange heat dips low in my belly. I'm made all the more tense with how close I lay next to my aggravating captor, our cuffed hands less than a foot away. Unlike me, the Huntsman is soundly asleep. How the hell he can find slumber so easily in our situation is beyond me.

I glance over at his dozing form. I've had my eyes open ever since he turned off the lamps in the room, so they are well adjusted to the dark by now. Neither of us lies beneath the blankets, since the room is warm enough without them, so I can see his figure in its entirety. I watch the slow rise and fall of his broad chest before my eyes rove up to his face and land on his mouth. The sight of his slightly parted lips paired with the sounds of pleasure echoing beyond the walls fills my mind with a sudden curiosity of how he might kiss—

I avert my eyes, forcing them to the ceiling. Why would I be curious about how he'd kiss? It doesn't matter that he's hand-some. That his beard is rather dashing, that his irises look like honey, and that his copper hair might be the prettiest shade I've ever seen. It certainly doesn't matter that he's strong and capable and killed an ogre to rescue me. He's my captor. A bounty hunter. And the gruffest son of a harpy I've ever had the displeasure to meet. Not to mention, he almost tried to kill me.

The reminder cools my blood just enough to allow me to look at him without any unwelcome fantasies plaguing my mind. I even manage to stare down at his trousers without thinking about what lies beneath his underbritches. Well, I mostly manage not to think about that. Most of my attention is on his nearest pocket.

I stare at it for a few moments, trying to recall which side of his trousers he put the key into. After our conversation, I have no intention of running away. Not until he tells me if he'll accept my proposition and let me help him find my father's killer. In other words, proving it was Tris. I need him. But right now, what I need more than anything is some blooming sleep. And I'm certain I'll sleep much better if I can free my wrist from my metal cuff and curl up on my side as far from the Huntsman as I can.

With slow moves, I inch slightly closer to him. He doesn't react, doesn't so much as draw a sharper breath. So I scoot closer, closer, trying to move the bed as little as possible. When only a few inches separate us, I bring a tentative hand toward his pocket. I hold my breath as I press my palm against his upper thigh. My eyes fly to his face, but he still doesn't react, just keeps breathing deeply, sleeping soundly. And yet my heart falls, for I don't feel the telltale shape of a key beneath my palm, not even his room key.

I slowly remove my hand and scowl at the opposite pocket, the one farthest away from me. I'd already suspected the key would be there, for I'm pretty sure I saw him pocket it with his free hand. That side of him will be much harder for me to reach without waking him.

I stare at him a few breaths longer before I dare scoot closer and lift myself to sitting. Every move is slow and careful as I do my best not to disturb his cuffed hand. When he still doesn't react, I reach across him and softly lay my hand on his thigh.

Once again, no reaction.

A devious grin tugs my lips as I finally feel what I'm looking for. This is the pocket with the key. The next challenge will be extracting it.

Recalling how tight his pants are, I know it won't be easy, especially with the unfortunate angle I'm at. There's only so much leverage I can get from our horizontal positions while avoiding touching him or draping myself across him.

I glare at the pocket in question. Is a slightly more comfortable sleeping arrangement worth an attempt?

The moans from the room next door reach a crescendo. My heart thuds in response, and now I just want a distraction. So into his pocket I shall go.

Pouring all my focus into my task, I angle myself closer and plant my cuffed hand as close to his side as I can without tugging our chain. Then, propping one knee next to his hip, I bring my other between his legs. I pause, waiting to see if he'll rouse, but he continues to sleep like a log. Confident that this man will sleep through anything, I shift my weight over him and bring my fingertips to his pocket's opening. Then, inch my inch, I slide my hand inside—

Before I know what's happening, I'm on my back, panting hard as the Huntsman looms over me. He has my wrists pinned over my head while his knees frame my hips. Only a fraction of his weight is upon me, for he remains partially on his side. His sudden closeness has my pulse racing. Adding to our suggestive position is my awareness of the way he hovers over me, his grip on my wrists, the sounds of panting pounding from behind the walls—no wait. The sound of heavy breathing isn't coming from outside the room, but from *him*. From *me*. Our chests heave together for several moments. An earthy scent like soil and fur mingling with wood smoke fills my lungs, so potent it has my lashes fluttering.

I'm frozen as I stare up at him, his face only inches away. That's when I realize...his eyes are closed. Is he still asleep?

His lips part and his low voice reverberates through me. "Go to sleep, Miss Snow."

With that, he rolls off me and returns to his previous position on his back. Soon his breathing steadies and his face goes slack again.

I blink up at the ceiling, my breaths still far from even. Every inch of my body that was pressed against his tingles. Whether with rage or shock or excitement, I know not. All I know is there's no way I'm going for that key again. He may be a sound sleeper, but his reflexes are too sharp, even during slumber.

Annoyance ripples through me, cutting through...whatever I started feeling when he rolled on top of me. How dare he sleep so deeply? How dare he fend off my attempts to gain some semblance of comfort? How dare he...be so large and heavy and...and to make my heart race?

I bite my bottom lip and slap my free hand over my forehead. It's the Crimson Malus, isn't it? My tincture is messing with my emotions, heightening my senses in the strangest ways. That's all it is. I probably took too much.

Or did I not take enough?

My fingers flinch toward my skirt pocket.

Maybe just one more drop. What's the worst that can happen? The last time I consumed more than three drops in the span of an hour, I slept longer than usual. Right now, I could use forced slumber.

I extract my vial with my free hand and place a single drop under my tongue. My body thrums with immediate relief, stripping me of all thoughts of my impossibly annoying, impossibly...handsome...no.

Impossibly...irresistible.

No.

My impossibly...

*Irritating...*

Bedmate.

∽

WHEN I WAKE, THE FIRST THING I'M AWARE OF IS THE HEAT. I open my eyes and find myself surrounded by flames. Red flames. Pink flames. I shutter my eyes against the blinding light of the inferno, but I find it isn't a fire that surrounds me at all. It's sunlight.

Morning heat and sunshine stream in through the open windows, setting the pink and red decor in the room glowing. I sit up in a rush and look over at the Huntsman.

His side of the bed is empty.

Then I realize my wrist is no longer cuffed. I'm alone in the room, alone in the bed, and the day is well past sunrise. A slight throbbing pulses in my temple, and I bring a hand to the side of my head. I don't remember a single thing after my last dose of my tincture, which means it must have sent me into a deep sleep.

But...where is the Huntsman?

I leave the bed and scan the room. It's my first time seeing it in the daylight, so I have to scan my surroundings a few times before I notice the open door to a modest washroom, the pile of clothing at the foot of the bed, and the piece of parchment sitting on top of the stack.

I go to it and lift the paper, finding a short note scrawled over it.

*Miss Snow,*
    *Do not run away or our deal is off. Bathe and dress. I'll return later.*
    —T

I do a double take at the letter *T* in place of a signature. What does the *T* stand for? He told me to call him Huntsman. I turn my attention to the stack of clothes, finding a lightweight cotton skirt and blouse, similar to the one I'm wearing now. Well, similar to how it was before it was torn and bloodied. My gaze wanders to the washroom, where I see a porcelain tub, already filled with steaming water. I release a sigh, my muscles uncoiling at the thought of a bath. Just looking at it makes me want to linger in the tub all day.

But I won't.

I'll bathe and dress as the Huntsman requested in his note, but I'll make it quick. If he isn't back by the time I'm finished, I'm not sitting in this room waiting for him all day.

I have very important things to do.

## 12

### THE HUNTSMAN

O f course Astrid Snow is gone. Of course she fled at her first chance to get away from me. She didn't even make it through a single night without trying to steal my key. Although I remained half asleep during last night's attempt, I vaguely recall the feeling of her hand dipping into my pocket, the startling realization that the girl was almost on top of me. I managed to turn the tables and frighten her from any further attempts, but there was a moment where—even in my half-asleep state—where Astrid's scent shifted into something that was almost...dare I say desire?

No, I dare not. *Astrid* and *desire* are two words I should go to great lengths to separate. In fact, desire is the last thing I need right now. The last thing this mission needs. I know just how detrimental such feelings can be. Romance, lust, love—even the platonic kind—blinds me. Clouds my senses, my thoughts, my ability to see and smell the truth. I learned that the hard way. With Father. With the woman I so stupidly thought I loved five years ago.

Besides, just because Astrid has filled my head with doubts over her guilt doesn't mean I don't still have a bargain to fulfill. If she isn't responsible for her father's murder, then I need to find out who is. It's the only way I can save both my life and Astrid's. Proof of the real killer is the only sure way to convince Tris to release me from my bargain—and clear Astrid of the charges against her.

However, if Miss Snow is guilty, I need to be able to perform my duties with a clear head.

There are only two ways this can end.

I either present the queen with the real killer or I deliver her stepdaughter into her custody.

Since Astrid has run away again, I suspect it will be the latter.

With my jaw clenched tight, I follow her scent trail from our bedroom at Lust, down to the first floor of the building, and out the front doors. From there I follow it along the walking paths to Department Gluttony. I enter the building, finding indoor storefronts to a grocer, a butcher, and other markets on the first floor. Astrid's scent leads me to the butcher, then right back out to the walking paths. I'm surprised when her scent trail has me doubling back toward Lust. I expected to find her beyond the hotel grounds, in the process of making her escape.

I pass the front of the brothel and enter the alley between Lust and the perimeter wall. It's the same location I first saw her and the site of the ogre's bloody demise. I already inspected the alley at first light, so I know all traces of the attack have been cleaned up.

I slow my pace, hearing the first strains of a soft, cooing voice that dissolves into a giggle. Astrid's scent grows sharper and softer at the same time, evoking aromas of morning dew on fresh grass and apple blossoms unfurling in a sunlit grove.

Then I see her.

She rises to her feet from behind the largest waste bin, a

wide smile playing over her lips—small lips the color of coral. Her heart-shaped face emanates joy in everything from her smile to the blushing apples of her cheeks, to her petite nose that wrinkles with laughter, to her gray eyes glittering with mirth. Dark lashes flutter closed as she brings an orange kitten to her cheek and nuzzles it.

That's when I realize something that sets my heart racing, thudding, hammering, rioting.

Not only do I see her, but I...*see* her.

As silent as I can, I step closer. Closer. Daring my eyes to tell me I'm mistaken. They don't.

Her every feature is clear, from her giddy expression to her short, blue-black hair. I study her raven strands, the cut that falls just above her nape, the wave of fringe swept off to one side of her forehead. She's dressed in the outfit I picked out for her this morning at Department Envy, and for once I'm able to take in more than just her posture. I see the way her blouse is left unbuttoned at her neck, the way sweat beads at the hollow of her clavicle, the slight swell of her bosom, the taper of her waist—

Her face swings toward mine. Like a door slamming shut, my view of her shifts into a sudden blur. My eyes return to her face, but the sight of it is no longer clear. I frown at her, trying to see beyond the haze while also committing what I just glimpsed to memory. It feels tenuous, as if any moment it will slip away. I suppose that isn't important. What matters is that, however briefly, I *saw* her.

What doesn't matter is that she's absolutely and undeniably lovely.

She backs up a step, her posture suddenly stiff. "I didn't run away."

I rouse myself from my thoughts and feign gruff nonchalance. Taking a few steps closer, I say, "It doesn't look that way to me."

She lifts her chin, tone laced with defiance. "I didn't know when you'd be back, and I wasn't about to be trapped in that stuffy room all day. Madame Desire doesn't like when guests stay past daybreak anyway."

"I doubt she'll mind what we do as guests. I purchased the room for an entire week." My lips lift into a grin I know will send her bristling. "Same goes for you."

She furrows her brow. "Same goes for..." Her words dissolve into a scoff. "You *purchased* me?"

"I paid for your company," I clarify. She opens her mouth to argue, but I speak first. "It's essential that I keep you close, especially at night. The thief clearly prefers to work under the cover of darkness, and I'll not have you endangered."

"I'd be flattered if I didn't know all you cared about is fulfilling your bargain."

"Don't bother feeling flattered at all. And if you don't want to return to the cuff, then I suggest making no argument about our sleeping arrangements."

She nuzzles the kitten again, who had begun to wiggle out of her grasp, and sets the mewling animal down. She dips into a crouch and allows all four kittens to climb up her skirts. The mother cat feasts on a plate of herring. "I'm being perfectly compliant, am I not? I didn't run away, and your note never stated I couldn't leave our room. I had important things to do."

I huff a laugh and tilt my head at the kittens. "*This* is important?"

"Yes, Huntsman. This among other things. I do have a job, you know."

Right. Astrid Snow is a matchmaker and not a courtesan like I originally thought. "Isn't proving your innocence a little more pressing than pairing up husbands and wives?"

She smiles wide. It's a grin I wish I could clearly see. What color were her lips? Ruby? No, coral. Even as I try to recall them, the memory dissolves like mist.

But what the blooming hell am I doing trying to remember her lips in the first place?

Gathering another kitten in her arms, a gray one this time, she stands and bounces on the balls of her feet. "Do you mean it? You're going to help me find the real killer? And I'm going to help you do it?"

I clench my jaw, cursing myself for having stated something that sounded so optimistic. There's a chance this could fail. That she's lying to my face. It wouldn't be the first time someone's deception has evaded my detection. "I'm going to find out who stole my Chariot and get it back, and you are going to come with me. You made a decent point last night when you said I might come across clues that mean more to you than to me. If someone is only using me to get to you, then we need to work together."

"Someone," she says, arching a brow, "like my stepmother."

"I will not entertain such a possibility until we've gathered more proof." A pit of dread forms in my stomach as I say it. Astrid made a few good points last night, ones that are almost too daunting to consider. While I strongly doubt Queen Tris had such sinister motives when she put me on the case, I can't ignore the possibility that she too is capable of deceiving me. If she truly hates her stepdaughter as much as Astrid thinks she does, then I suppose the queen could have tried to poison her. And if the poison killed the man she loved instead of her intended victim, then it makes sense she'd want revenge on Astrid at all costs, and to silence her before proof of her own guilt gets out.

The thing that doesn't make sense, though, is that the poisoner used Crimson Malus. Tris should have known better than to use it on someone with fae blood.

"We'll see justice served soon enough, Abernathy," she says to the gray kitten. Her voice is so light, so gleeful, I can't help but wonder how much of her tincture she's had today. I recall how slowly her wounds healed last night, despite her use of a poison renowned for its healing. Does she have no clue what's happening to her? What she's doing to herself? I suppose I wouldn't either if I hadn't already seen it happen firsthand.

But I have.

I shake my head. None of that matters right now.

"Are you done?" I ask, giving the kitten in her arms a pointed look.

"Hardly," she says. "Mama Cat hasn't finished her meal and I've only snuggled two kittens."

"You know stray cats can take care of themselves, right?"

She says nothing, only nuzzles the kitten again, giggling when it presses its paws to her chin and begins licking her lower lip.

I grimace. "That's disgusting."

"No, it's not. It's adorable."

"These are wild animals. They don't need to be fed and coddled and comforted. They survive well enough on their own without you feeding them."

"I like feeding them." She sets the gray kitten down and picks up the fluffy white one. "And Madeline likes me."

I hang my head and rub my brow. "This is exactly why fae began to change in the first place. Because of humans trying to *help*."

"I know," she says, and has the decency to sound somewhat ashamed.

Because I'm right. Long ago, Faerwyvae was only inhabited by fae, and all had only one physical form—their unseelie manifestation. Fae were animals. Spirits. Wild forces of nature. But then humans discovered the isle and began to interact with the fae. They taught us their language and brought food and clothing. Contact with such items began to change faekind. Soon we learned to manifest a second form modeled after human likeness. What followed was a bloody war that divided the isle, separating the humans from the fae. It wasn't until just over twenty years ago that another war brought the wall that divided our two people down. Since then, we've been united. The fae rule the isle, but the humans who live here flourish under their protection.

"I don't see you complaining about having a seelie form," Astrid says, glancing at me from head to toe. "Which body do you spend more time in? This one or the bear?"

I purse my lips, debating whether to answer her at all. But the pure curiosity in her voice has me speaking almost against my will. "This one, mostly," I say with a resigned sigh.

"Why? You're so cute as a bear." Her scent constricts with a hint of embarrassment, as if she hadn't meant to say that out loud.

I snort an involuntary laugh. "Yes, well, I spent the first several years of my life as a bear. But after I learned to shift, I didn't shift back often. Now I only do so when it suits my work as Huntsman."

"If I had an animal form, I don't think I'd ever shift. I envy animals. Not fae ones, I suppose, but true animals. They don't seem to have the same tendency to judge and scheme like people do." Her scent dips with a note of grief and longing.

"Don't envy them too much," I say, tone harsher than I intend. "Animals—whether fae or wild creatures—have their own dangers to contend with."

She scoffs. "I thought you said animals can take care of themselves." When I don't answer, she nuzzles the kitten and breathes in its scent. Something that almost makes me want to gag, considering the creature must smell like garbage.

"What is with you and animals?" I ask.

"I just said as much. I envy them."

"It's more than that. Your mood changes when you're around them." I watch for any sign that she realizes—for that single moment where she was distracted by her own joy—that I *saw* her.

She grins. "How could it not? I just...I've always loved soft things. The feeling of fur in particular. My very first memory as a baby is my father wrapping me in fur and holding me close. I was so warm then. So safe and cherished and protected. It was the most comfortable feeling in the world."

"I'm not so sure it was equally as comfortable for whatever beast the fur came from."

She lets out a groan. "Don't make me think of such sad things."

I'm about to counter that with a gibing retort when she takes a sudden step closer and holds the white kitten out toward me.

I stare at the ball of fluff. "What?"

"Hold her."

"Why would I?"

"Why wouldn't you?"

"Because she lives behind a refuse bin. You do recall I have a strong sense of smell, do you not?"

"Just hold a kitten, Huntsman. It will be good for you. Your grumpy act is getting old."

"If I hold a kitten, can we get on with our business?"

"Of course."

"Fine," I say through my teeth. The word is hardly out of my mouth before Astrid shoves the feline in my arms.

Astrid bends down and strokes the mother cat before picking up the fourth kitten, another gray one. Her voice takes on a ridiculously high pitch. "Oh, Natalie. How can anyone resist squeezing your sweet little brains right out?"

I pull my head back. "That's rather violent."

She scoffs. "It's just an expression. Don't you ever feel that way when you see something cute? The overwhelming urge to just...squeeze?"

"No."

"Hmm. Well, you must live a very boring life."

I'd tell her she's wrong, that serving as Huntsman is far from boring, but that's not entirely true. Sure, I'm constantly on the move, constantly on one mission or another, traveling to a different court every few weeks, enjoying free meals, fine clothes, and the fanciest hotels, all funded by the Alpha Council...but there's nothing fulfilling about this work. About my life these last five years. I have no permanent home. I'm forbidden from owning property or earning a single chip of my own. The work I'm forced to do suits my talents, but...it isn't what I want to do.

The tiny prick of claws against my chest steals me from my thoughts. The insufferable little beast has begun climbing my torso. Before I know what to do, she's perched on my shoulder like a damn pirate's bird. "What is she doing?"

"Aww, she likes you."

The kitten walks along my shoulder toward my neck and shoves her face into my cheek, rubbing the top of her head against my beard. An unexpected sensation brightens in my chest, summoning memories of a warm muzzle bumping up affectionately against mine, a comforting tongue grooming my fur, a plump belly to snuggle against.

Mother.

My heart constricts. Normally, I'd push such thoughts away, for sentimentality has no place in my mind while I'm working. But with the kitten now licking my cheek with her bristly tongue, I can't find the will to resist. A tender warmth radiates from my chest to my fingertips. I reach up a hand and pet the kitten. Once. Twice.

All right, so the little beast is soft.

Astrid's scent flares, the lemon brightening with fresh zest. I glance over to find her watching me with her hazy gaze, and realize my lips have stretched into a wide grin.

Training my features into a scowl, I gently lift the kitten off my shoulder and place her next to her mother. "Enough with this nonsense. Let's go."

"Very well," Astrid says, but there's something smug about her tone. She sets down her kitten as well, then offers each one several more pets.

"Miss Snow," I growl.

"Fine." With a huff, she leaves the kittens behind. As soon as she reaches my side, I take off. She quickens her pace to keep up with me. "Where are we going, Huntsman?"

We round the corner of Lust and head straight for Department Wrath. "It's time we had a chat with Madame Fury."

## 13

*ASTRID*

I stop in place for a few moments before I force my legs to move and catch up with the Huntsman again. A disbelieving laugh escapes my lips. "Chat with Madame Fury? Do you think it's going to be that simple?"

"Why wouldn't it be?" His tone is all confidence as he makes a beeline for Department Wrath's ticket counter. The window is empty, so he rings the bell on the counter a few times.

I glare at the side of his face. "Have you any clue how expensive a meeting with Madame Fury is? A petition costs just short of a hundred opal rounds."

Without looking at me, he takes his coin from his waistcoat pocket and flourishes it between two fingers. "I have the funds."

"Yes, well, even when one pays the fine, she has the right to refuse a meeting. If she does agree to one, she can schedule it whenever she likes. It could be set for weeks from now."

The Huntsman doesn't bother looking at all worried as the ticket seller approaches the window.

"How may I help you?" asks a female fae in seelie form. She

has small round eyes and two bunnylike ears sprouting off the top of her head, reminiscent of the desert cottontails I see hopping around the hotel grounds now and then. Unlike the kittens, they do not let me pet them.

"I need to speak with Madame Fury at once," the Huntsman says.

The ticket seller's eyes go wide. Her lips flicker with a half smile as if she can't tell whether he's joking. I cross my arms and give the Huntsman a pointed look, waiting for him to acknowledge I was right. When he neither looks my way nor takes back his outrageous request, the ticket seller says, "Sir, you cannot simply demand an audience with Madame Fury—"

Her voice cuts off as the Huntsman flashes his coin. He slides it through the slot at the bottom of the ticket window. The fae gingerly takes the coin in her hands and examines it. Then, with trembling fingers, she shoves the coin back under the slot and stammers, "Yes, sir. Right away, sir. Or...as...as soon as I can. Let me show you to the parlor where you can wait for her."

With a slow, crooked smile spreading across his lips, the Huntsman turns toward me and meets my eyes. "What did I say, Miss Snow? Simple."

~

A FEW MINUTES LATER, WE STAND IN THE PARLOR INSIDE Department Wrath. It's located on the main floor near the ticket counter, kept private behind two immense doors. The ticket seller left us alone, promising to do her best to secure a meeting. All we can do now is wait.

I can't bear to look at the Huntsman's gloating face, so I wander the elegant room, taking in the plush rugs, the mahogany furniture, the gilded portraits of fighters lining the walls. I've never entered Wrath through the front door, nor have

I been in this room before. It's meant as a place for esteemed guests and those with private boxes to await the start of the fights in style. Everyone else has to stand in line until the doors open. It reminds me of the two jobs I still need to finish. I never did get very far with Mr. Donnelly last night. Thanks to my captor.

I glance over my shoulder at him and find him watching me from a few feet away. It brings to mind how he looked when he caught me in the alley. I'd been so content with my fluffy friends, I hadn't noticed when he'd arrived. But when I did see him, I was startled to find him staring so intently.

It was almost as if he could *see* me.

I push the impossible thought from my mind, but it's replaced with another memory involving the Huntsman—how he looked when he held Madeline. For the briefest moment, he smiled. Not a smirk. Not a smug grin. A true and genuine smile. I must admit, it was easy on the eyes. I'm not one for swooning, but if ever I did, it would be over a smile like that.

But not *his* smile, of course. No, I couldn't swoon over *him*.

I lift my chin and turn my gaze to the nearest portrait. It's one of Helody, the griffin who fought the ogre last night. Her expression brims with pride while her sharp beak warns of her temper. Whoever the artist is, they captured her perfectly.

A stab of pain sinks my heart. I can't even think of the word *artist* without being reminded of my father. "I'm surprised you didn't come here without me," I say, mostly to distract myself from the grief that threatens to drag me down.

The Huntsman grunts in reply before gracing me with a true response. "Why do you say that?"

I wander to the next portrait, one of a unicorn who retired from fighting years ago. "Because you left without me this morning. What exactly were you doing?"

He scoffs. "Aside from getting us new clothing and arranging a much-needed bath for you?"

I scowl at the *much-needed bath* part, but I realize he too has cleaned up and wears fresh clothing. I wouldn't have noticed it isn't the same outfit he wore last night if not for the lack of tears. Much like yesterday, he's dressed in another all-black ensemble. His trousers hug his thighs while the open collar of his shirt reveals a musculature I hadn't glimpsed last night. He somehow manages to make such casual clothing look both formal and seductive at once. I scan his waistcoat for any sign that he still carries his handcuffs, but that summons my last memory of wearing them.

Me reaching for the key.

Him rolling on top of me...

Tearing my gaze away, I say, "Yes, aside from that."

He takes a step closer until we're side by side and assesses the portrait of the unicorn. "I left at first light to see if I could find any traces of the thief's false floral scent around the hotel grounds."

"Did you?"

He nods. "It was difficult because no matter where I caught the trail, it kept leading back to the garden. The thief clearly knows that forcing me so close to the garden confuses my senses. But I did manage to find the trail in other locations."

"Like where?"

"Your room."

I face him with a furrowed brow. "My room?"

"Based on the freshness of the scent trail, the thief visited your bedroom both before and after the attack. So it's a good thing we stayed at Department Lust."

I suppress a shudder. This proves the thief truly is after me. "Wait, how do you know where my room is?"

"The richness of your scent made it obvious," he says, tone matter-of-fact. "I knew where to find your room the day I arrived here."

"How long ago was that?"

"Four days."

I take an involuntary step away from him. "You could have broken into my room days ago and killed me in my sleep?"

His throat bobs before he replies. "Yes."

"Then why didn't you?" I'm not sure I want to know the answer.

He slowly slides his gaze away from me and settles it back on the portrait. "I tried, but I couldn't bring myself to act while you were sleeping."

I bring a hand to my chest and absently rub the flesh his fingers had tried to pierce last night. "You actually attempted it. To kill me while I was sleeping."

"Why should that surprise you?" His voice is neither sharp nor kind. Instead, it's more...tired. "I tried to kill you last night too."

"Yes, but at least I knew about it and had the chance to fight you off. I could have died in my sleep and never known about it." Panic crawls up my throat, making my fingers flinch for the tincture in my pocket. It takes all my restraint not to grab it and down a drop. I've already had three drops today. If I take another too soon, I might get lethargic. Then how will I be any help in proving Queen Tris' guilt?

"That is precisely why I didn't act. I decided you deserved a respectable death while you were awake and aware, not an execution while you were in such a vulnerable state." His voice catches on that last part, but he rushes to add, "Until we prove your innocence, I won't apologize for either attempt on your life."

My muscles relax the slightest bit. He said *until* we prove my innocence. Which suggests he expects to find proof that will exonerate me. "Very well. I suppose I can't hold it against you. However, I am rather cross that you went to investigate without me."

"Out of all the things you could be upset about, that is your primary grievance with me? I freed you from your cuff, at least."

"Yes, but I told you I wanted to work together."

"If you want to work together, then you must ensure from now on that you can rouse yourself from sleep before noon." He turns a stern look on me. "If you want to work with me, keep your wits sharp and stop relying on that poison."

I meet his gaze with a glare, my cheeks burning with indignation. "You don't understand."

"What I understand is that if you keep forcing your body to rely on Crimson Malus, then you'll soon find yourself in a sorry state. There's a reason your wounds didn't heal quickly last night—"

His voice cuts off as the door swings open.

We whirl away from each other and face the parlor entrance just as a figure strolls through the double doors and closes them behind her. Like Madame Desire, Madame Fury is tall and lithe. Her skin is orange while her hair and lashes are composed of ever-dancing flames. From what I've heard, all seven heads of the Seven Sins Hotel are sisters. I've only seen a few of them in person, but all are said to be sprites that each embody a different trait. Traits the humans call sins.

Everything from Madame Fury's fiery hair to her sharply pointed ears and fierce eyes evoke the spirit of wrath to its fullest.

I force a smile to my lips, summoning only pleasant emotions as I prepare to meet Fury's gaze. My magic hums around me, surging outward as soon as our eyes lock. She barely offers me more than a glance, but it's enough to form an impression. Now when I look at her, I see the qualities she likes most in herself—vindictiveness, strength, and wits. Qualities she'll now see in me.

With a smile that looks more like a sneer, she strolls to the center of the parlor. She's dressed in leather trousers and a form-fitting shirt, both of which are almost the same shade of orange as her skin.

"Thank you for meeting with us on such short notice, Madame Fury," the Huntsman says. "Charge whatever fee you require to the Alpha Council."

She angles her head at a sitting area and claims a large wingback chair. The flames of her hair crawl over the headrest but don't char the velvet fabric. "Take a seat. Let us get this over with. I do not take kindly to demands on my time, regardless of the fee paid."

The Huntsman and I each claim chairs at the opposite side of the tea table that separates us from the fae female. He reaches into the pocket of his waistcoat and shows her his coin. "I am here on behalf of the Alpha Council investigating a case—"

She interrupts him with a scoff. "I know who you are, and you're no detective, Huntsman. You're a bounty hunter. A conscripted one at that. Save me your posturing and get to the point."

His eyes widen briefly, as if he's surprised Fury knows who he is. Then he steels his expression, revealing only a hint of agitation as a tic forms at the corner of his jaw. He pockets his coin again. "Madame Fury, one of your fighters attacked me and my companion last night."

"A dreadful ogre attack. Yes, I heard about this. You killed Murtis, did you not?"

"I did."

"Then it seems justice has been served." She begins to rise from her seat, but the Huntsman speaks again, halting her.

"I am not finished, Madame Fury. Should you seek to evade punishment by the Alpha Council, you will grant me an audience until I have said my piece."

She barks a laugh, nonplussed by his threat. "If the Alpha Council wants to punish me, they can try. You'll find I have a certain amount of autonomy here, Huntsman. So long as I act in the name of wrath and justice, I am allowed to do as I please at the hotel."

"If you stand for wrath and justice, then you will aid our case. I believe the fae I killed was working at the behest of another. My true quarrel was not with the ogre, but the person who sent him. I need to find out who that was so I can see justice served."

Fury's lips lift into an amused smirk while her eyes glitter with a keen look. "What you fail to understand is that the attack *was* justice being served. The attack was an act of revenge, and you killed Murtis as a result. Fate has chosen her victor, and you have won. Take that and be satisfied."

The Huntsman narrows his eyes. "You know who sent Murtis, don't you? You sanctioned the attack."

"How could I not? Like I said, it was a matter of revenge, which I fully stand for. She petitioned me with her case, and I approved it. It was an unconventional duel, but still within my rights to approve."

My heart hammers against my ribs. I find myself gripping the armrests of my chair with all my strength. "Who petitioned you with her case?" I ask, even though I already know the answer. It was Queen Tris. She's here, in this very city, just like I theorized last night. I'm struck by a sudden spike of anger so strong it threatens to devour every ounce of calm my tincture has provided. Fury's answer will confirm that Tris has succeeded at the very thing I've fantasized about doing since I first set foot in Department Wrath. Tris didn't have to struggle to save money to meet with Fury. She didn't have to worry about making the perfect first impression to petition her case. She didn't need to figure out a way to tempt me to meet her face to face.

She took my ridiculous, impossible dream and turned it into a solid plan. Not only that, but she did it in a way that keeps her identity hidden. Keeps her name from being sullied.

Keeps her guilt a secret.

I take a deep breath, digging my fingers into the velvet armrest of my chair. The soft fabric manages to cool some of my anger.

Fury lifts her chin in defiance. "I will not tell you. I shouldn't have even said it was a *she*."

I bite the inside of my cheek against a fresh wave of rage. Based on Fury's fearless composure and the intelligent gleam in her eyes, I doubt anything she says is an accident. I'm willing to bet she wanted to bait us, tease us with the slightest hint of truth.

The Huntsman stiffens in his seat. "If you will not tell us who *she* is, at least tell me what case she petitioned you with. What exactly was this person's reason for orchestrating an attack against me?"

Amusement dances in Fury's eyes. "She said someone was planning to murder an innocent woman and asked permission to use one of my fighters to rescue her."

My stomach turns as I pore over her words. Since Tris can't lie, she used the truth to gain Fury's favor. I suppose being a royal didn't hurt either, even though the Spring Queen has no sway in the Fire Court.

"Madame Fury," the Huntsman says, "your petitioner tricked you into aiding an unjust cause."

"Do you deny it then? Were you not planning on murdering an innocent woman?"

He says nothing for a few tense moments. When he speaks, his voice is dark. Dangerous. "I will not deny that I held such intentions, only that a matter of innocence is yet to be established. Either way, I assure you that you were misled. The woman in question stands alive beside me, as you can clearly see. Not only that, but the ogre wounded her as well. If your petitioner was so concerned over my companion's well-being, she could have executed this supposed *rescue* by gentler means."

Fury cocks her head and assesses him from under her fiery lashes. "What an entertaining turn of events."

"Give me her name, Madame Fury."

"Or what? You'll report me to the Alpha Council? I've already told you, they won't care. I am in my rights here. The Seven Sins Hotel is a unique entity bound by special rules. It is both the risk and reward one takes when stepping foot onto this property."

My heart sinks. Fury is right. The hotel has certain privileges other parts of Faerwyvae don't. Nowhere else can one so freely gamble without limits on what one can wager. Nowhere else can one watch bloody fights involving fae magic and the threat of death. Nowhere else can one buy pleasure with a fae courtesan.

Fury brings a long finger to her chin and gives us a calculating look. "You know, Murtis was supposed to fight Helody this evening. I booked their fight to last two nights. It was hard enough to convince Helody to hold back during the first fight in order to make a two-night spectacle possible. Once she finds out Murtis died by someone else's hands, she'll be enraged. Besides, the show must go on."

I frown, trying to understand why she's telling us this. "Are you saying you fixed last night's duel just to give Murtis the chance to attack us?"

She barks a laugh. "Hardly. I'm a businesswoman and an entertainer. I planned a two-day fight between Helody and Murtis from the start. Murtis was always meant to yield during the first fight and agree to a second duel to commence the night after."

My heart sinks a little. It never occurred to me that any aspect of the fights at Department Wrath were staged. I've watched duels that lasted weeks at a time. I admit, it's disappointing to know the truth.

"How about this," Fury says. "I'll help you if you help me. Huntsman, you will fight in the pit tonight. You owe Helody as much, considering you killed Murtis."

The Huntsman's jaw shifts side to side. "Why the hell would I agree to do that?"

"Because if you fight Helody and win," she says, then slowly slides her gaze to me, "I'll let your female companion duel the woman whose identity you seek."

# 14

*ASTRID*

The Huntsman rises from his chair. "Absolutely not. Miss Snow will not fight in the ring."

My eyes dart from Madame Fury to my enraged companion. I don't know whether I should be more shocked over Fury's offer or the Huntsman's concern for me. Then I remind myself he doesn't care about *me* but fulfilling his bargain. If I'm violently slaughtered in the fighting pit, it might prove difficult to retrieve my heart.

Why hasn't he accepted the truth yet? Tris doesn't care about him bringing her my heart, for she's the one who expects to face me in the ring. She wants to do the killing herself. I don't believe for a minute that Fury's offer was her own idea. Tris orchestrated this entire situation.

Madame Fury gives a flippant shrug. "Why not?" Her gaze locks on mine. "She's a strong girl. She'd do well in the ring."

All I manage in reply is a huff of cold laughter. If only Fury knew I'm nothing like the mirrored reflection she sees now. I'm not strong like she is. I'm not even sure I have the fiercest wit that she values so highly in herself. I might be slightly vindictive, perhaps, but only a fraction of what Fury sees, and only where my father's murder is concerned. If I were more so, I wouldn't have run away from Fairweather Palace. I would have sought revenge on Tris right away instead of humoring an impossible fantasy about facing her in the ring someday...

My mind goes still at the last thought.

Isn't this what I've wished for? What I've dreamed of? Isn't this my secret reason for building a nest egg of opal rounds? In all my musings about facing Tris in the pit, getting her to agree to a duel was always the most unlikely factor. Surely a queen would rather send a champion in her stead than fight me face to face. Surely her hatred for me couldn't be so strong that she'd debase herself before an audience. But now...now I know I underestimated her enmity. She *wants* to face me head on. She wants to end my life with her own hands.

And what better place to do so than a court that is not her own, in a hotel bound by its own laws?

A spark of hope ignites in my chest. Not over the thought of her ending my life but the realization that my fancies weren't in vain. I *can* face her in the ring. That spark, however, is quickly extinguished by my dread. I may have imagined facing my stepmother, but my musings never took me far enough to form a concrete plan for victory. People like me never win duels against people like Tris. The strongest is always the victor. Or the one with the most magic. Or—

No, that's not true. A precedent has been set where a weaker fighter came out on top. It was the duel between the tiny fire sprite and the dragon. The sprite yielded. She lost the duel. But she got her opponent to confess to his crime. That was all she truly wanted.

Fury's voice snaps my attention back to her. "I can tell you're angry."

Surprise ripples through me. This is one of the rare occasions where I've heard the words *you are* followed by something true. I *am* angry. But...but...does my anger stand a chance against my stepmother? Tris is a royal. Fae monarchs have magic that allows them to tap into all four elements to some degree.

"This is ridiculous," the Huntsman says, shaking his head. "Tell me where to find the woman we seek—"

"I've given you my terms." Fury's voice turns sharp. "Agree to them or our mutual acquaintance will be back in the Spring Court before you catch another whiff of her presence here. And your little mystery will go unsolved."

My breath catches in my throat. Once again, I get the feeling that every word Fury says is calculated. Mentioning the Spring Court was no error on her part. She wanted to tempt us with another morsel that gets us closer to the truth...but not close enough.

Ignoring the Huntsman, who continues to stare daggers at her, Fury shifts in her seat and faces me. "I won't go so far as to say you must fight your opponent during your duel. That will be up to you and her. If this person truly cares about your welfare, then seeing you alive will be enough to put this misunderstanding to rest, and the audience can cheer for such a heartwarming reunion. But if it was a matter of me being deceived, then I expect the confrontation will be far more entertaining. Besides, if you were wronged, you'll want this chance at revenge."

"I don't know if I can beat her." The words leave my lips before I realize I've spoken them aloud.

"I'd say you're well matched. If I were a betting woman, I'd go to Department Greed and put all my opal rounds on you. You're stronger than your opponent."

I purse my lips to keep myself from confessing I'm nothing more than a half-human girl with useless magic.

Madame Fury rises to her feet with a weary sigh, clearly

annoyed by my lack of reply. "Decide in the next ten minutes. Whatever your choice, your time with me is up. Inform the ticket seller whether you will take my bargain or not. Good day."

She turns on her heel and marches out the door, leaving me and the Huntsman silent in her wake.

I sink into the back of my chair. My heart hammers so loud I can barely hear the Huntsman when he next speaks.

"This is ridiculous," he says through his teeth. "Never in all my time working for the Alpha Council have I been so rudely dismissed." He glances over at me, and his tone softens. "Come. We'll find another way to confirm the identity of our thief."

I swallow hard, knowing what I say next could be the stupidest thing I've ever uttered. "I think we should do it."

The Huntsman's expression shows just how ludicrous he finds my words. "Excuse me?"

"I think we should take Madame Fury's bargain."

"Like hell we should."

With a deep breath, I force myself to stand and meet his eyes. I don't bother feigning confidence, only sincerity. "I know I'm asking a lot of you to suggest that you face Helody—"

He scoffs. "You're asking a lot of *me*? It isn't me I'm worried about. You cannot fight Queen Tris and win."

My heart stutters at his words. "You believe me then? You believe I'm right about her guilt?"

He glances at his feet and runs a hand over his beard. "I shouldn't have said that. What I meant to say is *if* your opponent turns out to be Tris, you will be overpowered."

Despite his attempt to correct his statement, it doesn't stop an ember of hope from glowing in my chest. There's at least a part of him that believes me. It's enough to give me the courage I need to vocalize what's on my mind. "I have an idea, Huntsman."

"You can't fight her."

"It doesn't involve me fighting."

He furrows his brow but makes no further argument.

I take a few steps closer to him. "If you can find some way to defeat Helody—"

"You say that like it's impossible," he says, his tone bristling with affront.

I put my hands on my hips and lift a brow. "If you're not the least bit worried, then you've never seen her fight, nor must you know of her reputation."

He shrugs. "I've heard about it."

His arrogance has me clenching my jaw. "She's going to be harder to fight than an ogre."

"You doubt I can beat her?"

I give him a pointed look. "Yes, of course I do!"

A corner of his lips quirks up. "Just like you doubted my ability to secure a meeting with Madame Fury?"

"Huntsman," I say with a frustrated groan. "That was different. You really don't know what you're getting into with Helody."

"I thought you were supposed to convince me to fight her. Were you not just saying your idea revolves around me winning?"

Heat floods my cheeks. I don't know if he takes pleasure in aggravating me or if he's this quarrelsome with everyone. When I narrow my eyes at him, I see a hint of amusement playing over his lips. "This isn't a joke. You could get yourself killed trying to fight her."

"Is that concern over my life that I smell?"

I open and close my mouth several times before I form the right words. "Well...yes, I'm...I'm concerned for your life. If you die fighting Helody, I'll lose my chance to face Tris. That was part of Fury's bargain."

"I'll win, Miss Snow." This time there's no arrogance in his tone. No teasing. "I'll make sure of it. But what of you? How will you survive if you face Tris in the pit?"

"All I have to do is avoid any physical attacks while I trick her into making a public confession. Tris has access to magic using all four elements, but she isn't trained in combat."

"Neither are you."

"True, but I know how to make her flustered. I know what irritates her, what qualities of hers to insult. She speaks without thinking when she's angry with me. It's happened before. I can use that to my advantage. I can catch her off guard and get her to say something she'll regret. As soon as she confesses to having poisoned the pie that killed my father, I'll yield. We'll lose the duel but will be able to turn the case over to the Alpha Council."

"You're sure you can get her to confess?"

I'm not sure, but I don't say so. This plan is my best hope. "I'll do what I can. I've seen it done in the ring before. I know it's possible."

"What if her only crime is that she wholeheartedly believes you killed her husband and seeks revenge? A confession over that will not prove your innocence, nor will it protect you from being punished by her. The Alpha Council will not turn against one of their own under those circumstances. Are you sure you still want to go through with this?"

A surge of panic rushes through me. What if he's right? Even though I'm certain she killed my father—even if she'd only been trying to kill me—I must admit there's a chance I'm wrong. And if I am, facing her in the pit could be a death sentence. If she's innocent but thinks *I'm* guilty...

It's enough to make my head spin.

Still, I can't pass this opportunity up. If nothing else, perhaps I can plead my case and swear my innocence before an audience. That will have to count for something, won't it?

With a deep breath, I say, "I still want to do it."

The Huntsman assesses me for a few silent moments, then poses his next question. "What will you do if it isn't Tris you face in the pit? What if someone else stole my Chariot and set the ogre after us?"

"It has to be my stepmother. Everything lines up. She used a version of the truth to trick Fury into allowing her to use Murtis. A truth only Tris should know about. Fury all but gave Tris' identity away when she mentioned the Spring Court. Who else knows your weakness to floral aromas and the fact that you had a Chariot?"

"Just humor me," he says. "I will not agree to Fury's bargain unless your side of the plan is sound. What will you do if it isn't Tris?"

I nibble my lip, considering my answer, but there's only one I can give. "Then I'll yield right away. I have no need to win a duel. No insatiable desire for the prize money. Our goal in coming here was to learn the identity of the thief who stole your Chariot and sent the ogre after us. As soon as my opponent reveals herself in the pit, we'll have our answer. She may escape with the stolen travel device, but her identity should allow you to track her through traditional means, right?"

His expression brightens with something like approval. "It isn't a terrible plan. Especially since I still highly doubt it's Tris we're dealing with. And you're right. We came here to learn the thief's identity, not win duels."

"Well, *you* have to win a duel. All I have to do is yield."

"And possibly trick a fae queen into giving a murder confession."

My stomach turns. "Yes, and that."

He releases a heavy sigh. "You're certain about this? Even with the best plan, we can't escape an element of danger."

"Huntsman, if we don't prove my innocence, you're going to turn me over to my stepmother, and she wants me dead. I'd say you brought that element of danger straight to my doorstep already."

He gives me a half grin. Even though it looks nothing like the smile he wore in the alleyway earlier, it manages to tighten my belly. "Very well, Miss Snow. Tonight we duel."

## 15

### THE HUNTSMAN

ater that night, Astrid and I wait in the underbelly of Department Wrath for the match to begin. We stand in silence in a cool dark room constructed of sandstone walls, lit with a single lamp hanging overhead. A solid metal gate stands between us and the sandy floor of the arena, but the sound of chattering spectators has already risen loud enough to be heard through the door. The stadium must be filling up quickly. Soon the duel will commence.

And I'll be forced to fight a legend.

"Are you nervous, Huntsman?" Astrid stares at me from where she leans against the opposite wall. We're alone, yet we've kept our distance since entering the waiting room, each lost to our own thoughts and worries.

I'd like to tell her I'm not nervous at all, but that would be a lie. I hardly know what came over me when I boasted about my certainty that I could beat Helody. No, I suppose that isn't true either. I know exactly what drove me. It was the excitement of a wager placed, the thrill of a bet. Instead of money, I placed my life on the line. Even though I know it will be dangerous, I am determined to win. I must. "Don't worry about me. Worry about yourself."

"Well, I'm nervous." She pushes off from the wall and crosses her arms. She's dressed in loose linen trousers and a form-fitting wool top—an outfit she selected from Department Envy earlier today.

I'm dressed in similar attire. Both of our ensembles were chosen with the forthcoming duel in mind. Even though our plan means Astrid shouldn't have to fight at all, it's wisest to be practical. Cumbersome skirts will only get in the way should she need to dodge or run. Practical attire or no, her outfit makes it hard not to stare at how her shirt hugs every curve of her torso. Especially since her figure is all I can clearly see.

She nibbles her bottom lip. "There are so many ways this could go wrong."

"You're the one who said we should do this."

"Oh, I'm not having second thoughts. Only that...well, I'm just feeling a little panic, all right?" She reaches into her pocket and extracts her vial.

My shoulders tense as she begins twisting off the cap to her poison. In a few quick strides, I reach her and place a hand over her vial. "Don't."

She takes a step back and gives me an affronted look. "Excuse me?"

"Don't take more of that. I watched you take three drops two hours ago."

Her scent flares with guilt, then indignation. "I'm only going to take one drop. It will settle my nerves."

"It will do more than that."

She rolls her eyes. "It won't put me to sleep if that's what you're worried about. I'm plenty awake. A single drop will only ensure my mood is stable when I enter the ring."

I clench my jaw against everything I want to say. I know I

shouldn't get involved. What she does isn't any of my business.

And yet...

"You're slowly killing yourself," I say in a rush, my tone sharp. "Do you know that?"

She stares at me for a few moments, as if she can't tell if I'm joking. "Huntsman, I'm half fae. You know this. Crimson Malus can't kill me."

"Not like it can kill a human, no." My eyes land on her elbow where blood had ceaselessly gushed last night. "It may not instantaneously poison you, but it is killing you none-theless. Did you wonder why last night's wound didn't start healing until you took another dose? It's because your body has come to rely on the poison to heal at all. Your innate fae healing has been compromised. Soon your human healing will be as well. You'll get to the point where you won't be able to do a thing without it. You'll need more and more just to avoid common ailments your own immunity should be able to fight. But the more you take, the more your mental faculties will grow compromised too. You'll be fighting to survive and won't even be awake or aware enough to realize you're surviving at all."

Her scent profile contracts, a spike of bitter lemon that tells of her fear. She takes a step away from me. "How do you know?"

"I can smell it, Miss Snow. I can smell what it's doing to you." There's a deeper truth that I don't confess. That I've seen this happen once before.

She releases a trembling breath, and her hand closes tight around her vial. "Well, even if you are correct, I need it tonight."

"No, you don't."

"Yes, I do. What if the person I face in the pit isn't Tris? What if it's a stranger? It could work in my favor to make a posi-tive first impression."

I pin her with a stern look. "You don't need it for that."

Her scent turns angry, the morning dew shifting to the salt of a stormy sea. "Yes, I—"

"Your eyes are gray," I say it before I can stop myself. I still don't know why I'm getting so involved in her personal problems. I shouldn't care. Perhaps it's that ever-present instinct to protect her that has me unable to stand by and watch as she slowly poisons herself to death.

She slowly backs away from me until her shoulders press against the wall behind her. "What did you say?"

"Your eyes are gray." I say, punctuating each word as I shadow her retreat, closing in until only a foot of space remains between us. Since I've already gotten myself so stupidly involved, I might as well ensure she listens. "Your hair is black, tinged with the slightest bit of blue. It's cropped short to the nape of your neck."

She says nothing, only stands frozen before me, her hazy gaze locked on mine.

I lean closer until we're almost eye to eye and plant my hand on the wall next to her head. Breathing in deeply, I take in the intricacies of her scent—the shock, the fear, the trepidation. Mingled among the darker qualities is something small and bright. Something like hope.

I smirk. "I'm right, aren't I? Somewhere beyond this indistinct mask you wear are those gray irises."

Her chest pulses with sharp, short breaths. "How do you know?"

I strain my eyes to see through the haze, to glimpse the features I saw this morning. But the longer I look, the less of her I can decipher. The cloudier my memory of said features becomes. It's almost as if...she doesn't *want* me to see her. And the closer I lean, the deeper I look, the less she wants me to see. The thicker her magic becomes. She releases a shaky exhale. We stand so close, her warm breath brushes my face, my lips—

With a jolt, I straighten, realizing I'd leaned far closer than

I'd intended.

"You don't need this damn poison, Astrid," I say, swiping the vial from her now-limp fingers and tucking it back into her trouser pocket. Then I turn my back on her and stalk toward the gate.

Astrid follows hard on my heels and rounds me until we're face to face again. "You don't get to tell me what to do, nor do you have a right to comment on what's happening inside my body. Furthermore, since when are we so familiar that you can call me Astrid? You won't even tell me your real name. I'm left to call you Huntsman—"

"It's Torben," I bite out, if only to halt her tirade.

It works. She blinks at me a few times. Then her shoulders relax. "That's your name?"

"Torben Davenport."

"You have a surname even though you're full fae?"

Why the hell are we still talking? And why the hell do I feel so compelled to answer her? "My father adopted a surname after we took seelie form and entered human society," I say.

She cocks her head to the side, and her scent profile begins to mellow. The bitter lemon turns mild and sweet, and the stormy sea once again becomes morning dew. "I assume, since you called me Astrid, I can call you Torben? Or must I continue to call you Huntsman? Or shall I refer to you as Mr. Davenport?"

"Call me whatever. It matters not."

"Oh, I think it matters," she says, a note of teasing in her voice. Her sudden shift in mood makes me wonder if she took a dose of her tincture during the split second I had my back to her. Could she really be so pleased simply by knowing my name? She crosses her arms and pops a hip to the side. "If we're on a first-name basis, does that mean we're friends?"

"No."

"But we're more than cold acquaintances, and for the time

being, we aren't enemies. Are we allies then? Or partners!"

I find my heart skittering at the last word. I know she meant it in a business sense, but *partners* can have a romantic connotation when used a certain way. Based on the sudden spike of embarrassment in her scent, she's thinking the same thing.

I save her from stammering. "We're about to possibly get our asses thoroughly handed to us, so I'd rather not dally in talking of friendship."

She huffs. "What happened to your confidence that you could win?"

I open my mouth, a flippant retort brimming on my lips, when the sound of grating metal has my attention moving to the gate. With a rumble, it splits down the middle and begins to open.

Shit. Fuck. Blooming hell.

It's time.

I take a deep breath, but my senses are overwhelmed with a sudden influx of smell. Sand, sweat, and an assortment of food and refreshments from the concession stands mingle with subtler aromas, ones that tell of excitement, nervous anticipation, awe, mundane joy. They stream through the ever-widening gate, emanating from the spectators crowding the stands. It's enough to make my heart pound. To make me feel suddenly small and foolish and in way over my head.

Then the fragrance of apple blossoms cuts through everything else, narrowing down to a single scent profile behind me. A small, soft hand squeezes my fingers.

I turn to find Astrid, and she gives my hand another squeeze. "Good luck, Torben."

The sound of my name on her lips helps clear my mind further. I can do this. I must. For us both.

I give her a halfhearted smile that only tugs one side of my lips. "I'll try not to die."

With that, I stride under the open archway and into the pit.

# 16

*TORBEN*

I barely pay attention to the Master of Ceremonies as he welcomes the guests to the duel. Instead, all my attention is fixated on the griffin who paces at the opposite side of the pit, wings splayed out wide. She halts and snaps her beak in my direction, her front talons curling into the sand while her hind paws stomp in agitation. It's obvious she isn't pleased about seeing me in place of the ogre. I do my best to keep my composure, standing tall with my hands fisted at my sides. She returns to pacing as the Master of Ceremonies goes over the rules. I watch the griffin's every step, every move, calculating everything about her.

Despite having never stepped foot in Department Wrath before I came here to capture Astrid Snow, I've heard of Helody. Heard of her famed actions in this very pit. I've even bet on her matches a time or two, back when I used to frequent the gambling halls. Betting on events like races and fights wasn't the safest thing to gamble on, unlike my preferred vice— betting on card games where I could use my sense of smell to determine my opponents' bluffs—but it provided a thrill none-theless. And whenever I put a wager on Helody, I won. It was as close to a sure bet as it got.

Of course, I've since learned there is no such thing as a sure bet. No such thing as smelling every bluff, catching every deception. A hard lesson to learn, and one that cost me everything.

But now, the reminder that sure bets don't exist is all that keeps me on my feet. All that keeps me rooted in place as a vicious griffin hisses in my direction. My former self would have scoffed at the thought of betting in favor of her opponent.

But I'm not my former self. Torben Davenport lost his final wager and brought shame to the legacy his father built for him.

I, the Huntsman, will win.

It's my only choice.

"Begin!" the Master of Ceremony announces.

Blood rushes from my face, but I'm already poised for Helody's attack. She charges at me from the other side of the pit, her body quivering with rage. I sidestep at the last minute, and her talons meet only air.

She stomps back, blinking several times as if she can't fathom how she missed me. Clearly she thought this fight would be over in an instant. For her, that wouldn't be unprecedented.

She angles her body and shifts to the side. I mirror her moves, keeping several feet of space between us. She shifts the other direction, and again I do the same.

"I didn't expect you to have any skill," comes Helody's deep feminine voice. "It doesn't take much to kill a fool like Murtis."

I nearly bite back a cutting retort over how she wouldn't have needed two nights to fight her opponent if that were the case. But I hold my tongue, knowing it would be foolish to aggravate her further. Not only that, but my barb would be unfounded. I know she only kept herself from unleashing her full wrath on Murtis last night because Madame Fury demanded it.

We slowly begin to circle one another, analyzing each other's moves and reaction times. Helody keeps her head held high, her posture regal. Griffins are proud creatures. That's something I can work with.

"I respect you, Helody," I say, keeping my tone both firm and sincere.

"If that were true, you wouldn't have stolen my vengeance from me." She darts forward, beak snapping. I dodge to the side and swipe at her long neck with claw-tipped fingers. She eyes my claws until they shrink back into humanlike digits, but she doesn't close in for another attack. It was a test, then. She knows I have another form. One I haven't shown her yet.

My heart slams against my ribs. Everything inside me begs to shift fully into a bear. But I won't give her the satisfaction of analyzing all my capabilities. Not yet.

"I only killed Murtis because he attacked me and my companion," I say as we return to circling each other. "Our lives were in danger."

"He was mine to kill."

"I'm sorry I took that from you. Please know that he died a painful death."

"Your words do nothing to soften my heart, creature," she says. "I will kill you in his place. Make no mistake."

"I'd rather not kill you, Helody."

A low laugh rumbles in her chest. "You won't get the chance." She rises on her hind paws with a roar, wings spread wide, talons outstretched. Then, with a ferocity she hadn't yet shown, she charges.

With a shudder that ripples from my head to my toes, I turn myself over to my other half. My bear half.

Hands and feet turn to immense paws. My hide thickens as fur coats my body, replacing my clothing. My teeth grow longer, sharper, until they fill my muzzle. Helody's talons reach me just as my transformation is complete. She swipes a gash over my belly, then lurches back.

She'd been going for my neck, intending to sever my head from my shoulders, but that was when I was in my seelie form. Now that I'm a bear, we stand at the same height. And unlike other fae she's fought before—the ones she's famed for instantly decapitating—my neck isn't so easy to sever. She'll need more than a single swipe. More than all the rage she can muster. It would have been the same for her fight with Murtis, had she had the chance to finish the duel. It took more than one bite for me to cleave his head from his shoulders, and Helody would have struggled just the same. However, I am not as slow and lumbering as an ogre.

I will not be so easy to kill.

Before Helody has the chance to analyze the strengths and weaknesses of my changed form, I charge her. I shove her back with my wide paws, sending her skidding before I claw a gash in her neck. She slices open my torso, then my shoulder. I ignore the pain and continue to return every strike with one of my own. The air shifts around us, and I catch sight of her wings beating on each side of her. She's trying to lift herself out of my reach so I'll have nothing but razor-sharp talons to contend with.

Before she can take flight, I rise on my hind legs and charge in closer. A taloned foot sinks into my belly. She tries to use that to kick off into the air, but I hook my claws into her neck. With all my strength, I slam her down to the sandy floor. In turn, her talons open a wide gash from my stomach to my thigh. Warm blood streams down my legs as she thrashes out with all four limbs, catching me with talons and paws. One searing cut strikes me after the other, but I ignore it. Not because I'm not in danger. Full fae can succumb to blood loss just like humans can. It may not be as quick or as fatal, but if I lose enough blood, I could grow weak enough for Helody to deliver a killing blow.

But the same goes for Helody.

"Yield," I say, forcing my claws deeper into her neck, drawing just as much blood from her as she's drawing from me. I sink my weight onto her despite the relentless gashes from her talons.

"I will never yield," she hisses, even as blood seeps down her golden feathers. She bucks and scrapes, then finally lands a gash on the side of my face. With her hind paws, she scrambles against the floor until she's on her side. She lifts a wing into the air and begins to flap. It sends sand into my eyes and gives her the momentum she needs to wriggle the rest of the way out from under me.

I don't let her get far.

Shifting to the side, I reach for her wing and pin it to the ground. She cries out, and a spike of guilt clenches my heart. Wings are sensitive, and the way I crush hers now, clawing her feathers into the sandy floor, must be excruciating. She claws at my side, raking my hide with deep, agonizing cuts. I shift my hind paws to her wing and lunge for her torso. My claws find her chest, seeking the beat of her rage-filled heart. Once one paw is splayed over her thudding organ, I press the other to her neck, keeping her snapping beak from my face.

"Yield," I say again. I sink my claws into her chest, feeling a gush of blood seep against my paw.

She goes still for only a moment, and I smell the tang of fear mingling with the scent of her blood. Then she renews her struggle. Claws me, rakes me, kicks me. But it's no use. She can't get far with how I'm crushing her poor wings. With how I'm digging deeper into her chest, closing around her heart.

"Yield or I must kill you," I say, my tone tinged with desperation. "I don't want to do that. I meant it when I said I respect you."

"I will not yield. I have honor to uphold." She bucks against my grip, but my claws are clamped so tightly around her heart now, there's not much she can do that won't force me to rip out the living drum whether I want to or not.

"You have children, Helody," I say with a growl. "Is that not why you challenged Murtis? Because he tried to eat your daughter? If I kill you, who will protect her?"

"You will not kill me." She snaps her teeth at the paw holding down her neck and manages to free herself from my grip. But my other paw is still clenched around her heart. I give it a subtle squeeze and she lets out a hissing gasp.

I clamp my paw over her neck again. "There is no honor in leaving your children behind. Not if you have a choice."

Her blood continues to pour over my claws while my own streams down the gashes she continues to tear open in my hide.

Dread fills my heart and turns my stomach. When I agreed to fight Helody, I'd had every intention of forcing her to yield, not to kill her. Yet I knew there was a chance I'd have to end her life. It's a thought that sickens me, that forces tears to my eyes.

But it's her life or mine. Her life or Astrid's fate is sealed. And if Astrid is innocent...

The thought of her summons the scent of bitter lemons. Fear. It's so strong, it almost overpowers the tang of blood filling my nose.

My eyes fly to the archway I emerged from when the fight began. A latticed grate fills the dark gap, but beyond it I see Astrid watching me, fingers curled around the crisscrossed bars. Waiting to see if I'll win or lose, if her bold plan will succeed or fail. It all depends on what I do next.

For the love of the All of All, she needs me.

I return my gaze to Helody and receive a wide slash from my ear to my neck. Giving her heart another squeeze, I say, "There is no honor in killing a child's parent when one can avoid it." My voice trembles as I sink my claws tighter, deeper. "I don't want to take you from your children, Helody, but I will do what must be done. Know this, though. If you choose pride over survival, then you dishonor us both."

I squeeze her heart harder and begin to lift it from her chest. With one mighty pull, I'll have it out from beneath her ribs—

She freezes beneath me. Then slowly, she extracts her claws from my hide. Her scent flares with shame. Grief. Humility. When she speaks, her voice quavers. "I yield."

## 17

*ASTRID*

My hands are clenched so tightly around the bars of the grate, I've lost feeling in my fingers. I'd give anything to be in the stands right now, to sit in one of the coveted boxes where I'd have a better view of the pit. Torben and Helody are a tangle of bloody limbs at the center of the ring and have been struggling in nearly the same position for what feels like an eternity. There's so much blood and gore, I can't tell where one wound begins and another ends.

Then finally, they both freeze. I hold my breath, the sound of my racing heart filling my ears, sending my entire body trembling from its force.

Torben pushes away from the griffin. His front paw drips rivers of blood as he pulls it from Helody's chest. My eyes go wide as I seek any sign that he holds her heart. The way he'd splayed his paw over her feathered chest and dug his claws in deep...it's the same thing he tried to do to me when he first captured me last night. It was frightening to witness, for it only made me realize how easily he could have ended my life. How quickly he could have torn out my heart.

But now, as I stare at his bloody paw, I see no sign that he holds the griffin's most essential organ. After a few tense seconds, Helody shifts on the ground. As Torben backs away from her, Helody starts to right herself, wincing as she folds a crumpled wing to her side.

I stare open mouthed. They're both alive.

Helody limps back on all fours, then slowly dips into a shaky bow.

A *bow*. To Torben.

One of the proudest, fiercest fighters ever to grace the pit...yielded.

The pounding of my raging heart reaches a crescendo, its roar so loud I'd cover my ears if I could manage to pull my hands from the grate. Then I realize the sound is only partially from my heartbeat. Most of it is coming from the stands.

I tear my eyes from Torben to catch sight of angry faces and shaking fists. No one expected the duel to end this way, and most aren't happy about it.

I, on the other hand, am overwhelmed with something very close to happiness. If one could feel joy over such violence and bloodshed. And the fact that I'm now one step closer to having to face my stepmother.

Nausea turns my stomach at the thought, but I'm not given any more time to consider such a daunting prospect. The Master of Ceremonies flies down on his violet wings and lands on the floor near the two fighters. I can't hear him announce the winner over the disappointed shouts of the spectators, but soon the griffin and the bear begin making their way toward their opposite ends of the arena. The latticed grate slides open just as Torben lumbers toward it. It takes all my restraint not to run to him at once, especially as my eyes land on all the crimson gashes marring the bear's flank, his face, his neck.

Finally, he reaches the archway.

"Torben! Are you all right?"

As he enters the dark waiting room, the solid metal gate closes behind him, muffling the sounds of the audience. He releases a heavy breath and sits back on his haunches, head drooped low as if it's too much effort for him to lift it. It would be absolutely adorable to see a bear sitting like this if I weren't so worried over his fate. "You only have a few minutes to prepare," he says, his voice emanating from inside him. Blood trails down a particularly gruesome cut stretching from under his eye to his thick neck.

Unable to help myself any longer, I close the distance between us and press my hands gingerly to the side of his face, seeking any sign of how deep the cut is. "This isn't good. You're badly injured."

"I'll heal."

My eyes wander the rest of him, and I find hardly any part of his body that isn't covered in blood. Thank the All of All it isn't my own or I'd faint. I bring my attention back to the still-oozing gash on his face. "If your healing is so impressive, why is this one still bleeding?"

His chest rumbles with an irritated groan befitting a bear before he answers. "Even pureblood fae have limits to what our healing powers can accomplish. The more wounded a fae is, the harder our bodies have to work. Helody didn't hold back with those talons." He tries to make his voice sound light when he says the last part, but he comes across more somber than anything.

"None of your wounds were fatal?"

"Do I look like I'm missing a head or a heart? Only wounds with iron have long term lethal effects. A griffin's claws are nothing. I'll be healed in a matter of minutes."

"But Torben—"

"Worry about yourself," he says, tone sharper. Then it softens. "You don't have long. Once those gates open, it's your turn."

The blood drains from my face. I swallow hard.

"Besides," he says, once again attempting to sound lighthearted, "you're only worried about me because I'm a bear. If I were in my seelie form, you wouldn't care."

I huff. "That's not true at all. I'm not that callous, you know. Were you seelie, I'd be just as worried. We've established we're allies, have we not? Allies should care about each other's fates."

Torben shudders, and before I can blink, he stands before me in seelie form.

My breath catches as I find myself close to him, my hand on his jaw. It's exactly how we stood a second ago, but it feels different than it did when he was a bear. I nearly lurch a step back, but when I catch sight of his crooked grin, I know that's exactly what he expected me to do. He meant to catch me off guard. To fluster me with his sudden nearness.

So, forcing myself to act nonchalant, I step slightly closer, pretending to be preoccupied with inspecting the wound on his cheek. It doesn't take long before I'm not pretending at all. The gash looks far less severe and no longer actively gushes. Instead, the line begins shrinking before my eyes, his flesh weaving together until only dried blood remains.

"See," I say, patting his bearded jaw the same way I would have pet his soft pelt. "I care just fine." It's my turn to wear a smug grin now, knowing I beat him at his game. But when my eyes meet his, there's no taunting on his face. Instead, his expression is slack. Open. His body rigid aside from the pulse of his chest. A chest I can clearly see through the bloody tears in his shirt.

I clear my throat and step back from him, keeping my eyes anywhere but the firm musculature of his wide torso, the exposed skin over his thighs where his trousers have been torn to shreds. I hadn't expected his wounds to have affected his clothing, but it makes sense that they would. When fae shift from seelie to unseelie, their clothing merges with them, becoming part of their unseelie form. It stands to reason that anything done to their unseelie bodies is also done to their seelie bodies—clothing included. I'd have firsthand experience with this if I were like a normal half-fae girl and could shift at all.

"I'm glad you're healing," I say stiffly as heat burns my cheeks. Can he see how I blush? I remember what he said earlier about having glimpsed my true face. It shouldn't have been possible, and yet the prospect makes my cheeks flush deeper.

Damn him. Why does he have me so flustered right now?

"Get ready, Astrid." His voice rouses me from my embarrassment and brings my attention to the opening gate.

My stomach bottoms out, bringing back all the dread I felt before I became distracted by Torben's wounds...and his closeness. Now that my dire circumstances have returned to the forefront of my mind, I'm grateful for the brief respite the momentary distraction provided. It makes me wonder if he'd meant to distract me. That might be giving him too much credit, though. Could he really care about giving me a few moments of freedom from my worries? Doubtful.

"Remember our plan," Torben says. "Do not physically engage. Do nothing brash. Yield at once if it isn't your stepmother—"

"I know the plan, Huntsman," I say, my tone sharper than I intended it to be. "It's my plan, after all."

He says nothing more as I approach the archway and the sandy pit beyond. The Master of Ceremonies once again stands in the center of the ring, reviewing the *very special circumstances* of tonight's duel and the second spectacle that awaits.

My eyes lock on the opposite side of the pit, but the announcer's fluttering wings obscure my view.

"Astrid," Torben whispers. I feel a hand press lightly against my lower back.

I realize I'm still frozen under the archway, and the Master of Ceremonies has his hand extended my way. He must have announced me.

Torben speaks again. "You can do this."

On trembling legs that feel more like water than limbs, I step away from the doorway and into the pit. I'm greeted by silence. A glance into the stands reveals the stadium holds about a third less audience members than there had been for Torben's fight.

The scrape of metal screeches behind me, and I take a final look at Torben as the latticed grate slides shut. He gives me a nod from behind the woven bars.

Then, with a deep breath, I face forward again, just in time to watch the Master of Ceremonies leap into the air and fly back to wherever he perches during the fights. My stomach roils as I stare across the pit, seeing no sign of my opponent. I squint, seeking the slightest movement in the air. Queen Tris could be here in her unseelie form, a manifestation she rarely takes. I've only seen her in that form once, but I remember her looking like a tiny pixie with a twig-like body and a pink flower for a head. But no matter how intently I search, I see no sign of pixie wings fluttering about.

I frown. This isn't how these duels are supposed to go. The two fighters always exit their respective archways before the announcer flies off. I'm not even certain my opponent's name was announced yet. Madame Fury must have orchestrated this dramatic entrance for entertainment purposes.

I curl my fingers into fists, although I'm tempted to reach into my pocket and take several drops of my tincture. Thanks to Torben's interference, it's been hours since my last dose. I'd meant to take another during his fight, but I'd been unable to tear my eyes away from the duel.

Now I'm left with nothing but anxiety. Dread. An aching fear that tightens my chest.

What was I thinking? What was I thinking facing Tris like this?

Something shifts in the shadowed archway across from me. My mind goes still, but my heart turns wild. Thudding. Racing. Hammering as heavy as a drum.

A figure emerges into the arena.

I shutter my eyes, trying to reconcile what I see with what I expected. I anticipated a tall form with cherry blossoms for hair. Or perhaps a pixie with pink wings.

What I didn't expect was the human female with brown hair and wide, horrified eyes, trembling as her gaze meets mine.

My opponent isn't Queen Tris.

It's Marybeth.

My lady's maid.

## 18

ASTRID

My first reaction at seeing Marybeth is confusion. Is this a glamour? Has Queen Tris woven an enchantment so that I see a familiar figure?

But as the girl takes a few hesitant steps closer, her shoulders tensed almost as high as her ears, I know it's my lady's maid. This isn't some glamour conjured to trick me into letting my guard down. It's Marybeth. The only person I befriended since moving to Fairweather Palace. The only true friend I've ever had. I've trusted her with things I'd previously only told Father—about my magic, my horrible injury from the horse, the truth about the woman who caused that injury, my dependency on Crimson Malus.

She's always accepted me. Been kind to me.

What the blooming hell is she doing here?

"Astrid, thank goodness you're alive." Marybeth shifts as if to take another step closer, then seems to think better of it and brushes out the folds of her skirt instead. Unlike me, she's dressed in attire suited to a palace, not an arena. Her tartan skirt and lace blouse are similar to what she wears at Fair-weather Palace but are quite travel-worn. Her brown hair is pinned in her usual updo, revealing her round human ears, but loose tendrils stand in disarray around her face. Dark circles hover beneath her eyes, and her complexion is far more sallow than usual. She looks like she hasn't slept well in days. Her lips flick between a hesitant smile and a frown.

Understanding dawns as I try to piece together how—and why—she's here. Marybeth stole Torben's Chariot. She sent the ogre to attack him. It's possible she could have found out about the bargain Tris made with the Huntsman. She might have been present during his investigation and learned of his weakness to floral aromas.

It all makes a crushing, dreadful sort of sense. She really did come here to save me. Just like she told Madame Fury.

No wonder she's so flustered. She probably doesn't know how to treat me after what she did. After hearing that Torben and I are now working together. That I've been helping him hunt her down.

This is all just a huge misunderstanding.

My shoulders sag, and I'm not sure whether I feel relieved that I won't be facing Tris...or disappointed.

Someone makes a *boo*-ing sound from the stands, reminding me of our audience. This clearly wasn't the duel our spectators were hoping for. I ignore them as I jog forward to close the distance between me and Marybeth. Her lips stretch into a relieved smile as she extends a hand.

"Astrid," Torben's warning tone cuts through the growing sounds of displeasure radiating from the stands, but it's enough to halt my progress and keep me from taking her hand.

That's when I notice the silver hexagonal disc in her other palm. I frown at it. Could that be Torben's travel device? She must have taken it from her pocket when she smoothed down her skirt. I remember him describing the Chariot as small, easily mistakable as a snuff box or cosmetics compact. I'd already reasoned that Marybeth was the one who stole it, but seeing it now, seeing how she angles her arm to the side as if to obscure it from my view, makes my stomach harden around a pit of dread. It makes me wonder if perhaps I haven't pieced together *all* the answers.

Torben calls out again. "Yield!"

Another round of boos from the audience. "Fight already!" someone says from the nearest box.

"Yield, Astrid!" Torben says, tone deep and bellowing.

Marybeth's eyes flick toward the grate he stands behind, and her expression darkens.

I know I should listen to Torben. He's only reminding me of my own plan. Instead, I ask, "Marybeth, what are you doing here?"

She grins again as her attention returns to me, but there's a hint of sorrow in the upward turn of her lips. "I came to save you from the Huntsman."

I open my mouth, but I'm not sure what to say. I can't tell her she was wrong to worry over my fate. Torben had intended to kill me. He made a binding bargain with my stepmother that he'd bring her my heart. Marybeth had every right to worry.

My eyes narrow with suspicion. "You came to save me from the Huntsman...by sending a violent ogre after us. He hurt me, you know."

She wrings her hands. "You weren't supposed to be harmed. Murtis was supposed to kill the Huntsman. But if you were found in his custody, I ordered the ogre to get you away from him."

"Why?"

"So he could bring you to me." She stretches her open palm closer. "Come, I'll get you out of here. Grab my hand and I'll take you where it's safe."

I stare at her palm, making no move to take it. I may not

know how Torben's Chariot works, only that it allows for instantaneous travel, but I have a feeling that if I touch her hand, the device will activate. Part of me wants to allow that to happen, to let her take me to safety. But an equal part of me tenses with warning. Perhaps it's only from Torben's tone as he calls my name yet again.

Marybeth grits her teeth. "Why are you working with him, Astrid? The queen sent him to kill you."

"Yes, but...he didn't." My answer is weak and I know it.

"He still will. He has a bargain to fulfill. I don't know why he hasn't carried it out yet, but you must know that he will."

I nibble my bottom lip. Torben has admitted as much. Several times, in fact. And yet, beneath his gruff demeanor lies something else. He may not like to admit it, but there's a part of him that believes me. A part of him that wants to prove my innocence. Not only that, but he has the means to help me do so. He has the influence I need to bring my case to the Alpha Council once we find proof. It's a concept that now sends a wave of panic through me. Torben and I have less than two weeks to gather the evidence we need. This duel was supposed to bring me closer to exonerating myself. It was supposed to allow me to prove the queen's involvement with my father's death. But I was wrong. This wasn't the confrontation it was supposed to be. Just an inconvenient roadblock unwittingly created by my well-meaning friend. Now every second that ticks by feels like time wasted.

"Marybeth, it's hard to explain," I say. "The Huntsman is helping me prove my innocence."

"You can't trust him," she says.

Maybe she's right. Maybe I'm reading too much into Torben's moments of softness. In his accidental confessions that he believes me.

She thrusts out her hand again. "Let me save you, Astrid."

Maybe I should do what she says. Maybe I should let her

spirit me away from the Huntsman, far from where he can find us. I'd only have to hide until the seventeenth, when his broken bargain claims his life.

The thought makes my chest feel tight, but I remind myself that it will be my life instead if we can't prove my stepmother's guilt.

Marybeth takes a step closer, reaching for my wrist.

I glance at the silver disc in her hand again. Before she can touch my arm, I leap a step back. "Where would you take me?"

"Somewhere safe."

"Tell me where."

Her eyes dart toward the archway where Torben watches us. She lowers her voice. "If I say it out loud, he'll know."

"He can't hear us from there. Tell me where you'd take me or I'm not coming with you."

"All I can say is that it's safe." Her voice quavers with every word.

"Are you planning on taking me back to the Spring Court?"

She pales but says nothing.

My eyes turn to slits. "To Fairweather Palace?"

Again, no answer.

The hair at the back of my neck stands on end as I watch her tremble.

My throat feels as dry as the sand beneath my shoes as I state my next question. "Marybeth, are you working with Queen Tris?"

She opens her mouth, gaping for several seconds. Then she releases a strangled groan and shouts, "I can't tell you!"

My blood goes cold, as does my tone. "Did Queen Tris kill my father?"

Tears well in her eyes. She lowers her chin and shakes her head.

I'm not sure I believe her answer. "Do you know who killed him?"

Her throat bobs. When she speaks, her voice comes out quiet. Weak. "I don't remember doing it."

I blink at her, trying to comprehend what she means by that. The truth dawns like an iron blade to my heart. "Marybeth, did you kill him? Did you poison my pie?"

Her well of tears breaks, sending moisture streaming down her cheeks. Her voice catches on a sob. "I don't remember it, nor did I have a choice."

Rage roars through my body, heating my blood. "What do you mean you didn't have a choice?"

Marybeth falls to her knees. "I gave her my true name."

A wave of gasps rumbles from the stands followed by utter silence.

My body seizes up. The giving of one's true name was outlawed decades ago, as were all forms of mental compulsion. Before the last war united the humans and fae on the isle, humans lived in fear of fae compulsion. It was said a fae could compel a human simply by making eye contact with them. Such magic either no longer exists or has been rendered ineffective due to everyday precautions that have become commonplace since unification, such as fortifying all drinking water with Saint John's Wort—something known to ward against compulsion and other harmful fae magics. However, unlike regular compulsion, which was only said to last as long as eye contact was maintained, giving one's true name grants a fae permission to use compulsion on them indefinitely.

And where eye contact can be easily forced, giving one's true name can't be. It isn't about discovering some mystical secret name and gaining absolute control. It's a type of binding bargain that ignites when someone states a very specific phrase to a fae: *I give you my true name.* Children learn from an early age never to say these words to anyone, and never to confirm you've given your true name if asked, for that's one way a person can be tricked into igniting the magic. This means

Marybeth either entered the illegal bargain willingly or was stupid enough to be tricked.

Neither possibility manages to evoke feelings of sympathy as I stare down at the girl who was supposed to be my only friend. "You gave Queen Tris your true name, and she ordered you to try and kill me?"

She shakes her head. "I can't tell you. I'm forbidden from saying certain things. But the poison couldn't have killed you, Astrid. I knew it couldn't. Your life was spared. Don't you understand?"

What does that mean? Did she work within the bounds of my stepmother's commands? Did she use my tincture, knowing it wouldn't kill me?

But I told Marybeth I was making the pie for my father. She's the only one who knew. Which means even if she used Crimson Malus to execute my stepmother's commands in a way that wouldn't harm me, she still did it knowing it would kill my father instead. She had the opportunity to poison the pie too. Marybeth was amongst those my stepmother banished from the kitchen when we talked. But if the two are working together, Tris could have commanded Marybeth return after I stalked away in anger. Marybeth could have come into the kitchen before any of the other staff returned.

I curl my fingers so tight, my nails bite into my palms. Rage fills every ounce of my blood. "You killed my father," I say through my teeth.

"I didn't have control. I still don't have control. But I promise you, where we're going, you won't be harmed."

Every inch of my body burns with the heat of my anger. I'm hardly aware of how I lunge for the girl. Hardly aware of Torben's voice as he begs me to stop, begs me to step away and yield at once. I don't even know what I intend to do—strike her, shake her, slap her. All I know is that I can't stop my hands from moving, can't keep myself from grabbing the collar of her blouse and hauling her to her feet.

Still sobbing, she lets me drag her off her knees. I'm vaguely aware of a sudden roar of cheers echoing from the stands. They're finally getting the action they came for. I tighten my fist around Marybeth's collar, but my view of her is obscured by a sudden blast of blinding light. I feel her hand clamp tight around my forearm. The light grows brighter.

I close my eyelids against the blinding glare.

Torben's voice bellows out from the archway, cutting through the noise rising from the audience. "Madame Fury's parlor."

That's the last thing I hear before the roar of the stands is swallowed by silence.

The sandy floor of the pit shifts beneath my feet, turning hard in an instant. Soon the blinding light begins to fade.

I pry open my eyes to find Marybeth standing before me, her hand still clamped around my forearm. She glances wildly about. "No, no, no!"

I use her current preoccupation to wrench my arm free from her grip. Only then do I realize we're no longer in the fighting pit. Instead...

Torben's last words now make sense, as does Marybeth's agitation.

Marybeth didn't transport us to Fairweather Palace like she intended.

In fact, she didn't take us far at all.

She took us to Madame Fury's parlor.

## 19

ASTRID

I quickly scan my surroundings. Marybeth and I are alone in Madame Fury's parlor. It looks the same as it did earlier today when Torben and I came to speak with Fury, aside from the plates and glass tumblers littered about the room, remnants from the patrons who visited before the match.

"Damn it!" Marybeth says, stomping her foot. "He tricked me into visualizing the wrong place."

I back up to put several feet between us, stopping only when my hip comes up against a table laden with half-eaten pastries and melted fruity ices. My eyes catch on a glint of something silver beneath a crumbled cloth napkin—a butter knife. It isn't much, but it's something.

Clenching my hand around the hilt, I thrust it toward the other girl.

She gives me an exasperated look. "Astrid, we must hurry. I can only use the Chariot one more time before it needs to be charged under starlight. And I can only take you with me if we're touching. Now, put that down and be reasonable."

I huff a dark laugh. "Reasonable? You want me to be reasonable? How is this anything but a reasonable way to react to the person who murdered my father?"

Her chin quivers. "I didn't want to kill him."

"You were supposed to be my friend."

"I still am." She takes a step closer, but I take one too, thrusting the dull blade at her. Luckily, she seems wary enough to lurch back, even if it is just a butter knife. "Just please let me take you home. You'll be safe there."

I shake my head. "I can't believe a word that comes out of your mouth. You say you're my friend, that you came here to save me from the Huntsman, but then you try to take me back to my stepmother. To the very woman who wants me dead."

She opens her mouth but only manages a groan. "I wish I could tell you, but I can't. Just come with me and she'll explain everything."

"There's no explanation that will justify my father's death."

Renewed tears stream down Marybeth's cheeks again. "I know," she whispers. "He didn't deserve to die."

Her words send an ache to my heart. Not out of sympathy for her, but because she's right. He didn't deserve to die. A darker truth lurks just beneath that, one I don't want to face. I seek the rage I felt in the arena, if only to burn this new sensation away, but the sinister emotion wends its way through my blood and bones, filling me with a hollow ache. A dark void.

It's grief.

Memories flood my mind, of Father's slack face crisscrossed with black veins of poison. Then I recall the argument we had, how I shouted that he didn't care about me. I close my eyes against his wounded expression, but the vision is replaced by ones far more painful. Of happy moments. Of his smiling eyes and jovial voice. How he laughed when my rescued squirrel wreaked havoc on his studio and nibbled his tubes of paint. How I used to stand by his side while he worked on his portraits. How he'd affectionately pat me on the head whenever I shared my secret insights regarding his patrons' most cherished qualities. How he lifted me from the shore of my cruel mother's lake, halted my incessant cries as he wrapped me in the softest pelt and promised to love and care for me for the rest of his life.

He kept that promise, but I...

I killed him.

The poison was meant for me.

For *me*.

It should have been me.

My chest heaves with a jagged sob, one so violent it takes my breath away. My lungs feel too tight. My heart too sharp, too torn, too raw and exposed. I feel as if every ounce of sorrow I've avoided feeling since my father's death has struck me at once. It's a grief I can't bear to feel, for if I let it swallow me, I don't think I'll ever make my way out.

Do I deserve to come out of it?

Do I have any right to escape my stepmother's wrath?

The poison was meant for *me*.

It's something I've known from the start, just like I knew Tris had been behind the poisoning. But now the weight of having all my suspicions confirmed crushes me down. Down. It's too heavy. Far too heavy.

Another sob wracks through me, steeling my resolve. There's only one thing I can do.

I shove my hand into my trouser pocket. No sooner than I extract my tincture does the glass bottle leave my fingers. I blink through the haze of my tears and find Marybeth darting away from me, my vial in hand.

"Put the knife down, and I'll give you this back," she says.

Finally, the rage I'd sought returns, smoothing out the harshest edges of my grief. It gives me the courage to charge

Marybeth, thrusting out with my pathetic knife. With a squeal, she leaps back. Then her shout pierces the air. "I'll throw it!"

I freeze.

She holds out her hand to the side. "I'll throw this and smash it on the ground if you don't put down that knife and come with me."

My eyes lock on the vial, and panic crawls up my throat. I can't let her smash it. It's the only one I have left, and I still haven't figured out how to get more. And there's no way I'm going back to the Spring Court with her to get the ingredients I need to make it myself.

Marybeth's voice turns placating. "Come with me and you'll have access to all the Crimson Malus you want. You'll never have to feel pain again." I take a step forward, but she lifts her hand higher. "Drop the knife."

I open my palm, and my makeshift weapon clatters to the ground at my feet. Marybeth's shoulders slump with relief. She starts toward me, but my eyes remain firmly fixed on my tincture. I may have no intention of going with her, but I'm also not letting her smash my vial. I'll fight her if I need to. I'll hit her, claw her, do whatever I can—

The light she blinded me with in the arena returns. My stomach bottoms out. The glow must be a sign that the device is active. If she touches me, she'll take me with her. There's no way I'll be able to steal back my vial now. I can't even see where she is anymore.

The sound of shattering wood pierces the air. I startle and whirl toward it. The light from the Chariot quickly goes out, revealing Torben standing in the doorway, one of the wooden doors hanging from its hinges. His clothing is still bloodied from his fight with Helody, making him an image of pure rage as he strides into the room, chest heaving, fingers curled into fists at his sides.

"Are you hurt?" His eyes are locked on Marybeth, but I know his question is for me.

"No," I manage to say, "but she has my—"

Torben charges toward the girl. With a whimper, she throws my vial at him and retreats toward the other end of the room. I leap for my vial, my heart climbing into my throat. Just then, the blinding light returns. The sound of shattering glass reaches my ears just as something firm collides into me.

When the light abates, all I see is Torben. He must have been what I crashed into. I nearly trip in my haste to push away from him, but he steadies me on my feet.

"She's gone," Torben says through his teeth.

I glance around, but it isn't Marybeth I'm looking for.

My eyes fall on the shards of glass and the ruby liquid spreading over the floor beneath it.

My tincture.

It's...*no*. What will I do without it?

As if in answer, my well of grief returns, swallowing me whole.

THE NEXT THING I KNOW, I'M BLINKING INTO PALE MORNING light, a strange rumbling momentum thrumming beneath my body. My forehead is pressed to cool glass, and a blur of endless sandy dunes rushes by on the other side, illuminated with the glow of the rising sun. Bolting upright, I push away from the glass.

"Where am I?" As soon as I say it, my eyes land on the Huntsman.

"Train," he says. He sits across from me on a cushioned bench, one leg propped on his knee, his eyes fixed on a page in the broadsheets he's reading.

I take in my surroundings anew, noting the small, enclosed

room we're in, the thin sliding door opposite the window, and the rhythmic murmur of the train's motion. Turning my gaze back to Torben, I ask, "Why are we on a train? Where are we going?"

With a weary sigh, he folds his paper and gives me an exasperated look. "We're on our way to the Spring Court."

"You're taking me to the queen?" I half rise from my seat, but there's nowhere for me to go. Furthermore, the movement sends my head spinning. An ache pulses at my temple and behind my eyes. I lower myself back down and close my eyes against the wave of vertigo.

Torben's voice cuts through the melee of panic and pain. "I'm not taking you to your stepmother."

I pry my eyes open. "Then why are we going to the Spring Court?"

He pinches the bridge of his nose. "I've already told you at least half a dozen times."

I frown. What is he talking about? He hasn't told me anything. The last thing I remember...

The duel between Torben and Helody plays through my mind with perfect clarity, but the images that follow carry a cloud of dread.

I force the memories of my confrontation with Marybeth to speed by, giving myself no opportunity to dwell on them. Then I find my last clear memory.

I recall kneeling on the ground, sobbing as I stare at the shards of my broken tincture and the ruby liquid quickly spreading over the obsidian marble floor.

Why don't I remember anything after that?

Another stab of pain throbs through my temple, and I close my eyes once more. That's when I glimpse a fleeting image of me frantically trying to scoop the ruined tincture into my cupped palms and attempting to pour it into my mouth. When that didn't work, I...

I licked the poison from my fingertips.

Blooming hell. Not my finest moment.

And I wouldn't stop until Torben dragged me away from the broken vial. I recall kicking and screaming, then scrambling out of his arms. I nearly had my hands in the tincture once more, but this time he hefted me over his shoulder like a disobedient child and fled from Madame Fury's parlor. Patrons were only just then coming up the stairs from the fight. Thankfully, I don't think any of them caught sight of us. It's bad enough Torben had to see me like that.

I wince at the memories. That's the last thing I recall, so I must have fallen asleep afterward. And no wonder. The amount I remember licking from my fingers had to have been more than my usual two or three drops.

My cheeks flush with guilt as I hazard a peek at the Huntsman. He watches me with a neutral expression. After that spectacle, I wouldn't blame him for taking me back to my stepmother. But if he isn't, then what are we doing?

I sit up a little straighter, earning another sharp jab of pain radiating through my skull. A blanket I hadn't noticed I was covered in slips from my shoulders. Glancing down, I find myself dressed in a fresh blouse and skirt.

But...that's not what I was wearing last night.

My eyes fly back to Torben's. This time my cheeks flush for a different reason. "Huntsman, did you undress me while I was sleeping?"

He stiffens, and his expression turns indignant. "Of course I didn't. You did that just fine on your own."

I tilt my head back. "I don't remember..."

Another flash of memories surges through my mind, these ones hazier than the others.

Our bedroom in Department Lust.

Me swaying on my feet.

Torben handing me a pile of fresh clothing.

Me giggling and dropping the clothes to the ground.

Him averting his gaze just as I pull my shirt over my head.

*Wait until I'm out of the damn room, Astrid!*

My hand flies to my mouth. I'd give anything to shrink into a speck of dirt right now. The shirt I'd worn to the duel was not meant to be paired with a corset. It was thick, form fitting, and able to bind my breasts on its own. But I...I took it off...in front of Torben.

I shift to the side so I'm facing as far away from the Huntsman as I can, pretending to take a keen interest in the floral pattern on the seat beneath me. My fingers automatically reach for my chest, and I breathe a sigh of relief when I find the firm stays of my corset beneath the cotton blouse I wear. At least I managed to fully dress on my own.

I clear my throat and try to make my voice sound casual. "I don't remember anything from last night." Lies. I remember too much. "So please tell me why we're heading to the Spring Court."

Torben shifts slightly forward in his seat, but I refuse to meet his eyes. "We're going to prove your innocence."

## 20

*TORBEN*

Astrid's face whirls toward mine. "You mean it? You finally believe I'm innocent?"

I give her a reluctant nod. "I heard what Marybeth said to you in the ring. She may not have outright confessed, but it's clear she poisoned the pie that killed your father while she was under the influence of illegal compulsion."

Her lips pull into a smile, but she averts her gaze as if remembering she's supposed to be embarrassed in front of me right now. It's obvious she remembers more about her behavior from last night than she's letting on. As if on cue, her scent constricts. "Then why are we going to Spring?" she says, looking anywhere but at me. "Shouldn't we head straight for the Alpha Council's headquarters? Are the headquarters in Spring?"

The headquarters are in Spring, at the very center of the isle just north of the border of the Wind Court. But I'm not going to tell her that. "We aren't ready to take our case to the Alpha Council. Marybeth confessed to having given her name to a female in the Spring Court, but she never said to whom she gave it."

Astrid's brows knit together. She discards her previous embarrassment and faces me full on. "It was my stepmother. There's no doubt about it now."

"On the contrary, plenty of doubt remains. We need tangible proof."

"What other proof do you need? My lady's maid, a girl employed by my stepmother, murdered my—" Her scent profile shifts, the lemons turning bitter, the morning dew shifting into something murky like a bottomless swamp. Her breaths grow sharp as she reaches a hand into her skirt pocket. She doesn't act surprised at finding the pocket empty, which means she must remember her vial broke. That doesn't stop her from checking the other pocket. Her eyes glaze with a sudden sheen of tears. "Damn it!"

I lean forward and prop my elbows on my knees. "Astrid," I say, tone firm, "you're going to be all right."

"You don't know anything," she bites back, her voice edged with hysteria. Her scent twists again, flaring then contracting, over and over. It's a wild and chaotic medley, one I don't think she has any control over right now. It's the same scent she had last night when she was high on poison. She certainly had no control then.

Even though I could smell she was lying when she said she remembered nothing from the night before, I doubt she recalls it all. Based on how embarrassed she was after we discussed the clothing incident, I wouldn't be surprised if the full truth of last night's events prompted her to climb out the window of our moving train and throw herself upon the mercy of the dunes.

I, on the other hand, remember it all.

"You can't even see me," she said when I tried to leave the room while she was changing. "My magic won't let you. I could prance naked in a circle around you and all you'd see is your reflection."

It took all my restraint to keep silent then. The truth was, I could see her as plain as day. However much of the tincture she'd taken must have been enough to lower her defenses. Or diminish her magic, depending on how it works. Because when she stripped off that shirt, I saw everything. Not just a haze. Not just an impression of nudity.

All of it. Every curve, dip, and mound. Every shade of flesh, from her smooth skin to her coral lips and the rosy peaks of her breasts.

When I tried to leave, she stumbled over to stand between me and the door. I kept my eyes fixed on the top portion of the doorframe, but that only seemed to upset her.

"Even if you could see me, you wouldn't care," she said, her voice taking on a slight quaver. "You wouldn't even find me attractive, would you? It's because you don't like me at all. You think I'm annoying and...and you hate me."

That's when she dissolved into wailing tears.

"I don't hate you," I begrudgingly told her, but she wouldn't stop crying until I wrapped her in a loose hug. I patted her back, careful not to let too much of her naked flesh press against me. Not that there wasn't a strong urge to pull her close. But that would have been...disrespectful of her condition. And highly illogical.

"I don't want to wear clothes," she whined when she finally managed to dry her tears. Then her face brightened. "Huntsman! We should have sex!"

After that, I quite forcibly got her dressed with haste, aiding with everything from lacing up her corset to buttoning her damn shirt. She was asleep on her feet by the time I secured the last button, but that wasn't before she tried to tug off my shirt at the same time I was fastening hers.

The memory sends heat rising to my cheeks and a buzzing sensation to my chest.

Astrid scowls at me from the other bench as if the nature of my musings is clearly written over my face. Ever since she awoke, her magic has returned, so I'm once again left with only a vague awareness of her expressions. At least her scent has mellowed somewhat, which tells me her scowl is for a different reason that has nothing to do with me having seen her naked.

"If we still have so much proof left to find," she says, "then why are we going to the Spring Court? And..." She lets out a gasp. "My job! How could you just drag me away from the hotel like that? I have clients—"

"We already discussed this," I say. It was before the clothing incident, so I don't know why she doesn't remember. "I spoke with Madame Desire and told her to charge my account any fee for the inconvenience of losing you as an employee for the time being. She wasn't upset."

Astrid frowns. "She should have been. I'm quite good at what I do, you know."

"I'll take your word for it."

She gives me an assessing look. "Someone like you could use my services."

I bristle. "What the blooming fuck is that supposed to mean?"

"You just strike me as someone who could use a little passion in his life."

I open my mouth, on the verge of delivering some barbed quip, but I'm rendered mute as I recall her rather animated proposition last night. I'm particularly disturbed that the thought isn't at all unpleasant to me. Shouldn't it be? I was sent to hunt her down. I nearly attempted to rip her heart from her chest. Sure, I now know she isn't a murderer, and yet...

I blink at her a few times. Why would I even entertain such a thought? It's not like she meant what she said last night. She was out of her wits. There's no part of her that could possibly fancy the man who attempted to kill her. Not to mention, romance isn't in the cards for me. It hasn't been for years. I learned just how detrimental love can be when it comes to my senses, making me prone to deception, more susceptible to believing lies, more ignorant to truths lying just beneath the surface. The worst thing I could possibly do for Astrid Snow is fall in love with her. To prove her innocence, she needs me sharp. Clearheaded. Not a lust-driven imbecile who can't properly smell a truth from a lie.

Gathering my far more rational senses, I shake my head and shift my gaze to the window. "I'm not in the market for love."

Silence stretches between us before she speaks again. "Why not?"

"I'm enslaved to the Alpha Council for one hundred years, remember? My terms of service forbid me from marrying or owning property or doing much of anything a normal citizen would do. I have no permanent home. I constantly travel from city to city. Furthermore, my job comes with danger. Bringing a lover into my life...she'd only be put in danger too. It isn't unheard of for a bounty hunter to become the target of someone's wrath. I've hunted down people's husbands, wives, sons, daughters, friends. Some who were innocent and evading trial for personal reasons. If ever I made an enemy who sought revenge on me, they could hurt someone I loved to punish me. I would never put someone in that position. Ever. As much as it irks me at times that I'm disallowed from having any social or emotional ties, I understand the reasoning behind the rule. Being the Huntsman requires secrecy. Only the fae royals on the Alpha Council know my real name and the details of my past."

"And me," she says, drawing my attention back to her. "You told me your name."

I release a sigh. "I did. Keep it to yourself."

"All right." Her scent flutters with something soft and warm, bringing to mind apple blossoms opening beneath a bright ray of sunlight. Could she be pleased that she's one of the few who knows my name? Her voice takes on a tenuous quality. "So, what about after your term of service is complete? Will you seek love or matrimony then?"

"Doubtful."

"Why not?"

I shift uncomfortably in my seat. How the hell did we get on this topic? "I don't have the best experiences with romance and have no desire to repeat such mistakes again."

"What kind of mistakes?"

My chest tightens. "Gambling with my heart."

I feel the weight of her stare and smell the acrid scent of pity. "Does it have anything to do with how you came into debt?" Her voice is barely above a whisper.

I purse my lips. I know I don't have to answer her. There's only one reason I've let this conversation continue as long as it has—because talking about me is clearly keeping Astrid's emotional state steady. Something I know will eventually crash. She isn't the first Crimson Malus addict I've known. Maybe that sympathy is what frees my tongue.

"Yes."

Her scent brightens with curiosity. "What happened?"

I lean back and prop my ankle on my knee again. "I was eighteen years old when my father died and left me with a grand inheritance—Davenport Estate. Had I aged like the fae once did before the isle was unified, I would still have been a juvenile cub. But since I aged like a human, I was deemed old enough to bear the responsibilities Father left me with."

"How long ago was that?"

"Seven years ago."

Her eyes widen slightly. "That makes you old enough to have been born before the isle was unified. Yet you still aged like a human?"

I nod. "I was only three when the war ended and the wall came down. I believe my den's close proximity to a human city made me age as quickly as I did. Either that, or the fact that I was so young when the isle was unified."

"I wasn't aware that was possible."

"Neither were my parents," I say with a halfhearted chuckle. I don't blame Astrid for being surprised by anything regarding aging in Faerwyvae. Human-fae hybrids, like Astrid, seem to be the only ones whose aging was unaffected by the isle's unification. As far as anyone knows, part fae have always aged at the same rate humans do, stopping only when they reach maturity. As for the rest of us, there are still many mysteries we've yet to unravel.

Back when the isle was split by the wall that separated the humans from the fae, humans aged the same as they did everywhere else in the world, while pureblood fae aged very slowly until they reached maturity, after which they either stopped aging or experienced even slower aging than before. Once the isle was unified twenty-two years ago, humans and fae began affecting one another in strange new ways. Many pureblood fae born after unification aged at a humanlike rate until they reached maturity, while humans experienced a slow in aging, particularly those in close intimate relationships with a fae.

"So, how did you go from being a bear cub living in a den to the heir of a fortune that you somehow lost?"

My heart sinks at the question. I can't answer it without first telling her something I hate to talk about. I release a slow and heavy exhale. "My mother died when I was six years old."

Astrid's scent contracts. "I'm so sorry, Torben."

I shift in my seat as if that could disperse the uncomfortable weight of her pity. "Yes, well, her death frightened both me and Father equally. Faerwyvae had only been unified for three years at that point, and the isle was still adjusting. New borders were being drawn. Courts that had to be relocated after the wall went down were undergoing changes to climate and terrain."

"I was only just born at that point," Astrid says, "so I remember very little about what things were like back then."

"They were tumultuous times, to say the least, but my parents thought we could avoid anything to do with such post-war changes if we stayed in our same little den. That is, until a human city was built nearby. After that, we regularly encountered unexpected guests in what used to be our peaceful woods. To make matters worse, the land literally changed around us. Before unification, our den had been in the Earthen Court. After the war, the Earthen Court was relocated south, and Spring took over the land we lived on. Eternal spring was fine at first, but it made it difficult when it came time to hibernate. The energy was different. While the Earthen Court held a steady nature that made it easy to settle down and rest, the Spring Court was in a constant state of renewal and rebirth. Life, light, and color. After three years of trying and failing to adapt, we decided to migrate south to where the Earthen Court had moved. But on the way there..."

My throat closes up.

A sudden burst of resentment pierces my heart like a jagged thorn. Why am I even talking about this? Why am I subjecting myself to these memories, these old aches and pains, just to distract Astrid from feeling her own grief? I glance at the woman and find her nearly at the edge of her seat, her hands clasped to her heart.

My resentment softens.

I suppose I can express this next part. For her.

"On the way, Mother stepped into a hidden bear trap. An *iron* bear trap. It was located in lands that had once belonged to humans before unification. Even after all the efforts to eradicate every last bit of iron on the isle after the war, it was foolish to believe that nothing had been accidentally left behind. By the time Father and I got help, it was too late. Mother succumbed to iron poisoning and died."

My throat feels tight again, so I clear it with a subtle cough. I shift my gaze to the window and see golden dunes have given way to the pink and green of the Spring Court. I'm not sure whether I feel more anxious or relieved to know we'll soon be approaching our stop. Part of me wants to get out of this damn conversation, while the other part knows where we go next might be far more difficult to bear than tales of the past. Besides, if I don't tell Astrid now, she'll probably ask about it once we arrive at our destination. We'll be going to the very place our conversation has been orbiting around this entire time.

"What did you do after your mother died?" Astrid asks.

"We returned to our den in the Spring Court, but it wasn't long before Father decided it might be safer for us to enter society. More than that, I think he wanted to do whatever it took to separate himself from the life he lost—the life we'd shared with my mother. He couldn't tolerate being in his unseelie form without thinking of her. So we shifted into our seelie forms for the first time and entered the nearest city. Mother's death had one benefit, although I'm loath to even call it that. Because her death was caused by an illegal metal our fae royals had failed to locate and dispose of, we were financially compensated for our loss. That allowed us to enter society with some wealth. We both quickly learned how to navigate the rules of modern society. Father eventually bought an old manor just outside the city as well as the surrounding farmland. He named it Davenport Estate. After he took a gamble on a few new berry cultivars, our estate began to thrive."

Astrid's expression brightens. "Your farm grew berries?"

I allow myself the ghost of a smile. "The best berries. Bright, plump, and famously sweet."

"Wait! You're...you're Davenport Berries! I remember Davenport Berries from when I was little." Her lips dip into a frown. "It's starting to make sense why I haven't seen them around the last few years. I thought it was because I lived in a palace and didn't go to market anymore."

I shake my head. "When I gambled everything away, I lost the farms as well. No one has been keeping them up in my stead. I lost the crops once before that too. When Father died, so too did our berry crops. Someone had placed a blight curse on them, most likely a rival who sought to take advantage of Father's death and the period of vulnerability it left the estate in. I was in no way prepared to run the estate. Even less so when it came to cursed crops and the resulting plummet in finances. However, that's when I discovered gambling."

My stomach turns at the memory. "It started out innocently enough. I visited gambling halls as a means of escape from my responsibilities. Soon I learned I could use my sense of smell to gain the upper hand, particularly during certain card games. Since I maintained seelie form at all times during those days, no one knew I was a bear shifter. They only knew I was fae, not that I had any magical means of smelling lies. It didn't take long for me to reap financial benefits from my gambling activities, and that became a source of stability. Power. Control. I was able to recover financially, buy new crops, pay for countercurses to heal the damaged soil in the old plots. I was far from regaining the level of wealth Father had meant to leave me with, but I was getting there. Unfortunately, that's when I fell in love."

Astrid grimaces. "What happened?"

"Shannon Barrister happened." Even her name puts a sour

taste in my mouth. "I knew I needed a wife in order to fully step into the role Father left for me. By then, I understood the rules of society, and one of the primary expectations was marriage and securing an heir. I began courting Miss Barrister out of duty, but we quickly fell in love. There was only one thing standing in our way. Her parents wouldn't approve of a marriage with anyone earning less than eighty thousand rounds per year. Davenport Estate was still recovering, so I wasn't quite there, although I knew I would be soon. Had I been patient, I never would have made the mistake that cost me everything. Instead, I let greed guide me. I knew I could raise my wealth with a few risky bets. Miss Barrister encouraged me, expressing her eagerness to marry as soon as possible. She was the only person who knew about my keen sense of smell and how it helped me tell if people were lying. I never admitted to her that I used my magic to scent lies during card games, but she must have guessed as much."

Astrid worries her bottom lip. "Did she...betray you?"

"Yes," I say, though I hate to admit it. Hate to admit I was so blind. So stupidly confident. So pathetically infatuated that I didn't think to smell if my lover was lying. "Miss Barrister encouraged me to play against one of the most notorious gamblers two cities over. Frank Host was famed for his risky bets. His occasional losses were massive, but his wins were greater. So great, that he was sitting on an unbelievably large fortune at the time. One ripe for the taking. He was just the opponent I needed. Someone reckless enough to play against an equally reckless wager. So long as we played a game of bluffs and lies, I could win."

"But you didn't?"

"No. Miss Barrister told Mr. Host about my ability to sense lies. He used this knowledge to purposefully fluctuate his emotions during the game. I bet ten times the amount of money I had, and I lost. Shannon Barrister married Frank Host two months later."

Astrid's mouth falls open. "That's...that's despicable."

I shrug.

She slumps into her seat and crosses her arms. "I hate Shannon Barrister, and I don't even know her. No wonder you're such a grump."

I quirk a brow. "A grump?"

She doesn't bother looking apologetic over the insult as she meets my gaze. "But you know that wasn't love, Torben. She certainly didn't love you and she took advantage of your feelings for her. I agree she treated you poorly, but I don't think that experience should make you give up on love."

"Are you some expert on the topic?"

She gives me a haughty look. "I'm a matchmaker."

"Aside from helping other people fall in love. Do you know anything about it yourself?" My tone is meant to be teasing, and yet I can't help but tense up as I await her answer. Why am I so desperate to know about her love life?

She shrinks down a little. "Well, no. I've sworn off love. I can hardly find romance when all anyone else sees in me is their own reflection."

"Is that why you turned down Queen Tris' nephew?"

Her scent turns sharp. "That's precisely why. I could never love someone who has no clue as to who I really am. Which is everyone. That's why I like animals better than people—" She slaps her hand over her mouth, and her scent flares with panic. "Oh no! The kittens! I didn't even get to say goodbye. What are they going to do without me?"

I roll my eyes. I'm about to remind her that stray animals don't need her feeding them prime cuts of salmon in an alley, but as tears begin to well in her eyes and her scent plummets into sorrow, I find myself shoving my harsher instincts aside.

Instead, I reach for the small, blanket-covered crate on the bench next to me.

With a grumbling sigh, I place the crate beside her and remove the blanket.

She blinks at the barred crate and the five feline forms cuddled up asleep inside it. Her eyes glaze even further now as she faces me with a tremulous smile. "You brought them?"

"Because you wouldn't shut up about them." She'd complained about leaving the kittens behind several times last night, and again this morning when she briefly awoke before I carried her to the train station. Although, if she doesn't remember most of our other conversations from the night before, then she probably doesn't recall that one either. Nor does she appreciate how difficult it was to carry her sleeping body, a crate of kittens, and two suitcases across the city to Irridae Station.

Two of the kittens rouse from sleep, and Astrid opens the crate to let them crawl on her lap. Her scent brightens. The aroma is so heady, it does something funny to my heart.

I lift my broadsheets and return to reading. Now that she knows the kittens are here, she won't need me for conversation. Why didn't I just show her the damn creatures when she first awoke?

"You know, Torben," Astrid says from the other side of my broadsheets. She leans forward and tugs down my paper until I give in and meet her eyes.

"What?" My breath catches as I see her true face looking back at me. I try not to let the surprise show in my expression.

Her coral lips lift into a teasing grin. "I think I'm starting to like you."

With that, she releases the paper and turns her full attention to the kittens. I'm left watching her play with them, nuzzling their soft bodies against her cheeks, her words echoing in my head. I know they didn't mean anything. She was teasing. Taunting. She doesn't...*like* me. Why would I care either way?

I return my gaze to my paper, blocking her from view once more. No matter how I try to focus on the words before my eyes, the ones ringing through my ears take precedence. Regardless, I'm grateful that the broadsheets create a barrier between us, if only to hide the traitorous grin that tugs my lips.

## 21

*ASTRID*

Torben and I traverse an overgrown walkway toward a sprawling boarded-up building. "Welcome to my home," Torben says with a tired sigh. "The manor house of Davenport Estate."

I grimace at the peeling paint, the walls smothered in ivy, the shrubs that have nearly taken over the front stoop. Madeline purrs on my shoulder. Her siblings and Mama Cat are asleep in the crate Torben carries. I frown at him. "This is why we came to the Spring Court?"

"Not exactly." He sets the crate and two suitcases down at the bottom of the front steps, then strides up to the immense double doors. Wrapping his hands around one of the wooden planks nailed to the doorframe, he yanks it free in a single pull. "It's more that we need a place to stay. One that doesn't require payment. All charges made to the Alpha Council make our location easy to trace. Now that we suspect Queen Tris, we must evade even the Alpha Council knowing where we are."

I huff. "Oh, *now* that we suspect Queen Tris? I've suspected her all the while."

He says nothing in reply, only yanks free another board.

"If we can't use the Alpha Council's funds, how did we afford the train fare?"

"I had Madame Desire exchange a small amount of credit for opal chips. But we must spend them sparingly, hence why we're here and not some posh hotel." He glances over his shoulder as he frees the next board. "Are you asking because you find such accommodations beneath you, Your Highness?"

I burn him with a glare. "Don't you dare call me that again. And no, I find these accommodations just fine." To prove my point, I climb the first step toward the doors, keeping my palm underneath Madeline to prevent her from getting launched off my shoulder. Torben gives an amused smirk, then returns his attention to the planks. I take the opportunity to cast a wary glance at our surroundings. I have no qualms about staying in an abandoned manor. It's the safety of such a place I'm more concerned with. But as I look around, I find nothing more sinister than an unkempt lawn, unruly trees, and shrubs that have grown too wild for their own good. On our coach ride here, I saw very few homes, only gorgeous green countryside punctuated by pink and white fruit blossoms. The coach let us off a mile down the road, and we came across only a few country cottages between there and here. From where we are now, there's no sign of any other houses. No nosy neighbors to spy.

I can't help feeling exposed regardless. Then again, I've felt that way ever since Torben told me we were going to Spring. "Are you sure we should even be here? If all the fae royals know your true identity and past, then Tris must know about Davenport Estate. If she was responsible for doling out your punishment, then she probably knows more about it than anyone."

"She more than knows about it." His words end in a grunt as he frees the final plank. "She owns it."

My mouth falls open. "She what?"

With the pair of doors no longer boarded up, he turns one of the handles. When it doesn't budge, he throws his shoulder into the door and tries again. Finally, it swings open. He stares into the darkness beyond, making no move to step inside.

Tugging Madeline off my shoulder and cradling her against my chest where I can better hold her, I march up the remaining steps and burn Torben with a glare. "How is it a good idea to stay in a house Tris owns?"

He continues to stare into the dark foyer, hands curled into fists, shoulders tense. "She may own it," he says a bit absently, "but that's only because all my properties were seized when I gambled more money than I had. Since my debt and punishment fell under her jurisdiction, the deed to the estate automatically went to her."

"That still doesn't explain why we'd be safe here."

"She doesn't use this property," he says. "She hasn't done a single thing with the estate since it was transferred to her name."

"How are you so sure?"

His jaw shifts side to side. "She told me as much when we made our second bargain."

I swallow hard. "What second bargain?"

Finally, he turns his gaze to mine. "Our first bargain was that she'd end my sentence as Huntsman in exchange for me bringing her your heart. Our second bargain was that she'd return Davenport Estate to me if I handed over my Chariot once I finished my mission. She knew it was my goal to buy back the estate once my debts were paid and my punishment was served. When we made our second bargain, she confessed that she'd yet to do anything with the estate aside from having the manor boarded up. She promised I'd have it returned to me without me having to buy it back if I gave her my Chariot."

I give him a pointed look. "So that's the real reason you were so upset over losing it."

"Yes." He retrieves our luggage and cat crate from the base of the steps, then enters the house. "If anyone comes to find us here, she'll prove her guilt. If Marybeth truly is serving her, then she'll already have reported back everything that happened in Irridae. Tris will have guessed we'd suspect her by now. She might also guess we'd come here. If she's smart, she'll know better than to show her hand. If she isn't and sends someone after us, I'll deal with them swiftly and have even more proof to stack against her."

"That's not entirely comforting." I hold Madeline tighter as I follow behind him into the manor. Dust fills my nostrils along with the smell of mold. I imagine it must smell far worse to Torben. Fighting back a coughing fit, I say, "Also, that's not much of a plan. Please tell me you have a better scheme to prove my innocence than just using us as bait for my stepmother."

"I do have a plan." Torben continues down the foyer, and I keep as close to him as I can. Our only source of light is the meager glow peeking in from the boarded-up windows. Open doors line the halls, revealing a parlor, a large dining room, and a study. The rooms are mostly empty, aside from a few sparse pieces of furniture, all of which are draped in dusty sheets. The foyer opens to a wide space flanked by two immense mahogany staircases. He motions for me to follow him up the right side.

I stare daggers at his back as we climb the steps. "Care to share that plan, Huntsman?"

Each step he takes is slow, tense. He keeps his voice low. Probably to stop it from echoing so eerily. "I must make a report to Queen Tris as soon as possible. When I do, I'll try to get the proof we need."

"How? Isn't that dangerous? If Marybeth used the Chariot to get back to Fairweather Palace, Tris already knows we're working together. I told Marybeth you were helping me prove my innocence. If Tris thinks you suspect her, she could kill you at once before you get a chance to gather evidence against her."

"It's a risk," he says, "but she's too clever to act so brashly. She'll want to try and seem innocent for as long as she can. When I speak to her, I'll keep my senses open and smell for lies. I'll state things that should evoke an emotional response from her. I'll choose questions that require her to try and deceive me if she's guilty. If I'm successful, I'll get a confession from her."

"What if it doesn't work?"

"Then I'll gather as much information as I can and present it to the other royals on the Alpha Council. If we deliver enough proof to warrant an investigation, they'll take on a case against Queen Tris."

"Do we have enough time to do all that?" My stomach churns as I consider how little time we have left. Ten full days remain between now and the seventeenth. Even if Torben can convince the Alpha Council to investigate Tris as a potential murder suspect, will they be able to force her to revoke her bargain with Torben before it kills him? Or...or is he still planning on taking me back to her regardless of the outcome?

My chest tightens as I remind myself of the promise I made to him—that I'd go with him when the time came to fulfill his bargain. When I made that promise, doing so had seemed essential. A desperate offer to convince Torben to make me a temporary ally. Then again...he and I never made a binding pact. I may have offered the promise, but he never officially accepted it.

As we reach the top of the stairs, Torben heads straight for a closed door and pushes it open. I follow him into the room. It holds more furnishings than the other rooms I glimpsed on the floor below. Based on the cloth-covered shapes, there's a four-poster bed, a dresser, a chest, and a wardrobe.

Torben sets the crate and luggage on the bed and crosses the room to draw open moth-eaten drapes. Four sash windows line the far wall. Each is boarded up with a single plank cross-wise, allowing plenty of sunlight into the room. He proceeds to lift each bottom sash open, inviting some relief from the stifling, moldy air. Once he's finished opening all the windows, he pauses at the last one. His expression takes on a distant quality as he stares outside.

A heavy silence falls between us until it's pierced with waking kitten cries. I set Madeline on the bed and open the door of the crate. Mama Cat extends her body in a long stretch that ends in a yawn. Abernathy remains asleep while Natalie and Grigg happily pounce from the crate and begin investigating the bed. "Whose room was this?"

"Mine," he says, still looking out the window.

"So is this where you'll be staying while we're here?"

"No. I'll be staying in the parlor. This room is for you."

I'm about to ask why he'd stay in the parlor when there are bedrooms available, but his somber mood has me holding my tongue. After everything he told me on the train, it isn't hard to imagine how difficult it must be to be here. This is the home his deceased father left him. The home he lost in a reckless bet. A bet he'd made in the name of misplaced love. He must ache to see the manor in such disrepair, not to mention any painful memories it might hold.

I'm struck by a sudden urge to stand beside him, to offer him a consoling pat or weave my fingers through his. I shake the thought from my mind and approach the window farthest from him instead. Still, the space between us feels heavy. Weighted. Perhaps it's because of all that he divulged today. I'd be a fool to think sharing such private matters with me meant anything to him.

And yet...I can't help seeing him differently. Seeing a softness to his harsh edges. A warmth in his gruff bearing. A tender heart hiding inside that muscled chest. In this moment, I can almost see that strange impression I somehow formed on him —a weakness, a vulnerability. But like it always is when I manage to glimpse it, it feels thin, as if it doesn't truly represent him at all. Before my eyes, it fades away, replaced by an awareness of his broad shoulders, his sculpted thighs, his chiseled jaw. No, this man isn't weak at all. He's strong. Stoic, yes, but powerful. Intelligent. And that beautiful shade of copper in his hair—

Realizing I'm staring, I shift my gaze to the window. Thankfully, Torben doesn't seem to have noticed me at all and continues to look out at the scenery. The breeze funneling inside cools the sudden heat flushing my body and carries with it the scent of freshly cut grass and cherry blossoms. Beneath the plank crossing the window, I catch sight of the sunlit countryside. In the distance, rolling green hills span the width of my view. The shape of the hills has me tilting my head to the side. They look...familiar. But everything has looked familiar since we left the station at our stop.

I face Torben. "What part of the Spring Court is this?"

He shakes his head as if to clear it, then turns away from the window. Crossing his arms, he leans casually against the sill. "We're in Dewberry. It's just outside the city of—"

"Larklawn," I say at the same time he does. "That's the city you first lived in after you took seelie form?"

"Yes."

"After your mother died...when you were six years old."

A nod.

"Which was nineteen years ago."

"Roughly." He gives me an assessing look. "Have you been here before?"

I blink at him a few times, assessing everything he told me about his past under a new light. "Yes, I was born here. At Dewberry Lake."

He pulls his head back in surprise. "You were?"

I give a reluctant nod. My birthplace isn't something I like to think about much less talk about. But after all the personal details Torben has shared with me, I suppose I can do the same. "My mother was a lake sprite—the very spirit of Dewberry Lake."

"Your mother was the Dewberry Lake sprite? The sprite known for—"

"Making people fall in love with their own reflections and drowning," I finish for him, my lips pulled into a grimace. "That's her. Now you see where I get my awful magic from."

Torben stares at me with wide eyes. "How did your father come to sire a child with her?"

I shrug. "Father never explained the details and I certainly wasn't going to ask. All I know is that they fell in love while he was painting her. At first, he thought his subject was just a lake like any other and wanted to paint the source of the haunting tales that had circulated the city of Larklawn. What he didn't know was that the lake was my mother in her unseelie form. But when he returned to finish his painting, he got to see her seelie form. He always said she was terrifyingly beautiful and that he was never in danger of her. I've always assumed that he's immune to fae magic since he was always able to see me for who I really am."

"Didn't you tell me your mother abandoned you?" His brows knit with sympathy.

"I sure did," I say, tone wry to hide the anger that always fills my heart when I think about my mother. "I made such a poor impression on the female who birthed me that she didn't last a

year with me. She eventually left me on the lakeshore for my
father to find. He visited almost every day, but when he found
me alone with Mother refusing to emerge from the lake, Father
took me home. That's the memory I told you about, the one
involving Father wrapping me in fur."

I swallow the sudden ache in my throat. My eyes wander
the landscape, and I realize I'm searching for any sign of glittering blue hidden beneath the trees. Dewberry Lake must be
around here somewhere. Not that I want to go. We never
returned to the lake after that day when Father saved me from
my callous mother, and I'm glad. I hold no love for the fae who
so cruelly abandoned me.

I shutter my eyes and force myself away from the window.
When I return my gaze to Torben's, I find him watching me
with an expression I can't read. Every muscle in his body is
tense, his eyes wide, his brows knitting together to weave something like surprise. I shrink back beneath the intensity of his
stare. "What is it?"

He clears his throat and drags his eyes away from mine.
"Sorry," he says with a shake of his head. "I was...lost in my
thoughts. I'm also sorry your mother did that." He pins his
attention on the door at the other side of the room and begins
striding toward it. Just when I think he'll walk away, he pauses
under the doorway and glances back at me. "Do...do you know
that Dewberry Lake is gone?"

My breath catches in my throat.

He must see the answer on my face, for his eyes turn down
at the corners. "There are townhomes there now. The lake
hasn't been there for three years."

Does that mean...is my mother dead? I hate the way my
heart wrenches at the thought. Why should I care? Why should
it matter that my neglectful mother is gone? I'd trade her life a
thousand times over if it brought my father back.

I force my voice to sound far more playful than I feel. "Good riddance. I suppose that means fewer casualties for innocent lake-goers. You know what I do find strange, though? The fact that you and I must have lived in Larklawn at the same time. For at least a short while. Yet we never met." It's an obvious attempt at changing the subject.

Thankfully, Torben allows it. With a sideways grin, he says, "Strange indeed," before leaving me alone in my room.

## 22

*ASTRID*

I wake covered in a cold sweat, my body racked with
tremors. It takes me several moments to figure out where
I am. This isn't my bedroom at Department Sloth, nor is
it the room I shared with the Huntsman at Lust. Thoughts of
Torben clear my head slightly.

That's right. I'm at Davenport Manor. In his room. His bed.

I barely recall having fallen asleep, only that I was overcome with a massive wave of fatigue just before nightfall. I
knew where the sudden exhaustion had come from; I was
suffering from lack of Crimson Malus. Even before then, I was
keenly aware that I'd need to come up with a way to replace my
tincture—and fast. I'd planned on slipping out of the manor
when Torben was preoccupied so I could search for the fae
fruit. But by the time Torben finished seeking out fresh sheets
for the bed and handing me a meager meal of provisions he'd
brought with us from the hotel, I was hardly able to move. All I
could do was climb into bed and close my eyes.

Now that I'm awake, I regret having given in to slumber

before I could locate Crimson Malus. I regret that my tincture was shattered. I regret—

A wave of memory washes over me. Of my vial crashing to the ground. Of the sorrow I felt afterward as I was forced to feel the pain of my father's death all over again. Of my anger at hearing Marybeth's confession. I feel those same emotions roaring through me now. Grief, rage, pain, hatred. I squeeze my eyes shut and turn on my side, burying my face in the musty pillow as if that will extinguish the unwanted feelings. All it manages to do is send my stomach roiling.

I bite my lip and wait for the nausea to pass. When it does, I'm left coated in even more sweat than before, soaking the sheets beneath me. I whimper at the discomfort.

A gentle weight lands on my shoulder. I pry my eyes open to see little Natalie climbing on me. My heart softens, as do the sharpest edges of my pain. I reach a trembling hand to pet her and feel a slight glow of relief burning through my swarm of emotions.

That's all I need. Just a little relief so I can do what I need to do.

Biting my lip against a pulsing ache shattering my skull, I lift Natalie from my shoulder and push myself up to sitting. Even that small motion makes my bones feel weighted with iron, but I make myself rise to my feet next. I rub my arms against the chill, but I'm not sure if it's the air that's cold or something inside me. In contrast, every inch of my skin is hot with fever.

My stomach churns again as I slowly shuffle toward the window. I glance out at the night sky, the landscape bathed in shadows and moonlight. Somewhere out there must be a Crimson Malus tree. There must be. Now that I know where we are—in the very place I was born and not far from the city where I lived with Father for the first few years of my life—I feel confident I can find a tree. I know what they look like. They aren't exactly rare, although they are like a needle in a haystack amongst the cherry trees the Spring Court is famous for.

But...but I can find one. I *must* find one. I'll wander the woods all night if I have to.

Steeling my resolve, I make my way to the foot of the bed where a chest stands. Upon it, Torben left one of the suitcases he'd brought with us. It contains clothing he must have collected earlier this morning when I was still asleep. I don't have the patience to dig through everything and fully dress, so I grab the first practical thing I find—a silk robe—and wrap it over my nightdress. Then I gather my shoes, but I don't put them on. Instead, I carry them in one hand and cross the room to the door on silent feet.

What isn't so silent are the two mewling kittens circling my ankles. Were my situation not so dire, I'd reach down and pet them. However, I'm not sure I'd be able to do so without toppling over. Every step I take feels tenuous. So, as gently as I can, I scoot them away with my foot and sneak out the door, closing it behind me. Mama Cat and the other two kittens are snuggled up somewhere in the bedroom, so I don't feel too bad for closing them inside.

My progress is slow as I traverse the stairs. Sweat continues to bead over my skin, and now and then I'm struck with another wave of nausea. Eventually, I make it to the bottom without falling and breaking my neck. The next part, though, will require even more care.

I tiptoe down the foyer, heading straight for the front door. I'd prefer to use a back door, or any entrance not so near where Torben sleeps. Why he insisted on sleeping in the parlor while he put me in his former bedroom is beyond me. Perhaps it's to be close to the front door—the only entrance no longer boarded up—and able to quickly defend the manor should Queen Tris send anyone to see if we're here. The thought should have me scurrying back to my bedroom, both in fear of what could lurk outside at night and the fact that Torben might spring awake at the first sound of the door opening, but I'm too desperate to care. Too determined to stave off the emotions that threaten to crush me. I think the only reason they haven't yet is because I'm too preoccupied with what I'm doing. Or perhaps it's anticipation over Crimson Malus that has me keeping myself from falling apart.

I slow my pace as I reach the open door to the parlor. Holding my breath, I glance inside the room and find Torben sprawled over a sheet-covered divan. He's too large for it, with one leg hanging off the side, his foot planted on the floor. One arm is propped behind him while the other dangles off the edge. I watch him for a few heartbeats more, finding nothing to suggest he's awake, then finally continue toward the door. My heart slams against my ribs as I reach it. With careful movements, I set down my shoes and slide my feet into them. Then, extending a hand, I grasp the door handle.

*Please don't wake up. Please don't wake up.*

My main solace is my memory of how soundly Torben had slept the first night we spent at Lust. He didn't wake until I was halfway on top of him with my hand in his pocket. Even when he did wake, his eyes were still closed as if he'd only reacted from partial wakefulness. If it took that much to only half wake him, surely turning the door handle now—

"What are you doing?" Torben's voice comes from just behind me, too loud for the quiet foyer.

With a start, I whirl around. I was wrong in my assumption that he wouldn't be easy to wake. His eyes are wide open, his expression stern. The fright at having been caught is too much for me. My knees give out and I have to prop myself against the door to keep from sliding all the way to the ground. "What are...you...doing?" I say through chattering teeth. And how did he come up behind me so fast? So quietly?

"I caught your scent in my sleep," he says. "Now answer my question. What are you doing?"

Anger breaks through my momentary fear, clearing my mind a little more and giving strength to my legs. I force myself to straighten and push away from the door. It takes all my effort to speak without letting my teeth chatter again. "What right have you to ask like you're in charge of me?"

He crosses his arms. "I am in charge of you, Miss Snow. I was sent to kill you, and now I'm determined to protect you instead. At the risk of breaking a bargain that will end my life, mind you. Until we prove your innocence and your stepmother's guilt, your safety is my priority. Not to mention, this is my house."

I clench my jaw. "I wasn't aware it was a crime to leave."

"It is when your actions put us both in danger. Sneaking around in the middle of the night in the very court ruled by the woman who wants you dead is an act of grave stupidity."

I bristle, and my anger rises. I'm grateful for it. Grateful for how it burns away my nausea. Keeps the grief that lingers just beyond my awareness at bay. "Oh, so I'm stupid now?"

He takes a step closer. "You are if you were about to wander the woods in search of Crimson Malus."

Fury rises inside me like a vicious tide. I'm not sure what I'm angrier at—his know-it-all smugness or the fact that he's right. "You don't know what you're talking about. I was going out for air—"

"That's a lie."

I open my mouth but quickly snap it shut. The truth is, I have no argument against his allegations, and I hate it. I hate that he's right. I hate that he can smell my lies. I hate that my need for Crimson Malus is so strong that it's clouding my judgment, making me reckless. I hate that even though I know all that, I still want to creep from the estate and search for the fae fruit.

"Fine," I say, brushing past him with all the dignity I can muster. "If you're so determined to be my jailer, let me go back to my prison."

I manage only a few steps before his hand comes gently around my forearm. I pause, half out of exhaustion, half because there's something soothing about the sudden touch, the warmth of his skin that somehow cools my fever and burns away my cold sweat. He stands next to me, his eyes searing into my profile. My shoulders sag, my body desperate to lean into his solid form.

"It's almost out of your system," he says, tone soft. "Once it is, you'll be fine. This is the worst part, Astrid. You can get through it."

His words have my heart softening, my muscles uncoiling. I'm going to be fine. I can believe that...can't I?

A vision flashes before my mind's eye. Of Father's slack face, his pale skin. Of black veins dancing over his flesh, courtesy of a poison that had been meant for me...

I yank my arm out of Torben's grip, summoning my fury to burn the vision from my mind, to give me strength against the sorrow that seeks to claim me, body and soul.

"Stop talking about my situation like you know anything about it," I say through my teeth. "I'm not fine, Torben. I'm not going to be fine."

"Yes, you will be. It's the poison that's making you unwell, forcing you to rely on it. It's killing you."

"You don't know—"

"I do know." Torben's voice manages to rise without becoming a shout. "It's how my father died."

## 23

*ASTRID*

A new flood of convulsions has me in its grip. I take in Torben's tense shoulders, his expression that constantly shifts between sorrow and rage. Emotions that war within me as well. I swallow hard, but my voice still comes out with a tremor. "Your father died from Crimson Malus?"

He nods. When he speaks, his tone comes out cold. "My father, a pureblood fae bear shifter with the strongest constitution of anyone I've known, died from the very poison you're so fond of."

"I...I don't understand. How did that happen?"

He purses his lips as if he doesn't want to answer. Then, taking a step back, he rubs a hand over his jaw. "After my mother died," Torben says, voice softer now, "Father changed. At first, the changes were expected. He was grieving the same as I was. We were both getting used to our seelie bodies and living in human society. But as the years went on, his changes became drastic. Mood swings. Constant fatigue. He started handing over more of the estate's responsibilities to staff. Stopped teaching me how to properly take on his duties. Toward the end, he expressed neither grief nor joy. He ceased to show emotions at all. He'd always been a good and loving father, doing everything he could to give me a safe and thriving life in the wake of Mother's death. Crimson Malus changed that. By the time I found out about his use of the poison, it was too late. There was nothing I could do to help him."

"But...but he was full fae. It shouldn't have done anything to him."

"It affected him nonetheless. Using the poison for recreational purposes isn't unheard of for the fae, but most prefer the more potent effects of fruits like Honey Pyrus. Crimson Malus feels subtle in comparison. Nearly benign aside from a slight mellowing or lifting of the mood. That's what makes it seem safe. But it isn't safe. What's happening to you now is the same thing that happened to my father. The longer he used it, the more his body began to rely on it. His innate fae healing was destroyed. He started to weaken, catching every contagious ailment he came across—things no fae should be susceptible to in the first place. Eventually, no amount of Crimson Malus could help him recover. The worst part was, he didn't care. He was neither happy nor sad about his fate."

My heart hammers so hard I feel it might burst. While I ache for Torben's loss and fear what he's told me about the fatal consequences of my tincture, his story has also reminded me of my own loss. Of everything I'm trying not to feel right now. Desperation and panic claw their way up my throat, making it hard to breathe.

"Torben, I'm so sorry for what happened to your father," I say, trying to sound as sincere as I can, "but my situation isn't the same. I won't use my tincture forever."

He pins me with a knowing look. "You don't need it. Not now, not ever."

Anger cuts through my panic. What right does he have to decide what I do and don't need? "That's not true. If I don't get my tincture, I'll constantly be in danger, all because of my magic. It's dependent upon my mood, remember? Do you have any idea of what kinds of things I've been through because of it?"

He releases a heavy sigh, one that bears more pity than I can stand. "You don't need poison to control your magic. You can learn to allow others to see who you really are."

Another wave of rage courses through me, so fierce that my fingers curl into fists and drive my nails into my palms.

It's just like my father said during our last argument before he died.

*It's time you let someone other than me see you.*

I narrow my eyes to a scowl. All softness I felt for the Huntsman during his story about his father is gone. "You think I have *control* over my magic? You think it's only a matter of *wanting* to be seen? If what I wanted factored into my magic, would I have made enemies for my father and compromised his career time and time again? Would I have gotten myself trampled by a horse because another girl was jealous? Would I have made such a poor impression on my own mother that she abandoned me and left me to die?"

"No, Astrid, of course you couldn't control your magic when you were younger."

"It doesn't matter how you think my magic works. I'm the one who really knows. I'm the one who's had to deal with the consequences my whole life."

"Then you can deal with them now too. No amount of poison is going to change what has happened to you. Refusing to deal with those emotions won't help."

"You don't know—"

"Stop saying that," he says, taking a step closer until only a few inches separate us. His chest heaves as he stares down at me. "Stop saying I don't know what you're going through, because I do. You know I've been through what you have. When my mother died, my father and I ran away and tried to start new lives instead of dealing with the sorrow we left behind in our old one. When my father died, I turned to gambling to drown out my pain, and look where that got me. Losing everything had one benefit, though. It gave me no choice but to face the pains of my past. Trust me, Astrid, grieving is better than pushing your emotions away and making a mess of your life. I've been where you are, and I've gotten to the other side. I'm still grieving everything I've lost. It hurts. I won't lie and say that it doesn't. I will continue to grieve for my father, my mother, and my estate, to honor them with the emotions they're due. Don't make me grieve for you too."

His voice is so deep, so rich with agony, that it makes my knees quaver. I twist my face into a scowl to hide the way my lower lip trembles. "You would never grieve for me. You don't even know me. Everything you see in me is just your reflection—"

"That's kelpie shit and you know it. I've *seen* you. I've seen you lower your defenses and release your stranglehold on your magic. And I know you're strong enough. So toughen up and let yourself break like the rest of us."

"It's not that simple. If you think I can control my magic..." My breathing turns too sharp, too shallow. I can't bring myself to say the rest out loud. That if what he's suggesting is true, then that would mean...

That would mean none of the worst parts of my life ever had to happen.

I never had to be targeted by a jealous girl. Never had to be shoved from a horse and injured so badly that only poison could help me recover.

I never had to make myself an enemy of the queen.

I never had to...

Had to...

Be the cause of my father's death.

I lurch to the ground as my legs give out beneath me.

"No," I say, the word coming out with a sob. "I can't believe that. I can't believe I've had control all this time. Nor can I feel this...this grief." As the words leave my mouth, I feel it. The gaping pit of sorrow that's been waiting this entire time. I feel it claw its way up my legs, my thighs, my stomach, my heart. Constricting my throat, flooding my mind. "I...can't handle this feeling."

"Too bad." Torben's tone is soft, as gentle as a caress. I can't see him through my sheen of tears, but from the sound of his voice, he must be kneeling next to me. "That feeling is part of losing someone that you love. To ignore it is to dishonor their memory. You don't get a free pass. You don't get to run away and feel nothing. You will work through it. You're strong enough, and every day you'll get stronger."

*I'm not strong*, I try to say, but my lips no longer move. My stomach churns as my heart continues to feel like it's going to burst from my ribcage. Shadows whirl past my vision, obscured by the sheen of my tears. I'm vaguely aware of falling, of sliding to the floor, of cold marble pressed to my temple. Then arms. Strong arms lifting me from the ground.

The feeling of my head resting against Torben's chest is all that keeps me from losing myself to the full weight of my emotional agony. The thud of his heartbeat against my ear is like a melody. It recalls another time, another place, another set of arms. Of my first experience of safety, when Father lifted me from the lakeshore and laid me against his apron-covered chest, soothing me with his heart's lullaby the way Torben is doing now.

But no, that memory is wrong. I couldn't have felt Father's heartbeat through his apron. He'd wrapped me in fur. Wasn't it through the fur that I felt the thudding pulse?

My mind empties again as I feel something soft beneath me. A mattress. Torben's arms are no longer around me, no longer keeping me safe. I roll onto my side, but every part of my body aches. My skin is too hot, too cold, my sweat like needles. I continue to sob, to moan, but my pain refuses to relent. How much time has passed since Torben set me down? A minute? A second? A day?

The mattress sinks next to me, followed by a creaking sound. I'm barely able to cry out in alarm when the bed shudders beneath me, as if the frame has cracked. Then I realize why. An enormous warmth presses against my back, and I know at once it's Torben in his bear form. An earthy aroma invades my senses, and I turn toward it, finding his soft pelt. My body continues to throb, and my mind continues to spin, but I manage to lift a hand and run it down Torben's hide. The bed shifts again, and the bear rolls toward me. With one enormous paw, he presses me to his warm belly. Comfort unlike any I've felt settles over me. It doesn't numb my grief, nor does it lessen the effects of the Crimson Malus leaving my body. Instead, it dances with it, puts space between the uncomfortable feelings where there was none before. Again, Torben's heartbeat thuds against my cheek, this time coming from inside the body of a bear.

It brings me back to Father's arms again, to his heartbeat and the pelt...

No, his heartbeat *had* been thudding through his apron.

Hadn't it?

But I remember a pulse on the other side of the pelt. It was just like this. It was...

My memories unravel, taking a new shape they haven't before. Where once I recalled the feeling of my father's secure arms picking me up from the shore and wrapping me in fur, I feel the fur first. Fur with a soft, pulsing heartbeat, two rounded ears, and four gentle paws. It held an earthy-yet-pleasant aroma so like the one I smell now. I remember its sudden departure, the thud of paws retreating back into the woods. I heard foot-steps after that. Human ones. Then Father's strong arms lifted me from the ground and pressed me to his chest. Against his paint-splattered apron.

I never considered my beloved first memory of my father had been tangled. It was strange enough that I recalled anything from when I was a baby. There was no reason to try and look deeper. All I knew was that my first experience of comfort involved fur and my father's arms.

But all along, those had been two distinct memories.

The fur had never been a pelt. It was an animal. A bear cub.

A baby bear who lived in Dewberry the same year I was born.

The indecipherable look on Torben's face after I told him about where I was born is starting to make sense, as is the wry grin on his lips when I said it was strange we'd never met.

*Strange indeed.*

Now the truth snaps into place.

My first memory of comfort isn't of my father.

It's of Torben.

## 24

TORBEN

I've been at Davenport Estate for three days, but only now as I stand amongst overgrown berry fields does it truly smell like home. Closing my eyes, I tilt my head back, letting the morning sun warm my face. Scents of fresh strawberries, blackberries, and blueberries, as well as several rare fae fruit varieties, fill my nostrils. I could almost pretend I'm a young boy again, standing next to my father as he takes me on a tour of our farmlands and checking in with our workers. Before Crimson Malus made him distant. Before death took him away from me.

With a heavy sigh, I open my eyes and let my momentary fantasy fall away. Grim reality takes its place. What lies around me is not the farmland of my childhood, but an unkempt expanse of brambles and thorns. Many of the berry crops may have survived being abandoned, but they're hardly what I'd call cared for.

Despite the property's neglect, I'm surprised to find every inch of the estate's land intact. When Queen Tris tempted me into our bargain, promising to return Davenport Estate into my possession in exchange for my Chariot, she'd insisted that she'd neither sold nor altered the land in any way. It sounded too good to be true. Ever since, I've thought of ways she could have evaded the truth. I was half expecting to come here and find I'd been tricked. And yet, I've surveyed the land, the fields, the cottages that once housed estate staff and farmers, and have found everything just as I left it. Aside from being overrun by weeds and ivy. And being empty of people.

Guilt snags my heart when I think about everyone who found themselves suddenly unemployed after I lost the estate. If only Queen Tris had taken proper ownership of the land and kept the estate running, then at least I could release the guilt over having upended so many lives along with my own. Even if the queen had no desire to directly run the estate, she could have sold it and allowed it to continue thriving under someone else's management. I can't fathom why she didn't. Then again, her decision to allow it to fall into abandoned disrepair could have been a calculated move from the start. She may have planned all along to use the estate to eventually lure me into some kind of bargain.

If that's the case, her plan has worked. She trapped me in a bargain, tempting me with my fondness for risky bets. When I agreed to do what she asked, I thought I was only wagering my own life, my own failure, for I was so certain my target was guilty. I thought she was just a wretched girl who'd taken a father's love for granted and murdered him in cold blood.

But I was wrong. So, so wrong.

I gambled on both of our lives. And if I lose...

I shudder, my mind filling with thoughts of Astrid. She's been in and out of feverish sleep ever since her emotional breakdown three days ago. I've done my best to keep her comfortable, cooled her temperature with cold compresses, forced her to sip water during her few lucid moments. I went to town and bought her clean blankets. Aired out the room. Swept. Dusted. Did all I could to ensure she was recovering in as clean of an environment as I could provide. It's broken my heart to see her in such a state—almost as much as witnessing my abandoned farmland has. And there lies my dilemma. Which hurts me more? Astrid or my estate?

An uncomfortable truth has plagued me the last few days, a truth I hardly dare consider too long. But no matter how I try to ignore it, the fact remains: there's only one way I get my estate back. Only one way to earn an end to my hundred-year sentence as Huntsman and reclaim my freedom as a regular citizen.

I have to bring Astrid's heart to her stepmother.

A flash of heat surges through me, a mixture of rage and repulsion. Shaking the prospect from my head, I turn away from the field and march back toward the manor.

I can't turn Astrid over to her stepmother. It was easier when I was convinced Tris was innocent. Back then, I thought all I needed to do was prove Astrid was innocent too. All I'd have to do was bring evidence to the queen pointing to the true killer and present Astrid to her stepmother hale and whole. I'd fulfill our bargain—using Tris' own wording against her by bringing Astrid, heart intact—and save Astrid's life.

But if Tris is guilty, if she's truly as sinister and calculated as I'm starting to believe she is, then I can't rely on that plan. I can't present Astrid to a queen who wants her dead. My only option is to gather enough evidence to present to the other royals on the Alpha Council. Prove Tris tried to murder her own stepdaughter and accidentally killed her husband instead. Prove she used illegal magic to compel a human girl to do her dirty work. Prove that she sent me to find her stepdaughter, all so she could murder the girl herself before anyone discovered Tris' hidden guilt. Then I'll clear Astrid's name and save her life. I may save my own too. If the Alpha Council manages to condemn Tris for her crimes before my broken bargain claims my life, they could force her to revoke our pact.

But ending our bargain ends my chance at freedom too. My chance to reclaim Davenport Estate.

I clench my jaw. As desperate as I am to get my estate back, nothing is worth more than an innocent person's life. Not just any person's life either. Astrid's.

Her life is worth a thousand times more than an estate.

My certainty is so startling, I nearly stumble over the overgrown path I traverse. Had I considered such a prospect a week ago, I might have been swayed in the opposite direction. I never imagined anything could be more important than reclaiming my inheritance. Rebuilding my father's legacy. Making up for my terrible wrongs, my reckless gamble, my great shame.

But meeting Astrid changed things. Only a little at first, but after the other night, when I climbed on the bed in my bear form and felt her small body press against my belly...it broke something inside me. Or perhaps stitched it back together.

It made me remember things I'd long since forgotten.

A rustling sound comes from my right. I halt in place and turn toward it, breathing deeply. Every hair on my body stands on end as my senses go on high alert. The manor is within sight now, but the path to it is just as overgrown as the fields. I breathe deeply, smelling several animal aromas nearby. I'd been too preoccupied with my thoughts to notice before. Another rustling comes from the other side of a tall wall of shrubs that once were waist-high hedges. With slow, careful steps, I approach the source of the sound. I spread my fingers, ready to extend them into claws at the first sign of danger, and push the bushes aside.

A small brown shape freezes at the sight of me. The scent of panic fills my nostrils, but it floods me with relief. It's a damn rabbit. The creature bolts away faster than a train. Only then do I notice the family of deer farther out in the field. At my sudden appearance, they too leap away, darting toward the woods at the edge of the field, sending up a flurry of birds, and—is that a kelpie? At the far end near the tree line, a large, dark, equine form takes off with the rest of the startled creatures. I frown, debating whether to give chase, but Queen Tris isn't known to associate with ill-reputed unseelie fae, like kelpies. And I doubt she sent rabbits or deer families to hunt me and Astrid down either.

I return to the path toward the manor, shaking my head at my own jumpiness. As far as I can tell, Astrid and I are safe here. Every day since arriving at the estate, I've searched the property, seeking any scents that don't belong, smelling for hidden magics, traps, or enchantments. Each day I've found nothing but my neglected land and the wildlife that thinks it's a wonderland of free food. There's nothing to suggest Queen Tris knows I'm here or even suspects it. I've smelled neither Marybeth's false floral aroma nor her real one. The scents I've picked up are those belonging to animals and unseelie fae.

Still, the sooner we prove Astrid's innocence, the better.

ONCE INSIDE THE MANOR, I HEAD STRAIGHT FOR MY FORMER bedroom. As I reach the top step of the staircase, a soft sound reaches my ears. Astrid's scent fills my nostrils, telling me she's awake. My pulse kicks up. Is that a whimper I hear? Is she in pain? I all but run the rest of the way up the stairs, flinging open the door as soon as I reach it.

I halt just beyond the threshold as I take in the sight before me. I'd expected to find her coated in a sheen of sweat, lips pulled into a pained grimace. That's how she's looked during every moment of wakefulness the last couple days. Instead, I find her...smiling.

Four kittens pounce around her while Mama Cat—I

remember that's what Astrid calls her—lays on the center of her chest like it's her throne. That can't possibly be comfortable for Astrid, especially as weakened as she must be right now. My first instinct is to shoo the cat away, but Astrid's wide grin has me frozen in place. Not only is it the first time she's looked anything but miserable in days, but she's let down her magic, giving me one of those rare yet breathtaking glimpses of her true face. She's paler than before with half circles of violet hanging beneath her eyes, but there's a brightness to her that wasn't there before. Perhaps not even since I met her.

Slowly, she turns her gaze to mine. My heart sinks as her face falls beneath a haze. I continue to see her smile, but it has shifted from a clear vision to a soft impression. "Torben," she says, her voice coming out raspy. "How long have I been...recovering?"

"Almost three days." I approach the bed, finding an unexpected nervousness humming through me. It sends my heart pounding in a new rhythm. I try to offer a comforting smile only to realize that's not something I normally do. So I clear my throat and take a seat at the edge of the bed. The four kittens immediately swarm around me. I absently pet them, but my eyes are locked on Astrid. "How are you feeling?"

She gives a weak shrug. "Tired. But also...good. Surprisingly so."

"How is your temperature?"

"Fine, I think."

I lift a hand toward her. "May I?" My voice holds a tenuous quality, one that makes it sound foreign to my own ears. At her nod, I lay my hand gently over her forehead. My palm buzzes at the contact, at the feel of her soft skin. Her fever has abated, leaving only the appropriate amount of warmth emanating from her flesh. That doesn't explain why I suddenly feel as if I'm being burned by the sun. Heat glows from my chest, radiating down my arms, my hands. Despite my initial test of her temperature proving favorable, I find myself moving my hand to her cheek.

Her throat bobs. "How do I feel?"

"Good." The word comes out strained. "You feel...wonderful —I mean, your fever is gone." I wrench my hand away from her. *You feel wonderful?* What the hell was that supposed to mean? I reach for the side table and retrieve a glass of water. "Are you thirsty?"

She nods and tries to sit up. The movement finally forces Mama Cat off her chest, but she winces before she can fully sit.

"Here," I say as I prop pillows behind her until her upper body is more elevated. She accepts the cup and takes a few sips before handing it back to me. I exchange it for a bowl of fresh berries I picked early this morning before I began my survey of the property. "Hungry?"

She shakes her head and settles back into the pillows. Mama Cat climbs up and plants herself next to Astrid's head while the kittens continue to pounce. Madeline claws her way up my back and settles on my shoulder like she did when Astrid made me hold the little beast. I release a chuckle and give her a few pats, then return my attention to Astrid.

"I must check in with Queen Tris soon." I extract my coin from my waistcoat pocket. It rumbles with a subtle vibration, too minor to be seen with the naked eye, but enough to alert its holder. This is what happens when I'm being summoned by whichever royal I'm currently working for. When I had my Chariot, I checked in with Tris before she needed to summon me, all so I could flaunt the object I knew she so greatly desired. Now it's been buzzing for days. I expected as much. Even if Tris truly is controlling Marybeth and knows everything that happened at the Seven Sins, she'd still need to keep up appearances by demanding an update on my mission. I pocket the coin again. "I can't put it off too much longer or she will come looking for me."

Astrid's scent flares with panic. "All right. What will we do?"

"You still need to recover," I say, giving her a pointed look. "Until I get a confession from Tris, we can't have her knowing where you are. To keep her from suspecting that we're staying here, I need to check into a hotel for one night near the palace and pay with the Alpha Council's funds. I could bring you with me and set you up in your own room at a different hotel, but I believe you'll be safer here."

"I'm comfortable here," she says, "but are you certain Tris doesn't know where we are?"

"I can't be certain, but I've scented nothing to suggest anyone has set foot on this property. There are no suspicious aromas lingering, and I've found no scent of magic to suggest she's laid enchantments that could alert her of our presence."

"I'll stay here then."

Even though I know it's safest that she doesn't come with me and risk being seen by someone who recognizes her as the runaway princess—regardless of whatever false impression they've come to know her by—I can't help but feel empty knowing she'll be alone. Far from me. "If all goes according to plan, I won't be home until tomorrow night."

"I'll be fine," she says, but I barely hear it over the word that echoes through my mind.

Home.

I called the manor *home*.

It is my home, but it feels strange having said the word to Astrid as if...as if it were her home too. Or perhaps not strange, but entirely natural. Too natural.

I shove the thought away. "I'll leave you food and water. There's a stove downstairs if you'd like warm bathwater as well."

Her lips stretch into a wide grin. "I'm not a pet, Torben," she says, her tone light with taunting. "I'll be fine. I'll probably sleep the entire time you're gone."

She's probably right, yet I ache to think of her alone here. Regardless of what I've sensed so far, there is a chance of danger. Blooming hell, what I wouldn't give to just stay with her. To ensure she's truly recovered. There's another thought that crosses my mind—that she very well might leave the manor in search of Crimson Malus.

The thought has me bristling with a protective rage.

But if that's what she chooses to do, I can't stop her. I can only hope that having the poison out of her system will be enough to keep her from endangering herself with the drug.

Besides, I have a mission to do. And I'm running out of time. In just over a week, my bargain will claim my life unless it's fulfilled or revoked.

"I should prepare to leave, then," I say, lifting Madeline off my shoulder and setting her on the bed. I start to turn away from Astrid but feel her fingers come around my wrist. Her grip is weak but it stops me nonetheless. I shift back to face her.

"Torben..." Her mouth hangs open, but no more words leave her lips.

Furrowing my brow, I edge closer. "What is it?"

Her throat bobs several times, her scent flaring with a timid quality that matches how I've felt ever since seeing her awake. "It's just...the other night, I...remembered something. But I don't know if it was real."

My chest tightens. "What do you remember?"

Panic invades her scent profile, as does the tang of embarrassment. She keeps her eyes on the ceiling as she says, "I remembered being a baby...and...and my father coming to take me from the lake after my mother rejected me. But I remember something that happened before that." She pulls her blanket up to her chin and sinks deeper into her pillows.

Her words send my heart thudding wildly. I know exactly what she's referring to. I knew it as soon as I laid next to her as a bear, for it sparked my own memories.

"It was soon after my mother died," I say, my voice coming out with a slight tremble. "In fact, it was the day Father told me we'd be shifting from our unseelie forms and moving to the city of Larklawn. Even though I understood he thought we'd be safer joining human society in our seelie forms, I was upset Father didn't want us to return to our bear forms ever again. I ached at the thought that I'd no longer be the bear cub Mother once loved. So in my rebellion, I ran from Father. At first, I thought I'd run away. Live alone and raise myself. But as I wandered Dewberry Woods alone, my anger cooled and was quickly replaced with sorrow. By the time I made it to Dewberry Lake, I knew I wasn't going to run away. I was simply grieving. Saying goodbye to my last moments as a bear. It didn't take me long to realize I wasn't alone."

Astrid finally turns her gaze to me. Her wide eyes lock on mine.

"I heard a baby's cries at first," I say. "Then I found her. A small humanlike infant alone and helpless. Like I was. That's all I saw. A baby like me, someone who felt as weak and as vulnerable as I did."

I swallow hard. Now I know why I've always seen Astrid the way I have. Because she already made an impression on me long ago. Already sparked in me a need to protect her.

She was crying when we met, so her mood dictated she form a negative impression on me and reflect back my worst qualities. At the time, the qualities I disliked most in myself were that I was small, weak, and vulnerable. That I was hurting. That I was afraid. Now that I'm older and have processed much of my grief, I hold no resentment over such qualities. It makes sense why Astrid's magic provides such a hazy reflection. The impression we formed is old, based on the simple perception of a baby bear. A version of myself that I no longer am.

"I laid next to her," I say, my voice growing heavier with emotion. "Whether it was to comfort her or me, I didn't know. It just felt like the right thing to do. Soon, she stopped crying. She fell asleep. I did too. It wasn't until I heard human footsteps that I ran away. After that, a man picked up the baby and took her away from the lake."

Astrid's eyes well with tears. One trickles down her cheek. It takes all my restraint not to brush it away with my thumb. Something soft brushes over my hand, and I realize she's still holding my wrist. She absently strokes the back of my hand with her thumb, making me suppress a shudder. Her lips tremble as she speaks. "That was me."

"It was," I whisper, my own eyes stinging with a glaze of tears. "My last memory as a bear cub was of you."

## 25

*TORBEN*

The next day, I arrive at Fairweather Palace and am immediately escorted to the throne room to await my audience with Queen Tris. Two fae guards dressed in rose gold armor lead me up to the queen's empty throne and order me to stand before the dais. I do as I'm told and wait.

And wait.

And wait.

I keep my expression as neutral as I can. Even though no one but the two guards is present, I try not to reveal that I'm at all flustered by Tris' blatant show of disregard. I already expected as much before I arrived. As soon as I realized the guards were bringing me here instead of to the queen's private study where we normally meet, I knew she meant to put me in my place. Making me wait before her empty throne is meant to be a clear reminder that she's the one with the power. She holds my bargain. My very life is in her hands. And she is not a woman to take kindly to being ignored.

I half expect to be ambushed at any moment. For Tris to

march into the room with a dozen guards, ready to silence me while she has the chance. She must know by now that Astrid and I are working together. If she's as clever as I think she is, she'll know I suspect her. That I'm gathering evidence against her. My muscles are coiled tight, my limbs ready to spring into action at the slightest sign of attack. If Tris makes any such move, that will have to be proof enough to take to the Alpha Council. The challenge, of course, would be getting out alive.

I glance around the throne room, seeking exits. It's the first time I've been here, and if I weren't so on edge, it would be a sight to behold. The room is immense with floors of polished cherrywood and walls of rose quartz. Living cherry trees climb the walls, their boughs supporting the arched ceiling in place of support beams. I squint, seeking hidden assailants among their branches, but they appear empty. They smell empty too. The only nearby scents are those of the guards. Older aromas linger, the most persistent belonging to the queen. I sift through dozens upon dozens more, noting Marybeth's profile. It's less recent than I expected her trail to be, but that doesn't mean she isn't somewhere in the palace. I continue sifting through scent trail after scent trail until one makes my heart stumble.

Astrid.

It's old. Months old. I glance straight ahead where the scent is condensed. The queen's throne takes up most of my vision. It's a towering chair, the backrest made from crystal vines that sprout bright pink flowers, its base shaped like heavy roots that climb straight from the cherrywood floor. But behind the throne are two smaller, less elaborate chairs, both carved from milky white crystal. My eyes land on the left where Astrid's old scent lingers. The two smaller thrones must have once belonged to Astrid and her father. I'm surprised the queen gave Astrid a seat in the throne room at all.

Movement catches my eye, drawing my attention to a

hidden door at the back of the room. Queen Tris emerges in her seelie form—the only body I've ever seen her in. She's a pixie in her unseelie form, but the only evidence of her alternate manifestation is the enormous pair of pink wings folded down her back. Her skin is a rich brown textured in whorls and other bark-like patterns. Her hair is composed of brambles and blossoms, piled upon her head in an elegant updo. As soon as her eyes meet mine, I lower my gaze to the ground and take a knee. I continue to hold the position as she slowly makes her way to the throne. The pink hem of her spider silk gown brushes the floor in front of me.

She lowers herself onto her seat, her wings fanning out on each side of her to augment her regal appearance, but says nothing for several long seconds. Then finally, she demands, "Rise."

I do as I'm told and straighten to my full height. The queen stares at me through slitted lids, her pale pink irises flashing with annoyance. I breathe deeply, assessing her scent. I've met with her enough times to be familiar with her baseline aroma. Right now, it holds a bitter edge, but it says nothing that isn't already written over her face. Still, I keep myself attuned to the scent. Whatever happens next might be tantamount to proving Astrid's innocence and the queen's guilt. No matter what she does or doesn't say, I'll need to assess every rise and fall of her fragrance. Smell for every hint of deception.

She waves a dismissive hand at the two guards, and they exit out the hidden door, leaving me and the queen alone.

"You have much explaining to do, Huntsman," she says, tone icy. "When we last spoke, you told me you'd found my stepdaughter and were about to finish your mission. Ever since, you've given me nothing but silence when you were supposed to give me Astrid Snow's bleeding heart. Explain."

I read her aroma, surprised when I still find nothing

beyond irritation. Nothing to suggest she knows exactly what happened since our last conversation.

"There were complications," I say, choosing my words carefully. If she's going to feign ignorance for now, then I'll play a similar hand. No need to reveal all my cards at once and let her know I'm aware of the truth.

"I can't imagine any complications too great for you to overcome. What I find unsettling is that you've checked into a hotel in Bellabrook."

*Good, she already knows I stayed at a hotel in Bellabrook last night,* I note to myself. I hardly slept a wink in the luxury suite, mostly due to worry over leaving Astrid behind, but if it kept Tris from suspecting I've been at Davenport Estate—and that Astrid is there too—then it was worth it in the end.

The queen continues. "This tells me you did not travel by Chariot and that you've left my stepdaughter in Irridae. Why?"

"Miss Snow is no longer in Irridae."

Tris clenches the arms of her throne so tightly her knuckles turn pale. "Don't tell me you've lost her trail," she says through her teeth.

"I haven't."

"Are you suggesting she's in Bellabrook?"

"I'm suggesting that my mission is still underway."

"You're being rather evasive right now, and I do not appreciate it." Her voice trembles with suppressed rage, echoed by the agitated buzz of her wings. "And you haven't answered anything regarding the Chariot. Why is that?"

Is she asking about the Chariot because she truly doesn't know? Or is she baiting me because she *does* know? There's still nothing in her scent profile to suggest she's hiding anything. Or that she even knows I suspect her. "I no longer have it."

Her wings go still, and she leans forward in her throne so fast, I almost expect her to topple onto her face. "You what?"

Her shout echoes through the empty throne room, and her

scent rises with it. Her shock and anger seem genuine, which tells me she doesn't know Marybeth has the device now. That doesn't prove Tris isn't the one controlling the girl, however. Which means it's time to provoke her into giving me the truth. "That was another complication I ran into. Marybeth."

She blinks at me a few times. "Who is Marybeth?"

I frown. "Miss Snow's lady's maid."

"What does she have to do with anything?"

I watch her carefully, my breaths slow and steady to catch every possible shift in her aroma after what I say next. "Were you not aware that Marybeth came to Irridae City?"

"No, of course I wasn't."

My body goes still. She couldn't have stated such a thing if it wasn't true. Neither she nor I can lie. And there's still no change in her aroma. No hint of deception.

She speaks again. "What is all this nonsense about?"

"When was the last time you saw Marybeth?"

"Oh, am I being interrogated now?" she says with a huff.

"Knowing the answer might help my mission."

"Over a week ago," she finally says. "The girl requested time away to go to Greenhollow."

"What's in Greenhollow?" I recognize the name of the town. It isn't far from Larklawn.

"Her family lives there." She gives a flippant flutter of her hand. "Or something like that. She claimed grief over Astrid's disappearance and said she needed time with her loved ones."

"She hasn't returned?"

"No. Are you telling me that human girl has been harboring my stepdaughter?"

It takes me a few moments to decide how to answer. I could tell her the truth—that Marybeth confessed to poisoning the king at the command of another. If Tris' only crime is believing her stepdaughter guilty of murder and wanting her swiftly punished, then sharing what I know about Marybeth could get her to cooperate. It might even convince her to revoke my bargain and turn her misplaced hatred toward the guilty party instead.

Then again, would Tris believe me if I told her? Her hatred for her stepdaughter might be so strong that suggesting I believe Astrid was framed might only enrage her. She could refuse to believe Marybeth's confession had been anything but a lie. She could accuse me of being taken in by her scheming stepdaughter and send someone else to finish my job instead. Someone worse than me.

If Tris *is* guilty and is using deception to keep from admitting any involvement with the lady's maid, then telling her how much I know would certainly do more harm than good.

I cannot show my hand until I'm certain of winning. That means I need to find Marybeth and get her to prove who she's working for. In the meantime, I must keep Tris from getting too keen on what I'm really doing.

"What I know for certain," I say, every word carefully calculated, "is that Marybeth attempted to interfere with my capture of Miss Snow. She went to great lengths to try and prevent me from succeeding at taking her."

"What a deceitful little harpy," Tris says. "If she went to Irridae, then she lied to my face. I wouldn't be surprised if she's the wretch who snuck Astrid out of the palace in the first place. I'm willing to bet they've been working together all along."

It takes all my restraint to keep my hands from curling into fists. "Is there anything else you can tell me about Marybeth? Her surname? What family she comes from?"

"No," Tris says curtly.

Her answer sends me bristling. This is the first hint she's shown in favor of her guilt. If she refuses to cooperate regarding Marybeth...

"Is there anyone in the palace who might know more about her?" I ask, then quickly add, "If Marybeth were harboring

Astrid, more information could help find her." Not exactly a lie...if that *were* the case. Thank the All of All I'm able to evade the truth with clever wording.

Tris shrugs. "Ask my steward. She might have information on her. My stepdaughter's lady's maid has never been someone to concern myself with."

"Very well," I say. "I'll speak with your steward before I depart."

"Though perhaps I should have been concerned," she says as if I hadn't spoken. "You know, I didn't want a human girl serving as Astrid's lady's maid in the first place. If I'd had my way, I would have appointed one of my nieces to the job. But Edmund insisted—" Tris' voice breaks, and her scent constricts with a grief so deep it nearly chokes me. Her wings droop.

She shakes her head, but it does nothing to diminish the note of sorrow in her scent profile. "Regardless, Huntsman, seek whatever information you need to find my stepdaughter. But first, tell me what Marybeth has to do with your Chariot."

I don't have to feign my indignation when I confess the next part. "She broke into my hotel room at the Seven Sins and stole it while it was charging under starlight."

Her eyes go steely. "You lost the Chariot to a *human girl*?"

"I have every intention of getting it back."

"Be sure that you do. If you don't, you'll fail our second bargain."

I clench my jaw. "Understood."

"I hope you do understand. Your life depends on fulfilling two bargains now. You know what will happen if you break either one. You will die, Huntsman, and I will not shed a tear for you. But if you bring me Astrid's heart, I'll end your sentence, just as I said I would. I'll even be merciful and revoke our second bargain should it prove impossible to retrieve the Chariot. That, however, is the only mercy you'll get from me. If you fail our second bargain, I'll sell Davenport Estate to the highest bidder. And I'll make sure the bid is high indeed. That way, you might earn freedom with our first bargain, but you'll never earn enough to buy back what you lost. So if I were you, I'd get on with finding that Chariot as soon as you've killed my murderous stepdaughter. You only have one week left."

"I'm aware."

"Then be gone, Huntsman." With that, she leaves the throne and returns to the hidden door she came from.

The same two guards as before enter to escort me out of the throne room. I ask them to take me to speak with the palace steward, and they silently lead the way.

My mind reels with every step I take. The meeting didn't go how I expected at all. Despite the sliver of doubt I held regarding Tris' part in her husband's murder before today, I still felt mostly convinced everything was exactly as Astrid had said —that Tris was the one who had illegally compelled Marybeth. That she'd ordered the girl to poison Astrid's pie. That she'd forced her to go to Irridae, steal my Chariot, and take Astrid back to the queen. I'd hoped to at least get a partial admission from her today, or some tangible proof to convince the Alpha Council to open an investigation against her. But our conversation led to nothing of the sort. She gave me not even the barest hint that she was involved. Could she be so skilled at deception? The only time she seemed even remotely like a cruel, calculated killer was when she made the threat regarding our bargain.

The queen is a cold woman indeed, and perhaps she is calculating. But is she guilty of killing her husband? Of compelling a human to do her bidding all to punish the girl who was her originally intended victim?

And if not...then who is?

## 26

### ASTRID

I wake to a scratchy tongue grating against my eyelid. Blinking my eyes open, I catch Grigg standing on my forehead. I lift the fluffy orange kitten from my face and cradle him to my chest. As I run my palm over his soft coat, I'm startled by how much sensation I feel in my hands. In fact, every inch of my body seems awake, humming with energy, with feeling. I breathe easier. I see clearer. My blankets feel impossibly soft. The warm glow of the setting sun streaming through the windows seems to sparkle with a beauty I've never witnessed before.

It's been like this every time I've awoken the last two days. I've cycled through sleep and wakefulness more times than I can count, but each time I open my eyes from the dregs of slumber, I feel better than ever. As if each hour that passes, each hour that grows between my last dose of Crimson Malus, peels back another layer of a stifling cloak I hadn't been aware I was wearing. This time is no different. Now I feel as if I'm thinking clearly for the first time in years.

The first few days after my emotional breakdown in the foyer were nothing like this. I hardly remember them at all. I recall agony. Grief. Nightmares. So many nightmares. And Torben. I remember Torben lying next to me in his bear form when I was at my lowest. Mopping my sweat-soaked brow with a cool cloth. Helping me drink. Eat. Adjusting my pillows. Bringing fresh blankets that didn't smell of mold.

I roll onto my side—which sends Grigg scurrying away— and pull the blankets close to my chin. They smell of fresh clean cotton, which tells me Torben either purchased them new or dug them out of some well-preserved chest. Either way, it makes me realize just how much he fussed over me while I was recovering. Not to mention that memory I untangled.

The one of him.

The one he confirmed was real.

My heart does a strange flip in my chest, the feeling so wild and foreign I fear I'm having some sort of attack. But no, it is just a normal sensation. One I suppose I was never able to feel at such magnitude under the effects of my tincture.

I turn my gaze to the bedroom door, straining my ears for any sound of Torben, any sign that he's returned from speaking with my stepmother. All I hear is silence and the purr of Mama Cat curled up at the foot of the bed. Disappointment has my stomach sinking while anxious anticipation bubbles in my chest. He said he'd be home tonight. Which means he could be back at any minute.

Panic laces through me, sending me bolting upright to assess the state of the room. I grimace at the discolored cloth hanging over the side of the ewer, the half-eaten plate of berries sitting on the nightstand, the white nightgown crumpled on the floor, stained with something that looks an awful lot like vomit. What a mess I've made. I can only imagine what I must look like. What I must *smell* like.

That's all it takes to have me springing from bed and

rushing downstairs to find the stove to heat some water. It's about time I had a bath.

∼

AN HOUR LATER, I CAN SAFELY SAY I NO LONGER SMELL LIKE someone who's been bedridden for nearly a week. I've scrubbed myself clean, soaked my hair, done all that I could with boiled water and a washbasin. I'd have preferred a full bath in one of the many dusty tubs the manor has, but I don't know how plumbing works in homes that are supposed to be unoccupied. Same goes for electricity. I haven't dared touch a single light switch in case any usage of Faerwyvae's magic-infused utilities alert someone that Davenport Estate has been breached. Instead, I used only the well, the coal stove in the kitchen, and the oil lamp Torben left for me.

Now I stand naked in my room, letting the air dry my skin in the absence of anything appropriate to use as a towel. I frantically gather every discarded piece of clothing, searching for a nightgown that isn't dirty. It seems I went through every one Torben had packed for me, and left them all smelling of sweat and bile.

I shove aside my dirty clothing and sift through the items in the suitcase instead. Most are things I recognize—my lightweight skirts and blouses that I wore day to day at the hotel— which tells me Torben must have retrieved them from my room before we left Irridae. But there are also several new items. A lace blouse, a wool skirt, a tartan day dress. Clothing better suited to the cooler climate of the Spring Court, all as close to my size as an untailored article can be. They look brand new, which is oddly touching. It was one thing for him to buy me clothes after mine were ruined during the ogre fight, but to purchase me fine things like this...

My heart does another flip in my chest.

I gently fold my clothing and tuck it back into the suitcase. I'm about to simply wrap a sheet around myself in place of a nightdress when something catches my eye at the foot of the bed. I crouch down near one of the broken legs of the bedframe —courtesy of Torben lying on the bed in his bear form—and retrieve something made from rosy pink silk. It's a robe, the inside lined with plush velvet. I blink at it, wondering where it came from, only to recall having put it on the night I tried to sneak out in search of Crimson Malus. I'd hardly given it more than a cursory glance before I wrapped it around myself and snuck downstairs. Now that I'm in a proper frame of mind, I have the good sense to acknowledge how luxurious the robe is. Guilt pinches my chest at having found it crumpled on the floor.

Gingerly, I bring the robe to my nose and give it a hesitant sniff. Thankfully, it seems it was left in a tolerable state. I don the robe, shuddering as the velvet lining caresses my naked skin. It's the softest thing I've ever felt. Or does everything have the potential to feel like this? Have I been unwittingly numbed by my tincture? I tie the belt loosely around my waist, then run my fingers through my hair, combing my damp strands as well as I can. Halfway through, I find my eyelids fluttering shut. The feel of my fingertips against my scalp is highly soothing, sending shivers down my spine. I close my eyes and continue to massage my scalp. Flashes of feverish memories dance before my eyelids—of someone else's gentle touch. I see Torben using his strong, firm hands to gently smooth my brow, my cheek. I can almost feel him running his fingertips down the column of my neck—

My eyelids fly open, and I pause, the pads of my fingers hovering over the base of my throat.

That last part wasn't a memory, it was...more like a fantasy.

Why was I imagining that? Imagining...*him*? I do recall him comforting me during my convalescence, but his touch then had been practical. Clinical. Not a sensual featherlight pressure, running along my collarbone, then back up my neck only to trail down the curve of my shoulder—

My breath catches in my throat as I find my imagination has taken over yet again and my hands have moved with it. Hands I was fantasizing were *his*. I pause, my robe askew where I've bared my shoulder. A warm heat builds low in my belly, making my breaths turn sharp. My knees tremble so hard, I drop to the bed, sitting at the edge while I struggle to catch my breath. My skin tingles everywhere, eager for touch, to be brushed against, to be explored. No matter how hard I try to keep Torben's face at bay, I find my eyes closing again, imagining him standing before me, touching me, running one hand down between my breasts while his other skates up my leg from my knee to my inner thigh—

A whoosh of sound has me jumping to my feet. I open my eyes just in time to see Torben standing frozen in the doorway, one hand on the door handle, the other clenched to the frame as if he was in the middle of charging inside. His eyes are wide, shifting from panic to...

His gaze slides to my bare shoulder, my robe now hazardously low, exposing the upper curve of my breast.

"Sorry," he rushes to say as he looks hastily away. "I—I just got home. I thought you were in trouble. Your...your scent..." He clears his throat and takes a step back, his moves so uneven he stumbles.

I straighten my gown and gather my composure. I'm surprised I'm not more embarrassed. I know I should be. He must have glimpsed the position I was in. The placement of my hands. That is, if he could see me clearly. His flustered countenance tells me he could. Come to think of it, I don't feel the low hum of my magic like I normally do. Instead, all I feel is a different hum, a wave of heat radiating through me, building at my center and rippling out in every direction. It seems Torben's unexpected interruption did nothing to calm *that* sensation. If anything, it's only grown stronger.

Perhaps it's due to the nature of my brief fantasy, but I can't take my eyes off him. I take in the copper glint of his hair where it's touched by the dim lamplight. The sensuous curve of his lips. The close-cropped bronze beard adorning his sharp jaw. I knew he was handsome before, but right now...he's beautiful. Breathtaking. I'm certain he always was. I just haven't been so keenly aware of it until now.

He gives me a formal tilt of his head. "Pardon," he says and makes another attempt to back out of the doorway.

My pulse quickens at the thought of him leaving. I take a step closer. "How did it go with my stepmother?"

He freezes yet again. His throat bobs, and he meets my eyes only briefly. "Not as well as I had hoped. But we can talk about it in the morning. I should let you rest."

"I'm fully recovered. We can talk about it now."

His gaze locks on mine again, only to dip down to my lips. It seems to take him a momentous effort to drag his eyes away from them. "No, you must still be unwell. You seem...flushed."

"Flushed?" I echo, my voice suddenly pitched higher than normal. "Perhaps I'm just a little warm."

That seems to sober him from his flustered state. "Are you feverish again? Let me feel your temperature." I'm about to tell him it isn't necessary, but before I know it, he strides straight toward me and presses the back of his hand against my forehead. I stifle a gasp. The feel of his skin on mine sends a bolt of pleasure from my head to my toes. My eyelids grow heavy, sending my lashes fluttering as I lean into his touch. He pulls back, making me stumble forward, still seeking the pressure of his hand.

"Do that again," I say before I can stop myself.

"Astrid..." There's a note of warning in his voice, but I don't know what he's warning me against.

"Please," I say, my voice nearly breathless. "Touch me again."

His chest heaves while the rest of him goes rigid. Finally, he slowly lifts his hand and places it against my cheek. His skin is warm, his touch gentle yet steady. Nothing has ever felt so good in my life. Not even my fantasy about his fingertips dancing over my skin.

"Astrid, I..." Torben's voice is strained. "I can smell your arousal."

A flash of embarrassment courses through me, but it's nothing compared to the desire building inside me. I swallow hard. "So?"

"So..." He has to clear his throat a few times before he manages to say another word. "So this is highly inappropriate."

I almost pull my head back with the weight of my indignation, but the soft feel of his palm still cupping my cheek holds me in place. "Why?"

"Because of your condition."

I scoff. "My condition? You mean feeling well and healthy for the first time in years? Do you think I'm still under the effects of my tincture?"

"What I think is that you're in a highly sensitive state." His eyes dip to my lips again, and desire flashes in his eyes.

Perhaps that's what emboldens me to say what I do next. "I am. Every inch of my body is sensitive right now. Which is why I want you to put both of your hands on me."

His jaw shifts side to side as his breaths grow sharper, shakier. "It wouldn't be appropriate. You aren't thinking clearly."

My lips curl in what I hope to be a reassuring smile. "I promise you my mind is clear. It's never been so clear." I lift my chin, angling my face toward his, and lean closer. My mouth tingles, yearning to experience what his lips feel like, taste like. Everything inside me begs to press against him. It takes all my restraint to hold back, to let him make the next move. "Torben, I want you to touch me. Not just on my cheek."

His palm quavers against my skin, his flesh so hot it's almost scalding.

I close another inch between us. My pulse races as I lift one hand and place it over the center of his chest. I pause, waiting to see if he'll back away. When he doesn't, I reach for the belt of my robe. With a tug, the tie comes loose.

Torben steps back so suddenly, I'm startled in place. "No, I can't do this. I won't take advantage of your condition."

I bark a laugh. "You keep mentioning my *condition* like I'm some frail thing." As the words leave my mouth, I recall the memory I unearthed—of him as a cub comforting me on the lakeshore. The way we met explains why I've always been confused about the qualities I reflect back to him, why the hints of vulnerability and weakness I sometimes glimpse never match up with the version of him I know. It's because I formed that first impression when he was small. When we were both weak and vulnerable.

Which means that's all I can ever be. Something fragile and in need of protection. Not a sensual woman seeking the pleasurable touch of a highly attractive man.

I've never been more incensed by my own magic than I am now.

"Is that what it is?" I say, tone cold. "You don't find me desirable because you see me as weak and small. Because I'm nothing more than a reflection to you, and that reflection is not something to take pleasure in."

"That's not it," he says, and his tone is so firm I can't help but believe it's true. Not to mention he can't lie. "I see you clearly, Astrid."

The confirmation nearly fills me with panic, but my desire

is still too strong to allow anything else to remain present for long.

"And you are desirable," he says, tone hungry. Yearning.

"Then why—"

"Because I don't want you to do something you're going to regret."

"Then trust me when I say I want this." I hold his gaze, but the longer our eyes lock, the more resolute his expression becomes. The less desire I see in his eyes. Anger heats my blood, mingling with my arousal. I don't know whether I want to hurt him or seduce him. The latter urge wins out. Slowly, I part my robe to reveal a hint of skin and run a finger down my center from my neck to my stomach. There I splay my palm, my lashes fluttering at my own touch. "Either put your hands on me or leave. This is happening with or without you."

His fingers curl into fists as his eyes lock on the palm pressed over my abdomen. I move my hand lower, delighting in the widening of his eyes, the way his body surges forward the slightest inch.

Then—before I know it—he's gone.

Gone.

The slam of the door rings in my ears.

I blink at it, frozen in place. My heart sinks with guilt. Shame. I hadn't meant to drive him away, only to...to...

Oh, no. What did I do? What had I been thinking acting so bold with him? I'd been so enraptured by my own yearning for pleasure, by my awakening attraction to him, by my unexpected fantasy of his touch, that I hadn't had the presence of mind to remind myself he doesn't feel the same. He said I was desirable, but what does that mean? He could have said it to flatter me, evading the fact that while he may be able to state I'm desirable, he can't say I'm desirable *to him*.

I cover my face in my hands and release all my embarrassment in a muffled moan. My desire shrinks until it's barely a ball of heat lingering in my belly. I take a step back, ready to sink onto the bed and possibly disappear forever.

Then the door clangs open just as loudly as it had closed.

Torben's eyes lock on mine, chest heaving. On swift feet, he strides back into the room, gathers me in his arms, and presses his lips to mine.

## 27

*ASTRID*

My desire returns in a flash, hotter than it was before. My need to be touched and caressed ignites over every inch of my skin as Torben pulls me against him. He lifts me to my toes as I wrap my arms around his neck. His mouth is hard, unyielding, and I part my lips to allow our kiss to deepen. His tongue sweeps against mine, warm and eager. I arch against him as his hands move from my back to my bottom, then under my thighs. He hoists me off my feet, and I hook my legs around his waist. A moment later, I feel the mattress press against my back. My mind takes a fleeting turn to wonder where the kittens might be, but I hope they have enough sense to leave us alone for the time being.

Then my thoughts are fully taken by Torben. By the sensations tingling over my skin, warming my core. He hovers over me, but only part of his weight presses against me. My need for touch only grows, and I know then that I want more of him. All of him. My hands wind behind his neck, tangling in his hair. I shift my body to bear more of his weight, trying to express how much of him I need. He pulls his lips from mine, and I fear he'll break away and leave again. Instead, he studies my face. He runs a finger from my temple to my cheek, then down the column of my neck. A gasp escapes my lips.

His hand moves to the collar of my robe, still open but covering most of me. With agonizingly slow movements, he parts the fabric to the side, exposing my shoulder, then my upper chest, then the full curve of my breast. His gaze pauses there, drinking me in, before trailing back to my eyes. "You're beautiful, Astrid."

My heart slams against my ribs. I've heard that before. I've been told I'm beautiful more times than I can count, but never has that phrase been meant for *me*. It's always been about another's reflection.

But right now...

My magic is dormant. I know it is, by the absence of its hum. Torben can *see* me.

And he thinks I'm beautiful.

I pull him back down to me, claiming his lips and arching my bare chest against him. I yearn to feel the warmth of his skin against mine, to explore the planes of his torso with my newly sensitive palms. Keeping my hungry lips locked on his, I let my hands trail over his silk waistcoat. He pulls back just enough to unhook the buttons and throw the article of clothing onto the floor. He wasn't wearing a tie or cravat, so his shirt comes off next. My arms encircle his waist, and I pull him against me, delighting in the flex of his muscles against my palms. I run my hand down his spine while the other comes to the front of him. But as I cup his firm length, he freezes.

He pulls back and searches my eyes. Slowly, he reaches between us and removes my hand from the front of his pants. He pins my wrist over my head and gives me a light, teasing kiss on the tip of my nose. "No, Astrid," he says, voice heavy. "Tonight I'll give you only what you need and nothing more."

I don't know what he means by that. There's one thing I do know, though. "But I want...*that*." As I drop my eyes suggestively, I'm suddenly reminded of the first time I touched him there, when I retrieved the key to our handcuffs from his underbritches. It hadn't been the right time to fully appreciate the girth hidden within his trousers, but I hadn't failed to notice it either. Now I'm desperate to explore that which I once dismissed as only faintly intriguing. How have I ever been in his presence and not felt this fiery want?

He brings his lips to the corner of my mouth and plants another soft kiss. "If you still want more tomorrow, we'll talk. Tonight is just for you."

I'm about to argue that I want tonight to be for him too, but his next kiss closes over my lips. That's all it takes to quiet all possible complaints. But it doesn't stop me from trailing my hand down the front of him...

Again, he stops my hand. I grunt my disapproval, but he grips my hips in a way that has me gasping and turns me onto my side. He presses in close behind me and brings his lips to the back of my neck. Another sound leaves my lips, but this one isn't disapproving at all. I shudder as he trails a line of fire over my shoulder. One hand snakes underneath me and cups my breast while the other parts my robe open further. His strong hands caress my side, my hip. I arch my backside into him, feeling him stiffen against me. I'm half in pleasure, half in a rage that he won't just give me all of him now. Then his fingers skate over my hip and travel to my middle, pausing just at the apex of my thighs. I wriggle, needing his hand to move, to rove deeper. He chuckles into my hair, a devious sound that has me bucking against him.

"You're so impatient," he whispers in my ear.

"Why do you think that is?" I gasp back. "I haven't felt this good in years. I haven't known it was possible to feel this good, and now that I do, I only want to feel more—"

My words break off as he finally moves his hand, sliding his fingers over the warm center of me. He draws a slow circle over the most sensitive part of me, eliciting the most euphoric pleasure I've ever felt. A moan rises from my throat. I angle my body closer to him, parting my thighs to give him greater access. He slides his fingers deeper, his touch firmer, and coaxes a building wave of release. I'm on the edge of a vast chasm of pleasure, one so deep I feel as if stars are erupting before my eyes. And all I want is more. More. I reach my hand behind me, seeking the shape I feel driving against my backside. How he can handle not joining my pleasure right now is beyond me. But—just like before—he rebuffs my attempts to return the favor.

As if to distract me from my futile seduction, his fingers move faster, plunge deeper, making it impossible to do anything but ride the rising wave that courses through me. It builds and builds. I throw out an arm to grip the pillow, the sheets, whatever I can reach, as if that could possibly anchor me. Release tunnels through me, both beautiful and violent at once. I shudder with impossible ecstasy, again and again, until I'm left limp in its wake.

My limbs feel as if they're made from water as I lie still, catching my breath for what feels like an eternity. Torben kisses my shoulder, my neck, each press of his lips tender, soothing, easing me back down from my state of bliss. When I finally manage to move my body, I turn toward him.

He meets my eyes with an uncertain look. He almost seems...shy.

In the absence of my built-up desire, I feel timid too. I've never been with anyone like this. Not with someone who could see me. I almost expect for him to pull away, or for the hum of my magic to snap back in place. Neither happens.

I lift a hand and place it against his cheek. "Torben," I whisper, searching his eyes, his face, his lips. Even now that my pleasure has been thoroughly wrung from me, I still find the same dazzling beauty I noted when he first entered the room.

His lips curl into a warm smile, made even more stunning by the shyness that continues to play over his features.

My chest opens like a blooming rose, each petal unfurling as I look into his eyes. I lift my head to his and press a soft kiss to his lips. He returns the kiss with the same tenderness. It feels different from how he first kissed me. This feels...well, I'm not sure. But with how my heart glows in my chest, it almost feels like...

I can't finish the thought. Partly because I'm tired, but also because it's equal parts thrilling and terrifying to acknowledge what I'm starting to sense. Could I have feelings for this man? This fae male who was sent to kill me, who was supposed to be my enemy? This man who every day since we met has proven to be nothing like the callous brute I first thought he was?

And if so...does he feel the same?

A sobering thought tells me this could all be in my head, that my budding feelings could be one-sided. Torben wanted to wait until tomorrow before he'd let me touch him. Why? Did he just want to make sure my mind was clear? That I truly did want him that way?

Or was he not sure he wanted *me* in that way?

Did I...seduce him? Tempt him into doing something he wouldn't normally want to do?

The prospect is almost too humiliating to bear, but I don't get a chance to dwell on it long. Torben brings his lips to mine again, claiming them with more of that tender need.

I let my anxious musings go and lose myself in the kiss, committing the warmth of his lips to memory. Just in case I never feel them again. Just in case the morning light brings an end to whatever this was. I kiss him until I'm breathless. Until I can do nothing else but curl against him and lay my head on his broad chest, lulled to sleep by the beat of his heart.

## 28

*TORBEN*

Astrid fills my senses in every way possible. Each inhale I take fills my lungs with her aroma, her baseline scent profile mingling with the tang of sweat and a new smell—something powerfully sweet that lingers in the wake of her spent passion. The soft rhythm of her breaths, slow and steady in her slumber, hums through my ears. Her skin against mine feels more like an extension of my own flesh, some missing piece I've only just found again.

I angle my head and stare down at her sleeping form. She's half sprawled over my chest, her robe strewn only over her lower half. Her cheek is pressed to my pounding heart while one arm lies across me. She's been asleep for at least half an hour, and I've hardly dared move more than an inch lest I wake her. I'm too afraid that if I do, she'll roll away from me. And I'm not ready to feel her absence.

The way her presence consumes me in this moment is something I've never experienced before. I've felt lust. Pleasure. I've thought I'd experienced love. But this...this is...

More.

Different.

Frightening.

I didn't expect to feel this way. Not after what happened with my first paramour, Miss Barrister. I'd sworn off love after I learned she'd betrayed my secrets to Frank Host. While I can't blame her for the gamble I made that lost me everything—for that is my responsibility to bear—the part she played in my demise taught me love and deception are too intertwined. My love for her made me blind to her ulterior motives. My love for my father kept me from realizing he was suffering from addiction before my very eyes. His love for my mother sent him down a tunnel of grief he was never able to free himself from.

Love has never been a virtue in my life. And ever since I lost my freedom and was conscripted into serving the Alpha Council, it hasn't been a possibility either. I have no home. No money of my own. I'm disallowed from forging permanent ties, both as terms of my punishment and for practical reasons. The primary reason being my own and others' safety. I've found myself on the receiving end of threats and attempts at revenge, all for doing as I'm told as a bounty hunter. So long as I'm the Huntsman, I'll find myself in those same dangers again and again. And any dangers posed to me would surely transfer to a lover. I promised myself I'd never put someone I cared about in such a perilous position.

Which means Astrid...

She could never be...

Not unless...

I glance back down at her, and my mind empties. My sudden agitation uncoils. A grin tugs my lips as I study her peaceful face. This is a moment I must savor. Because the truth is, this could be the last time I feel her so close to me like this. In the morning, everything could change.

THE NEXT DAY, I STAND IN THE PARLOR, WATCHING THE SUNRISE through the slats of wood crisscrossing the windows. My ears are attuned to every sound, every possible footstep, as I wait with anxious anticipation for Astrid to wake. Only then will I know her true feelings.

*Not that they matter,* I remind myself for the hundredth time this morning. We have a mission. I'm enslaved to the council. If I fail my bargain, I die. If Queen Tris revokes it, I remain enslaved for another ninety-five years. What do feelings matter when there's no future for either of us?

Despite telling myself this over and over, I can't smother the strange spark of warmth that has made its home in my heart since last night. Perhaps it was there before and I just hadn't been aware of it. In fact, I didn't acknowledge it until after I coaxed out her pleasure—when she turned to me, uttered my name, and pressed her lips to mine. The kiss held so much tenderness I thought my heart would break. And as she fell asleep on my chest, I couldn't help feeling that what we'd done hadn't been only about pleasure. It held something deeper.

Of course, those far more pleasant thoughts fled me the instant I awoke this morning. It was just before dawn, and Astrid had rolled over some time in the night and was facing away from me. The sight of her back and the inches that separated us sent a wave of panic through me. Had she startled awake and regretted what we'd done? Did she feel embarrassed? Ashamed?

My logical side reminded me that she probably shifted positions without any knowledge of my presence at all, but that didn't stop my mind from spinning. Had I done the right thing by returning to her room and giving in to my aching desire to give her what her body wanted, despite my fears that she wasn't in a stable state of mind? Was I wrong to have stayed in bed with her afterward instead of leaving?

After that, it was impossible to get back to sleep. Besides, if Astrid did regret anything, I wanted to give her the chance to process it alone before seeing me again. So I bolted out of the room as quietly and as quickly as I could, then went about my daily routine. I checked the grounds, scenting the property for any sign of spies or trespassers.

Now, every minute that ticks by feels like agony. I *need* to know she doesn't regret our night together.

And—even though I know it's stupid—I want to know if it meant something more.

Gritting my teeth, I leave the window and stalk around the parlor, in search of anything that will busy both my hands and my mind. I move about the room, straightening the sheets covering the sparse furniture, even though they're already bloody straight enough. Finally, I reach a lumpy silhouette I don't recognize. My curiosity offers a welcome respite from thinking about Astrid, so I lift the sheet. Beneath it I find a side table cluttered with a broken vase, an empty picture frame, and a dusty wooden box.

My breath catches at the sight of the last item. It's a music box, one Father used to keep on the mantle in his study. When my inspection of his study proved it to be mostly empty, I'd assumed the box had been sold after the estate was seized, along with all our other valuable items and furnishing. Now that I behold it for the first time in five years, I realize it probably wouldn't fetch a high price. While it had been one of my most favorite items in the whole house, it's hardly more than a simple carved box with chipped polish.

My throat feels tight as I lift it and turn it over. On the bottom, there's a key. I turn it a few times, then set it upright on the table. A slow tune begins to play from the box, one that fills me with the most peaceful yet painful nostalgia. Even with the song's occasional mechanical hiccup, it sounds like a symphony to my ears. Father would play it for me when I was sad, especially when I missed being a bear.

As the song nears its end, the lid slowly swivels open on its hinges. Inside, a velvet compartment lies empty, but behind it dance three tiny carved figurines—bears—swirling over a painted landscape of mountains and trees.

I blink away the sudden sting that pricks my eyes.

"Good morning." Astrid's voice startles me. I'd been so enraptured by the music box, I hadn't scented her approach.

I close the lid to the box and whirl to face her, all my anxiety returning in a flash.

She stands in the doorway, fully dressed in a skirt and blouse, holding two kittens. A hesitant smile plays over her face. My first instinct is to rush to her, pull her into an embrace, and press my lips against hers. Isn't that how one should greet a lover they shared a bed with? Perhaps shared *more* than simply a bed with?

Then I notice the way her expression shifts in and out from behind a haze. Her magic is creeping forth. Magic I've started to suspect she unwittingly uses like a shield.

Does she feel like she needs a shield with me right now?

"Good morning," I echo back, hating the nervous tremble that infuses my tone. "Did you sleep well?"

A few uncomfortable beats of silence pass. Then, "I did." Her throat bobs, and the lemon in her scent turns bitter. "And you? Did you...sleep well?"

"Yes," I rush to say. "I slept very well."

Her eyes dart from me to the divan I normally sleep on. My pulse quickens. Does she think I spent the night here and not beside her? And if so, is she upset by that? Or relieved? Her scent suggests the former might be the case, so I take a step closer. "Astrid, last night—"

"Yes, about last night." Her tone has my words stuck in my

throat. She sets both kittens down and approaches me with hesitant steps. Her aroma deepens with what I recognize as embarrassment and a hint of shame. "If I...made you...if you felt like..." She bites her lip and wrings her hands. "I'm sorry."

Her apology echoes through my mind. She's sorry. She's sorry about last night. But what about it?

She clears her throat and speaks again. "You said that if I still felt...if I still wanted to..." She shifts from foot to foot. "That we'd talk in the morning."

"And?" I can barely work the word from my throat.

"And now..." She throws her head back with clear frustration, then gives a strained chuckle. "I'm really not good at this, Torben. Last night, I...well, last night was different. It was easier to express things because of...of how I felt."

*Last night was different.*

Does that mean she no longer feels the same? That she's just too anxious to vocalize it? The smell of her rising embarrassment only further illustrates the point. Disappointment courses through me, plummeting my heart to my feet. And yet, I feel some relief too. Accepting there might be feelings between us would only complicate our situation. There's very little chance that taking things further will end well for either of us. More important is the fact that love clouds my senses. I can't have...whatever *this* is putting Astrid at risk. I'd rather be rejected than compromise my ability to focus on our mission. Proving her innocence is my top priority.

"It's all right," I say, tone formal. "We both got carried away last night. We should keep things professional from now on. It's for the best that we keep our minds on the mission." The words almost pain me to say. Even though they're technically true, they're so at conflict with my heart it almost feels like a lie.

Astrid's face falls. "Oh."

My body goes rigid. Wait, did I misread her? Fuck.

I take a step closer, eager to close the distance between us.

*Do you have feelings for me?* The question is poised on my lips, but I find myself unable to utter it. Everything I said a moment ago remains true. It is best if we keep our minds on the mission.

But still...

Before I can consider saying anything more, she grins wide. It's a false grin, one shaped behind the haze of her magic. "Yes, that's what I was going to say too."

I refuse to breathe in. Refuse to smell if she's lying.

"Let's not talk about it anymore," she says with an uneasy laugh. "Instead, tell me how things went with my stepmother."

## 29

*ASTRID*

**M**y mouth falls open. "That's *all*? Did you even try to get a confession from her?" I seize hold of my irritation like an anchor. It roots me in place as I sit at the dusty wooden table in the manor's kitchen. Torben made us tea while he relayed everything that had happened when he met with my stepmother yesterday. I'm not sure if my anger would be so vast had this conversation happened yesterday. Before passion stirred inside me and brought about the most satisfying night of my life. Before I awoke alone, my mind just as clear as it had been the night before, but with more doubts filling it. More awareness of my desire-fueled actions and possible repercussions.

It had taken all my courage to decide to tell Torben the truth. That even though I no longer felt emboldened by the reckless intensity of last night's arousal, I still wanted him. More of him. All of him. I'd paced the bedroom for nearly an hour going over everything I planned to say as soon as I saw him. I had it all memorized. But when I entered the parlor, I was all but robbed of language. I tried so hard to say what I needed to say.

In the end, it didn't matter.

He didn't want me back.

It was clear he regretted what we'd done and probably still considers me an invalid. Or a seductress. I'm not sure what's worse.

Regardless, the irritation I feel for him now is far better than the hurt of his rejection. It keeps me from staring at his firm backside as he pours another cup of tea.

Then again...

What's the harm in looking when his back is turned? I bite my lip as I take in the tight trousers that had so recently been the bane of my existence. They still are, but now for a different reason.

"Our conversation didn't go the way I thought it would," he says, then turns away from the stove. I quickly lift my eyes to his face, but that only gives me a view of his lips. Lips that danced over my neck just last night. Lips I'll never get to feel again. He brings the chipped porcelain teacup to his mouth, and I've never been so envious of an inanimate object. He meets my gaze over the rim, and something stirs in his irises. I blink several times and pour all my attention into my own cup, pretending I find the faded blue design decorating the handle very interesting.

"Still," I say, trying to keep my voice level, "you could have tried harder to bait her into a confession."

He leans against the kitchen counter. "I didn't want her to suspect I know too much. If she's the one controlling Marybeth, then she's covered all her bases and made it so she can't be traced as her accomplice. The girl hasn't even returned to the palace since leaving Irridae with my Chariot."

My annoyance grows sharper. "What do you mean *if* she's the one controlling Marybeth?"

"There's still a chance it isn't Tris. Her scent gave no indication that she was deceiving me."

I rise to my feet and grip the edge of the table. "She *was*, Huntsman. No other explanation makes sense."

He shakes his head. "That kind of thinking could be our downfall. We're running out of time. We need to explore all possibilities."

"There's no one else it could be! I thought...I thought you believed me." Panic surges through my chest. Did last night make him doubt my innocence? Damn it, he was right. We should have kept things professional between us all along. I'm such a fool. A stupid, lustful fool!

The table thumps, startling me. I stare across it to find Torben facing me, hands planted on the tabletop, his discarded teacup rattling in its saucer. His gaze is hard, intense. "I do believe you, Astrid. Do not doubt that. *Never* doubt that. I will do anything to prove your innocence."

My heart slams against my ribs as I take in the depth of his tone, the fire in his expression. It makes me feel safe. Protected. Fiercely cared for. I have the strongest urge to crawl across the table and press my mouth to his. Hook my legs around his waist. Pull him down to me until there isn't an inch of space between us. What would it feel like to have him take me right here on this table?

I shake my head to banish such thoughts. It seems last night's pleasure did nothing to cool those heated fantasies of mine. Was I always this way? Or, more accurately, did I always have the potential to be like this, if I hadn't been numbed by my tincture all the time? I sit back down to hide the way my legs tremble. "Then what do we do next?"

"Marybeth is our target now," he says, still leaning against the table. "We need to find her as soon as possible. If we can deliver her to the Alpha Council, then perhaps they can find a way to break the compulsion she's under and get a confession about who she serves."

"How do we find her?"

"Tris said she has family in Greenhollow. She may have said that to throw me off her trail, but there's a chance we could find her there."

The name of the town sends a spike of alarm through me. "She has family in Greenhollow?"

"Yes. Does that town mean anything to you?"

I give a reluctant nod. "Father and I lived there for two years."

"Did you know Marybeth during that time?"

"No. I never met her before she was appointed as my maid."

Torben lowers himself into the seat across from me, expression keen. "How did she come into service at the palace?"

"Father asked Tris to appoint a human as my lady's maid. He thought it would be good for me to have a human companion, since I was raised mostly amongst human society. I'm not certain how Tris came to select Marybeth, but the few humans who serve at the palace come from elite families."

"Which the Hardings certainly are. They're one of the wealthiest families in the Spring Court."

My entire body goes cold. "What does Marybeth have to do with the Hardings?"

He furrows his brow. "Harding is her surname. Did you not know?"

I give a stiff shake of my head. "She never told me her surname. When we first met, she insisted on going by her first name only, like most fae do. How do *you* know it?"

"After I finished speaking with Tris yesterday, I looked at Marybeth's file. Her name is Marybeth Harding, daughter of Clayton and Trisha Harding. Her parents live in Newton's Crest. Her uncle, however, is Barton Harding, who lives in—"

"Greenhollow," I finish for him as my stomach ties itself

into knots.

"Which is where Tris stated Marybeth had asked to take leave to. It could be a clue or it could be an intentional diversion from the girl's true location, but I think it's worth investigating. Even more so if the Hardings hold any significance to you." When I say nothing, he adds, "Do they?"

All I can manage is a nod.

"Do you happen to have any enemies in that family? Anyone who might wish you harm?" From his careful tone, he seems to already suspect my answer.

I swallow hard. "Yes."

"Who?"

"Danielle Harding." The name grates like sandpaper against my tongue. "Barton Harding's daughter."

Torben watches me for a few moments. When he speaks, his voice is soft. "How did Danielle Harding become someone you consider an enemy?"

"How do you think?" I say, my tone flat. "Because of my magic."

"Will you tell me about it?"

I absently rub my ribs, feeling the ghost of a pain long since healed. Everything in me begs to stay silent. I don't want to talk about Danielle Harding. I can hardly stand to think about her.

But if Barton Harding is Marybeth's uncle...then Danielle is her cousin.

Marybeth has been related to my greatest nemesis—aside from the queen, of course—this entire time. She never spoke a word of it. Never hinted at being related to the Hardings. In fact, she rarely spoke about her past or her family at all. Only now does her insistence to go by her first name seem suspicious. If she knew of my history with the Hardings, then she might have hidden her familial ties on purpose. But was it out of shame? Fear that I'd hold the relationship against her? Or was it due to something far more sinister?

My stomach churns. I take a hasty sip of tea but it does nothing to settle my nausea. As I set my cup back down, it rattles against the saucer courtesy of my shaking hands.

I take a deep breath. "I can't tell you about Danielle Harding without first telling you about Lady Christine."

"Who's Lady Christine?"

"The first person I dared to share my secret with," I say. "Before we lived in Greenhollow, we lived in Kettings for a year. Lady Christine was Father's patroness there and introduced him to a plethora of elite clientele. I was thirteen then, and Father thought I should stop spending so much time using my magic to aid his paintings and start learning to be a lady. So he left me with Lady Christine during his painting sessions. I was to learn etiquette from her. At first, I hated it. Hated her. But soon I developed a fondness for the old widow. Enough that I shared the truth of my magic with her."

I take another sip of tea, but I hardly taste it. "I was surprised when she reacted so favorably to hearing about my powers. She was amused by my strange gift and soon made a game of it. She'd invite guests for tea. Guests whom she was eager to learn more about, especially those embroiled in scandal or who were the source of the latest gossip. Depending on what she wanted to learn about her guests, she'd have me shift my mood to make either a positive or negative impression. I was so pleased by Lady Christine's attention that I dutifully went along with it. But she began to change. She grew paranoid that I'd tell others about her secret, about our game, meanwhile growing resentful over the fact that she couldn't see my true face but I could see hers. She hated that I knew her best qualities—that she was haughty, self-assured, and ruthless. It enraged her to know everything she saw in me was only a reflection of the best in her. I suppose she found her reflection lacking. After a while, she refused my visits. Then she withdrew her support of my father entirely. Rumors spread about us, and Father lost most of his clientele."

Torben's eyes turn down at the corners. "Is that why you don't like telling others the truth about your magic? Because of what happened with Lady Christine?"

I nod. The pain of seeing someone I cared for and respected begin to look down on me with such disdain is still palpable, even after all this time. "After that, I vowed not to tell anyone about my magic again. The next time I broke my own rule was with Marybeth."

"How did she react?"

My chest tightens. "She accepted me. At least, I thought she did."

Torben taps his fingers against the tabletop, brows knitting together. "What does Lady Christine have to do with Danielle Harding?"

My body goes rigid. I suppose it's time to tell him the rest.

"After our falling out with Lady Christine, we moved to Greenhollow, where Father secured the patronage of Barton Harding. Mr. Harding was so taken by Father's talent that he treated him like more than just an artist. He treated him like a friend. Father once again wanted me to integrate with gentle society and encouraged me to befriend Danielle Harding, his patron's daughter. Unfortunately, we'd already met." I shift uncomfortably in my seat. "I didn't recognize her at first, but Danielle had once come to tea at Lady Christine's with her aunt."

"Was this aunt Marybeth's mother?"

I shake my head. "No, this was a Mrs. Tomlinson, Danielle's aunt on her mother's side."

Torben nods for me to continue my story.

I lift my teacup just to keep my hands busy. "I met Danielle on a visit where Lady Christine had instructed me to form a negative impression and learn our guest's least favorable qualities. Mrs. Tomlinson had been Lady Christine's target, not Danielle. Regardless, Danielle's opinion of me was solidified during that visit, and there was nothing I could do to change it thereafter. Even though our fathers encouraged us to develop an acquaintance, she only saw me as lustful and scheming. After two years of our forced friendship, she convinced herself I intended to steal her betrothed."

"What happened next?" When I don't immediately answer, he extends his hand across the table, as if he wants to reach for me. He halts halfway, then swiftly snatches it back to drum his fingers against the dusty wood surface instead. I try not to stare too long at those fluttering digits. Ones I now know are capable of far more useful feats than tapping out a beat on a table—

Blushing, I tear my eyes away from his hand. "Well, many small things happened next that made her my enemy, but I suppose the most significant is how it ended." My stomach churns again. I nibble my lip for several moments before I manage to say the rest. "I was invited riding one day. Danielle and I were accompanied by two other girls, but at a nod from Danielle, they left us alone. She confronted me about having stolen her betrothed's attention. Nothing of the sort had happened, but she was convinced I'd turned his head and that he was going to call off their betrothal for me. I tried to tell her it wasn't true. Tried to remind her I was only fifteen and far from being marriage minded, much less interested in a covert affair. She flew into a rage and forced her horse to sidle into mine. When she got close enough, she shoved me. I lost my seat and fell off my horse. The animal was so startled that it...that it..."

I close my eyes, remembering everything like it was yesterday. The agonizing crunch of hooves against my ribs. The searing pain that radiated through my body as both my legs were shattered.

Torben's voice cuts through the memory. "That's how you

were injured."

"Yes. The horse trampled me. I lost consciousness, but when I woke, I discovered my injury had caused a scandal. Danielle tried to profess that I'd fallen on my own. But as fate would have it, her betrothed had witnessed the entire fight from a distance. He saw her shove me. Shortly after, he called off their engagement. Father and I quickly relocated from Greenhollow to Tulias, the fae city where I was treated by the healer who helped me fully recover."

"I'm so sorry, Astrid," Torben says. I meet his eyes across the table and find them brimming with sincerity. Concern. Pain.

With a shrug, I say, "It's in the past."

"It might not be."

"What do you mean?"

He rubs his jaw. "Let me ask you this. Do the Hardings have anyone with fae blood in their family?"

"Why does that matter?" I ask, but I know the answer before he says a word. "You think one of the Hardings is controlling Marybeth?"

"It's possible, but only if any of them have fae blood. There needs to be at least some fae blood involved for compulsion to work."

I want to argue that it isn't possible at all. That Danielle already got her revenge against me. That she has no reason to hurt me further. That the culprit *has* to be my stepmother.

But I can say no such thing. Not with the chilling dread that sinks my stomach. Blooming hell. What if I was wrong all along?

I bite the inside of my cheek before answering. "The Hardings have two people with fae blood in the family."

"Who?"

"Sandy Harding is full fae."

"Danielle Harding's mother," Torben says.

I nod. "Which makes Danielle half fae."

## 30

*ASTRID*

Torben rises from the table in a rush. "I need to get to Greenhollow at once. Is Danielle Harding still unwed? Does she remain at the Hardings' manor?"

"I don't know," I say, getting up from the table with far less haste. Not because our situation isn't urgent, but because I'm still struggling to process the idea that someone other than Tris could be guilty of controlling Marybeth. I haven't seen Danielle Harding in four years. The scandal happened right before we moved to Tulias, which was where we lived when my father first became the queen's prized artisan. Could Danielle have held a grudge that long? Would she have gone so far as to make her cousin try and poison me?

I remember everything Marybeth said and try to reconcile it with this new possibility.

"I'll be back tonight." Torben's voice echoes from somewhere down the hall.

I stare at the empty kitchen doorway, realizing he's already left. I propel my feet after him, jogging to catch up. When I manage to find him, he's in the parlor, shrugging on his coat. I pin him with a glare. "What do you mean you'll be back tonight?"

"I'm leaving for Greenhollow at once. I'll try and speak with Barton Harding—perhaps his wife and daughter as well—and see if I can learn anything more. Marybeth might even be there. If she is, I'll be able to smell her. If she so much as tries to mask her scent with a potent floral aroma, I'll smell that too and know it's her."

I put my hands on my hips. "I missed the part where you decided to go without me."

He pauses in the middle of straightening his coat collar. His eyes lock on mine, making my breath catch in my throat. "It isn't safe for you to come."

"Well, I'm not staying here."

"Yes, you are. The Hardings know you. If Danielle recognized you after a brief meeting for tea at Lady Christine's, then her family will recognize you after everything that happened. From what you've told me, you can't change what others see once an impression has been formed."

"That's true, but—"

"And they know you as Astrid Snow, correct?"

"Yes, but...I can't just sit here and do nothing."

Torben finishes straightening his coat, then strides over to me. He stops a mere foot away. "That's exactly what you'll do. Even if the Hardings have nothing to do with your father's murder, we can't have any trail leading to your name or location."

My mouth falls open, but it takes several moments before I can summon an argument. "Huntsman, didn't our agreement state we'd investigate together? You could learn information that only means something to me. Remember?"

"I'll share everything I've learned afterward," he says. He holds my eyes for another beat, his gaze so intense it seems to steal all the air from the room. Then he brushes past me and into the foyer.

I follow hard on his heels. "Leaving me here when I was still recovering was one thing. I would have hindered more than helped. This time I really can help. I *need* to help."

He marches straight for the front door. "You can help by staying safe."

"Torben, please don't leave me here."

He must hear the desperation in my tone. Or smell it, perhaps. He pauses with his hand on the door handle, then slowly turns to face me.

I take my chance and close the distance between us. "Please let me help. This is my father's murder we're dealing with. Whatever happens to me doesn't matter—"

"It *does* matter." Torben's tone is sharp, icy. "I'm doing this for you."

I don't know how to take that. How to take the glimpses of fervent protectiveness I've seen all day. I try to remind myself it's simply because of my magic, because of that first impression I formed on him when I was just a baby. *He sees me as weak and vulnerable, remember?* But after what happened between us last night, it's hard to feel like that's the full truth.

Torben releases a heavy sigh and runs a hand down his face. "Fine," he says, the word almost a growl. "There's only one way I'll take you with me, and that is if you can control your magic and show your true face."

My eyes go wide. "What? Why?"

"Based on my experience with you, the absence of your magic removes the impressions you form as well. That means anyone who knows you only by their reflected perception won't recognize your true face. Keeping your magic at bay is the only way the Hardings won't see you as their version of Astrid Snow and spread word that the lost princess paid them a visit. But if you come with me, I can't go as the Huntsman. It will be too suspicious if I'm rumored to have been investigating with a female companion. If we go together, we'll need a ruse, and you'll need to do the lying for both of us."

I bite my lip, torn between my need to do whatever it takes to go with him and my stubborn desire to keep from admitting he's right about my magic. While I've come to accept the dangers of Crimson Malus and the fact that I can't rely on it to influence my mood, it still makes me sick to consider I have any sort of control over my magic. That I've had it all along. If I accept as much, then I accept responsibility for what Danielle did to me. For Lady Christine turning her back on me. For how Queen Tris has treated me.

And—ultimately—for my father's death.

My heart plummets, sending a wave of grief crashing through me. It threatens to pull me down, to send me right back to the foyer floor like it did just days ago. My fingers flinch toward my skirt pocket, but I already know my tincture isn't there. That relief is nowhere to be found. All I can do is feel it. Feel everything.

I close my eyes and take a trembling breath. Sorrow continues to writhe through me, digging its claws into my heart, clenching my lungs. I can't stop fidgeting, can't stop wishing I had my tincture. Even so, I remind myself I don't need it.

I don't.

I've felt this grief and survived. I'll survive again.

Strong hands frame my shoulders. My muscles uncoil at the feel of Torben's touch. At the earthy, woodsy scent of him. At his solid nearness. "Astrid," he says my name like a caress.

I open my eyes to find him watching me with concern. Holding his gaze, I breathe deeply, slowly. Until little by little, my sorrow drains from my heart, my lungs, my soul. I still feel it lingering at the edges of my awareness, but it's something that's always there. Something that might never leave. It's where my father's memory resides. But I feel stronger in its wake. Or perhaps it's Torben's touch that's making me feel that way.

Whatever the case, I grab hold of my strength and lift my chin with defiance. "I'll control it then."

He blinks a few times before his brows knit together. "What are you—"

"You said I could go with you if I control my magic. I'll do it."

Gently, he releases my shoulders and takes a step back, his expression turning steely. "Prove it."

Indignation bristles through me. "You're the one who thinks I can do it. You're the one who's seen my true face and insisted I have the ability to control my magic."

"And yet, you've been using said magic nearly the entire morning."

I open my mouth to argue, but he's right. I hadn't been aware of it until now, but I feel the hum of my magic dancing through my body, over my skin. It must have ignited without me realizing it. Probably during the conversation regarding our...relationship.

I clench my jaw, hating how powerless I feel with my magic. But if I want to convince Torben to let me come speak with the Hardings, I need to show him I'm the opposite of powerless.

*I've done it before*, I remind myself. I may not have been aware, but I have kept my magic at bay.

With a deep breath, I try to recall any instances where I didn't feel my powers humming around me. I certainly didn't last night when I was distracted by my own arousal. And I suppose I don't feel it when I'm alone. Or when I'm with the kittens. What is it about those moments that diminishes my ever-present magic?

I feel safe, I suppose.

Keeping that feeling in mind, I try to shove my magic away. But it seems the more I shove, the stronger the hum grows. I bite back a frustrated groan and try again. This time I don't pay attention to my magic at all. Instead, I turn myself over to safety and comfort. Torben's strong touch comes to mind, so I bring myself back to a few moments ago when his hands were on my shoulders.

Somehow, he's seen my true face more than anyone. Aside from Father, of course. With Torben, it's been natural. Accidental, perhaps. I've shown him the real me with no conscious effort on my part.

Like when he kissed me last night. When he held me in his arms.

The memories are like a soothing balm that make me feel as if I'm truly living them all over again. I feel the hum of my magic begin to quiet, shrink, so I lean into those memories more. The reminder of this morning's rejection threatens to shake my attention, but I refuse to dwell on it. Refuse to focus on anything but peace. Safety. Comfort. Pleasure.

I don't know how long I stand there, whether it's seconds, minutes, or hours, but soon I feel the hum of my magic dissipate.

Once I know it's fully gone, I open my eyes and meet Torben's gaze. A thrill runs through me as I find his eyes on my lips. I slowly tilt my head and don a careful smile, each move incremental as if the wrong breath could send my magic surging back. "See? I did it."

He studies my face, expression suddenly soft. "This will be dangerous," he says, voice strained. "Just because you've managed to control it now doesn't mean you won't slip up around the Hardings. You must understand the repercussions that could have."

My pulse quickens, partly because I know he's right, but also because he sounds like he's truly considering allowing me to come. I keep my breathing slow and steady, focusing on the absence of my magic. "I know it will be dangerous, but I need to do this. Please, Torben. Let me try."

He runs a hand over his beard, expression turning to steel, and releases a heavy sigh. "Fine. Don't make me regret bringing you."

## 31

*ASTRID*

I t feels strange being back in Greenhollow. I watch the familiar streets go by from my window in the small horse-drawn coach. We had to walk from Davenport Estate to downtown Larklawn on foot to procure the cab. Since Davenport is located in the countryside just outside the city, it was quite the walk. I expected Larklawn to hold some element of nostalgia when we arrived, considering it's where I spent the first few years of my life with Father, but it didn't. Turns out, I remember very little from my time there. Entering Greenhollow, on the other hand, brought memories back in an instant. Memories of attending dinners and luncheons with the Hardings. Memories of enduring Danielle's constant scorn.

Memories of how everything went so terribly wrong.

I feel the hum of my magic begin to return. Before it can fully snap into place, I reach inside my pocket until my fingers meet something soft buried at the bottom. Before we left the manor, Torben handed me a long strip of red velvet—a hair ribbon—and mumbled something about having bought it for me while I was recovering because he thought I'd find the texture pleasing. He was right. Even through my thin lace gloves, the feel of the soft fabric immediately sets my nerves at ease and helps me breathe my magic away. Thank the All of All it does. I know he's using the cab ride as a test of sorts, giving me the chance to practice my fledgling mastery over my magic. If I slip up or lose control completely between now and when we arrive at the Hardings, he'll surely make me wait in the cab.

I hazard a glance at Torben beside me. Our cab is a two-seater, which places us so close that the hem of my skirt brushes his legs. He stares out the window with a blank expression, posture tense. I can tell he's nervous about our meeting, but whether he's more anxious about what our visit will uncover or that he agreed to let me come along, I know not.

I return my attention to my window. Our cab has reached the end of town where the smaller homes give way to large manors and sprawling estates. My heart thuds faster and faster the closer we get to the Hardings' residence. Part of me hopes no one will be there to receive us, Danielle in particular, but that's a ridiculous notion. Even though I dread the thought of seeing Danielle again, if she's responsible for my father's death, we need to know about it. The sooner we solve his murder and prove my innocence, the better. It doesn't matter how uncomfortable it is for me. I need to do this. For Father.

The coach turns down a long drive flanked by immaculate shrubs. My heart leaps into my throat. We're here.

"Are you all right?"

I jump at the sound of Torben's voice but turn the sudden movement into a feigned attempt at smoothing my skirts. "Yes, I'm fine."

He shakes his head. "At least you're practiced at the lying part for today's scheme. Are you sure you can do this? You remember everything we talked about?"

I nod, a jagged motion. "Stay calm. Keep my magic at bay."

Torben releases a resigned sigh, then hands me something. It's his special coin. "You must do all the talking that involves a lie, but keep as close to the truth as you can. And be sure to show them this."

I take the coin from him and examine it up close. It's about half the size of my palm and bears an elegant *AC* on both sides. "This won't give you away? That you're the Huntsman?"

"No. It only shows that I'm working directly under the Alpha Council and am to be given any accommodations requested without question. Some know me by appearance, obviously, especially those I've worked with before. But a human family, even one with a pureblood fae matriarch, won't know me on sight. Especially if you manage our ruse well."

I slip the coin into the pocket of my wool coat next to my velvet ribbon. "Show them the coin. Do all the lying. Keep our ruse close to the truth. I can do that." Does he hear the note of panic in my voice? My magic threatens to ignite again, so I run my fingers over my ribbon.

*I can do this*, I tell myself. *This is just like one of my matchmaking investigations.*

The cab rolls to a stop before the Hardings' manor. My heart rages against my ribs.

*Just like matchmaking*, I repeat in my mind.

Except this time, I have to use my real face.

OUR RUSE GETS US THROUGH THE FRONT DOOR AND INTO THE parlor, courtesy of the maid who received us. Torben and I sit silently on a floral-patterned couch awaiting our hostess. According to the maid, we'll be meeting with Sandy Harding. Barton is out on business. It was almost too good to be true, for meeting with Sandy instead of Barton just might be in our favor. Since Mrs. Harding is full fae, she won't be able to lie.

Soon the parlor door opens to reveal a familiar female. We rise to our feet as Sandy Harding strolls into the room to greet us. She's a tall woman with curly brown hair assembled in an updo that reveals the tips of her pointed ears. That's the only clue that she's fae. I never learned what her unseelie form is, or what kind of elemental or animal affinity she favors, and there's nothing about her seelie form to suggest what it might be. She has no horns, no scales, no wings. No unique color of hair or skin. Her dress is elegant yet austere, its style the epitome of human modesty.

She meets my eyes, and the first test of my control begins. Will she recognize me? Can I maintain a strong enough hold on my magic to keep it from snapping into place? Eye contact is normally the trigger that raises my magic from a hum to a roar and ignites the magical impression, and as I lock eyes with our hostess, I feel my magic's pull. It lashes against its bonds like a tethered animal. The way my pulse races makes me feel as if I stand before a threat. But it's only eye contact. Not a true danger. Not a growl or a baring of teeth.

Have I always felt this way when I meet another's eyes?

I shake the question from my mind and take a deep, steady breath. Finally, Mrs. Harding shifts her gaze from me to Torben. Not an ounce of recognition flashes in her eyes.

I did it. Blooming hell, I really did it.

"How can I help you?" Sandy asks, tone uncertain. "My maid says you're here on an investigation."

Donning a polite smile, I say, "Yes, Mrs. Harding. I appreciate you receiving our visit unannounced. I'm Detective White and this is my partner, Detective Bjorn."

Her gaze shifts between us. "What is this about?"

With trembling hands, I extract Torben's coin from my pocket and flash it before her.

Mrs. Harding's eyes go wide before snapping back to mine. "You're with the Alpha Council?"

I return the coin to my pocket and deliver my next lines. Lines I rehearsed a thousand times in the cab. "Yes, and we're working on a case regarding a missing princess. Our case requires much discretion, so I'll need your binding promise that the topic of our visit today remains secret."

Her lips pull into a frown. "Should we wait for my hus—"

"Our matter is urgent," Torben interrupts, "and I do insist you cooperate."

Sandy purses her lips, then gives a resigned nod. "Very well. I promise to keep our conversation a secret."

Her promise leaves some room for deception, but I don't want to push her too far. At least we've covered our bases and lowered the chances that she'll turn our visit into gossip.

She gestures toward the couch for Torben and I to return to our seats. Meanwhile, she claims a chair across the tea table. I note the way she weaves her fingers in her lap. Is she just unsettled by our unexpected visit? Or does she suspect why we're here? "How may I assist your investigation?"

Torben asks the first question. "Have you ever been acquainted with Miss Astrid Snow?"

"Astrid Snow?" Sandy echoes, pulling her head back in surprise. Then realization seems to dawn. It quickly shifts to sympathy. "Oh. You said you were looking for a missing princess. I heard about Edmund Snow's death, as well as rumors that Miss Snow had run away."

"Will you answer the question, Mrs. Harding?" Torben says. I have to fight the urge not to elbow him in the side for his brusque tone.

"Apologies," Sandy rushes to say. "Yes, I have been acquainted with Miss Snow. She and her father were our dear friends a few years back."

"Were?" Torben echoes. "Did your friendship come to an end?"

Sandy waves a dismissive hand. "We didn't keep in touch after they moved from Greenhollow."

I narrow my eyes. That was a clever way to use the truth to avoid mentioning what happened between me and her daughter.

Torben must realize it too, and for a moment I fear he might comment on it. Instead, he moves on to our most pressing topic. "Marybeth Harding is your niece, correct?"

Sandy blinks a few times before answering. "She is."

"Were you aware that Miss Harding was Miss Snow's lady's maid at Fairweather Palace?"

"I was."

"When was the last time you saw her? Miss Harding, that is?"

Sandy stiffens. "What does my niece have to do with anything?"

When Torben doesn't answer right away, I realize it's because he can't. Not if we want to keep the truth to ourselves.

Which means it's my turn to deliver another almost-true lie. "Our intel tells us the two girls were close," I say. "We think Miss Harding might have information that could lead us to finding Miss Snow."

Mrs. Harding's eyes dart from me to Torben. "Then shouldn't you ask my niece directly?"

"We have," I say, "but as you can imagine she has been very distraught following the disappearance of her dear friend. We are reaching out to Miss Harding's closest family to see if she's said anything to anyone that could aid our investigation."

Her posture eases a little. "Well, I haven't seen or spoken to Marybeth since she took the position at the palace."

I assess her words for deception. "What about other correspondences? Letters?"

"No, we haven't corresponded by way of letter either."

While her answers have left some room for interpretation, it seems unlikely she's the one controlling Marybeth. Which leaves us one more suspect in the household.

Torben must come to the same conclusion I do. "May we speak with your daughter?"

She brings a hand to her chest, as if the question offends her. "My daughter?"

"She was friends with Miss Snow once, was she not?" Torben asks.

"Yes, but...but she won't know anything about the princess' whereabouts, I assure you."

"We'd like to speak with her directly, Mrs. Harding," I say, ignoring the way my stomach turns at the prospect.

Sandy shifts anxiously in her seat. "My daughter is not accepting visitors right now."

"I'll remind you we aren't casual callers," Torben says, tone cold. "Once again, I insist you cooperate. Our matter is timely."

A panicked look twists her face, but she says nothing.

Torben leans forward in his seat. "Mrs. Harding, are you hiding something from us?"

She averts her gaze, worrying her lip between her teeth.

"Mrs. Harding," Torben repeats, voice brimming with warning.

"All right," she bites out. "I'll take you to speak with Danielle. But..." She releases a trembling sigh. "I beg of you to respect my family's privacy. I know I have no right to extract a binding promise from agents of the Alpha Council, but please take nothing but what pertains to your case with you when you leave. My family...we will not tolerate rumors." She attempts to hold Torben's gaze but only manages to pale beneath his hard stare.

I try not to read too much into the terror in her eyes, try not to give it more meaning than it currently deserves. But try as I might, I can't help but wonder if we're moments away from unraveling everything.

I swallow down my tangle of emotions—fear mixed with dread and eager anticipation—and don what I hope is a reassuring grin. "I assure you, Mrs. Harding, we will act with tact and discretion. Once we leave here, we will share only what is essential to our case."

Sandy's lip quivers, but she nods. With stiff movements, she leaves her chair and motions for us to follow. She leads us out of the parlor and up a flight of stairs. I recognize these stairs, these halls. Not much has changed about the manor since I was last a guest here. That isn't at all comforting considering this is where I first regained consciousness after my accident. My magic rages at the edges of my consciousness, begging to return to its rightful place. Sweat beads at my brow with the effort it takes not to give in.

Sandy brings us to a wing of the manor far from the main part of the house. We stop before a door where a human maid stands in attendance.

"Danielle has visitors," Sandy says to the woman.

The maid gives us wide-eyed looks. "Oh, I don't think Miss Harding is—"

"They insist," Sandy says, her tone bristling with indignation. Not at her maid's impertinence...but ours.

"Very well," the maid says and bobs a curtsy. With trembling hands, she opens the door. Sandy rushes inside. Torben and I exchange a glance before following behind her.

We enter what appears to be a bedroom, one so sparse and drab it stands in stark contrast with the rest of the elegant manor. Here there are no gilded paintings, no polished marble floors. Instead, the wallpaper is peeling, the few furnishings are old and out of style, and the rugs are frayed and muted. Along the back wall are several large windows, but the curtains have been drawn shut save for one at the far end of the room. There sits a lone figure in a wicker chair, head bowed over a book in her lap, facing away from us.

"Danielle," Sandy says, "these detectives have come to ask you a few questions about Princess Astrid."

The figure doesn't move.

Sandy takes a few steps closer. "Danielle, did you hear—"

The girl bolts out of her chair and whirls to face us. My breath catches in my throat as I lay eyes on the woman who was once nearly the death of me. "Yes, I heard, Mother," she says with a sneer, then slams her book onto the seat of her chair. "Someone's here to talk to me about that lying harlot, Astrid Snow."

## 32

*ASTRID*

**D**anielle Harding looks nothing like the beautiful socialite I used to know. Her face is gaunt, her frame thin. Instead of the stunning gowns in bold patterns she once favored, she's outfitted in a simple gray dress. Her brown hair trails down her back in a thin braid, free from combs, bows, or dainty hats. I'm not sure what I expected to see when I encountered her, but it wasn't this.

My knees begin to tremble, and my magic surges against the thin walls of my control. I nearly give in, but something brushes against my fingers, distracting me. With a start, I glance down to find Torben's hand sliding into mine. He gives my palm a squeeze before letting go. That momentary pressure manages to steady me.

Keeping my composure as collected as I can, I tuck my hand into my pocket and run my fingers over my velvet ribbon, focusing on the soft texture through my lace gloves.

Danielle's gaze slides from her mother to me and Torben. I hold my breath, begging my magic to stay away as her eyes sweep over me. When no sign of recognition shows on her face, I let out a shaky exhale.

*I can do this. It worked on Sandy. It will work on Danielle.*

Danielle folds her arms over her chest. "So, is she dead yet? Did my former friend follow her father into the otherlife?"

"Danielle!" Sandy barks. "Don't say such rotten things! Astrid Snow is a princess."

She scoffs. "*Princess.* More like filthy scheming whore."

"Dan—"

"It's all right," I say, doing my best to keep my voice level. "Her personal opinion of Miss Snow will not factor into our investigation. We only wish to ask her a few questions."

Sandy turns to us with an apologetic look. "My daughter is unwell, as you can see. She has been for some years now."

"What's the matter with her, if you don't mind me inquiring?" Torben asks.

Sandy wrings her hands. "Well, you see...she..."

"Oh, did you not tell them, Mother?" Danielle's voice rings with feigned innocence. It's a familiar tone. One she used against me more times than I care to recall. "You didn't tell them that I'm the family's great shame? That I'm...how does the good doctor put it...*unhinged*?"

"That's enough," Sandy snaps at the girl, then turns a false smile to us. "You recall what I asked of you in the parlor? That you will take nothing from this conversation but what you deem relevant to your case?"

"We gave you our assurances," Torben says. "Now, if you will, please allow us some privacy to speak with your daughter."

Sandy looks as if she wants to argue, but she gives us a begrudging nod. "Behave," she mutters at her daughter, then exits the room.

My pulse races as I extend my hand toward a pair of chairs next to a meager hearth fire. "Shall we sit?"

Danielle says nothing, only stares at us with a haughty expression. That, it seems, hasn't changed.

Torben's jaw shifts side to side, his patience clearly wearing thin. "Miss Harding," he says, "when was the last time you saw or spoke to your cousin Marybeth?"

Danielle quirks a brow. "Marybeth? I thought this conversation was about Astrid Snow."

"It is, in a way," Torben says. "Marybeth Harding was Miss Snow's lady's maid. The two were friendly. Were you aware of this?"

She huffs a dark laugh. "That my cousin is a traitorous wretch? Yes, I'm aware."

"Why do you call her that?"

"Because she betrayed me."

"In what way?"

Danielle turns away from us and wanders over to her window. Silence falls over the room as we wait for her to speak again. In the absence of sound, my rapid heartbeat fills my ears. Several moments pass. When it doesn't appear that she'll speak again, Torben takes a few steps closer.

"Miss Harding," he says, "I insist you answer our questions. When did you last see or speak to Marybeth Harding? And by speak to, I mean all forms of correspondence, whether in person or by letter."

Danielle scowls at the window, her hands clenched tight around the edge of the sill.

I swallow hard and take a step forward. "Miss Harding—"

She whirls to face us. "Two years ago." She says it with such fury it sends a chill down my spine. "The last time I had any communication with my insipid cousin was two years ago when she wrote me a letter insisting Astrid Snow is—to use Marybeth's words—*a kind and wonderful person*."

"You didn't share the same opinion?" Torben asks.

"Of course not. I'm the only one who saw Astrid for what

she really was. She was nothing but a scheming, devious, lustful harpy. She envied me and everyone around her. She only wanted what others had. Things she had no right to lust after."

My knees buckle at the coldness in her tone. I can feel my walls growing thinner, my magic growing stronger, fiercer. So badly it wants to return, to surround me, to wrap me in a shield and stand between me and the other girl's chilling ire.

As if Torben can read my every thought, he shifts slightly until he's standing in front of me, meeting the full force of Danielle's scorn. "Did your cousin know of your history with Miss Snow when she accepted her position at the palace?"

"Yes, and she was supposed to be on my side. She knew what that girl did to me. She knew Astrid ruined my life."

*Astrid ruined my life.*

The words ring through my ears. With Torben blocking Danielle from view, I have nowhere else to look but the bedroom around us. It's small. Dark. Hidden in some far-off wing. These aren't the quarters Danielle used to reside in. This isn't the life she used to have.

Did I do this?

"My cousin was supposed to help me get revenge," Danielle says.

Torben stiffens. "How was she supposed to help you get revenge?"

"She was supposed to help me prove Astrid's true nature. Discover her secrets. Tell me everything she could find out about her. Instead, she betrayed me by becoming her *friend* instead." She delivers the word *friend* with no small amount of venom.

"I was told you pushed Miss Snow from a horse," Torben says, his tone just as dark as hers. "That she could have died from her injuries."

Danielle snorts a laugh. "I wish she had. Then perhaps her father would still be alive."

The mention of my father has me bolting out from behind Torben. "Why would you say that?" I ask, voice trembling.

She narrows her eyes at me, then assesses me from head to toe as if seeing me for the first time. The blood leaves my face. Do I still have control over my magic?

Danielle seems to lose interest in me and turns her gaze back to Torben. "It's obvious she killed her father. I knew she'd do something like that as soon as I heard Edmund had married the queen. She wouldn't be satisfied at being named a princess. No, she would want the queen's crown. She'd kill her father and her stepmother and seize the throne for herself." Her voice rises with hysteria. "I told everyone. *Everyone.* No one listened. Just like they didn't listen after the accident. How could they not see I was trying to protect everyone from her? Marybeth was the only person who ever believed me. But she too was won over by that evil, scheming whore."

Nausea turns in my gut as I take in the fervor in her eyes, the rage pulsing in the veins at her temples. I never saw this side of her when we were acquainted. She was paranoid, of course. Cruel. Cold. But never was she this...this...

"You think I'm unhinged too, don't you?" Her eyes lock on me again. "You think I'm the villain, but I assure you I'm not. I'm the victim. I was supposed to be a wife. A mother. Do you know what I got instead? What my parents have subjected me to? Bloodletting, exorcisms, purgatives, laudanum." She marches toward us. "I'm so *tired* of laudanum. I'm so fed up with being locked in this room!"

"Then perhaps you shouldn't have tried to murder a girl," Torben says without an ounce of sympathy.

She pulls her head back as if he'd slapped her. Then her lips curl into a too-pleasant smile. "I only wish the horse had crushed her skull."

With a growl, Torben leaps toward the girl, claws extending from his fingertips. I nearly trip in my haste to rush between them. His face twists into a snarl, his teeth elongating into pointed tips. I get in front of him and plant both hands on his chest. Pushing against him with all my might, I angle my face to his. "Torben! Don't!"

His chest heaves beneath my palms, his muscles quivering with rage, but he stops in place. His eyes, however, remain locked on the girl.

A sharp cackle pierces the air behind me. I turn to see Danielle chuckling, her face devoid of any concern over her life. Did she not see Torben's claws? His teeth? His rage? If so, she certainly didn't care.

I lower my voice. "I think we should go."

"You want to leave already?" Danielle says with a mock pout. She sobers from her laughing fit and turns her attention to me. As her eyes lock on mine, I feel the last of my control begin to melt away. Her gaze is too probing, too intense. It reminds me too much of how she looked just before she shoved me off the horse. I'd been struck by the bottomless rage in her eyes back then too. Or...perhaps not her eyes exactly, but what they'd reminded me of in that moment. Another pair of eyes linger at the edges of my memory, ones even more terrifying than Danielle's. A flash of green surrounding too-large pupils fills my mind, striking fear into my heart for reasons I don't understand.

I know I should calm down and breathe my magic away, but I can't, not after everything she said. Not with the guilt that weighs heavy in my heart.

That's all the permission my magic needs. It snaps into place, igniting between us. The hum of my power buzzes all around me like a cloak. Smothering yet protecting at the same time. I sink into the familiar comfort of being unseen. Of hiding behind a mask.

But as her face pales, my momentary relief is replaced with dread.

"You," Danielle says through her teeth. Then again, her voice a shout now. "It's you!"

Torben finally drags his attention from Danielle to me, and his expression turns panicked. "Shit."

"You ruined my life," Danielle cries out, her voice breaking on a sob. "Did you come to see what you did? Did you come to mock me?"

"No, I—"

Before I can finish, the door bursts open. Mrs. Harding and two maids rush inside and head straight for Danielle. Torben angles me behind him, hiding me from view. "This meeting is over," Sandy says, not bothering to glance our way. "I must ask you to leave now. Martha, get the laudanum."

"No!" Danielle shouts as Sandy and one of the maids restrain her flailing arms behind her back. "I don't want more laudanum! I want *her*. She's Astrid Snow. It's *her*."

"That's ridiculous," Sandy grinds out and forces her daughter to turn away from us.

That's the last thing I see before Torben ushers me out of the room. I'm in a daze as we hurry through the manor and out the front door. I barely notice when we return to the coach. Barely notice the tears streaming down my cheeks.

All I can see is Danielle's maniacal face, her thin frame, her dismal living quarters.

All I can hear is her voice.

*Astrid ruined my life.*

## 33

*ASTRID*

Torben and I don't speak during our ride home. He must sense that I couldn't talk if I tried. My throat is too tight, too dry, while my cheeks are too wet with tears. Instead of speaking, we sit next to each other in the coach, each looking out our respective windows. Halfway through our ride, I feel his hand fold around mine. He gives my palm a squeeze like he did in Danielle's bedroom, but this time he doesn't let go. This time he entwines our fingers as if he knows how badly I need to feel rooted to something right now.

There's a petty part of me that wants to pull away, to reject his kind gesture. I still haven't gotten over what he said to me this morning—that we should keep our relationship professional. And yet, I can't bring myself to leave the comfort of his grasp. So I don't.

Night has fallen by the time the cab lets us out in downtown Larklawn. Only then does Torben release my hand. From there, we walk back to the edge of town and into the countryside.

Once we draw near Davenport Estate, Torben gestures for me to follow him off the main road and onto a dirt path that winds through what looks like overgrown farmland. His estate's farmland, I assume.

"I want to walk the perimeter before we return to the manor," Torben says. His tone is so soft, so gentle, it's nearly unbearable. "Just to ensure no one has come stalking around the property in our absence. If they have, they'll have left a scent trail."

I follow him for several agonizingly silent minutes before I blurt out, "You can stop tiptoeing around me like I'm made of glass, you know. You don't have to keep quiet or talk to me in a half whisper, as if you fear I'll bolt away like a scared little deer. You don't have to—" I'm about to say *you don't have to hold my hand*, but I can't force the words from my lips.

He glances over his shoulder, and the moonlight overhead reveals a quirked brow. "I was speaking softly to keep from alerting any potential lurkers, but if you aren't wary of being attacked, by all means, I'll shout at you instead."

I open my mouth to argue but realize he's given me what I asked for.

He returns his attention to the path ahead, brushing aside stray branches and brambles where they've taken over the trail. "Also, I wanted to give you time to process what happened."

"Well, I have." That's a lie. Thankfully, Torben doesn't call me out on it.

"Then let's talk about what we've discovered. Despite Danielle having a firm motive to work against you, I find it unlikely she's the one controlling Marybeth. Not only was I unable to scent any lies coming from her, but she had no qualms about declaring her disdain for you in the first place. If she was involved in an attempt on your life—even one resulting in someone else's death—I think she'd admit it."

My stomach sours. Perhaps pretending I'm ready to talk about Danielle was the wrong choice. Still, if we are to find Marybeth and prove who's controlling her, we need to figure out what to do next. I release a heavy sigh. "You're probably right. I don't think we can consider Danielle a strong suspect. What's our next step?"

"I'm not sure yet." He slows his pace as he untangles a particularly unruly patch of overgrowth. Once he manages to part it from the path, he holds the gnarled greenery aside for me to pass. The space is so narrow I have no choice but to press myself against him as I scoot by. My chest brushes his and I hear him take in a sharp breath. The sound sends my pulse quickening, but I ignore it and proceed down the path. I take no more than five steps before I pull up short.

Before me stands a grove of cherry trees. Their pink blossoms glow under the moonlight while luminescent pink petals flutter amongst the boughs. Are those...pixies? Or some kind of flower sprite? Whatever they are, they're dainty and charming, lighting up the grove like a canopy of stars. The earth beneath the trees is overgrown with moss and weeds, which somehow only adds to the enchanting sight.

"Is this part of your property?" I ask.

Torben nods and enters the grove. One of the petal fae lands on his shoulder, and I see it has a plump, glowing, bee-like body and two pink wings that look exactly like the petals in the cherry trees. For as long as I've lived in the Spring Court, I've never seen this creature before.

Torben reaches overhead, which sends the little fae flying off, and plucks something from the nearest tree. He hands it to me—a cherry. He picks another and pops it into his mouth. "These were our specialty cherries. They seem to be flourishing even with such neglect, probably thanks to the cerapis sprites."

"Cerapis sprites? Is that what the glowing petal fae are?"

"They're only found around fae varieties of cherry trees and pollinate them. Even so, I'm surprised no one has come to chop this grove down or transplant it. Several of my berry crops have been robbed."

I stare down at the cherry he placed in my hand. The cerapis sprites who continue to flutter and buzz overhead illuminate the fruit's unique pale pink color speckled with little gold spots that glitter like starlight. "I've never seen anything like this."

"Try it," he says, then picks another for himself.

It almost seems a shame to eat something so pretty, but I oblige and bring it to my lips. The first taste nearly drags a moan from me. The flavor is sweet and tangy, the flesh reminiscent of a classic cherry but with a rosy floral aftertaste. I pluck out the seed and eat the rest. "I'm surprised you like these, what with your disdain for florals. In fact, I'm surprised you can tolerate standing in this grove."

As I meet his eyes, I find his are locked on my lips. There's something hungry about his expression. It makes every muscle in my body go still.

Blinking furiously, he tears his eyes away and leans against the trunk of a tree. "I told you. The smell of berry blossoms doesn't bother me, nor does it cloud my senses. And the taste..." His eyes slowly slide back to my lips as if caught by some magnetic force.

"You like the taste?"

"Yes." His answer is deep and throaty, and I can't help but feel like our conversation has shifted into something else. My skin starts to tingle, reminding me of the way it felt last night— as if a fire has been lit deep inside me, glowing from my very core. It builds so strong it nearly emboldens me to say something brash like I did the night before.

*Do you like my taste?*

*Will you taste me again?*

*Will you sample another part of me?*

Before I can utter something so daring and ludicrous, I purse my lips tight. Because what if I'm wrong? I was this morning.

As if in answer, he clears his throat and pushes off from the tree, then proceeds through the grove once more. "I don't smell any trespassers," he says. "We can head to the manor."

Disappointment weighs heavy in my stomach as I follow him. Yet I relish the hollow ache. After the condition I saw Danielle in today, I feel like I deserve it. Like I deserve all the pain I've experienced. Like I deserve nothing good or warm or—

Torben stops in front of me so suddenly, I nearly collide with him. At first, I think he's been alerted to a new scent, but when I glance up at him, I find all his attention is on me. His voice comes out with an edge. "What were you thinking about just now?"

I frown, confused by his sudden ire. "I'm not...I wasn't—"

"What were you thinking about?" he asks again, tone sharper.

A burst of anger rushes through me. I take a step away from him. "What right have you to ask?"

He shadows my step, and when I retreat from him again, he closes that distance too. My next step brings my back against one of the cherry trees. His voice deepens. "If you were thinking about anything that makes you feel guilty about what happened today, then stop."

That only perplexes me more. Why would he be mad that I feel guilty?

I refuse to let go of my anger. Not when sorrow rests on the other side. I'm not ready to return to sorrow. I tilt my head back and give him a defiant glare. "You saw what I did to that girl. What my magic did."

"You didn't do that, Astrid. *She* did."

I shake my head. "No. That was me. I can't hide from that responsibility any longer. You know why?"

His brows knit together in question.

I surge forward and pound a fist against his chest. He neither budges nor flinches, but the feel of my hand colliding with something firm helps channel my growing rage. "Because you were right, Torben. You were *right*."

"About what?"

"About—" In an instant, my anger cracks and sorrow comes flooding in. "About my magic," I say, my voice catching on a sob. "I *can* control it. I've been able to control it all along."

Torben steps in closer and presses his hand over mine—the one still curled into a fist on his chest. His other comes to rest on my cheek. "Just because you've learned to control your magic now doesn't mean you always could. It doesn't mean the past was your fault."

"But it was." Tears glaze my eyes, obscuring his features from view. In its place, I envision something else—two terrifying eyes. The same eyes I imagined in Danielle's bedroom. I can't see them clearly, can only feel the fear they ignite in me, the need to hide, the craving for a shield. Whether the eyes are from a memory or simply a conjuring of my mind, I know not. I do know one thing, though...

"I've been able to control it all along, I just didn't realize it until today. But now I know I'm the one who ignites my magic. I'm the one who keeps it wrapped around me at all times. I'm the one who...who...doesn't want to be seen."

I lower my head as another sob rips through me. "You were right. I *hate* that you were right."

"If I'm right, then you have nothing to feel guilty for. Nothing was your fault."

"No, that's the one part you're wrong about. It *is* my fault. Everything that has ever happened with my magic has been my fault."

Torben pulls me into his chest. I feel his lips come to the top of my head, feel his strong arms wrap me in an embrace far more comforting than any magic. "No, Astrid," he whispers into my hair. "You can't blame yourself for this. You didn't know how your magic worked."

"I ruined Danielle's life. She was a different person before—"

"She did that. Do you hear me? She ruined her own life. You had nothing to do with that. Everything she saw in you was *her* reflection. You didn't make her react the way she did. You didn't make her push you off a horse and nearly kill you."

"But I made her see that reflection. What if she'd have lived a normal and healthy life if she hadn't been forced into that situation?"

He strokes a hand down my back. "You can't think like that. You can't. Besides, there are plenty of people like Danielle in the world. Whether she encountered her worst qualities through your magic or someone who truly possessed them, she'd likely have reacted the same."

I know there's logic in his words, but I resist latching onto them. There's still a chance my magic is responsible for my father's death, even if in some roundabout way. If that proves to be the case, there will be no forgiving myself. Not if I've had the choice all along to keep from using my magic at all.

"Astrid," Torben growls in warning.

With a grunt, I pull myself out of his arms. I wipe furiously at my eyes but find my tears have dried. "Stop smelling my emotions."

He plants his hands on his hips. "Then stop being so damn hard on yourself!"

"You don't get to control me."

"Then get control of yourself."

I scoff. "You're one to talk when you're the one who nearly ripped out Danielle's throat."

He snaps his mouth shut, his face going ashen. It gives me no small amount of pleasure to see him at a loss for words.

I narrow my eyes. "Why did you try to attack her, anyway?"

His jaw shifts side to side before he answers. "I'm sorry. I lost control."

"Yes, but why?"

"Because she said vile things about you."

My irritation settles enough to allow my curiosity to grow. "Is it because of my magic? Because of how it makes you see me?"

I know the impression my magic creates disappears when I'm not using it, but my control slipped right before he lunged for her. Is that why he flew into a rage? Because he suddenly saw me as the crying babe he found on the lakeshore so many years ago?

"Astrid, I think you know we've moved well beyond a superficial impression by now. What I did had nothing to do with you being small or vulnerable."

"Then why?"

He steps in close again and lifts a tentative hand toward my face. I shudder as his palm settles against my cheek. He brushes his thumb lightly along my cheekbone. The gentle touch stands in stark contrast with the sudden darkening of his tone. "Because no one threatens your life in my presence unless they have a death wish. It's bad enough I had to stand before Queen Tris and hear the way she talks about you without being able to lift a hand against her."

My eyes go wide at such a fierce declaration. If this isn't my magic, then what is it?

I can't help but think of the night we shared, the tender way he kissed me before I fell asleep. The way my chest opened, the way I wondered if what we shared was more than...

I shake my head, reminding myself of what he said this morning. Steeling my nerve, I meet his eyes with a pointed look. "This isn't very professional, Huntsman," I say, tone mocking.

His hand freezes along my cheek. "Is that what you want?"

"It's what *you* want."

"You clearly don't know what I want." His voice is so deep it's almost a growl. My toes curl as a shudder runs down my back. He leans in closer, so close I can smell the sweet cherries on his breath. "I told you to come to me if you wanted more of me after last night. When you entered the parlor this morning and I scented your shame and embarrassment, I thought I knew your answer, which is why I said what I did. Even if I was wrong, I thought I was making the right choice. But now...now I'm not so sure."

"You're not sure about what?"

He trails his fingers from my cheek to the bottom of my ear, then brushes them along my jawbone. "Not sure if it matters that fate might tear us apart, either by danger, punishments, or deadly bargains. I'm not sure if I can live—whether a short life or a long one—without having more of you."

I stare up at him. Fire burns hot in my core, searing away all my hurt, all my grief, guilt, and sorrow. As I look into his honey-colored irises, I feel as if nothing else matters. Only this. This moment where I can stare into someone's eyes without feeling the need to hide. Where I can look at someone without seeing the qualities I reflect back. I'm not sure when I released my magic, but I know it's gone right now. Not even a hum of it remains.

"Astrid." The sound of my name on his lips sounds like a plea. A question. "I can see you right now. All of you. I see your gray eyes, your blue-black hair as dark as a midnight sky. I see your coral lips. Your flushed cheeks. And I see *you*. Your bravery. Your courage. You are so beautiful. So strong. Fragile too, but not weak. Never weak. You're incredible."

Tears prick my eyes at his words. How many times have I

wished I could hear *you are* followed by things that are true about me? How many times have I wished to be seen and accepted? All my life I thought I wanted those things, and yet I've hidden behind my magic. Unconsciously, perhaps, but I have. But with Torben...somehow with him, it's been easy.

But these things he sees in me now, true as he thinks they are, they aren't the full truth.

My lower lip quivers as I speak. "What I really am is a mess, Torben. I'm a tangle of emotions. I'm angry and ashamed. I've spent the last few years numbing myself with poison. I have magic that makes the people around me crazy. I have a...a strange fascination with soft things, and—"

My cheeks redden as a new realization dawns. "And...that's because of you. Because of my first memory. Which means I've basically been obsessed with you my whole life. That makes me rather strange, doesn't it?"

He lets out a laugh, and his eyes crinkle at the corners. "Astrid, you're allowed to be strange. You're allowed to be a mess. You can be all these things that are part of you. It won't stop me from loving everything about you."

My heart slams against my ribs. He said he loves everything about me. But does that mean he loves...*me*?

"Let's start over, Astrid. Tell me what you want. Tell me what you really wanted to say this morning."

All I hear is my raging heartbeat as I step in closer to him. A confession dances just beyond my lips but I don't know if I have the courage to say it. Because what I have to say goes beyond *want*. It's more than that. More than need. More than desire. I swallow hard, then bring my trembling hands to his torso. Keeping one palm steady on his abdomen, I slide the other up to his chest until it covers the organ thundering against the cage of his ribs. Then I lift my gaze to his, hoping he can read what I've spelled without words.

His lips turn up into a dazzling smile. "You want my heart?"

I nod, then finally manage to croak out, "Not just your body."

He presses his hand over mine and I feel his heart beat faster, wilder. "It's already yours, Astrid. My heart is already yours."

## 34

*ASTRID*

I feel as if I'm floating on air, drifting through the boughs of the cherry trees like the cerapis sprites that continue to dart through the blossoms overhead, illuminating the space around us. My heart feels as if it's glowing as bright as them too, warming my chest like the heat of the sun.

Torben tilts his head until our foreheads touch. His heart thuds heavier against my palm. "I was supposed to claim your heart," he whispers, a note of pain in his voice. "I hate that I agreed to perform such a vile act. I hate that I ever placed my hands upon you with that intent. Yet, in the end, you were the one who took my heart."

"I forgive you," I say, breathing in the scent of him, that rich woodsy, smoky fragrance. "But you're wrong, Torben. You did claim my heart. Just not in the way you expected to."

He angles his face closer to mine until our lips are almost touching. We share breath for several silent moments, our chests heaving. "Do you mean it?"

"I mean it. I...I'm in love with you, Torben."

He brings his lips to mine, a soft meeting of our mouths. It's nothing like the crushing kiss he gave me when he marched into my room last night, nor is it the hesitant tenderness we shared after he gave me pleasure. This kiss is gentle yet certain. A promise.

But I don't want gentle. Not now that I have his body against mine.

I pull my hands from his chest and wrap my arms around his neck. His rove to my back, pressing me against him until not an inch of space separates us. I part my lips, allowing our kiss to deepen, and his tongue sweeps against mine, painting it with the sweet, floral taste of cherries. I arch into him and slide my hands beneath the collar of his jacket, over his broad shoulders, tugging the fabric down with me. He pulls away from me enough to shrug the rest of the way out of his jacket, and I slip out of mine as well. Then his arms are around me again, gathering me against him as we meet in a kiss once more.

I feel my back come up against the trunk of a tree, and I surrender my weight to it, then to Torben as he hoists me up until we're eye to eye. I wrap my legs around his waist, shuddering as one of his hands slides beneath my crumpled skirt, running up the length of my silk hose to the bare flesh of my thigh exposed above them. His hand rounds the curve of my bottom and I moan against his mouth, cursing the layers of skirts and pants between us. He seems to share my frustration and gathers my hem in his other hand, dragging it higher until I'm bared against him. I bite my lip at the hardness that presses into my aching center, straining against his trousers.

His lips leave mine to trail down my jaw, my neck. His tongue sweeps along the sensitive flesh above the high lace collar of my blouse. He squeezes my bottom with both hands, and it only makes me want more of him, to feel every inch of his flesh bared against mine.

"Will you let me touch you this time?" I ask, my words breathless.

He brings his mouth back to mine, kissing me once. Twice. "Do you want to touch me?"

"Yes, I want to touch you. To see you. I want all of you."

He kisses me again, and I feel him smiling against my lips. Then his hand comes between us, working the buttons of his trousers. As soon as he frees himself, I slide my palm down his chest, his waist, until I finally reach what I've only had teasers of. I wrap my hand around him, exploring his smooth length.

"Astrid." My name comes out strained, almost a wince, and he nearly loses his footing. He shudders, one hand coming away from my backside to prop against the trunk of the tree, his chest heaving.

I release him and untangle my legs from around his waist. "Did I do something wrong?" I say as I plant my feet on the ground.

Eyes closed, he shakes his head, and I see a smile playing over his lips. A pair of cerapis sprites buzz behind him. Their light paired with the canopy of pink blossoms overhead tinge his copper strands a rosy hue. Blooming hell he's beautiful.

"No, Astrid," he says. "It's just...it's been many years since I've...since I've been touched. It almost feels too good."

"You haven't been with anyone since..." I don't even want to say her name out loud—the name of the wretched woman he once loved. The woman who betrayed him and tricked him into losing everything. I didn't like her when he told me about her before. With my heart now so fiercely entwined with his, I like her even less.

"Five years," he says.

I lift a hand to his face and run my fingers over his bearded jaw. When I speak, my voice is soft. "I won't hurt you like she did. I hope you know that."

He opens his eyes to meet mine, and there's something

pained in his expression. "Astrid, I don't know what we can be for each other."

I freeze, disappointment stabbing my chest.

"I love you," he rushes to say, then again, slower. "I love you, Astrid Snow. Don't misunderstand me. What I mean is...before we do this, before we become anything more to each other, we must acknowledge the truth. I still have a bargain to fulfill. When we prove your innocence, the queen might release me from said bargain. Or she might not. If she does, that doesn't mean I'm..."

I frown, piecing together what he can't bring himself to say. That's when I realize turning me over to my stepmother is the only way he *fulfills* his bargain. If she releases him from it, whether by free will or by order of the Alpha Council, he remains enslaved as Huntsman. I remember what he said about his life. That he has no home. That he's disallowed from forging social and emotional ties. How he said he'd never subject a lover to the dangers that come with his job.

Then there's the part I can't bear to think about. That if Tris refuses to dissolve their bargain, if we fail to find any proof of my innocence or of the killer's guilt, then...

Then Torben dies.

But no.

He won't. I will haul myself before the queen if that's what I must do. My chest tightens at such a terrifying thought, but if I must subject myself to Queen Tris' violent wrath to save Torben's life, I will.

Either way, I now understand why he rejected me this morning. And why he said what he did just before he confessed his feelings.

*I'm not sure if I can live—whether a short life or a long one—without having more of you.*

I feel the same now, but in far more certain terms.

"It doesn't matter how long either of our lives end up being," I say. "What I want is *this*. Now. If it's one of my last experiences—"

He covers my mouth with his. "Don't say it," he manages to say between kisses. "If you want whatever we can be for each other right now, for as long as we can, then let's not think about the future."

"Yes," I say against his lips. "Yes, I want this now. I want you for as long as we have together. If I have to wait ninety-five years for my next taste of you, I will."

I keep my next promise a secret. *If I have to die for you, I will.*

Out loud, I say, "Just give me what you can tonight."

He kisses me once more, long and lingering, before pulling away. For a moment, I fear he'll deny me, but the look in his eyes isn't rejection. It's hunger. Want. Need. My gaze drops to the length still exposed above his open trousers, and I gasp at the sight of it.

His lips curl into a devious grin as his fingers move to the buttons on his waistcoat. I bite my lip as I watch every slow movement he makes, my breaths growing sharper with every button he frees. Once his waistcoat is open, he drops it to the mossy ground. It lands with a far heavier thud than I expect. Then I note the brass chain peeking out beneath the brocade fabric—the cuffs we were once trapped in. He must have brought them to the Hardings in anticipation of a possible capture. The sight of them fills me with an odd fondness. I recall how angry I'd been to be chained to him, how desperate I was for the key.

Now the thought doesn't seem so bad at all.

Torben moves on to his shirt buttons, baring his muscled chest one inch at a time. My desire intensifies, mingling with the love that glows in my heart. Heat burns at my center, makes me ache with an unbearable want.

Torben's smirk deepens, showing me just how aware he is of the way his slow undressing tortures me. He reaches the final button of his shirt and throws the article to the floor. I watch every move and flex of his shoulders, every ripple of his abdomen. Then, finally, he slides his trousers the rest of the way down. I take in his thick, sculpted thighs, his roped calves. He's like a statue come to life. Or a stunning portrait of male perfection, framed by the beauty of the cherry tree grove around us.

How any foolish woman ever chose another man over him is beyond me. I would choose him a thousand times, even amongst the impossibly stunning attractiveness most fae males tend to possess. Torben is a beauty beyond all others. Rugged. Sharp. Dangerous. Honed to be lethal yet secretly soft.

I drag my eyes from his naked body and meet his gaze. From the way his chest heaves, he feels the same searing yearning as I do. I can wait no longer.

I tug off my blouse with haste, unable to tease him the same way he did me. With a rumbling growl, he closes the distance between us and helps me out of my skirt, hose, and corset until I'm just as bare as he is. The cool spring air dances over my skin, but with desire burning hot in my blood, I feel as if I'm standing beneath the Fire Court sun. He drinks me in, eyes sweeping from my head to my toes and back again. That's all I allow before I pull him to the ground beneath us. My back comes to a soft carpet of moss.

Torben hovers over me, first meeting my lips with a hungry kiss, then trailing his mouth down my neck. His hands explore my skin, running over my thighs, my hips, my breasts. He runs a thumb in an agonizingly slow circle over my nipple, eliciting a gasp from me. His mouth meets the other, his tongue flicking over the sensitive bud until I'm writhing against him. Then his lips trail to the underside of my breast, then down my stomach. He kisses the soft skin on each side of my inner thigh before sliding his tongue over the center of me. I throw my head back, arching off the ground as his mouth moves in ways I never imagined. It's even better than his fingers were.

Just when the pleasure grows nearly unbearable, I drag him up to me and wrap my hand around the length of him once more. He presses his lips to mine, groaning against my mouth. Then I guide him to my aching entrance. He pulls away, a question in his eyes, as if to be sure I'm certain. His irises glitter with light, with love, with the glow of the sprites buzzing high above him.

In answer, I buck against him, pulling him closer with my legs around his waist. Then, finally, he gives in. With one slow move, he thrusts into me, inch by inch, until he's seated to the hilt. The fullness of him is so right, so satisfying. He begins to move slowly, a gentle rhythm that feels nearly as torturous as his striptease. But as I writhe underneath him, pressing my hands into his lower back to push him deeper, faster, he quickens his pace. Soon our sweat-slicked bodies move in tandem. Our breaths mingle, our hearts thud in unison. My desire rises to an unbearable peak, roaring through my blood, erupting from my lips in moan after moan. Torben pulls back slightly, enough to meet my eyes. Where normally I feel the hum of my magic snap into place, with him I only feel warmth. Safety. A love that warms my chest more and more.

"I love you," he whispers.

That's all it takes to send me over the edge. Release tears through me, and he meets me with his own. Together we fall. Together we unravel. Together we burn and break. Once drained of pleasure and left limp in each other's arms, all I can think is that no matter what happens next, this was worth it. He was worth it. And if everything fails and I must die, then at least I'm happy to have lived. Truly lived. Not as someone else. Not as another's reflection.

Just me.

Existing *outside* another's eyes. Me, as I am, with all my messes, mistakes, and oddities.

For the very first time, I feel like I'm real.

## 35

*TORBEN*

I hadn't meant to tell her I loved her when we came to the grove. I hadn't meant to do anything but comfort her. But as a fae, I'm incapable of lying. And when it comes to Astrid, it seems I can't keep my deepest secrets at bay. Neither from her nor myself.

Now, as I hold her folded against my chest, my back sunk into the plush moss beneath us, it seems ludicrous that I'd even attempted to maintain my distance from her. I made it less than a day trying to keep our relationship *professional* before I gave in, heart, body, and soul. And fuck it all if it wasn't the best decision I ever made. Our future remains tenuous. Our fates uncertain. But the feeling of her warm body against mine, her sweet soft curves molded against all my firm edges, feels like the rightest thing in the world.

Astrid nuzzles closer to me and releases a contented sigh. I stare down at her, taking in her closed eyelids, the sweet smile playing over her swollen lips. The smell of her fills my senses, a fragrance so potent I could get drunk from it, live off it alone.

I run my fingers over the arm she has slung across my torso, and she shudders at my touch. "Should we return to the manor?" I ask, my voice hoarse in the wake of such expended pleasure. "You must be cold."

"I'm not," she whispers. "And I don't want to return. Not yet. I just want to stay like this a little while longer."

~

A LITTLE WHILE LONGER TURNS INTO DAYBREAK.

I wake with a start, confused by the canopy of pink blossoms overhead, the earthy mattress beneath me, until I find Astrid. She's still in my arms, still naked, still folded against my chest. I'm surprised the cool night air didn't eventually wake us, but with her body heat still entwined with mine, cocooned in the recess we've created in the mossy floor, I realize I'm not cold at all.

I shift slightly toward her, and she stirs. "Torben," she whispers, eyes still closed.

The sound of my name on her lips, uttered in the haze of sleep, sends my heart thudding. I'm almost of a mind to take her once more, here and now, but with the rising dawn, a sense of deepening urgency has settled itself in my gut.

We're running out of time. We have only five days until my bargain is due to be fulfilled. As much as I wish it were otherwise, we cannot linger in the throes of pleasure. Instead, we must use every remaining hour we have to prove Astrid's innocence. We must find Marybeth. It's the only chance either of us has.

I bring my lips to her forehead, and she finally opens her eyes. "Is it morning?"

"Yes. We should return to the manor."

"Must we?" She releases a pouty moan, one that has me tensing with want. As if sensing my waning resolve, she meets my gaze with a devious look. Then her lips come to mine, her kiss slow and soft. Last night's desire returns at once, and she climbs on top of me, straddling my hips, torso upright. The blush of the rising sun illuminates her smooth, bare flesh, the rosy buds at the tips of her breasts, the need in her half-lidded eyes.

She's beautiful. Desirable. The woman I love.

My body responds with a pulsing need, something she doesn't hesitate to utilize. She lowers herself onto me, and there's no going slow this time. No teasing. No pretense. Just our insatiable love. Our unyielding desire.

I turn myself over to it. To her.

Our mission can blooming wait.

WHEN WE'RE SPENT ONCE MORE, WE GO ABOUT COLLECTING OUR clothes strewn about the grove. They're slightly damp with morning dew, which makes for awkward dressing. Awkward and yet somehow erotic as we end up dressing each other between heated kisses.

Damn. What is it about this woman that distracts me so?

Thankfully—or perhaps unfortunately—we manage to keep our clothes on, reversing last night's slow undressing as we take turns doing the buttons on each other's shirts, each one secured with a kiss. When I reach the top button of Astrid's blouse, I plant a kiss at the base of her neck. As I help her into her coat, something red slips to the ground. It's the velvet ribbon I gave her. I hand it to her, and she runs her fingers over the soft length of it. Our eyes lock, and the suggestive tilt of her mouth nearly has me tearing off our clothes once more. I bite my lip to suppress the urge, but that only has her smile deepening.

She turns around, her backside brushing up against the

aching front of me, and glances coyly over her shoulder. "Will you tie it in my hair?"

I blink at her a few times, my love-addled brain struck dumb. Then I realize what she's referring to. I lift the ribbon and drape it over the crown of her head, bringing the ends to the nape of her neck. There I knot a bow to hang beneath the ends of her short tresses.

I bring my lips next to her ear. "There you go, Your Highness."

An affronted gasp bursts from her lips, and she turns to playfully swat my chest. "Did I not tell you once before never to call me that?"

"You are a princess."

"On technicality alone," she says, tone light. "I wouldn't be a royal at all if my father hadn't insisted." Her expression flickers for only a moment, her scent dipping with a note of grief before it brightens once more. "And it's not like you've ever treated me like one before."

"No?" I ask, wrapping my arms around her and pulling her into me. "Did I not serve you well last night? And this morning?"

She tilts her chin, eyes locking onto mine. "I suppose you did, but..." She wriggles against me, pressing into the part of me that burns for more of her. "Maybe you should serve me again before we return to the manor. Just to be sure you're doing a proper job."

I try to stifle a groan, but it comes out like a growl nonetheless. "You're insatiable."

She wraps her hands behind my neck. "To think the other night you suspected I was merely acting out of some strange side effect of Crimson Malus withdrawal. Do you see the error of your ways now?"

"I do. But as much as I want to service you all day," I plant a nipping kiss on the tip of her nose, "we do have a mission."

She sighs. "You're right. A rather life-or-death one."

I step back from her, an almost painful thing, and offer her my hand instead. She takes it and we finally drag ourselves away from the sanctity of our grove.

"The cerapis sprites are gone," she notes, glancing back at the trees.

"They're nocturnal."

She wrinkles her nose. "Do you think they...watched us?"

"I'm sure they did," I say with a chuckle. "But while they are fae creatures, cerapis sprites are prone to living more like insects than anything else. I'm not sure I've ever seen one speak or take seelie form."

Her scent dips with a note of mild panic. "I hope the kittens are all right. We left them alone since yesterday."

"I'm sure they'll be fine. I left them plenty of food, fresh dirt for their waste box. If that wasn't enough, I'm sure at least Mama Cat has already found a way out of the manor to feast on all the birds and rats she could want."

The manor comes into view now, beyond the overgrown shrubs and the expanse of unkempt berry crops that sprawl out before us. I breathe deeply, seeking any sign of trespassers like I do every morning. With Astrid at my side, it's a struggle to focus on any other aroma but hers. Her fragrance is so distracting, in fact, that I nearly miss the family of deer grazing at the edge of the berry field until we're nearly upon them. I wonder if it's the same family I frightened away a few days ago.

I pull up short, so as not to startle them again, and whisper to Astrid, "Look."

She follows my line of sight, then all but squeals at the sight of the doe and her two little fawns. "They're adorable," she says in a high-pitched whisper. "I want to pet their little faces so hard."

My chest rumbles with laughter. "Better not."

"You never let me have any fun," she says, tone light with

jest. "Do you always get such adorable wildlife on your property?"

I nod. "Bunnies, mostly. Deer quite often. And then some fae creatures too like the cerapis sprites. I even glimpsed a kelpie here the other day."

She pulls her head back. "A kelpie."

"It darted away as soon as it saw me."

Her eyes grow distant, and a shudder runs through her. "I met a kelpie once. They're frightening creatures, aren't they?"

I shrug. "Only if you agree to ride on their backs."

We proceed through the field, giving the deer plenty of space so as not to disturb their morning meal. Astrid stares wistfully at them until they're out of view.

When we reach the shrubs that skirt the manor, she asks, "What do you want to do? Once you're free?"

The question nearly makes me stumble. I pause. "Astrid…"

"I know, I know," she says. "Our future is uncertain. Yours. Mine. All of it. But let's just pretend. If you were freed from your term as Huntsman, what would you do?"

Part of me doesn't want to play her game, for the hope such meanderings bring is almost painful. But the smile on her face, the brightness of her scent…I've learned my lesson about trying to deny her anything.

I release a resigned sigh and push aside a few stray branches of a large shrub, allowing Astrid to enter the narrow trail I've managed to carve over the last few days. "If I were freed, I'd find work. Work that pays in chips or rounds, not years marked off a sentence like my current occupation offers. I'd work as hard as I could to buy back Davenport Estate."

"You've given up on getting the Chariot back?"

"No," I say. "I still intend to find Marybeth and get my Chariot back from her. Even so, whether I'm awarded owner-ship of my estate right away or am made to work for it, that is what I'll do. As soon as the estate is mine again, I'll start by working the land, even if I must tend every acre alone and by hand, until the farms are operational once more. Only then will I invest in the manor itself and bring on staff. I will build back everything my father left for me, bit by bit."

We reach the end of the trail that lets out onto the tangled lawn behind the manor. She glances at me, brow furrowed. "Is that really what you want? Not just to honor your father's memory?"

I ponder the question before I answer, seeking truth. "It is," I say, feeling a calm conviction fill me at the words. "Even if it weren't for the guilt I feel over my reckless actions, I've always loved the estate. The farms. The berries more than anything. The pride of growing something that brings joy to others. It was thanks to my sense of smell that we even chose our most popular berry varieties. I'd like to put my talents to work like that in the future. No more hunting down fugitives. More sniffing out the next most delectable fruit that will grow into something that makes others happy."

Her lips curl into a soft smile.

We round the manor toward the front door—still the only entrance I've unlocked. "What about you?" I ask. "What do you want once you're proven innocent?"

She slows her pace, eyes unfocused. Her words come out slow, uncertain. "I...I don't know. I've been so preoccupied with hiding and surviving my stepmother's wrath that I haven't given it much thought. I suppose I'll want to find a fulfilling way to use my magic. Something that feels true to who I am—like you and the berries. I've always loved when my magic was put to use. First with my father when I aided his paintings by using my magic on his clients so that he could paint their best qualities. Then at Department Lust when I played matchmaker. I don't know what I'd do next, but...I'd want to do something. Now that I can control my magic, I'd get to do that something as *me*."

I stop in place and tug her hand until she faces me. "You're going to be able to do that. I will prove your innocence if it's the last thing I do."

Astrid pales. "I don't want it to be the last thing you do. I want it to be the first of many, many more things that both of us do."

I bring my hand to her cheek. "So do I," I whisper, keeping the rest unspoken. That we might not have a choice. That only one of us might survive what happens next.

She lowers her eyes, and her scent dips, her expression suddenly hesitant. Shy. "Torben, do you think...I mean, would you be willing..."

"What?"

"If everything works the way we want it to, would you be willing to let me do my *something*...with you?"

I bring my finger beneath her chin and tilt her face until her eyes lock back on mine. "That goes without saying, Astrid. If I have my way, I want you by my side. And I want to be by your side, growing together. Learning more about one another. About ourselves."

She smiles, and the sight of it makes my chest feel pleasurably warm. "I want that too."

I lean in to kiss her, but as our lips meet, mine turn stiff. Every hair on my body stands on end.

That's when I smell something I should have noticed minutes ago. I would have, were I not so besotted with Astrid's aroma. So attuned to it.

She pulls back from me, frowning. "What's wrong?"

A growl rumbles deep in my chest as I gently push Astrid behind me and angle myself toward the figure that stands on the walkway leading to the manor.

I try to keep Astrid safely hidden, but she peeks around my arm. She breathes a gasp. "Marybeth."

## 36

*ASTRID*

My pulse quickens at the sight of my lady's maid. My former friend. She's dressed in the same skirt and blouse she wore in the fighting pit at Department Wrath, and the additional stains she's accumulated tell me she hasn't washed or changed. The dark circles under her eyes suggest she hasn't slept much either. She shifts anxiously from foot to foot, one hand clamped around the silver disc that is the Chariot, the other curled into a fist at her side.

I don't know how to feel at the sight of her, whether pity, rage, or fear is more appropriate. According to Danielle, Marybeth took the position as my maid with the intent to ruin me. To help her cousin get revenge all because she believed the rotten things Danielle said about me. Danielle did say Marybeth ended up changing her mind, but she ended up working against me anyway. How? Why? Marybeth's hands delivered the poison that killed my father. But who directed those hands?

Calm determination settles over me. This is our chance to

get answers. To solve the case that could set me and Torben free.

He must have the same thoughts as I do, for he reaches into his waistcoat and slowly extracts the handcuffs. "What are you doing here, Miss Harding?" he asks, voice level.

Marybeth reveals no surprise that he knows her surname. "I don't have long," she says, every word strained.

"Long before what?" Torben asks.

"Before the compulsion kicks in." She bites back a cry. "I'm fighting it. I've been fighting it, and she knows it. So she sent me on one last errand. If I succeed, she'll free me. If I don't, I...I die."

I come to stand beside Torben. He throws out an arm before me but doesn't try to shove me behind him. He probably knows it will do no good. This is my mission as much as it's his. "Who sent you?" I ask. "Who's controlling you, Marybeth? Who did you give the power of your true name to?"

She bites back another cry, her face going white as a sheet. She seems to be holding her breath, fighting to speak. Or not to. Then she falls to her knees on the stone walkway, head hanging low. "Tris!" she shouts, slamming a fist into the ground. "It's Queen Tris."

My blood goes cold.

"She's coming for you," she says in a rush. "She'll be here by morning to kill both of you if you refuse the offer she sent me to give."

Torben takes a slow step closer. With one hand, he holds an open cuff. His other offers a placating gesture. "We need you to come with us to the Alpha Council headquarters and tell the truth."

Her face snaps up. "I can't. I can never again say what I just did." Her words dissolve into a strangled cry. Tears stream down her cheeks. She forces herself back to her feet, stance unsteady. "I'm here to offer an ultimatum."

Torben edges closer, open hand still raised toward her, probably to distract her from the cuffs half hidden at his side. "What's the ultimatum?"

"Don't come any closer!" she shouts.

Torben and I pause.

She tosses the Chariot out to the side, where it's lost in the overgrown grass flanking the walkway. Torben's gaze snaps to where it lands, but he makes no move to retrieve it. "You get that, Huntsman," she says, then reaches into her skirt pocket and extracts a vial.

My heart races at the sight of it.

She holds the glass bottle out to me. "And you get this. But only if you come with me now."

An unexpected flash of temptation strikes me, summoning a wild, untamed, frantic hunger. It gnaws at my gut, my mind, my heart, promising peace. Safety. An end to grief. An end to sorrow and suffering.

I close my eyes and breathe the wretched urge away. It rakes invisible claws down my insides as it recedes, but when it's gone, I feel stronger. Relief sweeps through me. "I don't want that poison," I say through my teeth.

Marybeth sags, wavering on her feet. Then her hands come to the lid. She whimpers as she turns the cap. "If you don't come with me," she says, voice trembling, "then I must drink this."

Terror seizes me. Marybeth is fully human. If she drinks even a little bit of Crimson Malus, she'll die.

Just like my father.

A small part of me wants to let it happen. Wants to watch those veins of black crawl over her skin in retribution for what she did to my father. But that won't change that Marybeth was forced. That Tris has been orchestrating this all along. We need her alive to confess the truth.

She finishes removing the cap and brings the bottle toward her lips.

"I'll go with you!" I shout, and Marybeth pauses, her chest heaving, arms shaking.

"Astrid," Torben hisses, but he doesn't take his eyes off the other girl.

"It's all right," I whisper. "I'll go to her. When she's distracted, run for the Chariot, then grab hold of us both. Transport us to the Alpha Council, or wherever you can."

His jaw shifts side to side. "Something isn't right about this. Why did she toss away the Chariot? She can't take you anywhere without it. Can't outrun me."

He's right, and it fills my stomach with dread.

"I think Tris wants us to do exactly what we're about to do."

"But if you're holding the Chariot, you can control where we travel to, right?" My mind reels, seeking the hidden trap, for there must be one.

"Yes, but—"

"It's our only chance. We need her alive."

Marybeth cries out and lifts the bottle to her lips again.

"No!" I start toward her, and she freezes once more. "I'm coming with you! Take me anywhere you must. I'm not letting you die."

She pulls the bottle away from her face and tips her head back in an agonized sob. Torben takes his chance to dart toward the Chariot. "I'm not in control," Marybeth cries.

"I know," I say and grab her by the shoulders, if only to make it easier when Torben reaches us. My breath catches at how frail she feels beneath my hands. This is not the girl I've befriended over the past three years. This is a hollow shell of that person. Something used and abused. The realization sears my throat. "It's going to be all right," I whisper, not knowing whether it's a lie. "You're going to be all right."

From the corner of my eye, I see Torben snatch up the Chariot.

Marybeth lowers her head. Then, in a flash, she shoves me away. I stumble back, but before I can crash onto the stone walkway, I find Torben's arms encircling my waist.

"Don't trust me," comes Marybeth's strangled voice. Torben pulls me upright just in time for me to watch her tip the vial into her mouth and down its entire contents.

"NO!" Torben and I shout at once. We scramble toward her. She slides to her knees, body convulsing. Torben tries to help her gag, help her purge herself of the poison, but it's too late.

Too late.

The black veins have already traveled over her face, her neck, even her hands. A single drop could be lethal to a human. But the entire bottle?

I can do nothing but stare in horror. Nothing but watch as Crimson Malus—the very poison I once thought of as my savior, my safety, my friend—claims another life before my very eyes.

WHAT FOLLOWS IS A BLUR, EACH MOMENT NEARLY AS FUZZY AS MY poison withdrawals were. All I know is that, at some point, Torben lifts me in his arms and takes me to my room. I don't know whether I sleep or cry or simply stare at the ceiling. I don't notice if the kittens come to comfort me or if Torben lays by my side. All I feel is agony, tortured by the sight of Marybeth's death. Tormented by the echo of my father's too-similar demise.

I WAKE FEELING EMPTY AND RAW. AN ORANGE GLOW OF EVENING light pours through the boards covering the windows. Torben sits at the edge of the bed by my side, running a comforting hand over my hair. Everything that happened comes back in a flash, but I don't crumble this time. Will I always fall apart when I'm upset? I suppose death is hardly some small thing. Either way, it will probably take some time to get used to feeling the full expanse of my emotions, the good and the bad.

I angle myself closer to Torben. "Her body?"

"I've given her a temporary burial," he says, voice deep and soothing. "Once this is all sorted out, her family can collect her."

The concept is so grim, so disturbing, I nearly break into a sob. But I must keep my wits, for a while at least. I have too many unanswered questions swarming through my mind.

"I don't understand," I say. "Why did she drink the poison? I said I'd go with her. She still had a chance to steal back the Chariot and haul us straight to the queen."

A wrinkle forms between Torben's brows, his eyes distant. "I don't think Tris ever intended for Marybeth to live through this. She would have known I'd try to control the Chariot's destination. She knew Marybeth wouldn't succeed at bringing us to her. The ultimatum was an act."

"But why?"

"To kill our sole witness right in front of us and rob us of hope. It may also have been a test to confirm whether we're truly here or not. Tris will have felt Marybeth's death through the severing of the magical tie her compulsion formed. That will be enough to tell her she found us here. The only thing she didn't predict was that Marybeth would fight the compulsion and tell us the truth. Warn us that Tris will come for us in the morning. Either way, without Marybeth to confess...it's over. The queen has won."

I shake my head. "It can't be over. There must be another way—"

He closes his lips over mine. It's a slow kiss, one laced with sorrow. His lips are like a balm on my heart, and I give myself over to it, trying not to ponder what we'll find on the other side of our kiss, for only hopelessness awaits there.

Torben presses himself closer to me, cradling my cheek with one hand. He pulls back slightly to study my face, my eyes, my lips. "I love you, Astrid Snow. Never, ever forget that for as long as you live."

The sorrow in his voice expresses everything he doesn't say. That my life might not be long at all.

Nor his.

"I won't forget," I choke out. "I love you too."

His lips crush against mine, and I open my mouth for our kiss to deepen. He slides his hand down my waist, while the other wraps around my wrist and pins it overhead. It sparks a flash of desire inside me, even though my logical mind tells me this is hardly the time—

A metallic click sounds in my ears.

I freeze beneath Torben, watch as he pulls away from me. My eyes fall on the open brass cuff he holds in one hand. I don't need to look to know the other end is locked around my wrist.

My heart quickens and breaks at once. A question squeezes between my trembling lips. "What are you doing?"

His eyes turn down at the corners, glazed with unshed tears. He takes the Chariot from his waistcoat pocket. "Fulfilling my bargain."

## 37

*TORBEN*

**M**y heart feels as if it's been pierced by a thousand iron arrows. I don't know if Astrid will forgive me. If she'll understand why I'm doing what must be done. In the end, I suppose it doesn't matter. This is the only way.

We're out of time. Out of options.

The light of the Chariot goes out, and when it does, I'm grateful for the momentary searing blindness the device provides, for it seems to have burned away all remnants of my tears. It's done nothing to lighten the heaviness weighing on my heart, but I don't think anything will.

The queen's throne room forms around me in the wake of the Chariot's glow. It takes me a few moments to orient myself, and I find the room crowded—unlike the last time I was here. The sound of gasps fills my ears. Dozens of stunned figures gawk at me, some surprised, others affronted. It seems I've shown up during petitions with the queen. Good. At least now there are witnesses that I've been here.

Queen Tris sits upon her throne, her large pink wings splayed out wide, her eyes simmering with rage as they lock on mine. "What is the meaning of this?"

"I'm here to fulfill our bargain." The crowd parts to allow the queen full view of me. I lift the Chariot. "Both of them."

The queen pales, then barks, "Out! Everyone out."

Her guards rush into action, shuffling the muttering spectators out the doors. The silence left afterward is almost deafening. Threatening.

I lift my chin, determined to keep my composure. To allow as little victory to the queen as I can. "What? Didn't want an audience for such delicate subjects as murder and manipulation?"

She bares her teeth at me. "You said you came to fulfill both bargains. So where is she?"

It takes all my restraint not to leap at her, not to tear out her throat. Part of me wants to give in to the violent urge, even knowing the punishment I'd receive. But no. The result of such actions is definite. With what I'm about to do...there's still a chance. A slim chance. A meager, hopeless, desperate chance.

The queen's glare deepens. "Where is my stepdaughter's heart?"

I place my palm over my chest, over the thundering drum that rages inside. "Right here."

Her lips curl into a snarl as she studies my hand. "What nonsense is this?"

I swallow hard and deliver my words without quaver. "Astrid gave me her heart, and I gave her mine. You never stated I had to cut out her heart and leave her dead. You only said I must *bring you* her heart. So here it is. If you want it, you can rip it from my chest yourself."

She rises from her throne and folds her wings along her back. "You fool. You pitiful fool. You fell for her lies. Her charm. And now you want to sacrifice yourself for her?"

"Yes," I say, and I've never said something so true in all my life. "If you ever felt an ounce of true love for your husband, then you should understand. Love makes one go to great and terrible lengths for the object of their affection. It makes us hurt. Defend. Even kill. And yes—sacrifice. Accept death."

Her chest heaves as she watches me, eyes flashing with rage. Then she seems to gather her composure, expression turning cold, lips curling into a cruel smile. She strides down the dais and stands before me. "No wonder you lost everything to betting. This is your most idiotic gamble yet. In no way does this fulfill our bargain."

"Technically it does."

She scoffs. "If it did, you'd feel its absence. It would have broken at once."

She's right, and I hate to admit that. If my demonstration truly were enough to fulfill the terms of our bargain, I would have felt the relief that comes from the pact's severing. I would have felt an invisible tear in the magic that binds us.

"That must mean even you doubt your own sincerity," she says.

Once again, I must admit she's right. Fae magic is deeply entwined with personal intent. It's how fae can utilize deception, even with our inability to lie. So long as we can convince ourselves something is true, or that our words match up with some internal intent, we can state it aloud. That must be how Queen Tris deceived me before. She must have orchestrated everything in advance so that she could appear innocent. She controlled her scent to make me suspect she was being honest. She carefully chose words that aligned with her own version of the truth.

My intent isn't enough to fulfill our bargain. Even though I know Astrid gave me her heart—metaphorically—I know that's not what the queen truly wants. I can't fully convince myself it is, for deceiving myself has never been a strength. Only detecting the lies of others. Even that I've failed at, and this current failure is worse than all the rest. I could blame my feelings for Astrid for clouding my senses, but I know such thoughts are folly. Tris deceived me from the start, before I even met Astrid. Besides, I can no longer fault love for anything. Loving Astrid could never be a mistake.

Tris lets out a dark chuckle. "That means you need me to accept what you've offered for our bargain to be fulfilled."

"Will you?" I splay my hands wider over my chest. "Will you tear out my heart in place of hers and be satisfied?"

"No, Huntsman. Why would I? I want her dead. I want her punished for what she's done. I want her to suffer, and you were supposed to help make that happen."

It takes all my restraint to fight my rage at hearing Tris speak of Astrid in such a way. "I was wrong to accept your bargain," I say through my teeth. "I never should have agreed to such dark and underhanded methods."

"Dark and underhanded? Those are words reserved for my wretched stepdaughter, not me. How can you be such a fool, Huntsman? You will die because of her. Our bargain will claim you. We still have five more days, but if you refuse to fulfill it now, and I accept that our bargain has been broken, you will die at my feet within moments. Are you truly willing to do that?"

"Yes," I say, even though it makes my heart sink further. I knew there was little chance this would work. I knew Tris wouldn't let Astrid go so easily. But I never meant to survive this meeting with the queen. I only meant to give Astrid enough time to run. For the love of the All of All, she better fucking run.

Thoughts of her safely hidden away set my nerves at ease. Queen Tris will continue to hunt her, but Astrid is clever. She'll survive. She managed to survive me. She'll survive anyone else who comes for her as well. Now that she's learning to control her magic, she has an even greater chance.

But it does leave me curious about one thing...

"Why do you hate her so?" I ask.

Her answer comes out with a growl. "Because she killed my beloved Edmund."

"She didn't kill him, Tris, and you know it." My words are sharper than I've ever honed them before the queen. She takes a sudden step back as if sliced by their edges. "I ask you again, why do you hate her? What is it that you see when you look at her?"

"What does it matter to you? You're on the brink of death, Huntsman."

"Then offer the truth as my last request. What do you see when you look at Astrid Snow?"

She waves a flippant hand. "I see her beauty. Her pretty pink hair, her—"

"Not her appearance. What else do you see? What makes you so enraged when you look at the child of your beloved husband?"

Tris snaps her mouth shut. She blinks a few times, and her scent plummets. Her throat bobs, chin wobbling. She tears her gaze from mine. "I didn't always hate her," she whispers.

I'm stunned silent by the sudden shift in her countenance. The queen seems to fold in on herself, shoulders slumped forward.

"I loved her the moment I laid eyes on the girl," Tris says. "I was charmed by her. The same way you are now. She was the most beautiful thing I've ever seen. Her hair a prettier shade of pink than mine. Her rosebud lips so kind and smiling. When I looked at her, I saw everything Edmund loved about her. What *everyone* loved about her. She was so charming and graceful. And so utterly...lovable."

Her scent constricts, and she gathers some semblance of

her cold composure. "I resented how lovable she was. How effortlessly everyone was drawn to her. Edmund thought the world of his daughter. He'd accept no award as my husband unless I gave an equal boon to Astrid. I named her a princess so he'd accept being my king. I built her a throne so that he'd sit on his own."

My eyes fall on the two crystal thrones placed just behind the queen's. I wonder if Mr. Snow had originally asked for them both to flank the queen's, instead of being placed behind it. I imagine Tris wouldn't have allowed Astrid an equal place beside her.

Tris lifts her chin. "Astrid was so lovable to everyone around her, but I saw a secret side. She was haughty. She acted like she was better than everyone around her. Better than me. No one saw it. Edmund didn't believe me. Whenever we spoke of her, it felt like we were discussing two different people. And when it came to Astrid...well, she may have been lovable to everyone around her, but she certainly didn't love me. She acted like she was the queen of Fairweather Palace, demanding love and respect, charming my people, even my nephew. Then breaking their hearts one by one. That is why I began to hate her."

I fully understand why Astrid considers her magic a curse, why even positive first impressions have turned people against her. When I asked her about her relationship with Madame Desire, she said things tended to go badly when envy was involved—that one's best mirrored qualities eventually evoked negative feelings.

My heart aches for her. She's had to deal with this her entire life. With no one—*no one*—seeing the real her. Aside from her father. Now me.

One of whom has died. The other will soon be joining him.

Rage sparks in my chest, prompting truth to rise to my lips. "You're wrong about her."

"Excuse me?" She looks me over like I'm a speck of dirt. The curl of her upper lip illustrates the *best qualities* she must greatly treasure—arrogance, pride, haughtiness. Qualities she saw in Astrid and despised.

I know I have no right to confess what I'm about to say next. It isn't my confession to make. Not my truth to tell. And if I were to ask Astrid, I'm sure she'd tell me such a truth would be pointless to share, for it too has brought her much suffering.

But if there's a chance, even the slightest odds, that the truth could free Astrid from Tris' wrath, I must try. Even if it's the last wager I ever place.

"Everything you've seen in Astrid has been your reflection all along."

Her wings begin to buzz against her back in agitation. "What are you talking about?"

"Astrid is a mirror. That's her magic. And she's never known how to turn it off, how to control it. All she's ever had control over is what kind of impression people see. When she's in a positive mood, others see their best qualities reflected back. When she's in a negative mood, they see their worst."

Her wings go still. "I...I don't understand."

"You met Astrid when her father painted your portrait, correct?"

She nods.

"Because of her mood, Astrid formed a positive impression on you that day," I explain, "which means everything you've seen since has been your best qualities reflected back at you. When you saw her pink hair, that was your pink hair. When you saw her poppy-red lips, those were your lips. And when you saw how lovable she was, how everyone around her was drawn to her, every quality Edmund adored...that was *you*. You were the lovable one, the one your people and your husband cherished. All this time, you've let hatred grow in place of what should have been joy."

She throws her hands in the air, and her wings begin to buzz again. "I still don't understand what you're talking about."

"You were jealous of her. Envy grew over time. But you weren't envious of Astrid. You were envious of your own reflection. You've never met the real Astrid. You've never seen her true face. All you've ever seen is your reflection. Your hair, your lips, your charm, your lovability. All these things Edmund fell deeply in love with. They've always been *your* qualities. And you let what is good and true and wonderful fester in your heart. You let it turn you against a girl who could have been a daughter to you."

Her shoulders tremble. "I...I don't believe you."

"I can't lie, Your Majesty."

"But she can."

"I've seen it," I say, punctuating each word. "I've seen her magic in action. I promise you what I say is true; the Astrid you think you know is not the real her."

Her eyes widen a fraction at the word *promise*. Fae promises aren't given lightly, and she knows it. She takes a step away from me, her hand absently rubbing her heart. "But...but why didn't she tell me about her magic? Or anyone, for that matter. Did Edmund know?"

"Her father was one of the very few who knew. She never told many people because doing so has caused her pain in the past, as did her magic itself. Her magic is why she rejected your nephew—because he fell in love with a version of her that wasn't real. It's why she was so badly injured that she developed a Crimson Malus addiction. It's why she struggles to make friends. It's why you made yourself her enemy."

Tris shakes her head, as if that will help rid her of the truth. "She's...a mirror? You're certain?"

I nod.

Her lips pull into a pained grimace. "So as I've grown to hate her...I've hated...*me*?"

"That's the gist of it."

She puts a hand to her mouth, the other still clenched over heart. Her scent darkens with a chaotic medley of confusion, pain, and grief. Eyes unfocused, she backs up until her heels meet the bottom step of the dais. She drops to the step in a pool of pink silk, wings limp behind her, and cradles her face in her hands.

"What kind of monster am I?" comes her wailing voice. "What kind of person sees their own reflection and...and *hates* what they see?"

I'm stunned by her show of emotion. While I'd hoped my truth would get through to her, I hadn't fully believed it would, nor had I expected such a reaction. I feel only the slightest pity. The rest of me relishes the pain she's in.

Her shoulders heave as she cries into her hands. With slow, careful steps, I approach her sobbing form. Thrusting out the Chariot, I say, "Here. I've fulfilled our second bargain."

She lifts her face from her hands, blinking the sheen of glittering tears from her eyes. Her brows knit with confusion as she accepts the device.

"You agreed to return Davenport Estate to my name. Considering I'm about to die, that means nothing. But I request that you sell the property to someone who will take care of it, someone who will bring the crops out of their state of neglect and make them thrive again."

Tris turns the device over in her hands. "I can't keep this," she says, voice heavy with regret. "It belongs to the council."

I'm surprised by that. Chariots are rare and coveted. The Alpha Council is supposed to have ultimate control over who utilizes them, but I never expected Tris would have enough of a conscience not to keep it.

She sighs and rises unsteadily to her feet. Her voice comes out weak, flat. "I accept our second bargain as fulfilled and grant you full ownership of Davenport Estate."

Something snaps inside me like an invisible cord—the magical severing of our bond. I nod my thanks, despite how meaningless her gesture is mere seconds from the death she'll deliver next.

She opens her mouth to speak again, only to snap it shut. Finally, she meets my eyes. "You are certain Astrid didn't kill Edmund?"

I frown. Why would she ask me that? She damn well knows the answer. She has to know it was Marybeth acting on her orders. "I'm certain."

Her scent dips into sorrow once more. "Astrid gave you her heart, and you delivered yourself to me, heart intact. I accept this as your fulfillment of our first bargain. In return, I release you from your term as Huntsman."

Shock ripples through me, as does a surge of tingling power. It sends a shudder from the crown of my head to my toes as it dances over my skin, through my blood and bones. Layers upon layers of magic peel away, draining out of my feet until I'm left feeling lighter than I ever have before.

The bargain...

It's been fulfilled.

As is my term as Huntsman.

I can feel the absence of both, the void where the magic had once been.

Why...why did she do that? Why did she set me free? Doesn't she realize how much I know? What I could use against her now that I'm not bound by the ticking clock of our bargain?

Tris slowly returns to her throne, then sinks onto it. She looks tired. Drained. Is she going to turn herself in? Confess what she's done?

"If Astrid didn't kill Edmund," she asks, "then who did?"

My muscles tense. "Marybeth poisoned the pie. You know this."

She bolts upright in her seat. "Marybeth? The lady's maid you were asking about?"

My pulse kicks up. This could be a trick. A way to evade claiming responsibility for her part in Edmund's death. And yet, her scent holds no deception, only confusion. Shock. Is she deceiving me...again? Panic laces my words as I speak. "Did you or did you not send Marybeth to Davenport Estate this morning to deliver us an ultimatum?"

"No, of course not. I've still yet to see the girl since she left the palace almost two weeks ago."

"Marybeth didn't give you the power of her true name?"

"No," she says, bristling with ire. "I may be a wretched step-mother and—if it weren't for your interference and restraint—responsible for an unjust and deadly punishment, but...I would never compel a human. I may not trust them, but I've always fought to keep humans safe on the isle."

Her words echo through my ears until they're drowned out by the thudding of my heart.

My mind reels, traveling back to our meeting with Marybeth this morning. How she fought to tell the truth, fought to confess Tris' guilt. I'd known something was wrong, that we were playing into the very hands that sent the girl.

We were.

I know that now.

Marybeth hadn't been fighting compulsion to confess who she served. She delivered words that were meant to deceive us. Words only a person with the ability to lie could say.

I don't know who sent Marybeth.

But one thing is clear.

Astrid's in trouble.

## 38

*ASTRID*

I scream Torben's name again and again, even though I know it's no use. He's already gone. Whether I mean that in more ways than one, I don't want to know. Tears stream down my cheeks, my cries mingling with the haunting strain of music that fills the room, courtesy of the music box Torben placed on my lap after he closed the free end of my handcuffs to the bedpost. I hadn't noticed the little box when I first awoke. It wasn't until I was chained in place, straining against the brass cuff and begging Torben not to leave, not to do whatever reckless thing he was preparing to do, when I saw it. He lifted it from the bedside table, turned the key at the bottom, and set it in my lap.

I nearly chucked it across the room, but his warning stilled my hand. "The key to the handcuffs is inside," he rushed to say. "Don't you dare toss that away. Once the song comes to an end, the box will open. Then you can take the key and free yourself. Once you're free, run. Do not come after me. I'll already be at Fairweather Palace."

He flourished the Chariot held in his hand and left the rest unsaid—that if I tried to go after him, he'd likely already be dead by the time I reached my destination.

"No," I cried. "Torben, don't do this. We were supposed to work together."

I'd hoped he'd lean forward and comfort me then. If he did, I'd take the Chariot from him and force him to bring me along. He was never supposed to fulfill his bargain without me. I'd promised that if we didn't solve my father's murder and find a way to prove my innocence, I'd turn myself over to my step-mother willingly.

"We're out of time," he simply said, voice choked with regret.

"We still have five more days."

"No, Astrid, you heard Marybeth. Tris will be coming for us by morning. This is the only option that might save your life."

"Don't do this, Torben! If you face her, she'll kill you!"

"She most likely will. But there's a chance I can fulfill my bargain instead and save both of our lives. If so, I'll find you. If I manage to survive what I'm about to do, I'll follow your scent to the ends of the earth. There's nowhere you can go that I won't find you. So run, Astrid. Run."

That was the last thing he said to me before he strode from the bedroom and left me sobbing, tugging my cuffs with all my might. But I was still stuck when the light of the Chariot began to glow from the hallway, and I was still trapped by the time it went out.

Now I claw at the box, chipping my fingernails in my haste to pry open the lid. No matter what I do, it won't budge. Regardless of how futile my efforts are, I can't sit still. I can't simply wait while Torben sacrifices himself for me. There's no other way his meeting with the queen can end. She made it clear this morning that she intends to silence us. That she's willing to kill even those who serve her if it hides her guilt.

Whatever scheme Torben has up his sleeve, it won't convince her to spare his life.

The tune begins to slow, turning stuttered and haunting. My pulse riots. Every second that ticks by feels like an eternity. Mama Cat rubs my elbow as if she can sense my agitated mood, but not even her presence can calm me. Finally, the lid to the music box pops open. The first thing I see are three carved bears, mechanically moving in a sweet dance. I choke back a sob at the sight. Then my gaze lands on the brass key nestled in a velvet compartment. My fingers tremble as I extract the key and shove it into the lock on my cuffs. The process is too slow, too clumsy, but eventually I manage to open my bonds.

I spring from the bed at once, my steps made unsteady by how my body ripples with fury, heartache, and sorrow. Thankfully, I manage not to trip over my own feet as I don my shoes and rush down the stairs. With every shaking step, I try not to consider how much time has already passed, try not to imagine what Tris could do to Torben at merely the sight of him. What she already could have done.

I make it to the foyer and out the front door. Outside, the evening sky glows with the last blush of sunset. Only then does reality strike me in full force.

I stare down the walkway, Marybeth's corpse no longer draped across it, toward the main road. A road I'll have to take to Larklawn if I want to hail a cab. From there, the palace is at least an hour away.

My chest tightens, my own powerlessness a vise over my heart. All I want is to close the distance between me and Torben. Whether he still lives or not isn't something I can consider.

I just...I just need to...

A sob rips through me, so fierce it sends me to my knees.

What am I doing? What do I do?

A small voice answers in the back of my mind, telling me

Torben was right—that I should run. It's why he left to sacrifice himself for me. Barging into my stepmother's palace will only make his reckless actions meaningless.

But...

But I can't...

I can't give up on him.

And if it's already too late, if Queen Tris has silenced him and snuffed out his life, then...then I'll do whatever I can to face her one final time. I may not be strong, and I may not have the kind of magic that could help me win a fight, but I'll do whatever I must to take that wretched harpy down with me.

Wiping the back of my hand over my eyes, I force myself to my feet, fingers curling into fists.

Steeling my resolve, I start down the walkway—

And freeze.

A kelpie emerges from behind the shrubbery, cloaked in the darkening evening shadows. My heart leaps into my throat at the sight of his rippling mane, his ruby-red eyes. I've only ever met one kelpie before—the night I escaped the palace after my father died —and I can't help wondering if this is the same creature as before.

"You," the kelpie says, voice chilling and ethereal. "We've met before."

I take a step back, alarm bells ringing in my mind. It is the same creature. But why is he here? I breathe deeply and invite my magic to hum through my blood. My eyes lock on his, and my magic ignites.

The kelpie rumbles with a dark chuckle and takes a few slow steps closer, his mammoth hooves clopping against the stone walkway. Hooves that send my stomach churning. "You fooled me once. You will not fool me again."

I retreat closer to the manor. "What do you want?"

"The same thing I wanted then. To take you where you need to go."

"You mean, you want to murder me," I say. "I know what kelpies do. You'll allow me on your back, strangle my hands with your mane so I can't get free, and then sink me into the depths of the nearest water source."

"My kind has been known to enjoy such sport," the creature says, a note of wistfulness in his voice, "but that practice has been outlawed. Doing so could result in my own death sentence."

"You want me to believe you seek to be a glorified coach-and-four instead?"

"I will not drown you," the kelpie says, ignoring my last question. "In fact, I promise not to. I vow to take you where you need to go and release you at your destination alive and unharmed."

My mind whirls to process his words. Stating such a vow is as binding as a bargain. Should he so much as try to break his word, he'll die, strangled by his own fae magic. Could he have left room for deception? Part of me recoils to even consider the creature's offer, but this might be my one chance to reach Fairweather Palace before Torben is killed.

"Kelpies travel fast, don't they?" I ask.

"Faster than any creature on land. Faster than any animal underwater."

"And you'll take me anywhere that I choose? Alive and unharmed?"

"I've said as much already, but if you must hear it again, here it is. I promise to deliver you where you need to go alive and unharmed. I vow that my mane will not strangle your hands, nor will I drown you or so much as deposit you inside any body of water."

Warnings continue to blare through me, begging me to refuse, to run. But what other choice do I have? If I can save Torben, I must try.

"Fine." The word bursts from my lips with a heavy quaver. "Take me to Fairweather Palace."

The kelpie closes the remaining distance between us and lowers his head. My stomach turns as I approach the equine creature. I haven't so much as pet a horse since my accident, much less ridden one. The closest I get to horses these days is from the safety of a closed coach. I swallow down the bile that rises in my throat, then grip his thick black mane in my hands and heave myself onto his back. I sway in my seat before I manage a somewhat comfortable position. Then I hold my breath, waiting for the kelpie to go back on his word, to somehow break the binding magic of his promise. Any moment, his hair could wrap around my hands and lock me in an iron grip...

But it doesn't.

The kelpie's mane remains limp in my palms. Next thing I know, he takes off, sprinting faster than any horse I've ever ridden. The dark forest flies by in a green-black blur. Night has now fully fallen, leaving the moon to cast sinister shadows along our path. I keep my head low, fearing the greedy hands of wayward branches, but the kelpie manages to avoid them. I'm surprised by his smooth gait, his graceful shifts and turns that belie his large form.

I lose sense of time, lose all concept of direction or miles traveled. But after a while, the forest begins to thin, revealing a modest clearing just ahead. As we draw near, I catch sight of moonlight dancing over the surface of a small pond housed at the very center of the clearing. To my horror, the kelpie slows to a canter as he takes us straight toward the body of water.

My heart climbs into my throat, drumming out the beat of my terror.

"You promised you wouldn't drown me!" I shout, unwinding my hands from the creature's mane.

"I won't," he says. "I keep my promises, for I have no intention of dying."

Despite his words, he continues to head for the pond. I glance from the glistening water to the ground far below. A sickening vision floods my mind—of the last time I tumbled from an equine creature. The pain I felt as I struck the ground. The crunch of my ribs beneath massive hooves. The searing fire that surged through my shattered legs.

But I don't have time for fear. Forcing the memories away, I release the kelpie's mane. I half leap, half tumble from his back. My hip meets the ground first, then my shoulder. Fighting the pain that radiates through my bones, I scramble to my feet. The kelpie halts and rounds on me.

"You shouldn't have done that," he says, his tone unsettlingly calm.

"You shouldn't have deceived me," I say through my teeth. "How are you still alive? How can you survive a binding fae promise?" My eyes dart around the clearing, seeking a place to run, to hide. The pond is a mere few feet away, which still gives the kelpie a chance to drag me into its depths.

"I did not break my promise," he says. He takes a step, and I flinch. Then I realize he isn't stepping closer to me but toward the lake. "I brought you to where you needed to go, alive and unharmed, just like I promised. I was never going to deposit you inside the body of water, only at its shore."

"This isn't where I asked you to take me. I asked to go to Fairweather Palace."

"Yes, but that is not where you *needed* to go."

"And this is?"

"Yes." The kelpie retreats closer to the pond again. His rear hooves sink into the dark waters, sending a ripple outward. A second ripple forms at the pond's center, overwhelming the first as something begins to breach the surface.

I take another trembling step back. Then another.

A feminine figure rises from the pond and glides toward the shore. At first, she's nothing more than a liquid shape, feature-less and indistinguishable from the water she came from. Then the water sloughs off her, drip by drip, to reveal blue skin, pale lips, pointed ears, a nose. Finally, it drains from her upper face to unmask a pair of eyes.

Green eyes with too-large pupils.

Eyes that send me straight back to Danielle's bedroom where I glimpsed a memory of them.

And before that...

Long before that, when I first saw them...

Those terrifying eyes weren't conjured by my imagination. They belonged to a person all along.

I know who this fae female is.

Her lips curl into a smile that doesn't reach her sinister eyes. The last remnants of the water slide from her hair, revealing long blue-black strands the exact shade as mine. "Astrid," she croons, her voice like a hiss.

I can't bring myself to move. Can do nothing but stare at the fae who birthed me.

"It's me, Astrid," the fae says. "Don't you recognize me? I'm your mother."

## 39

*ASTRID*

I'm stunned silent. Frozen. I stare at the fae who is my mother, seeking anything I could possibly recognize from my brief time in her care. We look nothing alike, save for the hue of our hair. She's beautiful, just like Father said she was, with smooth blue skin and full lips. She wears a thin dress that appears to be woven from blue-green pond moss. It's sleeveless, draping over each breast before it connects beneath her belly button in a long, trailing skirt that clings to her sinuous curves. What Father failed to mention, however, is how frightening her particular quality of beauty is. Violence lurks just beneath the surface of her skin, her hair, her lips. I see it in the curl of her fingers, in the slight hunch of her slender shoulders, in the narrowing of her chartreuse eyes.

I suppress a shudder, the sight of those hauntingly familiar irises sending bile rising into my throat. With my magic still humming within me in the wake of my meeting with the kelpie, it needs no encouragement from me to surge outward and wrap around me. An impression locks into place—one of desperation, bloodlust, and a vast hollow emptiness. Are these what she considers her worst qualities? Or her best? Whatever this impression is, it had to have formed the first time we held each other's eyes.

Back when I was a baby.

Back before she left me abandoned on the lakeshore.

Unlike the threadbare impression I formed on Torben, this one hasn't been weakened by time. By change or growth. Whatever this impression is, it's just as valid as it was the day my magic created it.

A time or two I've let myself wonder what it might be like to be reunited with my mother. To see her again. Perhaps she'd have a reason for having left me the way she did. Perhaps none of the violent rumors of the sprite who haunted Dewberry Lake were true.

But as I stare at the female before me, I come to the same conclusion I always have before. That Father knew this woman better than anyone. He loved her. Made a baby with her. And he found her so dangerous that he saved me from her and never looked back.

This creature—mother or no—is lethal.

She continues to grin at me with that forced smile and spreads her arms out wide. "Come to me, Astrid." The gesture is meant to be welcoming, but the thought of meeting her in an embrace sends every hair on my body standing on end.

I glance from her to the kelpie at her side, calculating my chances of survival if I run. There's still somewhere I need to get to. The threat to Torben's life remains.

I swallow hard, burying as much of my fear as I can. "Why am I here? I'm in the middle of something very important."

She lowers her arms, releasing her welcoming gesture, and strokes the kelpie's mane instead. "I asked Vartul to bring you to me, alive and unharmed."

"Why?"

She scoffs. "What do you mean *why*? I'm your mother, Astrid. I gave you your name. I birthed you from the depths of my lake. What other reason do I need?"

"You've never been a mother to me," I say, voice quavering. "I don't even know your name. Father said you never told him."

"My name is Myrasa."

"Well, Myrasa, I would say it's lovely to meet you, but that would be a lie, and I'd rather not flatter you with false niceties."

Anger flashes through her eyes before she steels her expression beneath a deadly calm. "You have a sharp tongue, don't you?"

"Someone very important to me is in trouble," I say, "and your intervention may have already cost him his life. If it's no different to you, I'll be going."

I shift my stance, preparing to walk away. I hardly move an inch before the kelpie darts behind me. He sidles one way, then another, demonstrating his ability to block any route back into the woods.

I burn Myrasa with a glare. "Let me leave."

She lifts a thin blue-black brow. "You just met the mother you've been separated from for almost nineteen years, and this is your response?"

"I told you, you're no mother to me," I bite out. "You left me on the shore—"

"I simply set you aside so I could have a break from you," she says with a dismissive flutter of her hand.

Her words send a shard of glass to my chest. "A break from me," I echo.

She moves closer, leaving the pond to step barefoot onto the surrounding grass. "You were a very difficult child, Astrid."

A spark of rage ignites in my blood. "Then why bother seeing me now?"

Her smile shifts into something more like a snarl. "Because you're mine. Because you were taken from me—"

"You mean when my father saved me from you?"

She moves closer, each step making a squelching sound in the sodden grass. "He didn't save you. He abducted you. Stole you from me. That is why I had him killed."

My breath catches in my throat, so sudden it nearly chokes me. It takes me several moments to comprehend her vile words. "You...you're the one who orchestrated his murder?"

She lifts her chin. "It was nothing less than he deserved for stealing you from me."

My breaths come hard and fast, making my shoulders heave from the force. Truth dawns on me in a vicious, violent wave. "You're who Marybeth gave the power of her true name to. You made her poison the pie."

"Yes," she says without a hint of remorse. "Something happened the last time I saw you, daughter. I required much rest afterward, so I laid you on the shore. You couldn't shift like me, couldn't merge with the water like I could. Instead, you were forever in that frail humanlike body, desperate for air, wailing when you got even the slightest droplet of water in your lungs. Now do you understand why I left you alone while I rested? Do you understand why I was so upset that Edmund Snow stole you from me?"

"It doesn't explain why you killed him."

She scoffs. "Don't tell me you mourn for your captor."

"Captor? He was my rescuer! The only parent I ever had. You took him—my father, the person I loved most in the world —away from me. Yes, I mourn him."

"Edmund Snow wasn't your father, Astrid. Is that what he told you?" She releases a dark chuckle. "Lying humans."

My blood turns to ice. "What...what do you mean?"

"You truly thought he sired you?" She tuts, shaking her head. "No, Astrid. Edmund Snow never came near enough to so much as touch me. He always lingered around my lake, painting me from the shadows. There was nothing I could do to tempt him closer, for he knew what I was, what I'd done to a handful of unlucky fools who dared seek their reflection in my lake. I take it you know of my magic?"

I give a shaky nod, feeling as if I'm outside of my body. "You made people fall in love with their reflections. They'd fall into your lake and drown."

"That's part of it," Myrasa says. "Yes, those who looked into my lake and met my eyes were enchanted with an over- whelming feeling of love. An emotion so enticing they were immobilized, even once I started feeding off them."

"What do you mean you fed off them?" I knew her victims drowned, but their bodies were always recovered.

"I'm a water sprite, therefore emotion is my domain. I have the ability to feed off the emotions I evoke with my magic. That's how I survive. How I keep my lake full and expansive."

I note that the body of water behind her is hardly full or expansive, but I keep my observation to myself. "If all you needed was emotion to feed, then why did those who fell in love with their reflections also drown?"

"Not all of them did," she says. "It just so happens that most of whom I drained energy from fell into my lake."

"And you just let them?"

She shrugs, as if the human lives lost meant nothing. "I understood the dangers of growing too notorious. So, yes, if someone fell into my lake, I let them drown. But that's not the point I'm trying to make. We were supposed to be discussing your abductor, Edmund Snow, correct?"

I clench my jaw.

"Edmund was a prize I sought to claim," she says, "but no matter what I tried, I couldn't get him close enough to my lake to ensnare him. You see, my magic only works when at least part of my physical form is connected to my main body of water. Whether he knew this or was simply wary of me, he kept his admiration at a distance. When you were born, he came around even more frequently, watching us, painting us. And then he stole you."

"You left me alone and crying."

"I told you. I was resting. Something happened—"

"What? *What* happened? And if Edmund isn't my father, then who..." I can't bring myself to finish the question. My own words echo in my head.

*Edmund isn't my father.*

*Edmund isn't my...*

No. No matter what Myrasa says, Edmund Snow *was* my father in the only way that mattered.

"You want to know who your real father was?" she asks.

I'm not sure I'm ready for that, so I say nothing. Then a chilling thought occurs to me. I glance sidelong at the kelpie who continues to pace behind me.

Myrasa chuckles. "No, not Vartul. He's more of a business partner than a lover. Vartul serves me in any way I need. In return, I provide him with a body of water where he can safely feed."

It isn't hard to guess what she means by that. She allows him to feed off human victims in her pond—an illegal practice. The thought sends my stomach roiling.

"Your true father is just another dead man," she says. "They didn't all succumb to a limp stupor before they fell into my lake. I played with the handsome ones first."

For the love of the All of All, is this monster truly my mother? "So you murdered both of them. The man who sired me and the one who raised me."

Myrasa releases a grumbling sigh. "This isn't at all how our reunion was supposed to go."

"How did you think it would go? That I'd run into your arms and thank you for what you've done?" A sob heaves through my chest.

"I thought you would at least understand me. We're the same, Astrid. Creatures of powerful magic."

"I'm nothing like you! I've never wished for my magic to cause harm or distress. I've regretted every ounce of pain I've ever unwittingly inflicted upon anyone."

She narrows her eyes, distaste stretching her lips thin. "Causing harm and distress is the natural way of life. The prey must suffer so the predators can survive. All of us are prey to something. Doing what I do, feeding the way I choose, is my right. At least it should be."

"Murder should never be a right."

She scoffs. "Before the war, there weren't such harsh limitations on the fae like there are now. I fed on my own kind then, and I wasn't punished for it. Anyone foolish enough to visit my lake deserved to die. I didn't choose for human cities to grow around my lake, my forest. I didn't agree to let humans onto our land, to let them mingle with us. I didn't agree for my lake to fall under a seelie queen's jurisdiction, nor did I agree to follow her oppressive rules. Those choices weren't given to me. They happened to me. Why should I have to change?"

I feel only the slightest pinch of sympathy. I've heard about the struggles many fae have gone through—the unseelie in particular—in adapting to post-war changes. Courts shifted. Human cities sprouted where once there was only forest. The wildest of unseelie creatures were banished to lands that fell under the protection of each court's unseelie ruler. Those who didn't comply with the new rules were punished. So I can understand her frustration. But the way Myrasa kills is an unnecessary cruelty. If she only needs to touch her main body of water to use her magic, then there are other ways she can feed without killing people. She hid beneath the surface of the water on purpose. To kill.

But what she did to my father...that went beyond feeding.

"Perhaps I've misjudged you," Myrasa says. "Perhaps you

are softer than I thought you'd be. Regardless, I am glad for our reunion. You will forgive me in time."

"I will never forgive you," I say, my words laced with all my rage. All my grief. "My father meant the world to me, and you took him away. Why? Why, after so many years, did you suddenly want me back?"

"It's not as sudden as you think. I need you, Astrid."

*Need*. Not love. "Why?"

Her expression turns hard. "Because, daughter, you stole my magic."

## 40

*ASTRID*

A chill runs through me. "What do you mean I stole your magic?"

Myrasa extends a hand toward a low boulder and stump near her pond. "Let us sit down while we catch up. I know it isn't the fancy accommodations you're used to at the palace, but you'll have to forgive me for not being a queen." Her words sharpen to a bitter edge at the word *queen*.

"I'm not sitting down. And we aren't *catching up*. In fact, I can't...I can't be here—" Torben's face fills my mind, reminding me of his stupid, pointless sacrifice. Even with the knowledge that Tris isn't the one who killed my father, I harbor no hope that she'll let him go. I don't know exactly what he intended to do during his meeting with her, but from the hollow look in his eyes to the hopeless way he said he loved me before he left, I know he didn't plan on leaving the palace alive. My chest tightens as I wonder if it's already too late.

Even if it isn't...

I glance around the clearing, but the kelpie bares his sharp teeth in warning. There's no way I can outrun a kelpie. If I fought him off, tricked him again, I'd still have to make my way to Fairweather Palace. Still have to risk that Torben could already be...

Vertigo seizes me. I refuse to finish the thought as I sway on my feet.

"It's too late, Astrid," Myrasa says, her tone filled with false sympathy. "I know all about the queen's hate for you. And I know where your most recent captor went. He won't be coming for you, nor you for him."

Rage heats my blood, and I use it as an anchor. A tether to logic. It's all I can do not to give in to my grief. I fix Myrasa with a scowl. "You sent Marybeth to lie to us this morning, didn't you?"

"I sent her to free you from yet another man holding you captive."

"He wasn't—" I bite off my words, knowing there's no point in arguing with this creature. What I want from her now is the truth. "Did you force her to end her own life with the Crimson Malus?"

"I gave her a set of orders," Myrasa explains. "Words she must say. Words she cannot say. Being given the power of one's true name doesn't grant ultimate control, only the ability to compel the person through direct commands. So I had to make my orders very clear. I have from the start. One of her orders for this morning was to swallow the poison under two conditions. The first was if you refused to come with her. The second was if she said so much as three words that compromised you coming to me. It was a safeguard, should she find a way around the other words I ordered her not to say."

My breath hitches as I recall the last thing that left Marybeth's lips.

*Don't trust me.*

Three final words.

I thought she'd meant that I shouldn't trust her because she was taking me to Tris. Now I know she'd meant not to trust the words she'd said prior to that moment. I recall how she seemed to be fighting to speak. Struggling to get every word out. I'd thought she'd been battling her master's compulsion, but instead...

She'd been fighting *not* to speak. Fighting the scripted lie she'd been sent to deliver. A lie meant to separate me and Torben. A lie that would convince Torben we were out of time. The only way Myrasa could have predicted the scheme would work is if she knew what Torben meant to me. Not only that, but she had to have known where to find us in the first place.

That's when I recall what Torben said this morning—that he'd recently seen a kelpie on his property. I know now it hadn't been just any kelpie but Vartul, sent by Myrasa to spy on us. But how did he know to look for us at Davenport Estate?

Myrasa takes a step closer to me, and I stiffen. Thankfully, she doesn't draw nearer. Instead, she folds her hands at her waist. "I would have let the girl live if you'd come with her."

"I tried," I say. "I agreed, but she..."

"Ah." Myrasa's lips curl with amusement. "It was my second condition then."

"Which means you killed her."

She lets out an irritated sigh. "The girl was responsible for her own fate. She knew the dangers of giving away the power of her true name."

I narrow my eyes. "How did it happen? When?"

Myrasa gestures toward the boulder and stump again. "Can we sit? I'm not strong outside of my pond these days."

Something flares in my chest, a simmering combination of hope, rage, and...and something darker. Vengeance. It's what I once felt for Tris when I was certain she'd killed my father. It was what drew me to Wrath's fighting pit night after night, eager to learn whatever I could. I doubt much of what I learned will help me now, but at least I know the value of learning your opponent's weaknesses. And Myrasa just hinted at one of hers.

I fold my arms. "Fine."

Her smile stretches wide, but her cold eyes remain fixed on me as we take our places at her makeshift seating area—she on the boulder, me on the stump. "I'd offer you tea first, but I'm not some simpering human," she says, tone mocking.

"Just speak."

"Very well. You want to know about how your lady's maid came into my company?"

"I want to know everything."

She quirks a brow. "Are you certain? The truth can be a heavy burden to bear." When I refuse to acknowledge her question, she rolls her eyes and speaks. "I'd been looking for you for a year when your lady's maid and I crossed paths. That was two years ago. After searching for where Edmund had taken you, I discovered you'd become a princess, step-daughter to the Seelie Queen of Spring." She says the last part with a snarl. "I tried to come see you, but I couldn't so much as enter the palace grounds. They were warded with enchant-ments. Every fabricated request for a petition with the queen was denied. It seemed you rarely left the walls of the palace yourself, so I couldn't meet you face to face. So I waited. Settled a body of water nearby in the Fairweather Woods where I could watch for any potential leads that would help me get you back. That's when I discovered your maid often met with a human messenger after dark to exchange letters she couldn't send from inside the palace. I intercepted the first letter. It was written to a cousin of hers named Danielle. A young woman I'd heard about during my investigation to find you."

A pit forms in my stomach at the mention of Danielle. "What did the letter say?"

"That little friend of yours was selling your secrets. The

letter detailed your magic—something she'd recently learned about from you."

My chest tightens, part with sorrow, part with anger. I trusted Marybeth. Befriended her. I always thought she asked me questions out of genuine curiosity. I never suspected she was encouraging me to divulge my secrets so she could pass them on to Danielle.

But when Torben and I met with Sandy and Danielle, neither mentioned knowing about my magic. "You destroyed the letter, didn't you?"

She nods. "And ended the messenger's life. I saw both as a threat to you, and the same went for Marybeth. I was prepared to kill her when I next found her in the woods with a letter in hand. Vartul and I caught her, trapped her. But when I read her latest correspondence, I was surprised by what I found. In it, she expressed a refusal to divulge any more of your secrets. She insisted you were a good person and a kind friend and that she no longer believed what her cousin had told her about you. Seeing this, I realized I could make her an ally. So I...*persuaded* her to give me the power of her true name."

"You persuaded her." I give Myrasa a pointed look. "How?"

"I threatened her, all right? I said I'd go to the queen and reveal the maid's treachery. The girl would be executed for smuggling information about the princess out of the castle, but if she gave the power of her true name to me, I'd use her to reunite her beloved princess with her mother."

"She agreed, simple as that?"

Her lips curl up at the corners. "There may have been some...fear involved as well."

Vartul snickers behind me. I imagine they threatened Marybeth with a violent drowning to quicken her resolve.

Myrasa continues. "But yes, she agreed. She seemed almost happy to do so once I told her who Edmund Snow really was— your captor. After that, I utilized my control over the girl to gain information about you, the queen, and your so-called father. I learned about your reliance on Crimson Malus, about your stepmother's growing disdain for you. It took two years to finalize a plan, but once I had a clear vision of how to get you out of the palace, I executed it."

I curl my fingers into my palms until I feel the bite of my nails. "You mean you killed my father."

She lifts her chin. "I liberated you from your captor. From a false familial bond."

*This is the false familial bond,* I want to say, but I hold my tongue.

Her smug expression turns affronted as she speaks again. "Unfortunately, my plan didn't quite go as I'd foreseen. While Marybeth spirited you from the palace as ordered, you managed to trick Vartul. He was supposed to take you to me that night, but when you used your magic against him, he thought he'd found the wrong girl." She pauses to glare at the kelpie. "After that, I had to come up with a new plan. Marybeth's reports made me hopeless, as no one was able to find you. Until, finally, the Huntsman got involved."

My heart flips in my chest at the mention of Torben, but it quickly turns into a hollow ache.

"I ordered Marybeth to read his correspondences with the queen, to learn all she could about his mission, his whereabouts, his weaknesses. Whenever he showed up to the palace in person, she spied on his meetings with Tris. She learned about his possession of the Chariot, overheard him making a bargain to deliver the device to the queen in exchange for Davenport Estate. Marybeth also discovered that he'd located you in the Fire Court, in Irridae. That you'd made a new life for yourself at the Seven Sins Hotel." Her tone darkens, as does her expression. "That he was planning on ending your life within the following days. As soon as I learned where you were, I ordered Marybeth to take leave from the palace and get to

Irridae at once. Vartul took her to the border of the Fire Court, and she rode the train the rest of the way. I feared even then it might be too late. That...that you were lost to me."

Her eyes go unfocused, and my hate for the creature almost softens. Almost.

"Why didn't you simply come find me yourself?" I ask. "Or send your kelpie friend? Surely either of you would have been more formidable than a human girl."

"You'd be right about that, had you gone to any other court, but Vartul and I are both water fae. While water is known to overpower fire, there are instances where fire is detrimental to water. I couldn't have survived that hot and barren land. Vartul would have been weak outside of the pools and ponds throughout the court. So I sent your friend to save you instead. Someone you trusted. Someone who cared about you enough to work hard to save you regardless of the orders I gave. I told her to do whatever it took to kill the Huntsman before he killed you. Above all else, though, she was to bring you back to me."

Her eyes lock on mine, disgust curling her upper lip. "I should have known better. Should have foreseen that you'd fall in love with your captor yet again."

"Stop calling them that. Father and Torben—" I nearly choke on my words. For a moment, I wonder if she's right. Both men did abduct me in the strictest sense of the word. While Father's intentions had been noble from the start, Torben's weren't. I think back to our first meeting, how he handcuffed me and nearly went through with tearing out my heart. He'd been my enemy then, a man sent to murder me in cold blood.

And Myrasa is right. I fell in love with him.

I expect shame to sink my heart at the admission.

But it doesn't.

Instead, a lightness flutters through me. A comforting warmth.

Myrasa's words may be true, but they fail to account for

everything that happened between my first meeting with Torben and when I realized I loved him. Despite the bargain that could cost him his life, despite the prejudice he'd formed against me regarding my guilt, despite the fact that the same poison that killed my father laced my blood...

He stood by my side. Fought to prove my innocence. Befriended me. Comforted me in my time of need. Helped me get through one of the hardest experiences of my life. Not only that, but...

The feeling of fur against my cheek floods my memory—no, two memories. Of Torben lying next to me on the bed, calming my frayed mind while I was trapped in my grief. Of the baby bear snuggled up against my tiny, crying form while I was hurting and alone.

So yes, I fell in love with my captor. I've loved two of them in two different ways.

But both men have been so much more.

So. Much. More.

Myrasa places a hand on my shoulder. I stiffen at her touch, the coldness of her palm seeping through my blouse. "You're free from him now," she says. "It's time to take your rightful place at my side."

I shrug out of her grip and rise to my feet. "My place isn't—"

My words become lodged in my throat as Myrasa reaches into the folds of her mossy skirt and extracts a ruby red fruit. She thrusts the Crimson Malus toward me, a false smile dancing over her cruel lips. "Take it, daughter. Take one bite and all the pain you've endured will be gone. Take it and you'll be free from pain. Free from responsibility. You don't need to suffer any longer. You don't need to try and be anything you aren't. Instead, you can live carefree with me. No longer will you suffer the consequences of your magic. Instead, you will unleash your powers, use them as you see fit, punish those who treat you badly."

Hunger gnaws at my stomach, burns my blood. It isn't a true hunger but a lustful, insatiable beast. My eyes lock on the apple, on the promise of freedom from sorrow. Of a numbing of the pain that stabs my heart.

"One bite, my darling," Myrasa coos. "One bite and you'll feel free. The best part is you can have all you want of this. We'll relocate our pond to the very heart of a Crimson Malus grove. You will use your magic to attract food sources that will help me feed and grow stronger. In turn, I'll help you grow stronger, to gain more control over your magic. Together, we'll grow this pond into a lake like it once was. I *need* you, daughter."

The word *need* echoes through my mind, even as the dark hunger continues to writhe through me. My vision blurs at the edges, all color leached from the landscape in favor of the single ball of red held before me, radiating like a beacon under the moonlight.

I swallow the dryness in my throat, the thirst, the desperate longing for numb relief.

With a trembling hand, I accept the apple.

## 41

*ASTRID*

Myrasa's face brightens, eyes dancing with victory as she hands over the poisonous fruit.

I turn the apple over and over in my palm. Then, with as much force as I can muster, I toss it across the clearing and send it rolling into the shadows between the trees.

When I meet Myrasa's eyes, rage burns in them. I hold her cruel gaze without falter. "No," I say, my tone cold. Firm. Resolute. "No, I will not accept your offer of poison, nor will I stand at your side and let you use me how you see fit. Because you need me, right? You believe I stole your magic."

"You did steal it, daughter," she says, teeth bared. "When you were a babe and did nothing but cry and cry and cry, I tried to soothe you. But all you wanted was to be held, to be kept dry and constantly fed. Nothing I did seemed to calm you. For months I suffered, not knowing how to make you happy. So one day, I decided to try and use my magic on you."

I frown. "You...you tried to make me fall in love with my reflection?"

"Yes, but since I can only use my magic while touching water, I had to hold you while I stood in the lake. You were frightened of the lake, rejecting the very element that fuels your magic."

It isn't hard to imagine why I might have feared her lake, considering what she'd said about me disliking water in my lungs. She probably tried to force me to shift forms, dragging me under the surface to see if I'd finally become like her.

"All you did was cry," she says. "You wouldn't even open your eyes to look at me. Like you, I require eye contact to ignite my reflection magic. So, I admit, I resorted to draining your energy. I feed off love better than any other emotion, but I could still drain your fear. That seemed to frighten you more, but it got you to open your eyes. Finally, you looked at me and I was able to ignite my magic, to force you to feel love. But you had magic of your own, a kind I hadn't witnessed until that very moment. Suddenly, I saw you as a vile creature, an empty, hollow monster with nothing but desperation and bloodlust in her veins. In my shock, my magic surged out of my control. Instead of draining you, I began to drain myself. I nearly sapped myself dry as I held your gaze, and it wasn't until I dropped you that I was freed. You nearly fell into the lake, and I used the last of my energy to gather you back in my arms and place you on the shore. After that, I fell into a deep slumber as I recovered my energy. By the time I awoke, you were gone."

"Rescued by my father," I say, my tone flat to hide how unsettled I feel at her tale.

Myrasa scoffs. "I was grateful, at first. Not because I wanted you gone, but because I wasn't sure how long I'd slept. Even after I awoke, I remained weak. It took months to realize why. To accept that you'd taken my magic."

"I don't understand. How did I...take your magic?"

"It took me a long time to understand as well, and it wasn't until I read your maid's first letter that everything fell into place. You were a mirror, born with a magic much like my own. But instead of reflecting back one's best qualities and making them fall in love with themselves, you reflected back one's worst. And when we locked eyes and I used my magic on you, your mirror magic deflected it, deflected my draining of your energy, and forced me to drain myself instead. When I dropped you and severed our strange linking of powers, I'd unintentionally transferred my magic to you. From then on, you've carried both of our powers—the power to form a negative impression and a positive one."

My stomach turns at the thought of harboring this monster's magic. The same magic that sent countless victims to their deaths at the bottom of her lake. "But...but I can't drain others of energy...can I?"

The blood leaves my face.

Is that what I've been doing all along? Is that why people turn against me time after time? My mind spins at the prospect.

"No, Astrid, you did not take that part of my magic. Only my reflection magic."

My thoughts go still. I can't tell if I'm relieved. Discovering some dark and unknown layer to my magic would be agonizing to bear, but so is the confirmation that nothing else is responsible for all my relationships that have turned sour. Only me. Only my unintentional use of my magic.

"Even with my draining magic still intact," Myrasa says, "I grew weaker and weaker. I must be touching my body of water to feed, but without my reflection magic, I couldn't lure people close enough to my lake to drain them in the first place. Without adequate sustenance, my lake grew smaller and smaller. I began to sleep longer and longer. I didn't realize how close to death I'd become until Vartul paid me an unintended visit three years ago. He'd had someone on his back, but they were fighting against the bonds of his mane. Instead of taking them to one of the larger bodies of water far from seelie cities like he normally did, he risked killing his victim nearby in my pond. When I sensed the emotion of fear suddenly flooding my waters, I fed. Awoke.

"With my mind clear for the first time in almost two decades, I saw how meager my lake had become. I grieved for the magic I'd lost and knew I had to get it back. So Vartul and I struck a deal. He'd serve me, and I'd allow him to use my pond. We'd share each victim he caught. I'd drink their energy and he'd consume their bodies. It was but a temporary solution, for without my reflection magic, I couldn't devour love—the only truly nutritious emotion. No matter how much fear I've consumed these last few years, I haven't been able to grow larger than this." She waves a hand at her pond.

"But *you*," she says, expression brightening. "I knew you had what I needed to regain my former glory. I set off in search of you, trying to find out where you'd gone. My only clues were the human footprints I'd found when I first awoke from slumber. Even though I'd been too weak to follow them then, I'd noted how they'd approached my shore, right where I'd left you, then led back the other way. Edmund Snow was my primary lead, for he was the only person who frequented my lake on a regular basis, and he didn't return after I regained my meager consciousness. My investigation proved he now had a daughter named Astrid—the name I gave my own child. I knew then he was your captor. However, I was perplexed by every account I heard about you, for everyone described you differently. I suspected it had to do with your magic, but as I said before, it wasn't until I met your lady's maid that it all made sense."

"So you came after me not because I'm your daughter, but because you wanted your magic back."

"You make it sound like I feel no affection for you at all, but you're wrong. The more I learned about you, the more affection I felt. You seemed so much like me, leaving a trail of enemies behind as you moved from town to town, even making an enemy of the queen. I thought you knew what you were doing and treasured your powers the same way I always have." She gives me a pitying look. "Don't break my heart, daughter. Tell me I wasn't wrong. Tell me we can work together. Tell me you'll belong to me again."

I narrow my eyes. "I've never belonged to you, and I never will."

She lowers her head and releases a long sigh. Then she shifts toward her pond, stopping only when her left toe meets the water's edge. She doesn't lift her eyes to meet mine, but I see the sheen of tears that fills them. "Then I'll have to take my magic back by force."

## 42

*TORBEN*

Astrid's scent fills my lungs as I barrel through the forest in my unseelie form, paws tearing through soil as I race toward the woman I love. With every step I take, her scent grows stronger, fresher, closer. It's tangled with a secondary scent, one that has me alternating between fear and rage. I noticed it as soon as I arrived at Davenport Estate minutes ago. But I smelled it even before that. Breathed it in on my property just the other day when I was doing my rounds.

A kelpie.

It had seemed so benign then. Just an unseelie creature passing through along with all the other wildlife. But now... now I know its presence was purposeful. What exactly its motive was, I know not. But I'm desperate to find out.

The sound of rapidly beating wings buzzes in my ear, followed by a minuscule feminine voice. "You're going too fast, Huntsman. I can't keep up."

Irritation flashes through me. "I never said you had to come."

The tiny pixie scoffs. "That's no way to speak to your queen."

Tris is right, but I have no patience for guilt or formalities right now. My every thought revolves around Astrid, around the fear now sharpening in her scent trail. When I don't reply to the queen, she falls back to a more moderate pace.

As soon as I realized Astrid was in trouble and the queen wasn't the guilty party, I asked Tris to allow me to use the Chariot one last time. I had to explain my reasons—or as much of them as I could in a matter of anxiety-ridden seconds—and she insisted on escorting me herself. If finding Astrid meant finding the person who killed her husband, she wasn't willing to let me go alone. I'm surprised she didn't bring any of her guards. I can only guess it means she expects to confront the culprit—and deal with them—herself.

Well, she'll have to fly faster if she wants to dole out personal vengeance. I have no intention of slowing down for the pixie or waiting for her permission to act. As soon as I find Astrid, I won't hesitate to lay waste to that damned kelpie or anyone who has harmed so much as a hair on her head. Tris can lag behind and confront their bloody remains for all I care.

Astrid's scent turns sharper, her trail now mingling with the fragrance of her current profile. I'm close. So close. But the terror that pulses through her aroma, constricting it, strangling it...I can't help but fear I won't get there in time.

# 43

*ASTRID*

I gasp at the sudden pull that surges through me. It feels as if my lungs are being squeezed by iron, my blood drained of life, my bones sapped of energy. My mind spins, turning the moonlit clearing to black.

I don't realize I lost consciousness until I open my eyes and find myself lying on the muddy grass.

Myrasa crouches next to me, lips turned down at the corners. She lifts a slender hand to brush a strand of hair off my forehead. I try to flinch back from her, but I don't have the strength to move. My eyes flutter shut of their own accord, my eyelids too heavy.

"I don't like having to feed off you, my child," Myrasa says, her voice deceptively kind, "but I will do whatever it takes to get my magic back. It won't be like it was last time. You can't deflect my feeding magic now that I know what to expect. As long as I don't meet your eyes, I can feed off your energy without you mirroring my powers back at me and making me drain myself. There is no escape, Astrid. Not unless you agree to become a partner. A true daughter. Use your magic to help me lure true sustenance to my pond, and I will allow you to keep the powers you stole. Then we can become a family."

I try to speak, try to tell her that what she's asking of me makes a mockery of the word *family*, but even speaking is too difficult.

"If you will not willingly stand by my side, I will feed off you again and again until you return my magic to me." She strokes my hair again, her cold caress making my stomach roil. "So this is your true face. You're so beautiful, my daughter."

I realize then that my magic must have fled when I lost consciousness. Finally, I manage to open my eyes again. Her face swims before me, but as soon as those green irises become clear, a jolt of terror runs through me. On instinct, my magic snaps back into place.

She snatches her hand away from me, then lets out a low chuckle. "I still don't enjoy that side of your magic, Astrid, but now that I understand it, I won't let it thwart me. You've been wearing that face since you stepped into the clearing. Donning it again won't keep me at bay. Show me my worst qualities all you want. It won't change what must be done."

I struggle to move again, trying to force my lips, my hands —*anything*—to flinch or flutter. But I remain limp. Now I understand why so many of her victims drowned, lured to the edge of her lake and drained of energy, unable to fight the water that flooded their lungs. What a sad irony, that a creature who feeds off love has sent so many people to such a violent, unloving death. I doubt she's ever experienced real love herself.

But I have.

I think of Torben's face, his smile, the strength of his touch. The comforting warmth of his bear form. My mind goes to Father next. His loving, unwavering acceptance of me and my magic. His kindness. His bright and boisterous laugh.

A tingling rises to my lips, then spreads to my fingers and

toes. Slowly, inch by aching inch, strength returns to me. Not entirely, but enough to push myself to sitting. Then standing.

Myrasa rises to her feet too, looking me over through slitted lids. "You recovered quickly. Now, I ask you once more, will you cooperate? I don't want to have to drain you again."

I shake my head.

She flashes her teeth. "Then will you give me back my magic? This is your last chance, Astrid. You will force my hand after this."

"I don't know how to give it back," I say, my words heavy on my tongue. I sway on my feet but manage to plant them firmly on the grass. More and more of my strength builds inside me, warming me, steadying me. "Do you think I've wanted my magic all these years?"

"Haven't you?"

I'm about to deny it, but the truth weighs heavy on my shoulders. I *have* wanted my magic. Perhaps not consciously, but now that I understand how my strange powers work, I know I've unwittingly used my magic all my life to protect myself, to keep others at a distance. All because of Myrasa, because of her neglect, the abuse I don't even recall. Because of those terrifying eyes she forced me to gaze into as a babe, after she began to drain my energy. That was when I first used my magic. As a defense against her. It's why I've automatically used it again and again whenever I make eye contact with another. Father was the only person I ever felt safe enough with to keep my magic at bay. And Torben.

Thoughts of Torben send a shard of glass through my heart, reminding me of his precarious situation, of the sacrifice he left to make. But they fill me with a steady warmth too.

With a deep breath, I close my eyes, focusing only on feelings of love. Comfort. The feeling of fur beneath my hands. The tickle of kitten whiskers against my cheek. Memories of being cherished. Cared for. The scent of paint on canvas. The sound of Father's bellowing laugh.

Light blooms in my chest, unfurling outward until it banishes every dark feeling. Every fear. Every regret. My heart lifts, my mood shifts.

I open my eyes and meet Myrasa's. My magic hums all around me, and I know it's *her* magic this time. I've never tried to use my magic this way, to form a secondary impression. I always thought nothing could negate the first impression I form with my magic. But Torben proved that wrong. Torben proved I can release my magic and allow others to see the real me. So it stands to reason I can create a new impression as well. As I feel the strange shift in my power, I know it's working. The hum of my magic buzzes the same way it does when forming an impression on a new person for the first time.

I search Myrasa's face, expecting to find her best qualities written in her features...but I see nothing.

"Here's your magic," I say, my voice worn and tired. "I don't know how to give it back, but if you know how to take it, then do so. Take it and let me leave. Never come near me again."

She quirks a brow. "You aren't using my magic."

"I am."

"I don't see it. I don't see anything. You're...you're..." Her chest heaves with sharp breaths. "You're faceless. Featureless. I see nothing. *Nothing.*"

The truth slices through me like a cold knife. "There's nothing you love about yourself."

She takes a step back until both feet are submerged in pond water. Her expression turns panicked. "What are you talking about?"

"I'm using your magic and you see nothing. There are no qualities you cherish in yourself. Nothing to fall in love with."

"Perhaps my own magic doesn't work on me," she says, but the tremor in her voice reveals her doubt.

"That's why you feed off love," I say. Despite my hatred for this creature, true pity forms inside my heart. "Because you've never felt it. Never known it. Not for yourself or anyone else."

She squeezes her eyes shut as if she can't bear to look at me a second longer. "Quiet!"

I gasp as I'm once again struck by that surging pull. She wasn't closing her eyes because she couldn't look at me...but to drain me. I try to cry out, but my breath leaves my lungs. My energy melts out of me, sending my head spinning. I lurch on my feet, and my knees give way—

Something enormous barrels between me and Myrasa. Her draining magic cuts off, and I gather in heavy lungfuls of air. Only then do I dare to acknowledge what the large shape is that stands before me. I take in the brown fur, the four paws, the two rounded ears. My heart leaps at the impossible sight of the bear. *My* bear. It's...it's Torben. He's alive.

Rearing up on his hindquarters, he swipes at Myrasa's chest. A spray of blood arcs through the air before she splashes into the center of the pond. The bear turns toward me, and I close the distance between us, burying my hands in the fur around his neck.

"Torben!" The word bursts from my lips with a sob. "You're...you're really here."

He gently nudges my cheek with his muzzle. "Are you all right?"

I don't get the chance to answer. A pair of vicious hooves collide with Torben's head. I scramble back as Torben swipes a paw at the kelpie, grazing the creature's throat with his razor-sharp claws. Vartul lets out a guttural whinny but rears up and strikes Torben again. Torben retreats, but not to run away—to lure the kelpie away from me. I can't peel my eyes off them, off the spray of blood that seeps between the kelpie's teeth as he sinks them into Torben's neck. I cry out and start toward them, desperate to help Torben—

Hands come around my wrists, whirling me away from the fight. Myrasa stands before me, chest heaving, eyes flashing with rage. She tugs me toward the edge of the pond. "If you will not cooperate or give me back my magic, then you will return to me."

I dig my heels into the earth, fighting her painful hold, but the grass is too soft, too muddy, making me slide toward the bank instead. Her fingers tighten around my wrists, her grip so hard I fear my bones will snap.

"I wanted us to stand side by side," she says, dragging me closer. Her feet meet the edge of the pond. She tugs me again until my feet sink beneath the surface, my shoes filling with murky water. Another tug and we're knee deep. Then waist deep. "I wanted us to live as true mother and daughter. Instead, I will return you to the womb that created you. We will merge as one soul. One body. Perhaps I will birth you again after you've learned your lesson."

"What are you—" The surging pull strikes me again, but this time, we're nearly at the center of the pond.

I swallow hard at the chilling realization.

She's going to drown me.

"I'll die," I say, voice weak. My knees begin to give out, but Myrasa keeps me upright in her viselike grip.

"You'll be one with me," she says, her words strangled with tears. "I have to do this, Astrid. I need my magic or I'll never be whole. I'll never feel..."

A sickening sorrow plummets my heart. I know what she's refusing to say. It all makes sense now. Myrasa is incapable of feeling love. Not for herself or others. Whether by choice or by the cruel design of her nature, I know not, but feeding off another's love is the only way she can experience the emotion herself. The only way she can gain full strength. The only way to grow her body of water into a flourishing lake.

How different could things have been if she only knew how to love?

My throat constricts as tears spring to my eyes. Grief fills my blood, and my bones grow heavy with mourning. Mourning for my father. For the nameless man who sired me as well. Mourning for every life Myrasa has taken in her quest to feel love. And mourning for Myrasa herself. Because there's no doubt in my mind...

My mother must die.

Her grip begins to slacken around my wrists, her body shaking with sobs. "Goodbye, Astrid."

I feel myself sinking, my legs giving way as she continues to drain my energy, to feed off my agony, my fear, ounce by ounce. She releases one wrist, and I sink into the pond shoulder deep. I try to meet her eyes, try to do what I unknowingly did when I was a baby and deflect her magic by using her own reflection. But she keeps her gaze fixed firmly away from me.

With nothing left to do, I close my eyes and think of Torben. Father. The kittens. I think of strong arms and gentle touch. Of loving acceptance. Of smiles and laughter and all the things that ever made me feel loved. Warmth spreads through me, cutting through my fear. Mingling with my grief and mourning until it too becomes something sweeter. Something to be cherished.

Myrasa gasps, her body growing rigid at the sudden shift in emotions she's feeding from.

But as she continues to feed, my heart grows warmer, my body reclaiming its strength inch by inch. Not by some new magic but by the endless well that is the love I have inside of me. The love that can never be fully drained or obliterated. It's stronger than my fear. Stronger than Myrasa's magic.

Just as Myrasa releases my other wrist, I surge to my feet on steady legs, my shoes gaining purchase on the muddy pond floor. With all my strength, I shove Myrasa in the chest. She falls backward, arms pinwheeling as she tumbles into the pond. With her momentarily down, I seek out Torben. He and Vartul are still locked in combat at the far end of the clearing, filling it with a cacophony of growls and snarls and sprays of blood.

Myrasa rises to her feet, blocking my view. She's near the edge of the pond now, where the water is only knee deep. I reach for her, but the pull of her draining magic strikes me once more. My strength wavers, but I refocus on feelings of love. Warmth. Safety. I use all my remaining energy to barrel into her and push her the rest of the way out of the pond.

Her draining power cuts off.

If she can't touch her pond, she can't use her magic.

She chuckles as I haul myself off her and plant my feet in the mucky grass between her and the pond. "What are you going to do, daughter? You can't fight me. I'm stronger than you. You can't keep me out of my pond."

I clench my fingers into fists. I know she's right. Against her, I am just a half-human girl with no combat training. I don't have the power to drain victims like she does. But I must try to defeat her. I must keep her from hurting anyone else.

Steeling my resolve, I march toward her and thrust out my hand, wrapping it around her throat. She doesn't fight me. Doesn't claw my hands or wriggle beneath my grasp. Instead, she holds her ground, hands loose at her sides and...laughs.

"You aren't going to kill me, Astrid."

I try to squeeze tighter, but the feel of her pulse fluttering against my palm sends my stomach roiling. She's right. I...I can't do this.

Water flows over my hand. My eyes go wide as I watch her face melt from flesh to rivulets of clear water. It's the opposite of what happened when I first saw her emerge from the pond. Instead of turning from liquid to corporeal, she's shifting back to water. To her unseelie form. I snatch my hand away, scrambling back as her watery shape slinks across the grass back toward the pond.

No! If she touches the pond again, she'll have her magic.

And she won't hesitate to kill me.

I try to kick at her, to block her progress toward the pond, but she simply flows around my feet, avoiding my touch. Inches separate Myrasa from her power, and there's nothing I can do to stop her.

An animalistic wail of pain draws my eyes toward Torben and sends my heart climbing into my throat. Is he hurt? There's no movement. No flurry of hooves and claws, only hulking shadows and blood. Then I see him. Torben, still in bear form, is on the ground with the kelpie pinned beneath his paws. Lowering his head, he snaps his teeth over the kelpie's throat. A whinny pierces the air as Torben severs Vartul's head from his neck. The kelpie goes still.

Torben starts toward me. Just then, something heavy strikes my midsection and lifts me off my feet. I fight against it only to realize my assailant is a thick vine. And it isn't attacking me. Instead, it encircles my waist and sets me down several feet from the pond. The vine releases me and burrows into the earth. I'm about to rush back to the pond, back to where Myrasa continues to trickle toward her pond, when a familiar hand closes over my shoulder. I whirl around to find Torben now in seelie form.

"Wait," he says, voice tense with warning.

"But Myrasa. If she touches the pond..." I turn back toward where I last saw her liquid shape only to find flames bursting at the water's edge, inches from where I just stood. Inches from my mother's unseelie form.

Myrasa recoils from the wall of flame, leaping back and returning to her seelie form at once. She tries to dart around the flame, but the wall grows, spreads, encircles her. Steam rises where her body makes contact with the fire, and she flinches away.

A tiny, winged creature zips toward the flames. As it reaches them, it shifts into a female form. She stands tall before the fiery cage, her wings no longer tiny but large and folded against her back. Shock ripples through me at the sight of my stepmother.

She looks so out of place in her elegant gown, its hem soaking up the mud around her as her silk slippers sink into the grass. Tris stares daggers at the fae caught in the circle of flames. She lifts her hand, and several vines rise from the earth within the blazing enclosure. They wrap around Myrasa, lifting her off her feet. Myrasa's face begins to drip as she tries to turn to liquid once more, but flames now coat the ground beneath her, leaving nowhere to melt. Nowhere to escape. That's when I realize Tris is controlling both the fire and the vines. She's the one who lifted me away from the pond. She's the one who has Myrasa trapped.

I've known fae monarchs have access to all four elements, but I've never seen it in practice before. Never seen Tris utilize such gifts.

My stepmother meets Myrasa's eyes, her face composed, voice calm. Despite her controlled countenance, she's never seemed more terrifying than she does now.

"Your Majesty," Myrasa bites out, tone full of mockery. "Here to punish me—a creature of your own kind—for crimes committed against your precious humans?"

Tris ignores the question. "Did you orchestrate the murder of Edmund Snow?"

Myrasa winces as a tendril of fire licks up one of her legs, but she hides the expression behind a cold smile. "Yes."

The vines squeeze tighter, wrapping around her legs, her neck, her stomach.

I find myself trembling, unable to look away. Torben places

both hands on my shoulders, neither pulling me toward him nor keeping me still. Just...making me aware of his presence. Offering it.

Tris slowly turns to face me. Her composure cracks for the merest second, a frown tugging her lips as she meets my eyes. "I'm sorry," she whispers over the sound of crackling flames.

At first, I think she's apologizing for having wrongfully accused me. Then I see how her hand is curled as if around an invisible orb. She wrenches her arm back in a deliberate motion. A vine inside the circle of flames mirrors the gesture. But unlike the queen's hand, the vine's gnarled fingers aren't empty. Within them pulses a small, dark organ. Myrasa gasps. I do the same when I see the gaping cavity in her chest.

Tris isn't apologizing for what she accused me of.

She's apologizing for killing my mother.

Shifting my gaze to the queen, I give her a subtle nod.

Tris slowly faces Myrasa. "He was the love of my life."

"He was a filthy—" I'll never know what my mother was going to say, nor do I want to. For her last words are cut off as Tris closes her hand into a tight fist.

The vine does the same over the vacant, hollow heart until its pulse thuds no more.

---

## 44

*ASTRID*

The familiar halls of Fairweather Palace spark equal parts terror and nostalgia within me, even as dimly lit as they are now. It must be close to midnight, and most of the palace is sleeping. Much like it was the last time I was here—the night my father died and Marybeth spirited me out of the palace through the servants' quarters. It's hard to recall such things without seeing them in a new light. Now I know she only helped me escape because Myrasa had commanded her to do so.

I blink away the sudden image of flood and flames that threatens to invade my mind and focus on my surroundings. The two guards who flank me. The soft beat of my slippered feet thudding on the cherrywood floor. The rhythm of my pulse that quickens with every step that draws me closer to my destination.

I don't know where exactly I'm being taken, only that I'm meeting with the queen.

I haven't exchanged more than a few words with her since

arriving at the palace a few hours ago. Before that, everything is a blur. So much so that I hardly remember coming back here at all. All I know is my stepmother insisted we return to the palace with her. The kelpie had taken me far enough from Davenport Estate that we were just as far from there as we were from the palace. And apparently, even the queen's delivery of swift justice requires formalities—paperwork, debriefing, correspondences with the other royals on the Alpha Council. That's how it seemed, at least, when Tris had me escorted to my former bedroom upon arrival and whisked Torben away.

I'd been too exhausted to argue then. Too filthy to deny the opportunity for a proper bath. But now that I've cleaned up and briefly rested—however fitfully—I can't stop the nagging worry that I'm still in trouble. Tris may have discovered the identity of Father's real killer, but that doesn't mean she's ceased hating me. For all I know, she could blame me for this. Myrasa was my mother, after all. She killed Father because he took me from her.

What's more worrisome is that I haven't seen Torben since we first arrived. He'd squeezed my hand, a silent reassuring promise, before Tris mentioned something about needing to bring him before the Alpha Council.

We hadn't gotten a chance to speak much, not with how drained I felt. I'm still not entirely sure how Torben and Tris found me. How or why Tris showed up at the clearing at all, seemingly out of nowhere.

The two guards flanking me shift course, guiding me down a flight of stairs to the main floor. From there we make our way down a familiar path to a set of glass doors etched with cherry blossoms. It's the entrance to the gardens. The guards stop before the doors and pull them open.

"The queen will see you now," says one.

I glance from the two guards to the shadowed gardens

beyond. It must be close to midnight by now. Why does Tris want to speak with me out here?

Steeling my nerve, I step beyond the doors and onto the garden path. The night air is cool on my skin, making me wish I'd worn a coat. I changed into clean clothing upon arriving at the palace and taking a much-needed bath. It felt odd donning attire made for a princess after spending these last months as a fugitive, so I chose a simple tartan skirt and matching short jacket. It probably would have been most sensible to wear a nightdress, considering the late hour, but I had a feeling I wasn't getting restful sleep any time soon. Not until I knew whether I was a guest or a prisoner.

That very question rings through my mind as the garden path opens to the first courtyard and reveals the figure standing at the center. Queen Tris faces away from me, wrapped in a long pink brocade cloak trimmed in white fur. Her hair is more unkempt than I've ever seen it, her brambles hanging low and tangled on her head, the petals of her blossoms wilted.

I'm about to clear my throat and announce my arrival when my gaze snags on what has her attention fixed so firmly away from me. She stands before a rose quartz statue, and when I take in the smiling face carved into the figure's head, a sob nearly breaks from my chest. It's my father. He stands not with formidable pride nor terrifying grace like most royal statues I've seen, but with a calm confidence. A crown has been carved on his head, but instead of a scepter in his hand or some other regal symbol, he holds a paintbrush and palette.

My heart swells with a mixture of pain and joy at seeing him. The artist captured in art. It's...him. Beautiful. Kind. Accepting. I'm struck by how much he's done for me my whole life. Even when he insisted I befriend people when I only wanted to stay and help him paint, even when he encouraged me to leave the palace and do something for myself...it was always in my best interest. He knew what I still hadn't discovered—that I had the ability to show my true face. To open my heart and trust, just like how I'd learned to do with him. Tears prick my eyes as I recall how I rebelled against such a notion. How I said wretched things to him that last time we'd argued. Even more painful is how he bore it all with a sympathetic smile.

I let out a shaky breath and return my attention to the queen. She still hasn't noticed my arrival. I take a step closer and feel my magic hum around me, tightening, smothering, protecting. Anticipating the moment she turns around and meets my eyes.

I could keep it in place. I always have with Tris.

But this isn't who I want to be anymore. I don't need my magic to protect me, for I've faced the source of the very fear that created my dependence upon it. Now I know the truth. And I'm stronger than it.

With a slow exhale, I release my magic and approach the queen.

"Your Majesty," I say as I reach her side and dip into an ungraceful curtsy. It seems my months away from the palace have left me rusty.

She slowly turns to face me, and when her eyes meet mine, she furrows her brow. The urge to reach for my magic strikes me hard but I don't give in. Instead, I hold her gaze. Let her look at me.

"So this is what you truly look like," Tris says, her voice far softer than I've ever heard it. She doesn't seem surprised at all.

"Did...did you know..." I can't find the words to finish.

"Torben told me about your magic earlier today," she explains.

I'm surprised she called him *Torben* and not *Huntsman*. I've never heard him referred to by his first name. Aside from when I say it, of course. A pinch of anxiety runs through me now that she now knows my secret—a secret that has done me little good in the past when revealed. Even telling Marybeth proved to be detrimental. She may have accepted me and my magic, but she tried to pass the information on to my enemy. Myrasa's intervention was the only thing that kept it out of Danielle's clutches, but she too used the information with ill intent.

My stomach lurches at the thought of Myrasa. I breathe away memories of fire, blood, and vines. Of murky water and vicious green eyes—

"This was finished just yesterday," Tris says, freeing me from my dark thoughts. She turns her gaze to the statue.

I too study my father's likeness, grateful for a change of subject. Despite the way my muscles tense in the queen's presence, or how my stomach turns at the reminder of what happened earlier today, I can't help but feel a sense of ease fall over me as I stare at the statue. It's even more stunning up close. "The artist did a wonderful job."

"Yes, they did." Silence falls between us for several moments as we stand side by side, entranced by the figure we both loved. She turns to face me again. "I know you have a thousand reasons to hate me."

I don't know what to say to that. I can't deny it, so I stay silent.

She continues. "I can apologize for all of them but one. No matter how you might resent me, I will not apologize for killing your mother. As queen, it is my right to dole out judgment in my court as I see fit, so long as it is justified. Not only was she responsible for Edmund's death, but she posed a threat to you. To my court. I only regret that you witnessed what I did to her. No child should have to watch a parent die, much less both parents."

I'm taken aback. All I can do is stare, surprised by her candor. It wasn't exactly an apology, but what she said still holds value. "I don't blame you for her death," I finally say, and as the words leave my lips, I know they are true. "I thank you for it, for I don't think I could have done it myself."

"Nor should you be forced to bear such a burden," she says. "For everything else, Astrid, I am deeply sorry. I can't begin to express the shame I feel at how I've responded to your magic. Had I known the truth about you straight away..." She trails off as if reconsidering. "No, I suppose I can't be certain how I would have responded to that either. Knowing you could see the depths of my soul written on my face...I can't imagine what that would have been like. All I am certain of now is that I will never hold your magic against you, nor will I use you for your power. I promise."

I'm half in disbelief that I've heard her correctly. This female who I've considered my enemy, who I've hated as much as she's hated me...just made me a promise. A fae promise, a binding one. My throat tightens. "I appreciate that."

"Like I said before, you have a thousand reasons to hate me, and I fault you for none of them. But if you will allow me to make it up to you in the slightest way, I would be honored if you would...if you would allow me to get to know you as you truly are."

Emotions war within me, bitter rage mingling with a warm hope. I'm not ready to forgive her for how she's treated me, but I also can't deny the yearning for connection that's begun to take root in my heart. Before my hope can swell too large, I counter it with logic. "You are no longer bound to me by your marriage to my father, Your Majesty. You should know that... that he and I were never...he wasn't the man who sired me."

"But he *was* your father," she says, unsurprised by the news I delivered. Had she already known? Did Father tell her without ever telling me? I'm not sure how to feel about that.

Tris speaks again. "The ties of blood matter not to me, only that Edmund loved you as his daughter. You were his world well before I came into his life. He wanted everything for you. If he knew what I tried to make Torben Davenport do, he would..."

She brings a hand to her trembling lips and casts a tear-glazed glance at the statue. "He would surely despise me, but only half as much as I currently despise myself. I will carry that burden on my shoulders for a very long time."

"Please don't suffer my presence over some false sense of duty," I say, keeping my tone level despite the emotions still warring in my chest. "I won't hold you to it."

She turns her gaze back to me. "Astrid, I want you to remain my stepdaughter. I want to become worthy of being considered your stepmother. For Edmund, yes, but for myself as well. Perhaps even for you, if you'll allow it. I'm not asking you to forgive me. Only to...let me try. Let me get to know you."

In this moment, I wish I had Torben's sense of smell so I could decipher how she's truly feeling. As strong as my yearning for connection has grown, my suspicion is stronger. I've held onto it all my life, always waiting for others to turn on me.

But...things are different now. At least, I want them to be. I don't know what the future holds, how life will feel knowing I can show my true face. I don't know if it will be any easier to forge friendships or any harder to make enemies. There's a terrified part of me that thinks nothing will change. That all my difficulties stemmed not from my magic but me.

Even so, in the midst of this cold fear lies a bright light. A glimmer of steady truth. Falling in love with Torben was only a hint at what else is possible. There are other kinds of relationships to forge. Other connections to make. Other hearts to meet.

Maybe this—with my stepmother—is a good place to start.

I can't force a smile, but I can bring myself to nod. "All right," I say. "I...I'd like to get to know you too."

Tris' lips curl into an uncertain grin, and her eyes glaze with tears once more. "I see so much of him in you."

My heart stutters. I open my mouth to reiterate that my father and I were never related by blood, but I realize that isn't what she means. She doesn't see his likeness in me, but the parts of him I'll always carry. Qualities he infused in me through his kind nurturing.

She clears her throat and quickly swipes a finger beneath her lashes. "Now, if you follow the path to the left, you'll find someone I'm sure you're far more eager to see."

My pulse kicks up as I realize what she's hinting at. Taking her nod as my dismissal, I rush down the path she indicated. A small courtyard opens up to the side, alight with the glow of familiar petal-like fae creatures. The cerapis sprites buzz beneath an enormous cherry tree, its boughs arching overhead to create an umbrella over the clearing. My heart thuds heavily in my chest as my eyes land on the man who stands before the tree trunk.

Torben appears to have gotten cleaned up and changed since I last saw him, no longer dressed in the mud-splattered, bloodstained clothing he left the clearing in. I rush to him, colliding into his chest as he wraps me in his arms. I know it's only been a few hours since I've seen him, but it feels like a lifetime ago. Especially since I wasn't exactly in a clear frame of mind after everything that happened.

Now I breathe him in, luxuriating in the woodsy scent of him, the feel of his arms, the warmth of his breath against my hair as he utters my name again and again. We stay like that for several moments, falling into a comfortable silence, needing no words, only each other's embrace. But I know it can't last. Not when there's something I know I must say to him.

He must scent my shift in emotions, for he gently pulls back. His hands, however, remain on my shoulders, warm and strong. I tilt my chin to meet his eyes, their golden hue glittering beneath the glow of the sprites. The sight of him is so beautiful it nearly crumbles my resolve.

"I'm supposed to be mad at you," I say. I almost wince at my soft tone, for I don't sound mad at all.

His eyes turn down at the corners as understanding dawns. "For what I did to you today."

"For handcuffing me to the bed so you could sacrifice yourself." This time my words come out with the appropriate amount of sternness.

His jaw shifts side to side as if he's debating whether to argue. We both know he was only doing what he thought would save me. In the end, his meeting with Tris led them to the clearing. Led the queen to execute Myrasa.

Still, it doesn't excuse what he did. How he made me feel. I hold his gaze without falter. Without magic. "I never want you to make choices for me like that, regardless of whether you think it's in my best interest. You don't get to decide to sacrifice yourself for me."

His throat bobs. "I'm sorry, Astrid. Not just because my actions played into the very hands we were trying to escape. Not just because it got you captured by a kelpie and nearly killed. But because it was wrong of me. I could tell you why I did what I did, but you already know. And I..." He runs a hand through his hair, making his copper tresses stick out in a way that's annoyingly cute.

"You did what I would have done in your position too," I say, recalling the secret conclusion I came to last night when we confessed our feelings. I knew our future might be tenuous. I knew both of our fates hung in the balance. And I admitted to myself that I would turn myself over to the queen before letting Torben's life be claimed by a broken bargain. "Now that I know how it feels to be left like that, forced to survive while someone I love tries to trade my life for his, I know it's wrong."

He gives me a sad smile. "You're right. We agreed to

complete our mission together and I betrayed that. Betrayed your trust. I'm so sorry. I hope I can prove to you that I'm more than just a brutish Huntsman. I have a lot to learn about trusting others and opening my heart."

I return his smile. "So do I. Do you...think we can learn together?"

His grin widens. He reaches into his waistcoat pocket and extracts a piece of paper. When he unfolds it, I see it's the deed to Davenport Estate. "Only if you'll consider a humble farmer worthy of your affection."

My mouth falls open. "The queen returned the estate to you?"

"And freed me from my term as Huntsman, as promised."

"But you didn't fulfill your bargain."

He smirks. "I did. Both of them. I turned over the Chariot as well as Astrid Snow's heart." He pats his chest, which only makes me frown in confusion. "You gave me your heart, remember? And I gave you mine."

The words we exchanged in the cherry grove echo in my mind. "Clever, but I can't imagine Tris was at all amused by that."

"She wasn't, but she let me explain. I know it may not have been my place, but I told her about your magic. Told her that what she saw in you was only a reflection of herself. Those words...they changed something in her."

I can't help but agree after my conversation with the queen. That warm hope blooms in my chest again, clearing up the clouds of worry and fear that dance around the edges of my mind.

"She's been helping me finalize everything," he says. "That's where we've been these last few hours. Severing my ties with the Alpha Council, clearing my debts, getting the property officially transferred back to my name." His expression falls slightly. "In a way, I'm poorer now than I was during my service as Huntsman. I no longer have a special coin to flash about and pay for meals, lodgings, and clothing. Everything I want from now on, I must work for. It's just like we talked about this morning when you asked what I'd do with my freedom. Right now, I must work the land myself, till it by hand, care for it alone until—"

"You won't be alone," I say, giving him a playful shove. "Do you not recall what else we talked about this morning? How I asked if I could do my *something* alongside you doing yours?"

He gives me a wry grin, but there's a note of worry in his eyes. "Yes, I recall. However, you are a princess. I'm...I'm just..."

I step in closer, placing my hand over his heart. "You're just the man I love. And while I may be a princess, I'm not beholden to any promise to live here."

"You'd trade this luxury for a rundown manor and an unkempt farm?"

I quirk a brow. "I've worked in a brothel. I've befriended kittens who live behind waste bins. What makes you think I'm beneath working on a farm?"

"I don't want you to work on the farm," he says.

I open my mouth to argue, but he speaks first.

"I want you to do that *something* you spoke of this morning. Find a way to use your magic that feels fulfilling. You may work by my side if you wish, but I think it's more important that you live for *you* right now. It's what your father wanted, and it's what I want too."

His grim, resolute tone has panic tightening my chest. "Are you...breaking up with me? Or putting us on a break?" I gasp. "Wait, were we ever courting? I...I never really gave it much thought, considering—"

He swallows my words with a kiss and lifts me in his arms. "I'm saying no such thing, Astrid," he whispers against my lips. "I want you to be my mate if you'll have me."

My heart leaps at the word *mate*. Fae don't refer to just

anyone they're romantically entangled with as their mate. It's a term given only to committed partnerships. It's less official and less permanent than marriage, but for some fae, it's the highest form of commitment they participate in. Not even two weeks ago I was convinced I'd never experience love. Never know what it was like to be truly seen and loved for who I am.

But now...

Now love warms my chest, spilling outward until I feel like I'm the one glowing instead of the cerapis sprites.

"We can grow side by side," Torben says. "We can grow together—entwined or parallel. But we don't have to do the same thing. Or...or become the same tree."

I understand what he means now, and I realize I do have much to grow and learn. Already I nearly tried to do what I've always done—to latch onto the one person who sees me, to mold myself around what they do. But Father wanted more for me, and if I'm being honest...so do I.

"You're right," I say, and the admission sends a chill through me. A shudder of awe over the possibilities that await. The terrifying prospect that comes with having a future I never thought I'd have.

Everything that comes next—every joy, success, or failure—will be planted by me. *Me.* As I truly am. I don't know what it will be like, but I'm ready for it. To go on this journey with myself. And him.

"I accept you, humble farmer Torben Davenport," I say, tone mocking, "but I have conditions. Well, one."

He pulls back enough to meet my eyes. "What's that?"

"How many kittens can I have?"

His chest rumbles with laughter as he presses his lips to mine once more. "As many kittens as you want."

# EPILOGUE

## ONE YEAR LATER

*ASTRID*

Thousands of people have seen my face, and of those thousands, only a handful know what I truly look like. A year has passed since I learned how to control my magic. To some degree, at least. It isn't always easy. Sometimes, when meeting a new stranger, something about their countenance, the curl of their lips, the tilt of their chin, will have me reaching for my magic when I lock eyes with them. Now, though, I know how to let it go.

I know that I'm safe.

Safe to be seen.

That sense of safety, however, still feels tenuous around one person.

Queen Tris.

Anxiety tickles my chest as I wait in the parlor inside

Davenport Manor. Any moment my stepmother will arrive. Even though she's kept her promise to me over the last year, I can't help but be reminded now and then of how things used to be. How I previously perceived her...and how she perceived me. I think I'm close to forgiving her. Or maybe I have already. Maybe that's why I invite her to tea once a month.

Or perhaps it's because she's now Davenport Estate's largest investor.

The door to the parlor opens, and the estate's steward, Mrs. Morrison, announces my royal guest. I rise from my seat on the divan—the same one Torben used as a bed when we first arrived at the boarded-up manor, only refurbished—and brace myself. My magic tickles the edge of my awareness, but I breathe it away.

"Her Majesty, Queen Tris," Mrs. Morrison says, dipping into a curtsy as my stepmother enters the parlor. The queen looks as elegant as always, the pink blossoms that comprise her hair in full bloom. I dip into a curtsy and am about to rise when Mrs. Morrison speaks again. "And Her Highness, Princess Maisie of the Sea Court."

I nearly fall out of my elegant pose as a fae female enters behind the queen. She looks to be my age, but her pointed ears tell me she's full fae, so she could be ancient for all I know. Regardless, the casual way she carries herself paired with the loose silk trousers and unbuttoned vest she wears immediately sets me at ease.

Tris approaches me and plants a kiss on my cheek, one more practiced than affectionate, but it's a gesture I appreciate, even as it makes me seize up a little. "Hello, Astrid. I hope you don't mind that I brought a guest."

Princess Maisie comes to greet me next, but instead of saying any normal sort of greeting, she stares down at my chest and blurts out, "Oooh are those silvaran oyster pearls?"

It takes me a moment to realize what she's talking about. I glance down at my dress, a confection of silky-smooth gold chiffon and ivory lace, and notice the buttons running from the plunging neckline to my midsection. I hadn't noticed before, but they are in fact pearls.

"Um...yes?" I say, my answer pitched more like a question. I honestly don't know whether they're silvaran oyster pearls, for I'm more interested in the tactile experience of my attire than any shiny decorations they possess. Although, I am starting to appreciate fashion—a new experience for me. Before I learned to control my magic, I always wore what was either most comfortable or most readily at my disposal. Now that I know people can see what I truly look like—not to mention having a stepmother who insists on sending famous dressmakers to outfit me when she's feeling generous—I've begun to take pride in my appearance. Even better is the fact that I've discovered some of the most delectably comfortable fabrics I never knew existed before now.

I smooth my hands over my silky skirt, letting the softness of the chiffon calm my nerves.

Maisie releases a longing sigh, her eyes still locked on my chest. "What I wouldn't give to pluck one of those buttons off your dress and pocket it. I miss having someone to chide me over such instincts and tell me not to steal things."

I slide my gaze to my stepmother and give her a questioning look.

"That's why we're here," Tris says. "Maisie's father, King Ronan, is a dear friend of mine, and when he mentioned his daughter was wanting a pet, I knew exactly where to take her."

"Yes, that's right." Maisie meets my eyes for the first time, and her grin widens.

I'm not entirely sure what a pet has to do with Maisie wishing she had someone to tell her not to steal things, but at least I understand the nature of her visit. I return her grin.

"My husband and I—" Maisie cuts off with a snort of laughter. "That's so strange that I get to call him that now." She extends her hand and wiggles her fingers, drawing attention to the pink pearl and diamonds gracing a rose gold band. "We got married by a unicorn at a twenty-four-hour wedding chapel last week."

"Congratulations," I say. Though I must admit, her demeanor, while charming, has me a little flustered. I'm still not used to how open some people are. Or how random. I frown as I try to piece together what she's saying. "So...you decided to celebrate by getting a pet?"

"Yes, and I hear you're something of a matchmaker."

A sense of calm confidence settles over me, mingling with the budding excitement that always grows when I'm presented with a new client. "That I am."

I LEAD TRIS AND MAISIE FROM THE PARLOR AND INTO THE FOYER. Maids and butlers bustle by, pausing to curtsy before scurrying off to fulfill the manor's many duties.

"Davenport Manor is nearly indistinguishable from the condition it was in a year ago," Tris says to Maisie, a note of smug pride in her voice. "My stepdaughter has worked tirelessly to make good on the investments I've put into the place. However," she turns her gaze to me, "I had thought you and Torben would be living here yourselves when I made those investments."

I suppress an internal groan. We've had this conversation a thousand times. "Yes, but turning the manor into a bed and breakfast makes your investment multiply. Income from our guests helps keep the manor running, and serving breakfast highlighting products from Davenport Berries supports the farms. Besides, Torben and I don't need all this space to ourselves."

"If you say so," Tris says, tone curt.

We approach the end of the foyer where it opens up to what is now a lobby. A wide mahogany desk rests at the base of the two staircases. I smile at the little troll working the desk. He beams before bowing for my two guests. Not for me, though. I don't allow such genuflecting from the manor's staff. Here I don't have to be a princess.

I turn toward the eastern wing, the only part of the manor that hasn't been requisitioned for the bed and breakfast. As we approach our destination, I know it's time to do what I do best.

Focusing on pleasant feelings—love, comfort, safety—I summon my magic and look over at Princess Maisie. "What kind of pet are you looking for?"

She meets my eyes, and an impression forms. I see loyalty in her eyes, emotional resilience in the set of her shoulders, humor at the corners of her lips. "Something I can carry," she says. "I'd like it to have a certain heft, if that makes sense. And I want it to enjoy a good snuggle."

"Do you have a preference of what type of animal?" I ask, shifting my magic yet again. This time I allow my emotions to dip. Not too far, for I've practiced enough to spark a change of impression with only a subtle alteration of mood.

She taps a finger to her chin, and I see a stubborn quality in the set of her jaw, a hint of resentment clouding her chest, and envy. A lot of envy. That must have to do with her mention of stealing things. Whatever the case, nothing that I see makes her a bad person. Only a real one. Like all of us.

"Maybe a dog?" she says. "Or a turtle."

I release my magic and a laugh too. "A dog or a turtle," I echo. "Well, I don't have any turtles currently, but there are plenty of dogs."

We reach the part of the wing where glass doors line the

walls, giving us a full view of the adorable residents within each room. The first doors we pass showcase indoor felines, caught in the act of play or slumber. Their rooms boast carved climbing posts, cushy toys, and beds built on shelves and windowsills. The next set of rooms are for outdoor cats. These rooms contain much of the same items as the previous but have the added benefit of small doors built into the far wall to allow easy access outside. Next, we bypass the handful of rooms reserved for fae creature and wildlife rehabilitation, then our healing and surgery rooms where the animal doctors I've partnered with work. Finally, we reach the dog rooms. No sooner than we stop before the doors do dozens of pups eagerly approach, tails wagging, tongues lolling.

Maisie all but skips from door to door, exclaiming over each dog's cuteness. Perhaps she's a kindred spirit after all. Tris maintains a much more reserved composure beside me.

"Do any catch your eye?" I ask, coming up beside Maisie as I find her returning to one door in particular for the fifth time. I like to allow my clients to show me their preferences before I assess the appropriateness of the match.

Maisie crouches down and presses a palm to the door, giggling as three small dogs lick the glass on the other side. "Why can't I just have them all?"

I laugh, for it's a sentiment I can relate to. In fact, it's taking all my restraint not to turn into a squealing mess and dive headfirst into the nearest room to start a puppy pile. But I've learned to keep my wits when I have clients present. Even more so when Tris is around. I'll save the squealing, snuggling, and puppy piles for after they leave.

"If you aren't drawn to any dog in particular, I think your needs and temperament match well with Charlotte." I point at the middle dog, a squished-face pup with a plump belly that should provide that heft she mentioned. "She's a year old and loves to snuggle and be carried. She also needs plenty of exercise, though. Oh, and she enjoys playing in the water." I add the last part as I recall Mrs. Morrison announcing her as a princess of the Sea Court.

Maisie turns a teary-eyed grin at me. "She's perfect! Can I play with her before I decide?"

I lead Maisie and Charlotte into a private playroom where the princess can get to know the dog one on one. As I close the glass door and watch Charlotte smother a giggling Maisie with kisses, I know it will be a perfect pairing. I have instincts for matches like that. Setting adoptable animals up with hopeful owners is a thousand times more satisfying than matchmaking lovers ever was.

Tris clears her throat to remind me she's still here. I turn to face her and find her shifting from foot to foot, her haughty composure faltering. "Do you think..." She trails off then tries again. "Do you think you might have a match for me?"

My lips stretch wide. To be honest, I've been waiting for this question for months. I already know her well enough to pair her with the perfect animal companion. I gesture for her to follow me farther down the hall. "How do you feel about a bird?"

$\sim$

## TORBEN

I crouch down and pluck a round yellow berry from the short bush before me. Bringing it to my nose, I assess its scent, a rich profile of sweet strawberry mingling with clove-like spice. I pop it into my mouth, and the first bite brings a smile spreading across my lips. The taste is similar to its scent, but with a creamy vanilla note thrown in.

"Perfect," I say to myself and pluck three more to give to Astrid later.

As soon as I think her name, her scent floats upon my awareness, overpowering the soil, leaves, and berries around me. I turn to find her strolling toward me from the manor. The afternoon sun sends her golden gown glittering and highlights the hint of blue in her short dark tresses. I don't think I'll ever get over how lovely she is. I still recall what it was like when she hid her face from me. From the world. Of course, hiding herself behind her magic gave me a chance to get to know her from an entirely different angle—from the inside first. That's not something I can regret.

I close the distance between us and hand her one of the bright yellow berries. She takes it from me, frowning. "Are you sure that's ripe?"

"Trust me."

She winces before popping the fruit into her mouth. Her expression quickly turns to pleasure as she bites into the berry. "Blooming hell," she mutters and snatches the other two from me.

My lips curl into a smirk. "I take it you like the taste?"

She doesn't miss the suggestive lilt to my words and looks up at me from under her lashes. "I like the taste. But there's something else I'd rather taste more."

Heat stirs in my chest, and I don't hesitate to gather her into my arms and press my lips to hers. She moans softly against my lips, and I deepen our kiss, lifting her slightly off her feet. She throws her arms around my neck, pressing herself against me. I pull her closer, lift her higher, tempted to heft her all the way up until her legs are wrapped around my waist.

But...we have an audience. I can smell the attention of the field workers and laborers nearby, although most are merely amused by our display of affection. It wouldn't be the first time they've witnessed us in such a state.

Setting her back on her feet, I pull my lips far enough from hers to whisper, "You smell like dog."

She lets out a mock gasp and swats me on the shoulder. "I...
have no excuse. I may or may not have initiated a puppy pile."

I chuckle. "Please tell me you got your stepmother to join."

"Of course not. I waited until she left, thank you very much.
But I did manage to send her home with a blue budgie."

I pull my head back in genuine shock. "You actually
convinced her to adopt a pet?"

"I think a bird will suit her."

"You might be right," I say.

"Do you still have work to do, or..." She cocks her head to
the side, and I know what she's suggesting.

I gather my hand in hers. "No, we can go home."

We lace our fingers together and make our way between berry
plots, stopping to nod or chat with our workers along the way.
Astrid spots our lead horticulturist and leaves me briefly to gush
about the delectable berry she just sampled. I'm constantly
surprised by how friendly she's become. I know it's hard for her at
times, what with her past and lingering fears, but she's overcome
them in ways I never expected, always making an effort to ensure
our business partners, workers, and staff feel appreciated. I admit,
I'm a little behind when it comes to such affability. Taking on the
mantle of Huntsman made me curt and distant, and I wasn't
exactly social before that, either. I think that's why I liked the
gambling halls so much then. I was able to interact with people
without actually having to befriend any of them. But I'm learning.

Astrid returns to me, and we continue on our way. Soon the
forever-pink petals of our cherry grove peek above a row of
well-trimmed hedges. It's the only part of the farm I keep to
myself. Not that I don't trust anyone else to care for the cherry
trees. It's more that this grove has special meaning to me now.
It's where I first told Astrid I loved her.

It's also where we've built our tiny home—a single-story
stone cottage. A low fence and wall of shrubs surround the

cottage and grove, giving us a private space, even when the farm is at its busiest. The cottage was completed six months ago, and thank the All of All it was, for that was when the manor began to really take off as a bed and breakfast. Now that it's so busy, I can't imagine living there.

At first I thought Astrid would be disappointed when I suggested living separate from the manor, but she wasn't. Only concerned that I might be pushing away my past. I had to assure her that as much as I loved my former home and appreciated what my father left me, my heart has always belonged to the farm. I wanted to be more central on the property, especially in the beginning when it was only me and Astrid working the land. That didn't last long, though. Not when Tris was desperate to make amends for how she treated Astrid. It seems the queen feels most comfortable expressing her feelings through money rather than words. Either way, the estate wouldn't be where it is now if it weren't for her many investments.

We enter the front gate and are immediately greeted by four cats. Mama Cat doesn't bother joining the welcome party, for she's comfortably sprawled out on the front stoop. Instead, she flops her tail in greeting. The four kittens—rather large now, and not quite kittens at all—weave around our ankles. Astrid kneels down and nuzzles three of the kittens while the fourth — Madeline, of course—climbs up my leg until I set her on my shoulder. It turns out she hasn't outgrown thinking she's a parrot.

Once the kittens get bored of us, I start toward the little brown door to enter our cottage, but Astrid tugs my hand. "Let's not go in yet," she says, eyes glinting with mischief.

My heart quickens as she tugs me again, toward the pink trees beside our home. I follow her beyond the second gate and into our secluded grove. There are no cerapis sprites fluttering about, since they're nocturnal, but plenty of bees and butter-flies buzz over our heads.

Astrid releases my hand and stops at the center of the grove. When she turns to face me, her coral lips are quirked in a crooked smile. "Torben, did you know these," she runs a finger down the front of her dress along the row of tiny buttons, "are silvaran oyster pearls?"

I lift a brow, my sideways grin mirroring hers. "I did not."

She runs her finger back up the row, then flicks open the top button. Holding my gaze, she undoes another. Then another. My breath catches in my throat when I realize she's bare underneath. I know she's been experimenting with fae fashions lately, many of which favor a lack of corset, but I'm still not used to it. And that's in no way a complaint.

An ache pulses down the front of me, and I bite my lip as she finishes undoing her pearl buttons. She tilts her head to the side and parts the front of her dress, exposing her delectably round breasts. "Maybe you should take a closer look."

That's all the permission I need. With a growl I close the distance between us and lift her up beneath her thighs. Then, pressing her back lightly against the trunk of the nearest tree, I nip the base of her ear. "You're insatiable."

"Only for you." Her eyes search mine, and her teasing tone turns serious. "I love you, Torben."

Those words are a nectar like nothing else, and I'll never cease being awed by them. Honored by them. I'll never take them for granted, never stop trying to earn them, live up to them.

Maybe I never stopped being a betting man, for even after a year of opening my heart, I'm still fully aware that love is a daily gamble. I know someday I could lose her. Hurt her. She could hurt me. Love is always a risk. We'll fight, we'll argue. But I will bet time and time again that we will always return to one another.

Always.

It's a frightening concept. A beautiful one too. In the end, it doesn't matter if I lose this bet. Only that I've placed the wager. That I return to the table every day with my whole heart. My whole love. And truly give my all.

"I love you too, Astrid," I say. Then, sealing my bet, I press my lips to hers and entwine myself in our love.

# NOT READY TO LEAVE FAERWYVAE?

Keep the magic alive! More books in the *Entangled with Fae* series are coming! Next up is a Sleeping Beauty retelling starring Briony Rose, a character briefly introduced in *Kiss of the Selkie*. Haven't read *Kiss of the Selkie* yet? Now is the perfect time. It's all about Maisie, the princess you met in the epilogue of this book.

You can also take a trip to Faerwyvae's past with *The Fair Isle Trilogy*, which takes place twenty-two years before *A Taste of Poison*. Epic magic and enemies-to-lovers romance await!

# ALSO BY TESSONJA ODETTE

Entangled with Fae - fae romance

Curse of the Wolf King: A Beauty and the Beast Retelling

Heart of the Raven Prince: A Cinderella Retelling

Kiss of the Selkie: A Little Mermaid Retelling

— And more —

The Fair Isle Trilogy - fae fantasy

To Carve a Fae Heart

To Wear a Fae Crown

To Spark a Fae War

STANDALONE FAE ROMANCE NOVELLA SET IN FAERWYVAE

Married by Scandal

Prophecy of the Forgotten Fae - epic fantasy

A Throne of Shadows

A Cage of Crystal

A Fate of Flame

YA DYSTOPIAN PSYCHOLOGICAL THRILLER

Twisting Minds

# ABOUT THE AUTHOR

Tessonja Odette is a fantasy author living in Seattle with her family, her pets, and ample amounts of chocolate. When she isn't writing, she's watching cat videos, petting dogs, having dance parties in the kitchen with her daughter, or pursuing her many creative hobbies. Read more about Tessonja at www.tessonjaodette.com

instagram.com/tessonja

facebook.com/tessonjaodette

tiktok.com/@tessonja

twitter.com/tessonjaodette

CPSIA information can be obtained
at www.ICGtesting.com
Printed in the USA
LVHW040255170723
752491LV00089B/299/J